THE
CHILD
INSIDE

SUZANNE BUGLER

PAN BOOKS

First published in Great Britain 2012 by Pan Books
an imprint of Pan Macmillan, a division of Macmillan Publishers Limited
Pan Macmillan, 20 New Wharf Road, London N1 9RR
Basingstoke and Oxford
Associated companies throughout the world
www.panmacmillan.com

ISBN 978-0-330-51091-2

3 5 7 9 8 6 4 2

A CIP catalogue record for this book is available from
the British Library.

Typeset by Ellipsis Digital Limited, Glasgow
Printed and bound by CPI Group (UK) Ltd, Croydon, CR0 4YY

Visit **www.panmacmillan.com** to read more about all our books
and to buy them. You will also find features, author interviews and
news of any author events, and you can sign up for e-newsletters
so that you're always first to hear about our new releases.

Acknowledgements

With thanks to Sara Menguc, Jenny Geras and the staff at Macmillan. Thanks also to my husband Nick, and to my family and friends for their love and support.

PROLOGUE

I walked out of that hospital into the hazy sunlight, and I forced myself to smile. Other people were smiling, so I did, too. And I walked tall, even though it hurt. Andrew walked beside me, with Jonathan bounding along beside him. I did not look at them. I did not want to see them, or hear them, though see them and hear them I would, for evermore.

The car was in the long-stay car park, around the side of the building. I let myself into the passenger seat and waited, while Andrew put Jonathan and my overnight bag into the back. And then he got in, and he took a long, deep breath.

'You okay?' he said.

And I said, 'I'm fine.'

ONE

The house is in one of those tree-lined avenues between Kew
Gardens and the station. I find it easily enough. I got the
address from the class list and looked it up in the *A–Z*, and
when I spoke to Oliver's mother on the phone to confirm
she said, 'Oh, you can't miss us, we're the one on the corner
with the huge skip outside.'

So I find it easily enough, but because of the skip there's
nowhere to park. There's no space on the road, never mind
the fact that it's all permit holders only around here, and
that the drive outside the house, where we would have pulled
in, has got the skip on it. So I end up driving all the way to
the end of the road and across and around again, with
Jonathan whining in the back, 'Can't you just park?' and
'We're *miles* away now.'

I find a meter eventually, in the next street. And as I dig
around in my bag for change, Jonathan says, 'Why couldn't
you just drop me outside? I don't want you coming in.'

I look up and see his face in the mirror, pink-cheeked and
scowling.

'I have to come in,' I say. 'I'm not just going to drive off
and leave you there.'

3

'Well, don't stay then,' he says anxiously. 'And don't start talking.'

'Jono, I have to be polite,' I say gently.

And he says, 'And don't call me Jono.'

He does not mean to hurt me. He does not mean to be rude. I tell myself this, and yet my heart slides into a lost place deep inside me, a place where once there was warmth and need.

We let ourselves out of the car and I lock it behind me; the bolts click loudly in the quiet street. My son cannot bear to look at me. Instead he stands there, staring at his feet and wrestling with his demons, as I feed coins into the meter, and on the five-minute walk back towards Oliver's house he keeps a constant two steps ahead of me. But when we get to the house he hesitates; he doesn't want me with him, yet he cannot bring himself to walk up the pathway without me and stops, reluctantly, to let me go first.

'Well, go on then,' I say, stopping too.

It's a big house, as are all the houses in this street: Victorian and double-fronted with a wide front porch. But it isn't the house that's making him nervous; lots of his new friends at his new school live in big houses. He's getting used to that, I think, and so am I. After all, if you scrimp and save and push to get your child into a private school, he's bound to make friends with kids who live in bigger houses than his, have better holidays and flasher cars. No, it isn't the house that's the problem; it's me. That I exist. That he even needs to have a mother at all.

He rings the doorbell and his neck is stiff with shame.

They have one of those intercom things. A woman's voice crackles through it and I have to lean over Jonathan's head to say, 'Hi, it's us. It's Jonathan.'

And then the intercom buzzes and Jonathan shoves me back with his elbows, hissing, '*Shush!*', his pink cheeks turning scarlet, and the door clicks and swings open.

Oliver is standing there, and behind him his mother. We haven't met before. She is tall and thin with fine blonde hair, and she sticks out a confident hand. 'Hi,' she says, 'I'm Amy.'

And I say, 'Rachel. It's nice to meet you.' Her hand is cool and smooth in mine; I grasp it and let it go. She folds her arms then, languidly, across her stomach, and leans slightly to one side. I find myself mirroring her movements, though I am not so thin, or so at ease.

'Sorry about the skip,' she says. 'Did you find somewhere to park? It's a nightmare around here.'

'Just up the road,' I lie. And to Jonathan, who is disappearing up the stairs with Oliver, I call, 'Bye, Jono,' followed needlessly by 'I'll come back for you later.'

How desperate I sound. And how I could kick myself for calling him Jono in public. He doesn't reply. He runs up the stairs away from me. I can sense his anger from right down here.

Amy gives me a thin and, I suspect, slightly condescending smile.

'He'll be fine,' she says, as if I thought he wouldn't be.

And I should go now. I should smile back and say, 'I'll pick him up at six, shall I?' and make to dash off, as if there's something I must do, somewhere I must be. But I don't. Instead I do what Jono hates me doing – I linger as if I daren't let him go. And I try to chat.

'You've got a lovely house,' I say.

And Amy shrugs and looks about her, a little startled, as if she really hadn't noticed, and says, 'Thanks.'

Still I don't go.

5

'It needs a lot of work, though,' she says.

The hallway is wide, with rooms off to both sides and stairs up the middle. Further down I spot the evidence of decorators: a stepladder and paint pots along the side, and on the wall three large different-coloured swatches splashed out to view. I spot this and I latch on.

'You're choosing colours!' I gasp, on a catch of breath, and clasp together my hands. My enthusiasm has her turning, looking where I am looking.

'Yes,' she says and takes a few steps backwards down the hall, and I follow her, deeper into her house. 'Can't make up my mind between these two.' She points at the wall with a manicured finger and we stand there, side by side, contemplating the three shades of cream. She's taller than me, and out of the corner of my eye I can see the steady rise and fall of her chest inside her close-fitting sweater. She smells of lemons.

'I just adore decorating,' I say. 'We've just finished doing our house.'

'Really?' She's not as interested as I'd hoped. So I try harder.

'It is difficult, though. Choosing the right colour. You wouldn't think one shade would make a difference, but it does.'

'Mmm,' she says. 'It bores me stupid. Clive's the fussy one. He thinks all these colours are wrong.'

'Is Clive your husband?' I ask, and this is my cue for her to say, *Yes, and you know he'd love to meet you. You must come round sometime, you and your husband. You must come round for dinner.* And through my head runs a whole host of fantasies, of her family and ours, sharing summer barbecues and lazy afternoons drinking wine and laughing while the children play; of trips to the beach, where the men and boys horse around catching balls, and she and I laze and gossip on stripy towels, in charge of the picnic. We could be like those people in restaurants on Sundays: those families who always know people and come out in their crowds, to spread themselves noisily around the long, central tables and throw order after smiling order at the red-faced, overworked waiter – *Would you mind . . . ?; Could you just . . . ?* – while families like mine are squeezed onto the tiny tables in the corner, to quietly watch and wait, and envy.

She doesn't say anything of the sort, of course. She doesn't even offer me a coffee. And why should she? She'll have her friends. She'll have her busy, busy life.

Upstairs a door opens and I hear the children's footsteps running across the landing. Jonathan will be furious if he catches me still here.

I see Amy look at her watch, and quickly I say, 'Goodness, is that the time?' And, as I should have said five minutes ago, 'I really must be going. I'll come back at six, shall I?'

'No hurry,' Amy says, and she leads me back to the door. Her smile is pleasant, but distant. 'Clive and I aren't going out until eight. You can make it six-thirty.'

It's not much after three, but whatever light there was is rapidly fading. It's a dull, cold day, and everything is clouded with greyness. I walk briskly away from their house, but as soon as I am out of sight I slow right down, dragging out the distance back to my car. I've got nearly three and a half hours until I can collect Jonathan again, but what am I going to do in that time? It would take me half an hour to get home, and more than that to come back again later, because by then it will be busier on the roads. And what would I do at home anyway? Empty the dishwasher. Sort out the washing. Kill time till it is time to return.

Andrew is at home, but he will be sweeping up the last of the leaves and after that, maybe, fixing the shed door. Out there in the cold and the dark, straining his eyes under the outside light. Without Jono there we are middle-aged too soon, each of us silent in our isolation, him outside the house, me within it.

I could drive into Richmond and go shopping, but it is the first Saturday in December; the place will be packed and bustling with the heave of Christmas, and I am not in the mood. And so I just walk, wandering through these elegant streets crammed with gorgeous, elegant houses, and imagining what it must be like to live here. The roads all loop around and link together, and the second time I pass my car I stop, and feed the meter till six, after which parking is free. It's getting really dark now and the street lights are on; and the lights inside people's houses, too, giving me a good view. I see blonde-haired teenagers watching football on enormous TVs; polished tables on which there might be a large glass bowl or a vase of flowers – roses or white lilies, cut and arranged, bought from a proper florist; thin women in twos and threes, talking to each other, and to small children, who are dressed in soft, thick cotton and candy-striped wool. I see husbands, walking through their living rooms, cracking open a beer and talking on the phone.

I see. As always, I see.

I pass a good hour in this way. Then I wander over towards the station where the shops are, and such lovely shops. Specialist food shops and gift shops, and a quaint old-fashioned bookshop. I while away another hour, thinking how nice it must be for the lucky people who live here to have all this on their doorstep. While I am browsing, some of those lucky people saunter in and greet the shopkeepers by their names, and so they are greeted back.

Good to see you, Mike.

Miserable result, Don. Chelsea lost it in the second half. Got any of those sage-and-rosemary sausages left?

In the grocer's a man wanders in with a child on his shoulders, both of them wearing neither coat nor shoes, to pick up a couple of artichokes. I watch as they leave again; I watch the way he ambles across the road in his cashmere socks, wrapped in a shroud of insouciance. In a gift shop I admire soft leather bags with frightening price tags, and hand-made jewellery of the sort I would never dare wear. The woman sitting at the desk smiles at me and says hello, but I can see in her eyes that she's clocked me, that she knows I don't belong around here.

It's gone five now. The shops are starting to close. There's a coffee shop with a delicatessen at the back; I go in there and order a cappuccino just as they are starting to wipe down. The only other customers are a young woman and a child, spread messily around a circular table right in the middle. The woman is saying, 'No, Polly, don't do that. There's a good girl. No, Polly, no,' while the child picks up lumps of cake and throws them on the floor. The child reaches out a chocolatey hand to me as I walk past, and grins a chocolatey grin; I dodge around them, pick up an old copy of the *Daily Mail* and sit myself by the window.

The paper is just for cover; I don't read it. I'm listening to that mother and the way she talks to her child; listening and remembering what it was like to be so blanketed. I can almost hear my own voice superimposed over hers, saying, *There, now, Jono. Good boy, Jono. That's right, that's a clever boy.* And I feel the sweet-sad prickle of loss.

But soon they leave, packing themselves up, with a zipping up of coats and the scraping back of chairs, and leaving behind them a cold blast of air and a sudden quiet. I watch as one of the girls comes out resignedly from behind the counter with a J-cloth in one hand and cleaning spray in the other to tackle the mess left on that table. I listen to the hiss-hiss-hiss of the spray and the clatter of the plates and cups as she piles them up, and I'm thinking that I will have to be leaving soon, too.

But just then the automatic doors slide open again and somebody else walks in, and this, I feel, gives me licence to stay a moment longer. It's an old woman, wrapped against the cold in a marbled brown fur coat and hat – real fur, by the look of it, which surprises me, even for around here. Though I have to say it looks like she's had the coat forever; the fur has that mangy, slightly matted look that comes from having been alive once, and then dead for so long. Anyone dressed like that would get your attention, and I watch her march up to the counter and start ordering various items from the display cabinets, taking her time to point and delib-erate and eventually make her choices in a voice that is clipped and precise, but with an underlying scratch, catching on the vowels. She wants some ham to be sliced, and so the machine that had been cleaned and covered in a red checked cloth and put away for the night has to be unwrapped again and brought back out. The girl behind the counter sets about doing this with an audible sigh, and I see her look at the other girl and roll her eyes. And this makes me feel sorry for the old woman, fur coat or not.

I watch, as she is so begrudgingly served, and I find myself intrigued by her. She is quite tall, and her legs – where I can see them sticking out from under that coat – are painfully thin, and clad in tights so laddered as to be almost shredded. Her shoes, which are suede with a buttoned strap across the top, would have been gorgeous once upon a time, but are badly worn down now at the heel, so that the material is ruched and torn. And yet I notice that the finger with which she points, as she makes her requests, sports a diamond ring so enormous that it almost covers her knuckle.

And when she leaves, carrying her purchases inside a woven canvas bag that she loops over her wrist, she glances at me briefly and I catch the glacial blue of her eyes. Startlingly blue, in the naked paleness of her face. Then she passes me by with her worn heels clacking on the tiled floor, and the doors swoosh open for her and she's gone, out into the dark street. I sit and watch through the window as she looks twice and then steps out into the road.

And suddenly the girl at the till exclaims, 'Oh no!'

'What?' says the other girl, and I turn away from the window and back to them.

'She's left her card, again. Mrs Reiber. She's gone without her card.' She holds the credit card up in annoyance, and the other girl sighs and throws down her cleaning cloth.

'I'll go,' she says, like she's said it a hundred times before, and she grabs the card and straight away she's round from behind the counter and out of the shop with it, running after the woman.

And I'm thinking, *Reiber, Reiber*, and my heart is fluttering as if there's a butterfly trapped inside my chest. I shove back my chair and stick my arms into my coat, and scramble my purse out of my bag with trembling, clumsy hands.

'Keep the change,' I say to the girl at the till because I don't want to wait. And I rush out the door, just as the other

11

girl comes back in, her face flushed from the cold and from running.

I cross the road where the woman crossed; from there the road curves round onto the main street and then you can go either left or right. I think I might have lost her, but just then I see her: she's crossed over again and she's just turning into one of the side roads, going the same way that I will have to go when I head back to collect Jonathan. I walk fast, to catch her up. And still I'm thinking, *Reiber, Reiber.* How many people have that name? The only Reibers I ever knew lived in Oakley, in Surrey, and that, of course, was a long time ago.

I want to see her face again. I want to see her eyes.

I cross over the road and follow where she turned. She's just ahead of me now and I slow down a little. I walk just a few paces behind her, and I study the shape of her, and the way she walks. I look for clues. I walk softly in my quiet, flat boots, but even so I feel that she must sense me being there behind her, scrutinizing her like this, and I think that she will turn. *Then* I will see her eyes.

But how could I possibly recognize her? How could I know if it really is *her*? And what could I say? *Are you Mrs Reiber? Are you Vanessa's mother?*

How could I ever ask her that?

I only ever met Vanessa's mother two or three times, and then in passing, just as she walked through the kitchen or the living room of their house in Oakley, leaving one of Vanessa's parties to go off to another party of her own, throwing out intonations: *Be good, darlings*, and *Don't stay up too late!* I remember her laugh, rich and throaty, and the way she moved like an actress; I remember her voice, the easy, boarding-school drawl.

I think of this woman in the delicatessen, asking her questions and ordering her ham. I recall her voice, the precision of it, so English. But don't all people of a certain class sound the same?

Vanessa's mother had auburn hair, I remember, but she may well have dyed it. This woman's hair is hidden under her hat. But this woman is old – older than Vanessa's mother would be now, surely? Though maybe not. I need to see her face again; I need a second look. I mean, it isn't inconceivable that Mrs Reiber – *my* Mrs Reiber – should live in Kew now. More likely that than that she'd have stayed on in Oakley, surely?

But is it her?

On she walks, with her heels clacking hollowly on the concrete pavement. But look at the state of her shoes, and those poor ripped tights. Why would Vanessa's mother be dressed like that? Why would any woman with a diamond the size of a conker on her finger be dressed like that? But *Vanessa's mother*?

I think perhaps I'll cross the road and walk on ahead, then cross back again and return so that I'll get to walk past the woman, face to face. I need to see her eyes again. Vanessa had the most amazing eyes: clear pale blue. Like that stone you can get, aquamarine. Vanessa was the most beautiful person I have ever seen.

But then the woman abruptly stops, and so I stop, too. And my heart, which has been beating fast and steadily, cranks up a notch; I can almost hear it in the sudden silence of the street. She turns – not to me, but to the gate on her left, which creaks as she pushes it open. It's a waist-high black iron gate, attached to the railings enclosing a small front garden, dense with exotic plants: palm grasses and some kind of cactus reaching up its cowboy-film arms, and a monkey tree, crowding down over the path. Without looking in my direction, she closes the gate behind her and makes her way through this miniature jungle to the front door. She can't have seen me, and now I do cross the road, for fear of being caught spying, and I saunter on past, as nonchalantly as possible. And in a little while I saunter back again. She's gone inside the house now; there's a light on, in the hall. I can see the glow of it through the small window on the black front door, and faintly, through the bigger window to the side. Like Oliver's, it's a Victorian house, though narrower, with one big bay window at the front. As I loiter outside, another light comes on and the bay is lit up; I see her walk into the room then and approach the window. Startled, I react like a thief and catch myself slinking into the shadows, head bowed. I glance up one more time as I pass by, and see her reaching up an arm to draw the curtains, and as she does so she peers out with her face close up to the glass, squinting into the darkness, as if at last she can sense that I'm there. And I fancy that I can see her eyes. I can't, of course, not from here, not in the dark. But I fancy that I can.

Her eyes were the first thing I noticed about Vanessa. You couldn't not notice them. You couldn't not be stunned. Not just by the colour, but by the shape of them too, oval as almonds. She had sharp features, witch-like almost, and the palest skin. And when you'd got over this, there was the hair – masses of it, long and thick, and as yellow as gold. She was so beautiful that the first time I met her I could barely speak. First I felt astonished by her, and then unnerved, in a whispering, glance-over-your-shoulder kind of way. And that unnerved feeling never left me. She wasn't of this world; I'll say it now, but I knew it then, too.

Now, I walk on by, but I imagine that woman is at the window, watching me. I feel the pull of her imagined stare at my shoulders. My head is racing with the things I might say – that she might say – and I turn around, and I am convinced that it *is* Vanessa's mother, and that she will be there, beckoning me, recognition warm upon her face. *Rachel*, she will say. *Rachel*. And that will be enough.

But what I see is a dark and empty street, and that house, like most of the houses, is curtained up against the night now. And the fact of it is that even if that woman is Vanessa's mother, she wouldn't know me. Vanessa had so many friends; they came and went through her house in Oakley as easily as if it was their own. They slept there; they came for party after party. Friends called Fay and Annabel and Dominic and Tristram – see, I remember their names. And they called Vanessa's mother by her first name – Yolande. See, I remember that, too.

Oh, Yolande, they said, *I'm going to get completely drunk tonight*. And *Yolande, you've got to lend me that dress, it's gorgeous!*

Vanessa's mother might have recognized and remembered any one of those other friends, but not me. She probably never noticed me at all. Why would she?

I was just the one on the edge of things; the hanger-on.

I am late getting back for Jono. I manage to get myself lost, taking a wrong turning here, heading down a wrong street there. I walk myself into a circle, till I come across my car and work out where I am.

It's twenty to seven when I ring the bell. Amy opens the door promptly, as if she has been waiting. People like Amy don't expect people like me to be late, to have other things to do.

'Was there a lot of traffic?' she asks, and her smile is a little thin.

'No, I ...' I start to tell her – *what*? That I wandered around just killing time till I took it upon myself to follow some complete stranger, onto whom I projected the most ridiculous of dreams? 'Sorry,' I say. 'I got delayed.'

Jono is ready. Out he comes from the room to the left of the hall with his shoes already on, scowling at me, and we say our goodbyes.

Out in the street he says, 'What did you have to go and call me Jono for?'

'I'm sorry, Jonathan,' I say.

'Oliver laughed at me.'

'I'm sure he didn't.'

'Yes, he did. And he'll go telling everyone at school, and they'll all laugh at me, too.'

I sigh. 'For God's sake, Jonathan, do you have to be so sensitive?'

And he shuts up. Normally I'd launch into a long-winded explanation about friends not being your friends if they laugh at you, and how you mustn't show that you mind when people tease you, and so on and so on, but not today. Today I can't be doing with the arguing and the apologizing and the general wrenching that is my relationship with my son. I am too busy thinking about that woman, and about Vanessa. I am too busy sounding together in my head the connections: the blue eyes, the name, the fact that that woman would be the same age or thereabouts. These things cannot surely be mere coincidence?

I cannot let it go. Jono throws himself sulkily into the back of the car and I start it up, and drive back the way I walked, back towards that house. I drive slowly; I want to remember the way, I want to be sure of it, so I can find it again. And as I come to the house I slow right down and Jonathan wails, 'What are you *doing*?' and slams himself against the back seat in impatience.

I stare at that house. I lock it in my memory. The dust-faded black of the paintwork around the windows; the secretive, muted glow of the light from within. But when I try to imagine what it might be like inside, it is the house in Oakley that I see. I see the den downstairs in the basement where no adults ever ventured – and no wonder, Vanessa said, because the whole place was haunted as hell. *We* went down there, but we'd be sure to be drunk or stoned and always in a crowd. I see the living room upstairs with the balcony overlooking the green, and Vanessa's bedroom with the bunk beds that she used for sleepovers pressed up against the wall, and her own bed, queen-sized with its pale-yellow duvet and her old blue rabbit seated upon the pillow. I picture us, six of us at least, crammed onto the top bunk with our legs hanging over the side, jostling for space, saying, *Move up, I can't move*, but loving the closeness, all of us, just loving it. I picture Vanessa, lying on her bed, propped up on one elbow and watching us, cat-like. *Plenty of room down here*, she'd purr, but if any of us ventured down she'd pounce on us, tickling us to death and doing that thing she did with her nails, sticking them in you – one, two, three, four in a row and then all over again, one, two, three, four – till your muscles turned to mush, and you were helpless, begging her to stop. She said her dad had taught her to do that; it was a trick he'd picked up in Thailand.

And I picture Vanessa's mother opening the front door to more guests and sending them up the stairs to join us. 'She's entertaining in her bedroom,' I hear her call in her lush, theatrical drawl.

And Vanessa laughing back, 'Mummy! You make me sound like a whore!'

'Can we just *go*?' Jonathan pleads now behind me, and I drag my eyes away from that house and look at him in the mirror. I see his face flushed and petulant. He is tired. He wants to go home. Jonathan lives in a world where there is just himself to think about; just his own wants and needs, and I am merely ancillary to that world. That I could be anything more than just his mother – nurturer, facilitator, recipient of blame – is unthinkable to Jonathan. That there could ever have been anything more to my life would never enter his head. It's just not possible.

Andrew is sitting at the kitchen table, attending to some mail. He looks up when we come in.

'Hello, Jono,' he says. 'Have a good time, old boy?'

I notice that Jonathan doesn't scold his father for the use of his nickname. I notice also the way in which Andrew's face lights up when he looks at his son, his eyes warm with open love, a hunger almost. This must be the same expression that I wear, too, when I look at Jono. We feast upon our son. We drink him in, his every move. He is the essence of our lives, our morning, noon and night. Is he happy, is he hungry, is he doing well at school? Does he have enough friends, too many video games, the right things to eat? We worry and we fret and it holds us together.

And this is what Jonathan must see: two sad and anxious people forever watching him. This is what he rebels against.

'I'm going upstairs,' he says now, and pulls away.

That light in Andrew's eyes dims a little when he looks at me. His face becomes guarded, and careful. 'What did you do?' he asks.

And I say, 'Christmas shopping.'

And he accepts this. He doesn't probe for more. He doesn't say, *But where did you go?* or *What did you buy?* Andrew always accepts what I say without question, and I don't know if that is because he trusts me, or because he doesn't really care.

He turns back to his letters now, and I open the fridge to take out the chicken and peppers for supper. I put a pan upon the hob for rice, I turn on the oven, I start to chop, and Andrew sorts his papers into piles. For a moment I want to tell him about what happened in Kew, about the woman and how I followed her. *Do you think it could be Vanessa's mother?* I want to ask.

And he would say, *Who is Vanessa?*

And I would tell him. I would; I would tell him.

But Andrew doesn't ask. 'I'll go and see what Jono's up to,' he says, and he leaves me alone.

Later, I lie in my bed with my body very, very still. I am not asleep, but I am not fully awake, either. I lie on my back, and sink myself away.

Vaguely I am aware of the click of the bedroom door as Andrew opens it, and of the pause as he checks that I am asleep. Then he creeps in, and from my still place I open my eyes for a moment and watch as he undresses, careful to make no noise. I see the shadow of him, stooping in the dark, struggling to pull first his socks and then his trousers off over his feet. He goes into our bathroom and I listen to the running

SUZANNE BUGLER

of taps, the brushing of teeth. When he comes back out, he closes the door quietly behind him, and again he pauses and I know that he is looking at me. I am so still that I am barely breathing and behind my closed eyes the darkness is a funnel, spiralling away, like space, going on and on.

I feel the dip of the bed as Andrew gets in beside me, and the gentle tug of the duvet. I hear him sigh. And so we lie there, both of us, each locking the other out. I wish that he would touch me, but I cannot make the first move. I cannot bring myself to come back to him. And soon he is asleep, as he supposes me to be. And then I am truly alone.

I picture myself inside an envelope; I tuck myself in, the sides, the bottom, the top. I fold myself away. But the ghosts come anyway, weaving their way through my dreams.

TWO

I was fifteen when I met Vanessa. I knew her for less than a year. I was a friend by association, that's all. A friend of a friend.

And yet.

She was Leanne's friend, from school. Leanne lived opposite me, in the big house with the mismatched extension over the garage. And we were like sisters, Leanne and me, wandering in and out of each other's houses, sharing each other's things. Like sisters, and yet so different; her family so unlike mine. I think of her parents – so glamorous, so modern, so often not there. I think of Leanne and me, creeping into her parents' bedroom and opening her mother's wardrobe to see all those dresses hanging there, so many of them, shimmering and sparkling and swooshing against each other as we touched them. I think of the ashtrays on the bedside tables, and the glasses, and the decanter half-full of wine, and of her mother's jewellery box (the size of our TV), with all its drawers and trays and secret compartments crammed with earrings and bracelets and beads.

And I remember one summer's evening, just as the sun was going down; I must have been about ten, and I was balanced on the wall outside our house. My parents were

21

out there, too, watering the garden; I remember the soft, gentle hiss of the hosepipe, and the patter of water hitting the grass. As usual, I was looking over at Leanne's house in the expectation of something happening. And then a taxi pulled up in our quiet, dull street and the driver got out and knocked on Leanne's front door, and my parents stopped what they were doing and stood there and stared. And they carried on staring as Leanne's parents emerged from the house, her mother in a long blue dress, her father in a dinner suit with a white jacket and tie. And so we were all staring: me in admiration, my parents in a sort of dumbfounded amazement.

'Well, hello there,' Leanne's father called, and he raised an arm high in an exaggerated greeting. And then Leanne's mother bent down and got into the car, and Leanne's father patted her cheekily on the bottom and got in, too. And we heard them laughing.

I watched them drive away.

'More money than sense,' my father said.

And my mother said, 'Mmm.'

I think of this now. I think of them all with fondness: my parents so quiet, so very, very ordinary; Leanne's parents, so not the same.

I went to the comprehensive in Ashcroft where we lived, along with most of the kids from our junior school, but Leanne's parents sent her to the private girls' school in Westbury. And whereas I grew up skulking around Ashcroft at night with my school friends, finding dark corners in which to drink cheap vodka from the bottle and smoke cigarettes bought by the ten, Leanne's friends – well, they were from a different world entirely.

She told me about them. About Annabel, whose father

was a record producer and was forever having pop stars round to their house; and about Fay, who'd lived in Kenya till she was eleven and could speak Swahili. About the boys they passed around among themselves – friends of Vanessa's brother mostly, so easy, so happy to be shared. And about Vanessa, of course, whose house they all went to in Oakley.

Soon I started going to the parties, too.

I remember the first one, the first time I met Vanessa. She opened the door to Leanne and me; she draped her thin arms around our shoulders, said, 'Hi, come in, *come in* . . .' I remember the clink of her bracelets next to my ear, and against my face the soft press of her hair, which she'd back-combed into a wild Pre-Raphaelite mass. She smelled of White Linen, though I didn't know it at the time. I didn't know it until years later, when I was walking through a department store and the girl on the Estée Lauder counter slipped a perfume sample into my bag, and when I got home and split it open, it was like she was there in my room: Vanessa, the smell of her, the sound of her voice, the memory of her, so real. For years I kept that tiny perfume bottle. For years and years, long after the scent had all faded away.

She was dressed all in blue – I remember that, too – in a baby-cord jacket and matching low-waisted trousers, and on her feet the most amazing shoes: six-inch cherry-red patent stilettos that made her taller than ever. And there was me, in a black ra-ra skirt and ballet pumps. We followed her down to the den in the basement, and there they all were, all these people I'd heard so much about. There was Annabel, so out of it already, hugging me like she'd known me all her life and saying, 'Rachel, your skirt is so sweet . . .' And Tristram – who, according to rumour, had three testicles and there-fore three times the sex drive – sitting on a sofa with one ankle crossed over his knee, and patting the cushion next to him, saying, 'Rachel, Rachel, come over here with me.' Tristram, with his huge brown eyes fringed with such thick, dark lashes. Tristram, who two years later sat alone in his bedroom and inhaled the butane gas from a lighter refill, and turned blue, and died. I did sit next to him for a while, and he did put his arm around me. His body, next to mine, was warm in his soft cotton shirt.

And there was Vanessa saying, 'Be careful, Rachel, he's a naughty boy.' And to Tristram, laughingly, 'You leave my friend alone.'

My friend, my friend.

When the party got going, they drank cocktails mixed with tequila and vermouth and fizzy white wine, and Vanessa made punch, into which everything went. And the girls smoked Consulate menthol cigarettes because they came in all different colours to match their clothes, and *everyone* smoked dope. Vanessa's brother had a deck system, complete with projecting lights that flashed over the people dancing in the middle of the room; and around the edges of the room, where it was dark, people melded down together in twos. You couldn't see who was with whom, but it didn't matter because it felt just like *everyone* was with *everyone*.

There were so many parties. They blend into one in my head. Entering Vanessa's house was like entering a different universe and I loved it. I loved all those people. I loved Vanessa, with her circus of beautiful dreams.

This is all so long ago. I think of them all, bursting across my life like an explosion of elusive colour, so far from everything else that I've ever known. So far from now. I think of Vanessa, sitting on a stool in the centre of the room, with the party going on around her. Perched there so still, with her legs crossed over, just watching, and laughing. I see her face, so ethereal, so serene in its beauty; I see her skin the colour of milk, stretched tight across her bones, and her eyes, so guileless, so blue. And when she closed those eyes she saw lights, flashing behind her eyelids, and she'd carry on seeing them, long after the party was over. She told us all about it: sparkling orange lights, fizzing up inside her eyes, bright as fireworks.

'Rachel,' she said to me once, with her arm draped around my shoulder and her breath whispering across my cheek, 'do you believe in ghosts? I have a ghost. I see it all the time.' She took her arm away from my shoulder and held her two index fingers up in front of us. 'It goes like this,' she said. And she drew an S-shape in the air with her fingers. 'It starts just like two dots, then they join together and make this shape.' She moved those fingers fast, swirling them through the air. 'Like a genie.' And she started laughing. 'I think it must be my guardian angel.'

She started seeing double. There you'd be, talking to her, and her eyes would roll inwards so that she'd be almost cross-eyed. I saw it happen.

'Stop it,' I laughed.

And she laughed back, 'I can't.'

We all knew that house was haunted. Vanessa heard voices, calling her at night. Leanne said she came to school one day with a huge great bruise on her cheek; she'd woken up, apparently, to hear someone calling her name, over and over. And then she got out of bed and walked smack into the wall, because she couldn't see where she was going.

25

'Even the cat won't sleep in Vanessa's room now,' Leanne said.

So we planned to have a seance. Me, Vanessa and Leanne. It was my idea, because I believed in all that stuff back then. Ghosts, dreams, the whole lot. Show me your hand, I'd say, and I'll read your future. Write me a sentence, and I'll see through your lies. And if there was chill in the room I'd feel it. A bad omen, tapping on my shoulder.

But it never happened. It turned out there were no ghosts at all.

Vanessa had a brain tumour, spreading its roots inside her head.

She ended up so boss-eyed that she started walking into things. Her mother took her to the doctor, the doctor sent her for a scan. And there it was, the size of a plum. That's what caused the bright lights. That's what doubled her vision. No ghosts, no guardian angels, just cancer, eating its way down her spine.

I couldn't stop thinking about her. About Vanessa with her beautiful thick, long hair, spun out like gold. I thought of it being hacked away and of her head being broken into; of her paper-white skin and her thin, delicate bones. I thought of the bright lights that she saw and of the voices calling her at night. *Vanessa, Vanessa.*

I mouthed her name, whispered it over and over.

And I remembered how I felt that first time I met her; like she was too beautiful to be real.

She died on the first Sunday in November, a week after her sixteenth birthday. I didn't go to the funeral. I wasn't invited.

Yolande sent out the invitations, but she didn't send one

to me. Why would she? She didn't know my name or where I lived. I doubt if she'd even noticed me at all, on the few times that she'd passed me, drifting through her house.

Leanne told me about it afterwards. Apparently everyone from their class went and the church was packed.

But I had been at college that day. I cried, but I cried on my own when I walked through the woods at lunchtime. My grief was aimless; it had no home.

I wasn't part of their world. I'd just been there for a while, that's all.

THREE

The run-up to Christmas is busy – busier than ever, now that Jono is at Hensham Boys'. As well as all the shopping for food and presents, there are the end-of-term events to attend: concerts and carol services, and extra activities for Jono. Things to remember; that he has after-school rehearsals on Tuesdays and Thursdays, rugby practice on Wednesdays, school Christmas lunch on the last Tuesday of term, class party on the last Thursday, uniform not needed on that last Thursday, half-day on the penultimate Monday (concert in the evening) and again on the very last day, when the boys will all leave before lunch.

So much to remember. So much for me to write all over my calendar, as if it was me having such a busy life, and not just Jono. At this time of year, as at Easter, and in the run-up to summer, I am almost able to convince myself that it really is a full-time job looking after a child. Even just one child.

There is a class get-together, for the mums. Stephanie Rawlings, the class rep, is hosting it. My invitation comes home via Jono.

We're meeting for drinks at my place, Thursday night.
Do hope you can make it. RSVP Stephanie.
PS Husbands welcome, but not essential!

Which means of course: don't bring yours, if you have
one. After all, who's interested in husbands? It's each other
we want to size up. I analyse this invitation. From it I glean
that some of the mums already know each other well – hence
the use of the word 'we', as in *We're meeting for drinks*. And
so I am aware that there is already a tight club formed, of
which I am not a part, though I am invited along now to
observe. And I note that there is no phone number after
Stephanie's name, but this is no accident. Everyone who is
anyone will have Stephanie's number already keyed into their
phone. To admit that you haven't is to admit that you are a
no one.

Stupidly, I point this out to Andrew.

'Do you have to read so much into things?' he says, and
immediately he regrets it. He knows it was the wrong thing
to say. He knows this because he sees my face, which I turn
away from him.

'Don't just dismiss me,' I say.

'I'm not dismissing you,' he says. 'But why even go, if you
dislike them so much?'

'I don't dislike them. I don't even know them.'

I look up Stephanie's number on the class list, and phone
her, and get the answerphone. 'Hi,' I say in my breeziest voice.
'It's Rachel Morgan here. Thank you so much for the invitation. I'd love to come. Look forward to seeing you.'

I spend forever thinking what to wear. I stand in front of
the mirror in various possible outfits adopting various different
poses, trying to make myself appear confident and capable,

friendly and relaxed. I have clothes especially for such occasions, clothes bought in the shops that other women shop in, in the styles that other women wear. The right trousers, the right sweaters, the right jackets and the right heels. The uniform of the middle-class mother. I look at myself in the mirror and I see myself disappear.

'Where are you going?' Jono asks suspiciously when I kiss him goodbye.

'To drinks at Stephanie Rawlings's house,' I say. 'Your friend Isaac's mum.'

Jono grunts and says, 'Isaac's not my friend.'

Stephanie lives in Richmond, in a house that makes Amy's look suburban. The inner circle are already there when I arrive, gathered in Stephanie's vast steel-and-glass kitchen. A teenage girl answers the door to me and I can hear them straight away, the easy laughter, the smooth, confident voices. I fix a smile on my face and ignore the butterflies breaking loose in my stomach, and walk into this huge, echoing space. There are ten or so women standing in the middle of the room, sipping wine and chatting animatedly, and apparently admiring the domed glass ceiling above the dining table. Amy is there, and Stephanie of course, and I recognize a few of the other faces from various school things, but there is no one I really know.

Stephanie separates herself from the group when she sees me. Like a perfect hostess, she sweeps over to me and says, 'Hi, now you must be . . . ?'

'Rachel,' I say. 'Rachel Morgan. Jonathan's mum.'

'Yes, of course,' she says. 'Let me get you a drink. Did Lucy let you in?'

'Is Lucy your daughter?' I ask.

'One of them,' she says and hands me a glass of champagne,

which I clutch in front of me like a shield. 'Now, I'm sure you must know everyone.'

The others stop talking as we approach. I feel them scrutinizing me.

'This is Rachel, everyone,' Stephanie says by way of introduction.

And stupidly, infuriatingly, as if it weren't enough that I am simply Rachel, as if I can't exist just by being Rachel, I have to go and qualify this by adding, once again, 'Jonathan's mum.'

The woman to the left of me says, 'Hi, I'm Nicola. I don't think we've met.' She puts out her hand for me, but she doesn't tell me whose mother she is. It is assumed I should already know. 'We were just discussing the square footage of this house,' she says. 'Lizzie's just bought a new house, and we were trying to work out if it's the same size, overall, as this.'

'What's your square footage?' asks the woman on the other side of Nicola, whose name I also do not know.

I'm not sure if she is being serious. 'I really wouldn't have a clue,' I say.

'Well, where do you live?' She's an incredibly thin woman with piercing blue eyes and pale blonde hair scraped back in a twist.

'In Surbiton,' I say.

She waits for clarification.

'London Road,' I add, a little reluctantly.

'Oh, I know!' exclaims one of the other women, because they are all listening, all wanting to know. 'Those 1930s houses. Yes, we looked at one of those before we bought our last house, but we thought the bedrooms were too small. And there was only one bathroom.'

I can't stop myself from saying, somewhat defensively, 'We've got two.'

'You must have extended then,' she says, dismissively.

'Do you work, Rachel?' Nicola asks.

'No, not really.' I force myself to laugh. 'Unless you call running around after Jono work.'

She smiles a short, quick smile. 'What about your husband? What does he do?'

'He's an accountant.'

'Oh, in the City?' asks the woman with the intense blue eyes.

'No,' I say. 'He works for a telecoms firm in Guildford.'

I see the sums going on in her eyes. I swear, I literally see them.

'Oh,' she says. 'That's nice.' And she turns to speak to someone else. She is done with me.

My heart is thumping. I drink my champagne and wish that I could have another, but I'm driving. And then I thank God that I am driving, so that I can get away from here, soon.

Still, I try not to give up.

'Jono had a lovely time at your house the other day,' I say to Amy. 'I'm so glad they're friends.'

'Oh, yes,' says Amy. 'Oli has so many friends. He always has had. Steph and I were just saying, he and Isaac are quite a pair, aren't they, Steph?'

'What?' says Stephanie, who had been talking to someone else.

'Oli and Isaac,' says Amy. 'Ever since prep school.'

'Oh God, yes,' laughs Stephanie. 'The terrible twosome, always have been.'

And thus Jonathan is excluded, along with me. We are put

in our place. And isn't that the trouble – that people like me, and my family, should always stay in their place on the side-lines, on the outside, forever looking in, and longing. I hate myself for even trying. I hate myself that I should care.

Suddenly I see myself at Vanessa's house, at sixteen years old, doing my best to join in with the rest of them. I see myself admiring them so with their easy drugs and their easy sex. I see myself so enchanted; passing around the joint, sniffing up the coke, knocking back the tequila, doing what-ever I could to be like them. I was *infatuated*, almost. But it didn't work. Not really. I only had to speak to one of them to know that I didn't belong. But these women now, they'd have been perfectly at home in Vanessa's living room. They'd have been to the right schools, spoken the right language.

And yet Vanessa herself, how different she was.

Vanessa didn't cut me and measure me. Vanessa didn't judge me or shut me out. She was far, far above all these people and above those people, too, back then; those needy, drugged-up kids filling up her house weekend after weekend.

But Vanessa went and died, and I didn't even get to say goodbye.

I leave as soon as I politely can, but instead of going straight home I take a detour. I can't help myself. It is not far from Richmond to Kew, and within minutes I am driving slowly through the quiet streets to Mrs Reiber's house.

I can't stop thinking about Vanessa, and about that old woman, questioning myself over and over: is it her? Is it Vanessa's mother? It is as though a door has opened in my mind and the past has come spilling out. I cannot just shut it again. I cannot just let it go.

Andrew says I am obsessive. He says it all the time. He

hurls it at me as an accusation when we're rowing, and when we're not rowing he aims it lower, in a voice of pseudo-concern, though really it's to undermine me and keep me down.

Rachel, don't be so obsessive about things.

Rachel, you're obsessing again.

Andrew with his cool, calm reasonableness. Andrew who doesn't fight properly, out in the open, but stands before me like an implacable wall, frustrating me all the further. Andrew who freezes me out with his silence, and turns away from me in bed.

But Andrew isn't here to stop me now. He isn't here to know.

I crawl past Mrs Reiber's house. Twice I drive around the block. I do not know what my purpose is.

On my third time round I pull up, opposite the house. There is nowhere to park on the street, so I block someone's drive, and I turn off the engine, and the lights. I feel like some kind of stalker. I feel like I am half-mad, but there is no one to see me, no one to know. And so I sit there, and I stare at the house, and I ask myself again and again: is it her? There is a light on in the living room, and another upstairs. The curtains are all drawn. I wonder what she is doing in there; I wonder if she is alone.

Sometimes, after Vanessa died, I'd get a bus into Oakley and walk past her house. I could get a bus there from near my college, and sometimes I did, instead of going home. I'd get off the bus, walk to the cricket green and sit myself on a bench. Her house was one of only five town houses, the second one in from the right. On the first floor, where the living room was, there was a small balcony, overlooking the green, with full-length windows that you could open and step out of. From my bench on the green the glass looked black, but the light moved across it so that it seemed to move, like sunlight on oil. I imagined I could see her there, waving. I imagined she knew I was there. I wanted her to know.

And then I'd walk down into the village, past the sweet shop and the baker's and the smart ladies' dress shop; I'd walk where she would have walked. And it was as if she was in the air all around me. I expected to turn a corner and see her.

Suddenly I realize that the person whose driveway I am parked across is watching me. The front-room curtains have been pulled apart and there is a man standing there, with his hands on his hips. Quickly I dig my phone out of my bag and put it to my ear, as if I am making a call, then I put it away again and start up the car. He watches me the whole time. I look over my shoulder, careful not to catch his eye, and pull away.

And then I drive around the block again.

When I come back round, the man is gone and his curtains are closed. Even so, just to be safe, I stop across the next driveway along. From here I can still see Mrs Reiber's house, though to do so I have to turn in my seat. In the short time it took for me to go once around the block the downstairs lights have all been turned off, and just that one upstairs light remains on, as far as I can see. It is gone eleven now; she will be going to bed. As I watch, I see the shadow of a shape moving behind the curtains in the upstairs window. Suddenly the curtains are opened a little, and there she is, looking down at the street. I can just make out her face, ghostly, lit up from behind. She glances up and down the road, as if searching for something, as if she knows she is

SUZANNE BUGLER

being watched. I slink down in my seat and my heart is pounding. The next time I look round the curtains are closed again, and the shadow behind them has gone.

I know I should go. I know I should just stop being so stupid and go home. But I can't. It's like a door has opened inside my head, and I can hear them all, see them all. Leanne, at fifteen, squeezed into the tightest, tightest jeans with her layered fair hair crimped into zigzags, throwing her head back and laughing, open-mouthed, her breath smelling of peppermint; Annabel, barely five feet tall, with her cute baby face, wrapping her arm cat-like around mine, or Vanessa's or Dominic's. Annabel, always keen to get the dope out, and always there would be a little cube of dope to be found, maybe in Dominic's pocket, or Tristram's. 'Ooh, goody,' she'd purr, like a child after sweets. And brown-haired, brown-eyed Fay, who preferred to sniff coke because the dope made her cough, but who could down a bottle of wine and still seem completely sober. And the boys, so good-looking, all of them, gilded and interchangeable, so willing to be passed around. How sophisticated they all seemed to me.

And again and again Vanessa, so quixotic, so slightly removed, presiding over them all like a queen. I picture her; I can feel her, see her, smell her. And now I can hear her, too; laughing, putting her arm around my shoulder and whispering, 'God, Rachel, how bad you must think we all are!'

But I didn't think they were bad. I thought they were wonderful, like butterflies flying close to the sun.

I never saw any of them again, but I did hear about them, for a while, from Leanne.

I heard that Dominic got too heavily into drugs and was expelled from school, and drifted away. Annabel went the same way till at eighteen she shot herself up with a dirty needle and died of blood-poisoning in her boyfriend's Notting Hill flat. That one made the papers: *Record Producer's Daughter in Heroin OD*. Only it wasn't an overdose, it was a stupid, careless infection.

Tristram got no further than sniffing the gas from aerosols. I do not know what became of Fay, or any of the others.

Not long after Vanessa died, Leanne sat sobbing on my bed. 'I feel like I'm losing everything,' she cried. 'I don't know what to do.' She had hold of my hands in hers, clinging on like she never wanted to let go. He skin slid against mine, damp and clammy and hot. 'We'll always be friends, you and me, won't we?' she said. 'We'll always be friends.'

But our lives took very different paths, and Leanne drifted away, too, moving from job to job and town to town.

And now I do not even know where she lives.

A movement behind me catches my eye in the mirror; it is that man, the one who was watching me earlier. He must have seen me drive around again and park up. As I have been watching Mrs Reiber's house he has been watching me, and now here he is, wrapping his coat around his body as he approaches my car. Before I can do anything he's tapping on the window and peering in, suspicion on his face.

I open the window just a crack. I force my face into a smile.

'Can I help you, miss?' he asks.

And I say, 'No, no, I'm fine, thank you,' and I start up the car. He waits for me to say something more, but I don't and he stands there, watching after me, as I drive away.

*

It is a half-hour drive back to Surbiton. I flick through the radio channels searching for distraction, but then there are too many voices, crowding out my head, and too much music that I don't want to hear. So I switch the radio off again and I focus on the sounds of the car. Houses, cars, street lights pass me by, and I wish that I could drive forever, on and on, never arriving, never finishing anywhere. I wish that I could empty my head into silence.

I did not lose Leanne; she lost me. I tried to keep her. Through university, through my first job in Paris, my second job in London. I did not see her much, but I kept in touch. Her parents moved away from Ashcroft long ago, and Leanne moved around from flat to flat, but I managed to keep track of her for a while. The last time I saw her was at my wedding, to which she came drunk and angry. I kissed her on the cheek and she smelled of bitterness and decay.

'Well, that's you sold out, then,' she said.

A lifetime has passed since then.

I drive on home, but the ghosts come with me, clamouring inside my head.

I had this notion, this secret promise that I made to myself. I thought that if ever I had a daughter I would name her Vanessa. It would be my gift, secretly given. No one need know why, but me. And it is such a beautiful name, Vanessa; see how it rolls across the tongue.

But my daughter died inside me, at seven months. Exactly three years, three months and two days after Jono was born.

By then we knew her; we'd named her, too. At three months, and at four months, we saw her moving on the scan. Andrew held my hand and squeezed it, and to little Jono, who wriggled and kicked in his daddy's arms, he said, 'Look, Jonny-boy, there's your baby sister.'

But at seven months she wasn't moving. No one knew why. I had to push her out with the gas-and-air mask clamped to my face and the midwife saying over and over, 'Come on now, there's a good girl, push now, nearly over.'

I remember the pain, punishing its way through my body, and then the silence. I remember Andrew crying, and trying not to let me see.

It filled me with revulsion that I could give birth to something dead. It is such an oxymoron, so very wrong. I took home my cheated and empty body, and my breasts cruelly leaking their unwanted milk, and I tried to forget. And Andrew and I, we moved around each other carefully, so very, very numb. And one tentative month moved into another, and then into a year and another year. How can you grieve for something that wasn't wholly real? And how can you move on, if you cannot even grieve?

Hers is the ghost that cries loudest. Hers is the ghost that will not let me go.

'You're late,' Andrew says when I get home.

He is in bed, with the duvet tucked up under his arms, reading the review section of the paper. I thought he would be asleep.

'Were you worried?' I ask, and slowly, discreetly, I start to undress.

He doesn't look up. 'No,' he says, and then, 'How was your evening?'

'Hell,' I say.

'Why's that?' he asks, and he turns the page on his paper. 'Were they not your sort?'

'I don't have a sort,' I snap back. Somehow, he makes me feel that it's me who is at fault. And I don't know, maybe it is.

He doesn't say anything else, and I disappear into the bathroom. When I come out he has turned off the light, and I slip in beside him in the dark. I long for comfort. I long for him to touch me. Surprisingly, then, he does. He rolls towards me and places his hand on my stomach. I feel it there, warm and heavy, the dry touch of his skin. I do not move, I do not speak. There is a lump in my throat the size of a grapefruit and I can barely breathe. His fingers start to creep upwards, towards my breast, but it is a slow, uncertain journey and his hesitation fills me with rage. I pull away. I turn over. And I hear him sigh.

I pretend that I am asleep. I squeeze shut my eyes and cry silent, angry tears. What I want – what I want more than anything – is for him just to grab me and fuck me. To really fuck me until I can't think any more, until the ghosts in my head are left mute and silent. Not this. Not this timid hand upon my skin, touching me like I might break. I am so angry I could kick and scream and rip him apart. I cannot stand it. This constant apology, going on and on, torturing me.

FOUR

I decide to go and see Mrs Reiber. To visit her properly, and knock on her door and introduce myself.

I decide this in a rare moment of rational clarity. I do not need to stalk and creep and crowd out the shadows of my head with haunting speculation. I can take control. I can go up to her front door with the confidence and purposefulness of any other woman, and when she opens the door I can smile assuredly and simply ask her. *Excuse me, are you Mrs Reiber? Mrs Yolande Reiber?*

I can do it.

And then she will answer, and then I will know.

I think I will wait until Jonathan is next invited to Oliver's house, but the invitation doesn't come soon enough. It is our turn to have Oliver next, and we do, the following Saturday, and when his mother comes to collect him I have coffee brewing, the house is tidy, there are flowers in a vase in the hall. See me, I want to say; see me and see how much you could make me one of your friends.

But Amy is too busy to stop. She waits impatiently by the front door with the key to her Mercedes dangling from her finger while I call the boys down.

'They've had a great time,' I say. 'Let's get them together again soon.'

She smiles politely. 'It'll have to be after Christmas now,' she says. 'We don't have a minute until then.'

And I know I have been too keen.

'Are you going away?' I ask.

And she says, 'Oh, no, we're at home. How about you?'

'We're at home too,' I say, and I try not to feel hurt that her family will be at home, and my family will be at home, yet there still isn't time for her son to see mine. 'Just us and the grandparents.' How dull that sounds. 'And hopefully we'll see my sister sometime, too.'

'We're having sixteen for Christmas lunch,' Amy says casually as the boys finally drag themselves down the stairs. 'And ten of those are staying.'

'Goodness,' I say and feel the familiar mean tug of inadequacy. I cannot imagine cooking for sixteen. Eight is my maximum. Apart from anything else, where would you sit them all? Where would you find the cupboard space for all those plates?

We say our goodbyes, and I watch them drive away in Amy's black Mercedes, and when I close the door there is that sinking feeling in my stomach. I catch a glimpse of Jonathan's face before he disappears back upstairs again, and I realize that he feels the same. Our house is so quiet. I picture Amy's house on Christmas Day. I picture an endless, solid oak table laid up for sixteen, with gleaming silverware and polished glasses, beautiful white and gold china layered up in each place and linen napkins. I picture candles lit and glowing, and holly leaves and berries, artfully strewn. Do they have crackers, people like Amy? I think not, somehow.

They'd have something else in place of crackers, but I can't think what, because I do not know.

I picture happy children dressed in velvet, playing hide-and-seek. I picture beautiful women in beautiful dresses sipping champagne by the fireplace, and men setting up train tracks, and laughing. There's a huge tree of course, and someone is playing Christmassy tunes on the piano. Everyone is wrapped in a warm, muted glow. No one is harassed. No one is pink and frazzled from the cooking. I picture Amy's husband – in my imagination he is tall, square-jawed and blonde, like the men you see in catalogues advertising cufflinks and ties – looping a relaxed and lazy arm around her slim waist, pulling her to him, kissing her on the neck, around which is draped her Christmas present, something gold, something diamond.

I walk the length of my house and I am tormented by my imaginings. I stop in the conservatory, at the back of the house, and I stand there and look out. It is dark outside, but Andrew has all the outdoor lights on. He has his toolkit out on the patio table, and a variety of items that need his attention; Jono's football boots that need restudding, golf clubs that need cleaning, and parts of the lawn mower that need I do not know what. And there he is, frowning over some dirty piece of metal that he rubs and scrubs as though to bring it back to life. My husband. It startles me to see him looking so old; in less than five years he will be fifty and the lines of our marriage are etched heavily on his face. You think you have forever. You think you have forever, and yet there is Andrew, out there in the cold and the dark, looking for things to fix.

At what point does your life reach crisis? At what point do you realize that you will never go anywhere, never see anything, never be anything other than this, the appendage and extension of others?

I see Andrew out there and I feel the chains clamping me down. Never will I spontaneously hop on a train to Edinburgh or Paris, or a plane to Berlin or Milan – never will I go anywhere, just on a whim. There is Jono to think about, Andrew to think about. I am like a child, having to ask. And should I ask, then like a child I will face the madness of rhetorical questions: *Is that really what you want? Do you think that's a good idea?*

The holidays that we do go on are a compromise. They are about Jono, and about us and Jono. Will he be bored? Will there be enough for him to do? I am what I always am, but in another place. I am a body with no arms, no legs, no wings. My right to my own life was cut short, the day that I gave birth.

Sometimes I think what it would be like if there was just me and Jono. Sometimes I think life would be a whole lot easier without Andrew here to police us. We could eat what we want, when we want. I need not seem to care so much if Jono hasn't eaten enough vegetables, or cleaned his teeth. It would be like the few times when Andrew goes away on business; Jono and I, we stay up past his bedtime watching films when there's just us. We don't argue when we are alone; there's no need. Without Andrew, Jono's need to punish me is diminished. Without Andrew, my need to suffer, too, is gone.

But I stand here now and I look at Andrew out there in his own isolation, and I am sure that he feels just the same way about me.

*

My decision to visit Mrs Reiber eats away at me. I cannot wait until Jonathan is next invited to Oliver's; I need to visit her soon, before I change my mind.

So on Monday morning, when Andrew is at work and Jono is at school and I have the expanse of the week ahead of me to fill with a million trivial chores and errands, I stand in my bedroom and consider my reflection in the mirror. My stomach is alive with nerves, but my eyes are bright with determination. I have taken a lot of care over my clothes, and my make-up. I am wearing a dark-green woollen dress that brings out the green of my eyes, and grey woollen tights. Over this I will wear my best coat, and high-heeled boots. I do not normally wear heels in the daytime, but I feel the need to impress. I do not want to feel dowdy and insignificant, and dowdy and insignificant is, regrettably, how I have come to feel.

It is a damp day, so I have left my hair to go wavy. I stare at myself and take a deep breath. I look okay. But Vanessa was stunning. Had she lived, she would never have let herself fade into domesticity, I'm sure of it. She would be living somewhere amazing: Chelsea maybe, or a big house in the country. She would have a handsome husband, several beautiful children; she would be adored. I picture her as I think she would have been, dressed in expensively cut jeans and a loose white shirt, with that incredible hair flowing down her back. I picture her in a gorgeous blue and green woven coat, and genuine Louboutin shoes, with a large, soft bag over her arm, shopping in New Bond Street, or marching up Sloane Street to Harvey Nichols.

I turn away from my mirror and stare out of my bedroom window at the drizzle, dampening up the street in a fog of greyness. And quickly I pick up my coat and my bag and I leave, before I lose my nerve.

Driving to Kew, I have a sense of purpose. I need not think. In fact, I am quite enjoying it, being dressed up as I am, and having somewhere to go. Normally my Mondays are a heavy weight of loneliness, of house-tidying and supermarket trips and longed-for and then frighteningly disappointing solitude. I have friends, of course I do, but they are scattered far and wide. I see them rarely. We are all, it would seem, too busy with our lives, though for me such busyness is a charade, an excuse to hide behind. My world has shrunk in on itself, with Jono at its centre. Look outwards and I might catch myself looking away.

I park alongside the wall to Kew Gardens, because here parking is free and available; I get out of my car and there are other women parking up and getting out of their cars, too. Young women with small children, setting off for a walk, and slightly older women like myself, heading for the Tube station to go shopping in town. I feel like I am one of them: busy, with somewhere to go. I click shut my car and walk as briskly as my boots will allow, and still I need not think. I am vague about the exact direction to Mrs Reiber's house from here, but I find my way. I cross at the lights, and enter the quagmire of close, interwoven streets; I pass Amy's house and walk onwards. My boots are starting to pinch a little, and my confidence is starting to waver. The young women with their children will be in the park now; the other women on their way to shopping in town. I am alone. I cannot pretend that I am anyone, or like anyone, else. My heels clack clumsily on the pavement; I am hot inside my clothes.

Outside Mrs Reiber's house I stop. My teeth are clamped tight and I am tense from head to toe. The truth is that I haven't a clue what I am going to say to her. She may not even be in, of course, and then I will have had a wasted journey and will have spent so much time on my appearance for nothing. But I am not going to give up now. Absolutely not.

I push open the gate and march purposefully up to the front door, bending my head low to avoid the thick reaching branches of the monkey tree. On the doorstep I take a deep breath and ring the bell. Through the heavy black wood of the front door I can hear it ringing, deep inside the house. My heart starts pounding and I feel a little sick suddenly, with nerves. I take another deep breath, and I wait; she doesn't come. My finger is still positioned over the doorbell; before I have time to turn and run, I force myself to press it again. I listen to the ring, and then almost straight away I hear foot-steps approaching the other side of the door, and then it is slowly opening and there she is. She keeps one hand on the lock and opens the door just enough so that she can see me, but the view behind her is obscured, and she looks at me with hostile blue eyes.

'Yes?' she says, and she is wary, ready to shut the door again, fast. And no wonder; I am a stranger. And I am standing there on her doorstep, struggling to say anything. Because it is her – I'm sure of it. It is the eyes, the paleness of her skin, the cheekbones, everything. It has to be her. I wish I'd looked properly at Vanessa's mother all those years ago. I wish I hadn't shied away; I wish I'd really taken notice and stored her face away in my memory, so that now I could retrieve it and consult and compare.

I try to smile, but I find that I can't. My cheeks are numb; my whole mouth has turned to jelly.

'Yes?' she says again and she is frowning at me. 'Can I help you?'

She's about to close the door. She looks agitated, annoyed.

'Mrs Reiber?' I force the words out, but my voice cracks and wobbles and suddenly, to my deep and furious shame, I am crying. I am unable to stop myself. I put my wrist to my face and try to stem the tears with my coat sleeve. The door is open wider now; she is staring at me, alarmed. 'Mrs Reiber, I'm so sorry,' I manage to say on a shaking breath. 'I knew Vanessa.'

She says nothing. There is no sudden gasp of breath, nothing. Desperately I try to control myself. I wanted to be calm and composed, and I feel so stupid now, and so, so embarrassed. I look at her through my blurred and watery eyes. There is a stillness to her, but that is all. I wonder if I have got it wrong, and I have no idea what I should try to say or do next.

'I knew a girl called Vanessa Reiber,' I say shakily. 'And I thought that you might be her mother. That is why I'm here. I'm sorry.' My throat is burning up again with tears, and I am about to turn and leave when at last she opens the door a little further and steps to one side.

And she says, 'Oh dear. I think you'd better come in.'

The house is long; it seems to go back forever. She walks slowly down the hall in worn old slippers that slap, slap, slap against the black and white tiles of the floor, and I follow her, my own heels clicking noisily. She is wearing very old tights again, not laddered this time, but pulled and bobbled, and there is a piece of red fluff caught in a snag on the back of her left leg. I find this so sad, so hard to understand. She is painfully thin, her body swamped in a brown woollen skirt and a matching jacket, such country clothes, such typical, predictable clothes for a woman of a certain age. But Vanessa's mother wouldn't dress like this, surely? Vanessa's mother was so flamboyant, so theatrical. She dressed up, all the time. But of all these things it is the woman's hair that upsets and perturbs me the most; it hangs and clings to her shoulders in a series of lank, unkempt straggles. And it's so grey – white almost; silver – the colour that blonde hair turns when it ages.

Vanessa's mother had auburn hair. But did she? Weren't there photos of her scattered about the house at Oakley, photos from when she was young, photos of her with Vanessa's father, and with her children when they were small, and didn't she have fair hair then? They were black-and-white photos, from what I remember, but even so, you could tell. Auburn hair would have come out darker, much darker in a photograph.

So I stare at this hair and I'm wondering, and I'm looking for clues. We walk the length of the house, through the kitchen and another short connecting hallway and into a sort of small sitting room right at the back. Vanessa's house was modern and bright, but this place is so dark and enclosed, and there is a strange, cloying smell that I can't quite place. She gestures for me to sit and so I do, on the edge of a small leather sofa that is cracked and peeling along its arms. The seat of it creaks and gives under me, the cushion letting out its breath on a sigh. There is a large, pale rug on the floor and I rest my feet on it nervously, afraid that my boots will leave marks. I try to compose myself. I am desperate to look around, but I can't while she is standing there observing me.

Eventually she says, 'Can I get you a drink?'

And I say, 'Oh, thank you so much, a glass of water would be lovely.'

It is too hot in the room and as soon as she is gone, I stand up and take off my coat, but then I think that that might look presumptuous, as if I am making myself too at home, so I put it back on again. I can hear her in the kitchen, taking out glasses and running the tap. Quickly I glance around, but there is not much to see. The room is pretty small, with just these two mismatched sofas, each pitched at an angle to each other, and a rectangular, dark-wood side table between them at one end, so that the three items make a sort of triangle: sofa, table, sofa. And behind the table, with not enough room to get around there and open it, is a lone and heavily curtained glass-panelled door, leading on to the darkness of the garden. There is a tall lamp with a nondescript gold shade in one corner, and against the wall behind my sofa is a bookcase, but I can see nothing of interest on it: no photos, no give-away clues. All in all, it is a pretty characterless space, and I wonder why she chose to bring me here, all the way to the back of the house, rather than into the living room at the front, with the bay overlooking the street. Somehow I think that is the room I would have liked to have seen.

When she returns from the kitchen I am perched on my seat again, with my hands clutched in my lap. And I have been rehearsing my speech in my head.

'Thank you,' I say as she puts two glasses of water complete with ice and lemon on the table. And then she carefully sits herself opposite me, and looks at me, and waits.

'I must apologize for just turning up like this,' I say. 'You must think me very strange.' I smile, and she smiles back, but it is a polite smile, giving nothing away. 'The other day

I was in the cafe by the station,' I say, 'when you left your card. And I heard them say your name – Mrs Reiber—' I break off. How am I to continue without giving away the fact that I followed her? She sits so still before me, impassive, waiting for me to go on. 'Well, I . . . It's just it's such an unusual name, and I knew someone called Vanessa Reiber a long time ago, and I thought, I wondered . . .'

Her face is totally expressionless. Suddenly I am overwhelmed by the terrible fear that I may have got this all wrong. There is a long, awkward silence during which all I can hear is my heart, banging against my ribs. It is so hot in the room and the atmosphere is close and airless. My skin prickles under my dress and I can feel my feet starting to swell inside my boots. Eventually Mrs Reiber turns her head to look in the direction of the glass door, across which the curtains are still partially drawn. There is a faint, thin smile on her mouth, but I feel that this is a fixed expression, worn like a mask, and as I study her I see a quick, fleeting frown cross her eyes.

'Dear me,' she says. 'I think we are in for more rain.' And then she turns back to me and asks, 'Did you have to come far?'

'No, not too far. I – I live in Surbiton.'

She smiles, she nods, as though this is of some interest to her, as though we are here to make small talk. And I am thrown by this. I wonder if she is – well, *confused*. I feel that perhaps I should just give up and leave, and yet . . . and yet, I can't.

I swallow back my doubts and say, 'Please don't be offended. And well, forgive me if I'm wrong, but I knew Vanessa. Vanessa Reiber. I was a friend, sort of. I was Leanne's friend, and I came to the house a few times, in Oakley. When Vanessa died I was very ... sad.' How pathetic I sound. And if this woman is Vanessa's mother, what on earth do I expect her to say to that? Suddenly I wonder what it is that I am trying to achieve. 'I was very fond of Vanessa,' I say and I pinch my nails into my hands. *Fond?* What kind of a word is that? 'When I heard your name I thought – Vanessa's mother was called Yolande. Yolande Reiber.'

She listens to my speech with that mask-smile fixed firmly in place. But she says nothing; not that she is Yolande Reiber, not that she isn't. I don't know what to do. I feel such helplessness, spiralling inside my head.

'And if you were her mother, I just wanted you to know that I thought Vanessa was special. Very special.' That lump is swelling up inside my throat again. I swallow hard to contain it.

'It's very kind of you to say so,' Mrs Reiber says. 'But I am afraid that you have had a wasted journey. I do not have a daughter.' I stare at her and she stares back, her eyes unreadable.

'But—' I start, but she cuts me short.

'And I never have had.' She says it with such finality. And to make sure that I realize the conversation is now over, she breaks my stare and looks back out at the garden. 'I do hope you make it home before the rain,' she says.

I walk away from that house feeling numb. I am too miserable for words. It is raining now, that low-cloud persistent rain that looks as though it's not much more than a heavy drizzle, but in fact gets you soaked. I do have an umbrella in my bag, but I cannot be bothered to get it out and the rain is working its way through my hair to my head, where I can feel it trickling against my scalp. My boots are killing me now, pinching and rubbing against my toes; every step is a punishment, but it's a punishment I make myself endure. I feel I deserve it for being such a fool.

I walk to the end of the road and turn right, not really thinking which way I should be going. I have nothing particularly to do; no need to be anywhere until later this afternoon, when Jono comes home. And now I feel totally robbed of the day's purpose. I end up at the road leading to the station, where all those lovely shops are, and I cross over and walk towards them. The Christmas lights are on, even at this time of day, inside the shop windows and outside too, draped around the lamp posts. All very tasteful, but then of course it would be, here. I am too wet to go inside the shops so I just walk slowly, and look in the windows. And once again I feel myself to be outside life, looking in. At the gift shop I stop, and I look at the beautiful jewellery and the leather bags so artfully displayed. And then I catch sight of my reflection, of my glum, distorted face and my hair stuck wetly to my head, and I am overcome with a wave of self-loathing.

Who am I to try and link my life to Vanessa's – then, or now? I am just a middle-aged woman out of nowhere. I am what you become when you disappear.

I turn away from the shops and then cross back over the main road, and head back in the general direction of my car. And I try to walk tall, with dignity, as if I have the right to these streets, whilst inside I feel like an impostor. Niggling through my self-pity now is anger, worming its way like a thread.

Let us not forget that Vanessa's mother never did notice me. I may have been in her house on various occasions; I may have sat on her furniture, laughed with her children, drunk the booze in her dining room, but she always walked past me as if I didn't exist.

And she didn't invite me to the funeral.

And that woman back there, *that* Mrs Reiber – she was lying. She is Vanessa's mother. I know it. I know it in my bones.

It feels like the hugest of snubs.

I tuck the hurt up inside me where it festers and throbs like a deep, hidden boil. And I go about my life, as I always do. This is such a busy time of year and there is so much that I have to do. I make my lists. There are cards to be sent, there is food shopping to plan and buy, presents still to be bought and wrapped, as well as things for the house to be done: new napkins to be chosen and something festive for the table, the decorations to be brought down and updated where necessary, bed linen to be aired and ironed for the spare room in which Andrew's mother will stay. All this as well as so many school things to attend to: rugby matches to pick up from, the end-of-term art exhibition, the concert, and so on. I write things on my calendar and systematically I cross them off again, as evidence of my validity. And I tell myself that I could not possibly do all this *and* work.

Vaguely, like whispering ghosts at the corner of my mind, I remember a time when Christmas was all about lunches and parties and actually having a good time, instead of merely trying to buy one in the endless queues of supermarkets and department stores. But that was before.

I did work. Even after Jono was born. Not full-time then, but three days a week. For three days a week I catalogued antiques at an auction house in Burlington Gardens, and I was still me. I put Jono in the nursery and caught the train and then the Tube to my office in Piccadilly, with nothing in my arms except my handbag. I could have been anyone, then, and when there was just me, I thought I was someone. When I became pregnant again I saw no reason not to carry on. I had it all, as they say, back then: husband, family, career. I had the best of everything.

But when I lay on that hospital bed with my belly all slimed up with gel, with the midwife pressing the scanner into my flesh and dragging it about while she frowned at the screen in silence, I felt my life stop, like the hands of a clock. I'd felt so buoyant, so confident until then. I remember that I looked at Andrew for reassurance, but he wouldn't look back at me; he was staring at the screen with his eyes, and the skin on his face seeming to be drawn back in a parody of cartoon shock. I wanted almost to laugh. I wanted to scream, *No, no, you've got it wrong, everything is fine.* And I wanted to slap the midwife, who was now leaning over me with a little trumpet thing like a kid's toy held to her ear, which she moved about on my stomach, listening, listening. Pressing it down, listening. For how long was she going to do this? Her hair, which was long and dark and tied back in a ponytail, fell forward and strands of it stuck to the gunk on my stomach and dragged, like seaweed, as she moved.

'I can't find a heartbeat,' she said at last, and I did slap her then, and I did scream.

I couldn't go back to work. I couldn't bear to see all those familiar faces, avoiding mine. I couldn't make that journey, walk those familiar privileged streets so alive with certainty and optimism; I couldn't go back. That part of my life was over. It was dead, burnt in an incinerator in some far corner of the hospital grounds.

I couldn't leave Jono at the nursery. I just couldn't do it.

At first, I clung to Andrew and I cried and cried and he held me, and did his best to comfort me. He never said, *You have to*; he never pushed me out, back into the world, back onto the bicycle, so to speak, that I had so catastrophically fallen off. He just held me. And he said it was okay, although it wasn't. Of course it wasn't.

And so we turned our eyes to Jono. I became the full-time mother I had never wanted to be, but I could see no other way. I knew – we both knew – that if we looked away for even a second, we could lose him too.

Now, I serve up for Jono his sausages and his broccoli and his roast potatoes, and I sit myself down opposite him to watch him eat. And he says, 'How come Dad gives you more money than he gives me?'

I am taken aback. At first, I laugh. He is, after all, just a child. 'He doesn't give me money,' I say. 'It's *our* money. We share.'

'Dad earns it,' he says. 'So why do you get more than me?'

'Jono, what you get is pocket money. And your father goes out to work, but I work just as hard here, at home, looking after you.'

'No, you don't.' He cuts off a lump of sausage, and spears it. 'You just do what all mums do.'

Why does it hurt me so when my child speaks to me like this? Why do I feel that these comments of his are so accurately, sharply aimed right at the centre of my love for him? I look at him, methodically working his way through the food I so lovingly prepared, and I can't stop my eyes from smarting. He knows that he hurts me; that's why he does it.

'Jono,' I say, knowing that I shouldn't even try to justify myself like this, 'I used to go out to work. I had a job that

I enjoyed very much. But I gave it up, because it would have meant leaving you with child-minders, and I didn't want to have to do that. I wouldn't have been here for you in the holidays, or after school. I wouldn't even have been able to take you to school.'

'I get the coach,' he says, in a bored, indifferent voice.

'Yes, but when you were at junior school.'

He shrugs, and sticks a potato in his mouth. And I feel the heat rising in my face.

'I thought it would be better for you to be brought up by your mother rather than by a succession of strangers,' I say tightly. 'Don't you agree?'

Again he shrugs. And he almost smirks. 'Your choice,' he says indifferently.

Which are the same words that his father used, when I said that I couldn't go back to work, when I sat sobbing on our bed and pleading, *How can I go? How can I leave Jono in the care of strangers?*

Andrew sat beside me. He stroked my back, stiffly, mechanically, as if he'd read it in a book, an instruction manual: when the wife is sad and in need of comfort, she will need to be stroked. And he said, *It's your choice.*

But it didn't feel like a choice. Quite the opposite, in fact. It felt like all my choices had been taken away.

Jono finishes eating and lets his knife and fork clatter onto the plate. I cannot bear to look at him any more. 'You know I did have a life of my own once,' I say as I pick up his plate. 'A very good life.'

And he says, 'Well, what did you give it up for, then?'

FIVE

Jono will be thirteen in March. On June the seventh it will be ten years since my daughter was taken out of my womb. I do not know what has happened to the years. I do not know what has happened to me.

I look at myself in the mirror and it is the same face, but a still version. As if a mask of me, a cardboard copy, has been stuck on over the gap underneath. Once, I was walking past the shops and a young man – a good few years younger than me – started walking alongside me and trying to chat me up.

'You're gorgeous,' he said. 'But you've lost your sparkle. All you married women, you lose your sparkle. It's criminal. I don't know what your husbands are doing. Come out with me, love, and I'll put the sparkle back in your eyes.' And he persisted, trotting alongside me for the full length of the High Street while I did my best to ignore him. 'Go on, love, what do you say? Come and have a drink with me and I'll make you smile.'

I told Andrew. I wanted to know what he would say. I wanted him to laugh, of course, but a little part of me also wanted him to grab hold of me and kiss me and set about putting the sparkle back for himself.

But Andrew was not impressed. He tutted. He barely looked at me. And he said, 'Oh, Rachel, don't tell me you'd fall for that old line?'

To which I replied, 'No, of course not.' But I couldn't help wondering: *had* the sparkle gone from my eyes? And was it really that obvious?

And this was three, maybe four, years ago. I turned forty the September before last. Who will ever care about the sparkle in my eyes now?

On the wall in our spare room we have one of those wide glass photo frames that takes three photos, all in a row. We've had it for years. I bought it in a trendy little shop near my office, not long after we were married, and I put in it my three favourite photos of us at the time. There's one of us from our honeymoon, taken by a stranger outside St Mark's in Venice; I am holding onto my sunhat, to stop it blowing away, and Andrew is holding onto me. And he's looking at me like he can't believe I'm there. The middle one is from another holiday; this time we are balanced on the edge of a sailing boat, our faces sun-kissed and smiling, our hair whipping in the wind. You can see we have nothing to worry about. You can see it's just us, and whatever we want to be, wherever we want to go. The third photo is my favourite, though. In this, we are at Andrew's firm's Christmas party one year, long ago. We are sitting at a table among the debris of empty glasses and streamers, and we are flushed from laughing. I am wearing a black strapless dress and my hair, which was longer then, is curling loosely around my shoulders. We have our heads together for the photo and Andrew has his arm around me, squeezing me tight. We look so young, we look so in love, and see – I definitely hadn't lost my sparkle then.

These photos have been relegated to the spare room. In our old house they were on the landing, and before that, when we lived in our flat in Chiswick, they were in the hall. But gradually photos of Jono overtook their importance: photos of Jono as a baby, as a toddler, and of us with him, on holidays, in the garden, in the park. In these photos Andrew and I are merely the props, the supporting roles; we are smiling at him, we are holding him up, we are saying: look, here he is, our wonderful son.

We fill our home with photos of Jono. We cannot see enough of him. Photos of just the two of us don't seem relevant any more. They seem out of date, embarrassing almost. Like a too-old woman in a miniskirt and high heels, they no longer seem to fit.

The spare room is where I do the ironing. That is the only reason, really, that I am ever in there for any length of time. And those faces look down at me from the wall then, like actors in a film. Sometimes I cannot meet their eyes. They are strangers to me now, those people. They are the salt, rubbed into the wounds.

Now, I walk into the spare room with my arms laden with various Christmas purchases, and I look at these photos. The house is quiet; it is the middle of the day in the middle of the week, and as usual I am alone. And for some reason the silence is all wrong, as if really there is noise there – many, many layers of busy, vibrating noise – but it has been snapped off, as if someone has flicked off the volume switch. Carefully, I place my purchases down on the trunk among all the other packages and gifts all waiting to be wrapped, and then I stand and I look at those photos. Really look, as I haven't for a long time. And it is as if I am there again. I hear the noise from the boat; the sweet chink of the stays knocking against the mast and the ripple of the sail, the slap of sea against wood, and our voices, high-pitched, snatched out and away on the wind. I hear the sudden, feverish clamour of a thousand pigeons taking flight in St Mark's Square simultaneously with the echoing clang of the bell in the clock tower, chiming out the hour, and to the side of me the orchestra outside Harry's Bar striking up the violins to Verdi. And the voices, so many of them, in so many different languages: a group of French students singing the chorus of some unknown pop song; the vendors, selling corn for the pigeons and strips of postcards; the American guy taking our photo, saying, *Okay, you look great now*, and my own voice, then, squealing as I nearly lose my hat, and Andrew, laughing in my ear.

I hear all these sounds. I hear them all at once. As if they had been trapped all this time inside a locked glass box, but now the lid is off and out they all come, all of them, bursting out.

And that party – there was a live band playing blues music; they were brilliant, I remember. Andrew and I had only just sat down for a minute. See how flushed we are; I can hear our heartbeats pounding, the fast rush of our breath. I hear the music, I feel it, buzzing through my body. I hear the splash and the glug of glasses being refilled, of voices laughing, shouting to be heard.

And Andrew and me. Andrew and me.

I feel his hand on my skin, his body warm and sure next to mine.

Once, we had a terrible row. Before Jono was born. Before we were even married; we were living together, in our flat in Chiswick, and we were standing in our narrow hallway having this row. I cannot remember what it was about, just the fierceness of it, the danger of it in that tight, close space. I remember Andrew's face, looming up in front of mine, shouting, flushed with anger.

I kicked him, on the shin. I was wearing shoes, and I kicked him hard. He completely crumpled for a second as if his strings had been cut, and then he rose back up, right up, as if in slow motion, and then he grabbed me – literally grabbed me – by the collar of my shirt, fisting his hand into the material, and boom, boom, boomed me along the length of the wall, like a rag doll, saying, 'Don't–you–ever–do–that–again.' *Spitting* out the words. I ended up at the other end of the hall, still pinned to the wall by his hand. It was as if he didn't know what to do next, as if he was frozen now by his own reaction.

He didn't hurt me. Oh no. He *thrilled* me. I was racked up, horny as hell. All that power so almost unleashed, all that *passion*. But that is the difference between Andrew and me.

I saw the anger drain out of his eyes.

And he let go of me, then, in horror. He turned away from me. And he's never done anything like that since; whenever we have argued – however much I have goaded and pushed – he has never lost control. But, oh, how I wish that he would.

Later, I am sitting at the dining table, methodically sticking stamps onto Christmas cards when my sister Janice phones.

'What you doing?' she asks.

And I say, 'Oh, nothing much. The usual, you know. Getting ready for Christmas.'

'Mm,' Janice says, not impressed. She was married once herself, but not for long. She has no children. She lives on her own in north London, and teaches English at a comprehensive school. 'Guess what?' she says now. 'I'm off to Paris for the weekend.'

'Really?' I say. 'Who with?'

'Aha.'

'You've got a new man,' I state. 'What's his name?'

'Paul,' she says, a little nonchalantly.

'Must be serious if he's taking you off to Paris. Will we meet him over Christmas?'

'Not sure,' she goes on. 'There is one little snag.'

'Oh?'

'He's married.'

'Oh, Janice, no.'

'Oh, don't go all pious on me,' she says.

'I'm not, but . . . How come he's going to go to Paris for the weekend if he's married?'

'It's complicated,' she says.

'You mean he told his wife it's a business trip,' I state. 'How very original.'

And now her tone changes entirely. 'We can't all be happily married with our happy little families,' she says. And that is me labelled, whether or not it is true. I tell myself it is envy that makes her say things like that, however misplaced I think her envy might be. We don't talk about my marriage; we don't talk about my feelings at all. How's Jonathan? she'll ask. How's Andrew? But that is all. And I'll say: fine, thank you – and that is it. That's all she wants to hear. Anything else is off-limits, has been since her divorce.

I wish we could talk. I wish I could tell her things.

Now, to change the subject as much as anything, I ask, 'Do you remember Leanne, from across the road from us in Ashcroft?'

'Of course I do,' she says. 'Why do you ask?'

'I was just thinking about her, that's all.'

Janice laughs. 'I remember when her dad bought that fancy car. Pissed our dad off no end.' She pauses. 'Funny girl, Leanne, from what I remember. A bit screwed up, wouldn't you say? I wonder what became of her.'

I wonder it too.

I wonder how it came to be that for such a short time that small group of people came together and shone as brightly as the stars. And then, one by one, they all fell away, like lights going out in the dark.

I sit at the computer and I google Leanne's name. Nothing comes up. There are a couple of other people with the same name – one in America, one playing hockey for a school in Scotland – but not her. Not my Leanne. I even look up her old school, but she's not there, and neither is Fay. It's very strange, looking at the listed names of her year group; some of them have written about what they are doing now, and I can't resist clicking on a few and having a read. I wonder if any of them remember their dead classmates, Vanessa and Annabel. I wonder if they ever give them a thought.

And I think of those lives, cut off so very young.

Suddenly I remember Vanessa's brother, Simon. His name jumps into my head on a burst of adrenalin; I cannot believe I didn't think of him before. I key in his name and there he is.

Simon Reiber, of Sutton and Wright Associates,
    Fenchurch Street ...
Simon Reiber, new partner at Sutton and Wright ...
Simon Reiber, litigation expert, Sutton and Wright ...

Three entries. One person. It has to be him.

I feel a sudden rush of euphoria. For some reason I was afraid that he would be dead too, or just vanished without a trace, but there he is, very much alive. I'm so pleased. So pleased and so very, very relieved.

Vanessa's little brother.

I hardly knew him. I can't even picture what he looked like, except that he was blonde like her, and tall and thin. Gangly, in fact. I remember him trying to mix records on his music deck at those parties like a DJ. And I remember that his face would turn scarlet if one of the girls teased him.

'Oh, Simon, you're so cute,' crooned Fay.

And Vanessa said, 'He's too young for you. Keep off!'

I sit back in the chair, and I read his name, over and over. And I repeat it to myself. *Simon Reiber, Simon Reiber.* I scroll down the list, but there is nothing else, nothing to tell me anything else about him, just his professional listing. But I have no doubt that it is him. How could it not be?

And now I remember the school that he went to: St Dunstan's out near Oxshott. A few of the boys that Vanessa knew went there. I type in St Dunstan's on the schools site and search for him. He was two years younger than Vanessa, I think, but he isn't listed under his year group. I search through some of the other years, just in case, but find nothing. I do see a couple of other names that I think I recognize, but I can't really be sure. And then I look at the school photographs, posted there by ex-pupils. And he is mentioned; there is photo of about fifteen boys wearing cagoules over their uniforms and standing in the rain in front of a coach. The caption underneath says *Second-year geography field trip*, and there are the various boys' names (including his), written, I assume, in order. The photo is small, and not very clear. I zoom in as far as I can, but still their faces are tiny, peeping out from under their hoods, and blurred by the rain. The list of names suggests that he is the third one in from the right. I lean close to the screen and scrutinize the picture till my eyes hurt. The boy is pale, fine-boned and grinning. Yes, I think that it is him; I'm pretty sure of it. He'd have been twelve years old, thirteen at the most. I look at that smile, at that careless, boyish grin. His sister was alive still, then.

I think of him, going about his boyish life, laughing, mucking around, with nothing more on his mind than any other boy of that age. And I think how horribly all that would have changed.

And now I think of that old woman in Kew; I think of her sitting there in that small, claustrophobic sitting room, listening to my speech about how I knew Vanessa. I think of her impassiveness, of the distance in her cool blue eyes. I was so sure that she was Vanessa's mother, yet why would she deny it, and how could she be so unmoved?

But of course if she is Vanessa's mother, she'll be Simon's mother, too. I need to know. I cannot let it go.

SIX

I take her a gift this time. Just some chocolates that I pick up from one of those lovely shops by the station; hand-made truffles wrapped up in a cute little box with a bow. And it gives me a bit of confidence, coming out of that shop with my parcel tucked into its small paper bag with pink-ribbon handles. Today, I am the sort of person who makes such purchases. I am a person with a mission.

I walk briskly towards her house. I know my way around these streets now, and that familiarity allows me to adopt an air of assurance, I feel. Why, anyone passing me by might even think I actually lived around here.

I am little nervous by the time I reach Mrs Reiber's house, but I shovel that hesitation down inside me. Act the part, I tell myself; act it, and you will be it. So I press my finger hard on her doorbell and paste a smile firmly on my face while I wait for her to answer. I do not even allow myself to consider that she might not be at home. Jonathan breaks up in less than a week and after that I will be housebound, unable to escape, and if she is not in now I will have to come back tomorrow, before the Christmas concert, and that will hardly give me any time at all. But thankfully she is in. The door is unlatched and I pin that smile back, further into my cheeks.

She sees that it's me, and for a moment she looks afraid. Or annoyed. I'm not sure which. But then she slaps her own mask into place: that cold and empty smile. She doesn't speak, though, and she doesn't open the door any wider.

'Mrs Reiber,' I say on a deep breath, 'hello.' And quickly I hold out my offering. 'I bought you these,' I say, 'as a thank you for being so kind to me the other day. And as an apology for just turning up like that and for, well, for being so upset.'

For the count of one, two, three, four seconds we stay exactly like that: me proffering my gift, she holding onto the door that she peers around, and not taking it. But I hold my nerve. 'You do remember me, Mrs Reiber? I was here the other day.'

Now she does look annoyed. 'Yes, yes, of course I remember,' she says, and somewhat unwillingly she loosens one hand from the door and takes my held-out gift. 'Thank you,' she says. 'There was no need.'

And then another five, ten seconds pass and that smile on my face is cutting in like a grimace now. No doubt she wants to close the door and have me gone, whereas I am of course hoping that she will invite me in again. That, however, is not looking very likely. And so I say, 'I hope you don't mind me coming to visit you again.'

'Well, no,' she says a little reluctantly. 'I don't get many visitors.' And as if her manners won't allow her to do other-wise, at last she says, 'Would you like to come in?'

And I see this as a clue, as more than a clue – as evidence. I mean, surely she wouldn't let me back into her house if she wasn't Vanessa's mother? I could be anyone. I could mean her all manner of harm.

This time as I follow her down the hallway I say, 'You have a lovely house. Have you lived here very long?' Clues,

clues, I am fishing for clues. But she doesn't answer. The door to the living room is open slightly and I try to glance in as we pass; I catch a glimpse of green carpet, green walls and a large, dark wooden bureau. I wish that we were going in there, but she takes me to that room at the back again. I look around the kitchen as we walk through and I see a stack of papers piled up on the side next to a near-empty whisky bottle, and on the windowsill above the sink that diamond ring is perched; the glint of it catches my eye in the general gloom. And again I think, what is she doing letting a stranger into her house? There is no evidence of cooking or food preparation in the kitchen, none at all. But that is how it must be, to be lonely and old.

But she isn't that old, not really.

She's wearing that's suit again, and now I notice that although it's expensive, the wool has worn shiny and thin at the back of the skirt, and at the elbows, too, the material is starting to fray. And I can smell her slightly, a faint, sour smell like old milk. At first I think that it isn't her, but then I realize that it is and this shocks me, really shocks me. How could Vanessa's mother let herself come to this? Vanessa's mother with her beautiful clothes and her expensive perfume, the skin on her face and on her arms so polished and smooth, like a film star, always on show.

I sit down on that old leather sofa again, and she sits herself opposite me. I am careful not to appear as if I am staring as I look at her face. She wears no make-up, and her skin, as well as her hair, is badly neglected: dry and flaking, almost powder-like, across her cheekbones. And her lips are cracked and sore; there are tiny red lines bleeding into the corners of her mouth. I try not to stare, but it's hard not to, and my heart is wrenched to see such neglect.

She really isn't that old. Certainly not much older than my own mother, who runs about Ashcroft still, busying herself with the bridge club and the Women's Guild and gets her hair done, without fail, once a week. Age is a state of mind, my mother says. Behave like an old person and you'll become one.

'Perhaps you would like a cup of tea,' Mrs Reiber says, and I wonder by her tone if maybe I have been staring.

'No, no, please,' I say, 'I don't want to put you to the trouble.' And my heart starts speeding up. 'Mrs Reiber,' I say, I *have* to say, 'if there is anything I can do for you, anything at all while I am here, then please, I would be so glad to help. Do you need any shopping or – or can I help you prepare some lunch?' I feel the colour flooding into my face. She is sitting perfectly still and is staring at me with those stony blue eyes.

'I am quite capable of looking after myself, thank you,' she says.

'Yes, yes, of course,' I say, though I think that quite clearly she isn't. 'But if there is anything – I would love to help, that's all . . .' There is a long, awkward pause.

'Kew is very convenient,' she says at last. 'I can get everything that I need from the shops nearby.' Her voice is cold, and defensive, and so I tread more carefully.

'It's lovely around here,' I agree. 'And the shops by the station are gorgeous. My son has a friend who lives just near here,' I say. 'Kew is a very nice place.' She doesn't respond, but I carry on. I try to make chat. 'The Gardens are lovely, of course, although I haven't been to them for a few years. We used to come with our son, Jonathan, sometimes, when he was small. He loved the greenhouse.' I am waffling on; is this a good thing or a bad thing? I don't know. She is so closed, and unreadable. She invited me in, but she isn't exactly friendly. 'Do you have a son?' I ask, and I catch her off guard.

'Oh yes, I have a son,' she says and I hear the bitterness, sharpening her words. My heart starts to thump.

'Will you be seeing him over Christmas?' I ask tentatively.

'Oh, I expect so,' she says somewhat coolly. 'I believe that is what he has in mind.'

'Mrs Reiber,' I dare to say, 'is your son called Simon?'

'Why do you ask?' She stares at me now, her eyes flashing, intense. She sits up on that sofa, her body rigid, and her hands clasped tightly in her lap.

I feel the skin under my hair start to prickle and my heart starts to pound. 'It's just that . . . Vanessa had a brother called Simon,' I say and it comes out on a whisper almost, my throat dry suddenly, and tight.

And she turns on me.

'Who are you?' she demands. 'Who are you?' Her voice is shrill and angry and she unlocks her hands from her lap and starts clutching around on the sofa beside her, as if searching for something to grab.

'Mrs Reiber, I told you; I'm Rachel.'

'I know what you told me, but who are you really? Coming here with all these questions!' She snatches up a leaflet, advertising takeaway pizzas of all things, that was lying on the end of her sofa, and starts scrunching it and ripping it between her fingers.

'Mrs Reiber, I'm a friend of Vanessa's. Please, won't you just tell me: are you Vanessa's mother?'

'What do you want?' she shrieks. 'What do you want from me?'

'I don't want anything. Really, please . . . I'm sorry, I don't want to upset you—'

'Did Simon send you?'

'No,' I say. 'Mrs Reiber, please, if you are Vanessa's mother—'

'I do not have a daughter!' She stands up, and the shredded remains of that leaflet flutter to the ground from her lap like confetti.

'Mrs Reiber, please—'

'I do not have a daughter!' she cries. 'Now, please, just go!'

I've no choice but to stand up too. She is pointing towards the door and her hand is shaking. Her eyes are bright with anger and fear and her face is white, totally drained of all colour.

'I'm so sorry,' I say. 'So sorry.' And I keep saying it as I walk through the kitchen and the hall. 'I'm so sorry. I didn't mean to upset you.'

She follows me halfway down the hall, no further. She's still pointing with that finger, her arm outstretched, saying, 'Go. Just go.' When I reach the front door I look back and I see her there, this sad and broken woman, and my heart is wrenched. 'I loved Vanessa,' I say before I open the door, and my voice cracks over the words. It's true; I did love her. I loved her so simply, on a burst of pure feeling. Joy, without demands, without need. She was like a star, Vanessa; a star shining brightness into the humdrum greyness of my other- wise so ordinary life.

And now her mother stands there like an animal cornered. She stabs at the air in front of her with her finger. 'Go,' she shouts and her voice is hoarse and cracked. 'Just leave me alone.'

*

I almost stagger away from that house. My heart is racing and I breathe fast, with the cold air ripping down my hot, tight throat. I feel that everyone in the street will have heard her shouting at me, and will now be looking out of their windows to see what's going on, to see who it is that has upset that old woman so. And so I scuttle away with my head down, not looking at those houses, not looking anywhere except at the pavement in front of me. The street is quiet, but inside my head I can hear her voice still, echoing over and over: *Go, go, just leave me alone.*

I am so ashamed and so humiliated, and I fold my arms across my body and pinch and twist at the skin of my forearms through the sleeves of my coat. She made me feel like some kind of pariah, practically throwing me out like that. The shame of it turns and knots inside me. How could she treat me like that? *Why* would she treat me like that? Am I so unsavoury to her that it is inconceivable that her daughter would have me for a friend? And why would she think Simon had sent me? That is, of course, if her son *is* Simon.

But of course he is.

Am I mad? Am I making this whole thing up? A horrible coldness cramps across my shoulders and I huddle into my coat. What if I am all wrong? What if she is just a lonely old woman and nothing to do with Vanessa, and here I am turning up with my accusations and my prying? Then she would react like that. She would want me out of her house.

Doubt drags inside my stomach.

What if I have just fabricated the whole thing? What if I heard that woman's name, and latched on, and now I'm just looking for proof, when really there is none? There are coincidences, that's all, and not many of them. And you can read what you want into coincidences. You can believe what you want to believe. Suddenly I see a horrible image of myself, distorted and cloudy, as if I'm looking through the bottom of a glass. I see myself on that hospital bed as first that midwife, then a doctor and then Andrew himself tried to tell me my baby had no heartbeat. One by one they said it, and then one by one they all said it again, as if they thought I had trouble hearing. But they were wrong. Only that morning I'd felt my baby moving. And I could feel it again right then.

'Look, see, she moved!' I cried. I prodded my stomach with the palm of my hand. My stomach moved; I could see that it moved. I prodded it again.

'Rachel . . .' Andrew said, and his voice was thick and clogged with anguish. I looked at him, but he looked away and his lower lip was wobbling like crazy.

'Look!' I screamed at him. 'Look, she's moving!'

The midwife said, 'Hush, now, hush,' or some other such nonsense, and tried to cover me with a blanket, but I pushed her away, and the doctor made his excuses and left the room.

'I'll give you a few minutes,' he said on his way out, but what kind of a cop-out was that?

'She's moving!' I screamed, but no one would hear me. I shoved at the mound of my stomach, I pushed at it and pummelled it with my hands. 'How can she be dead if she's moving?'

And I see myself crying and wailing like a mad thing, with the snot and the tears all mingling with the dribble running out of my mouth. I see myself unrecognizable, out of control, alternately clutching and slapping at my stomach, and Andrew standing there in the corner with his hand across his eyes, quietly crying.

What is the truth if you cannot see it? What is the truth anyway if you just turn away?

They didn't take her out straight away. I had to be booked in. Andrew and I had to leave that small room, and walk to the in-patients desk with the midwife and book me a bed. I had to stop screaming and pull myself together and walk through the waiting area filled with other pregnant women, all looking at me with their horrified eyes.

And the woman at the desk asked me if tomorrow would be convenient. I was lucky, she said, they'd got a cancellation.

'*Lucky?*' I shrieked at her. 'How am I lucky? And what do you mean you've had a cancellation? Is some other woman's baby not dead after all?'

'Ssh, Rachel, please . . .' Andrew said and put his hand on my forearm. The midwife, standing the other side of me, did the same, so there I was, pinned between them with both of them holding onto my arms, ready to trap me, ready to hold me down.

We had to go home, and pack a bag. Andrew had to collect Jono from my parents' house, and make arrangements for him to come back again, the next day. I couldn't bear to see them. I waited in the car. And then there was Jono, oblivious, demanding his place in life as usual. He wanted feeding, he wanted attention, he wanted to play. He wanted *things*. I moved about our house with our dead baby inside me. I sat on the toilet, and tried to push her out. But she clung on. She clung on all night, and why would she do that if she was dead?

'Rachel, the doctor said she could have been dead for days,' Andrew said later in the middle of a long, sleepless night, doing his best to reason, doing his best to accept what we'd been told. But I couldn't accept.

'I think I'd know if my baby was dead, don't you?' I cried. 'I think I'd be the one to know. *Why* would she be dead?'

Andrew sighed and quoted banalities into the void. 'These

things just happen sometimes,' he said in his weary, robot's voice. 'It's nobody's fault.'

And the next day he drove me back to that hospital, and parked the car in the in-patients area, and carried my bag packed with my nightie and my towel and the oversized sanitary pads that I would still, apparently, be needing, and steered me zombie-like to the maternity ward. And there I was shown my bed, at the end of a ward in which there were other women, in various stages of labour. I saw some of them look at me, as if there was a sign over my head saying, *This woman's baby is dead*. The midwife pulled the curtain around my bed, to underline my isolation, and gave me a drug, to get things going. I was too numb to cry, too numb to do anything other than what I was told: to undress, to take the pill and keep on breathing.

The midwife patted my arm. 'Don't worry,' she said. 'It'll all be over in an hour or two.'

But my poor baby didn't want to come out. She clung on, with every wave of searing pain. Andrew walked me along the corridor and we stopped at the window and stared out a day that was shrouded in a ghostly, threading mist. Up and down the corridor we walked, up and down, in a horrible, endless limbo, until somebody decided it was *time for us to go*. Panic gripped me then, digging its nails into my chest, and I clung to Andrew.

'I can't do it,' I cried. 'I can't.'

And he said back, 'You have to.'

The delivery suite was eerily quiet, a shell of cold steel, rigged up for battle. No beeping monitors like I'd needed for Jono, no chat from the midwife, no bustling in and out. When Jono was born there was a radio playing, I remember: Capital, with its non-stop pop and banter. But into this silence we came now, interrupting its sterility with our broken voices and our helplessness; the midwife with her hushed instructions, Andrew with his stilted attempts at encouragement, parroting whatever the midwife said – and I wished he'd shut up, my God I wished he'd shut up – and me, howling out my pain on a pethidine-laced haze.

And soon, too soon, the silence.

I did not see my baby. I felt her wrenching her way out of my body, and then the smallness of her, slippery against my thighs.

I couldn't look. I heard Andrew gasp and choke on a sob, and the midwife saying, 'She's beautiful. A beautiful little girl. Would you like to hold her?'

I lay there with my eyes squeezed shut.

'Rachel? Rachel?' Andrew said, and his voice was thin and weak as a punctured tyre. I heard the quiver of his breath. If I looked at him I'd see him crying, I'd see him crying with our dead baby in his arms.

How much time passed? I did not open my eyes. At some point, they took her away. And then they wheeled me back down to the ward and pulled those curtains around me again, and Andrew went home and left me there. All night I heard the whispers and the moans and the snores of other women, and all night the silence of myself. My body throbbed, stripped out with rawness, bleeding. My breasts tingled and fizzed like a pair of showgirls, waiting for their cue to perform.

'You get some rest,' the midwife said. 'It's all over now.'

When Andrew turned up the next morning to take me home he brought Jono with him, to cheer me up, he said. And so I had to smile, and be normal. I had to be Mummy, Jono's mummy. And so it would seem that the midwife was right: it was all over now.

'How are you feeling?' Andrew asked.

And dutifully I replied, 'Fine.'

What more could be said, with Jono there to distract us, to keep us on track? We put our parent hats on, Andrew and I, and we kept them on for evermore.

I do not know what my baby daughter looked like, but I see her every day. I see her as I imagine she'd be now, at nine years old with a gap-toothed smile and her soft brown hair tied back in a pink and white band, wisps of it escaping and fluttering on the breeze. I hear her voice as she chatters away, saying, *Mummy, Mummy*; I hear her laughing and I hear her cry.

Every day I hear her cry.

How can I ever know what is true and what isn't? Life drifts along, one lie upon another, whatever I choose to make of it, whatever I convince myself that it should be.

Sometimes, in the darkest of nights, I dream that something has happened to Jono. I dream this in an abstract kind of way; I am never with him at the time. But I get the phone call, or the knock at the door. But then, instead of answering that phone or opening that door, I see myself outside suddenly walking instead, walking for mile upon mile along a green windswept cliff top. And I know that if I can just keep on walking, I will never hear the bad news. If I just keep walking, Jono will be safe. Because how can anything have happened to Jono if I cannot be told?

What is the truth if you never let yourself hear it? What is the truth if you just keep on walking away?

*

And who is lying now? Is it Mrs Reiber, telling me she isn't Vanessa's mother when my instincts are screaming to me that she is?

Or is it me? Am I lying to myself? Am I seeing what I want to see?

All these thoughts and all these questions; they plait themselves around me. They tangle with my doubts, and with my sense of myself as a copy of a person, a series of arms and legs and body parts stapled together to make up the image of a whole.

SEVEN

The next day, at three o'clock, Andrew and I take our places in the huge and ridiculously crowded church of St Mark's in Hensham for Jono's school Christmas concert. It is the lower school only today; the upper school will be doing the same thing again tomorrow, but even so the church is absolutely packed. We are greeted on the way in by the PTA elite, handing out programmes and ushering us down the aisles in search of somewhere to sit or stand.

'Good grief,' says Andrew, as if he's forgotten what it was like last year. 'Did you know it would be this busy?'

'That's why I said we should get here early,' I say a little sharply. 'To get a seat.' I force a smile onto my face. I do not want people to see us arguing.

We end up having to stand at the back of the far-left aisle, with our view pretty much obscured by a pillar. I can't even see Jono, though he is up there somewhere, crammed onto the stage, one of however many boys in identikit blazers and ties.

I am tired from standing even before the headmaster has finished his speech, but it would not do to slouch, so I do my best to stand tall and look interested and proud, even though I can barely see a thing past that pillar. I hear how well the boys are doing, and how privileged they are to be at Hensham Boys', but that such privilege carries with it its own duties, to which they all must aspire. It's quite a good speech, pitched perfectly at the wallets of the fathers. This year's charity, apparently, is the new music block, although – from what I remember – the existing music block, next to the dining hall, is not exactly old. It certainly looked pretty impressive to me when I saw it on the open day, with all its sound equipment and every instrument you could think of, ready and waiting to be played. At my school you carted your own recorder or flute or guitar, or whatever, in on a Wednesday and played it in one of the maths' classrooms at lunchtime, if you felt so inclined. But still, we must always strive to do more, as the headmaster says, and around me I see heads nodding in agreement. I look at Andrew, and even he is nodding and looking beyond that pillar in a wistful, misty-eyed way. He went to a grammar school in the Midlands somewhere, before they were abolished. A boys' grammar school. Maybe this all takes him back, down a rose-coloured memory lane. It certainly takes Jono forward, away from us.

But who am I to complain? This is what I bought into. This is what I wanted for my precious, only son.

The boys start to sing, accompanied by the junior orchestra, and many of the parents join in. We have the words in our programmes. Rousing numbers, all of them: 'Once in Royal David's City', 'Hark the Herald Angels' and the like, and, of course, good old 'Jerusalem', though I've never heard that one at a Christmas concert before. A small blonde boy gives an angelic rendition of 'Away in a Manger' and I swear there isn't a dry eye in the church. I look around, I see all these people, these lucky, chosen people puffed up with pride for their lucky, chosen sons, and even though I am in theory one of them – after all, I am here, and my son, too, is here – I feel like an alien, I feel like an impostor, a fake. So many blonde heads, so many expensive wool and silk jackets and beautiful scarves, so many men with the permanently tanned necks of those who ski and sun, and ski again; the glint of jewellery, the flash of a BlackBerry discreetly tended. I look around, I stand among these people. I am here, I am here, and yet I am not.

I look at Andrew again. He is tilted slightly backwards on his heels, totally enthralled. He is oblivious to me, and to the turmoil inside my head. He worked at home this morning, so that he would be ready for this. He shut himself in the study and I moved about the house with my demons raging inside me. If he loved me, he would see how tense I am. If there was any connection at all, surely, he would feel it. But he shuts himself away. He cuts himself off. I am best avoided, or handled at a distance, as though with gloves.

I look down suddenly. And I see with a jolt of embarrassment that slaps its cringing arms across my shoulders that Andrew is wearing the wrong shoes. He is wearing the soft-soled comfy slip-ons that he bought for weekends. They stick out from the bottom of his trousers like a pair of old man's easy-fit. It took me an age to decide what to wear; I even washed my hair again, and redid my make-up, and now I am standing here, crippling my feet in a pair of suede high heels, but there is Andrew, dressed for comfort and quite blatantly so. He doesn't care. He doesn't even realize. Shame grabs me by the shoulders and hangs me strapped like a puppet. I nudge him and he looks at me.

'You're wearing the wrong shoes!' I hiss in a whisper.

And he just looks at me, incredulously.

'Your shoes!' I whisper. 'Why didn't you put your smart shoes on?'

Andrew glances down at his feet and then back at me. Irritation cobwebs his forehead and he mouths at me to shush. And then he turns away from me and back to the stage, angling himself so that his shoulders are distinctly there between us. My heart is thumping. I am doubly embarrassed; first by Andrew's shoes, and now by this show of hostility. I imagine everyone is watching us, and noticing. This is not how I wanted us to be. What I wanted was for us to be united and serene, as benevolently happy as all these other perfect parents around us. I wanted us to fit in.

I suffer through the rest of the concert. I am ashamed of myself for being ashamed. I know I am wrong even to care about something as trivial as shoes, and the truth is that I wish I was more like Andrew and that I *didn't* care. But I can't help thinking that the other women – women like Amy and Stephanie – will be looking at us and later, talking about us and rolling their eyes. *Did you see her husband?* they might say. *Did you see his shoes? And did you see the way he told her to be quiet?* They, of course, will have perfectly turned-out husbands, as polished as themselves. Men who wear custom-made clothes during the week and Paul Smith at the weekend. Men who wear their shoes as if they own the world, and not as if they were just heading off to the garden centre.

They will know, as I know, that I will never be one of them.

When the concert is over, and we have all applauded the boys, the headmaster and – bizarrely – ourselves, the boys are released to locate their parents in the audience. Ten minutes of jovial chaos ensues as boys force their way through the baying and beckoning crowds, accompanied by more bursts of spontaneous applause and shouts of, *Well done, William/ Harry/George. Brilliant performance! Your parents are just over there. Tell them we'll meet you outside in five/in the restaurant/back at yours.*

Like one vast family, they collect and come together. And within this moving sea Andrew and I stand and wait, as Jonathan peels his way towards us. He greets us woodenly. As I was ashamed of Andrew, he is ashamed of us both.

'Well done, Jono,' Andrew says and makes to give Jono a quick, matey hug, but Jono recoils as though burnt.

'Get *off*,' he hisses, and he looks shiftily around lest any of his friends should have witnessed his dad's monumental gaffe.

The colour rises from the collar of Andrew's shirt, up his neck, up the sides of his face. He hesitates, he tries to laugh. I know how hurt he is. I know it, because I feel it too, a swift, sharp blow to the heart.

'Can we just *go*?' Jono whines, and his face is pulled in like a prune, dark with embarrassment. Around us the masses are still basking in the communal hug of congratulation, but we three, we slink out from that church unnoticed, each of us an island, each of us alone. I walk behind Andrew; I see the stiff set of his shoulders, and the back of his neck so vulnerable somehow, and flushed still. I see him, my husband, and I feel for him. Tears prickle in my eyes. I long to touch him. I long to put my arm through his and rest my head on his shoulder; I wish that we could lean together, laugh together. I am a bitch for minding about his shoes. He is a good man. He is a good, kind, caring man, but the truth is – the awful, terrifying and heartbreaking truth of it is – that he is lost to me, as I am to him. We lost each other, a long time ago.

*

Christmas arrives and with it Lois, Andrew's mother. She lives near Leicester, in the small, neat bungalow in which Andrew grew up. On Christmas Eve Andrew drives all the way there and back to collect her, and on the day after Boxing Day he will do the same again to return her, because she will not, thankfully, leave the cat for longer than that.

It is of course a good thing that Andrew will make this journey for his mother, and I hope that one day, if necessary, Jono would do the same for me. Andrew is setting his son a good example. But in those three hours or so alone together in the car Andrew becomes entirely hers again. Andrew is her only son, as Jono is ours. When Andrew was ten his father died, and then there were just the two of them in that claustrophobic, lace-trimmed bungalow, and now of course his mother is alone, apart from her cat, and whatever scraps of our lives we throw her way. On the rare occasions when I am with her I see the horrible potential that life has for repeating itself. I see the way she looks at Andrew, as though through a mirror in which longing and pain are equally reflected. And I see the way that he becomes around her: reduced and pulled back; the ghost of the umbilical cord still caught around his neck.

But that is not all.

Like Andrew, and like Jono too, she is tall and thin and dark, and so I, by physical default, am the outsider. I am outnumbered by the strong, commendable Morgan genes. I feel that she regards my lack of height, my tendency to freckle and my rather thick, wavy hair as combined proof of my failings.

At Jono's christening Lois got hold of Jonathan and rocked him in her vice-like arms. 'He looks just like his father. Just like him,' she said proudly, to anyone who was listening. And then, as if it was meant to be amusing, 'And I think we're all rather relieved about that!'

I have never forgiven her.

On Christmas morning the three of us watch as Jono opens his presents. Lois is properly dressed already, but the rest of us are not and I am very aware of my messy hair and my pale, soft skin under my bathrobe. Jono performs for us; he reverts to childishness, ripping paper off presents and letting it pile up discarded around him. Each unwrapped present he holds in both hands for the necessary amount of time before moving on to the next; I can almost see him counting out the seconds in his head. 'Thanks,' he says as he works his way through. 'Thanks, that's cool.'

And then my parents arrive later in the morning, and we do it all again. Now there are five people, all with their eyes on Jono. He is like a monkey in the spotlight. I see the stress of the circus, pink upon his cheeks.

There is a present for me, from Andrew. He has bought me earrings, small gold moon-shaped drops. I make a big show of putting them on. I look in the mirror. I tuck my hair behind my ear; I preen. I behave like a woman who is loved. My parents tell me how lucky I am. Lois tells me how lucky I am. Andrew basks in their approval like a boy who has done well at school. I have bought him a jumper, and a kit for cleaning his golf clubs. I do not hear anyone telling him how lucky he is, but these things of course are not so special.

My sister was unable to come. She decided to spend Christmas in Devon, instead, with friends. I try not to think of her going for long walks on a windswept beach, or lazing by the roar of an open fire. I try not to think of Amy, either, and her house filled with the exhilarating noise and laughter of sixteen people. I spend much of the day in the kitchen. Andrew has our guests to entertain, and a Meccano rocket-launcher to build with Jono. And I find that there is only so long that I can bear to be in the living room with them all, yet another pair of eyes upon Jono. I cook lunch, I serve lunch, I eat, I clear away. It goes as smoothly as ever it could. My son sits or moves among us – the pet, the idol, the raison d'être. One day he will escape all this; he will leave as soon as he is able. The inevitability of that is a large, immovable rock in the pathway of everything that I do.

Later, when it is over, and my parents have gone home and Jono is curled up in front of a film in his pyjamas, Lois decides it is time for her to go to bed.

'Thank you for a very nice day,' she says to Andrew.

And Andrew says, 'You're very welcome,' followed by the measure of all nice days: 'I think Jono enjoyed himself.'

She turns to me then, and I think that she is going to thank me, too, for after all, I did all the work. But instead she pulls a very wistful face and says, 'You want to make the most of Jonathan while you can, Rachel. Before you know it, some woman will come along and steal him away from you, and you won't like that, I can tell you.'

'Did you hear her?' I ask Andrew, when she's gone upstairs.

'She didn't mean anything by it,' he says. We are in the kitchen, putting away the last of the plates.

'She didn't even thank me. She just thanked you.'

'Don't be like that now,' Andrew says in his patient but warning voice, as if I am the one who is wrong, as if he is being patient with *me*. His tone goads me.

'When Jonathan gets married, I'll have the sense to make

a friend of his wife,' I snap. 'I'll be her best friend.' I swallow hard. 'She'll be the daughter I never had.'

I see the weariness cross his face; I swear, he almost rolls his eyes. 'But what if you don't like her?' he says so calmly, so apparently reasonably. He says it as if I don't know that it's meant to hurt.

'That won't even come into it,' I snap. 'But is that what you're saying? That your mum doesn't like me?'

'I'm saying it's hard for her, that's all. I'm her only child.'

'Oh yes,' I say. 'And Jono is mine.'

The unsaid words hang between us.

Andrew carries on putting away the crockery, and then he moves on to the glasses, his contribution to the day's meal. I stand there, mute now, and I watch him. He moves so precisely, so controlled. Inside I am bubbling with a rage I cannot define.

When there is nothing more to be done in the kitchen Andrew very carefully folds up the tea towel and places it on its rail. His composure infuriates me. I want to see him undone.

'It isn't my fault that Jono is an only child,' I say and my voice is loaded.

'No,' Andrew says. 'I suppose, like everything else, it's mine.'

My heart is thumping. 'Babies don't conceive themselves, you know.'

He looks at me coldly. 'And is that supposed to be a turn-on?'

The anger inside me floods over into despair and I feel tears rush into my eyes.

But we cannot argue, we cannot even talk, with Jono still up and Lois in the house, no doubt with her ear against her door. Andrew sighs, and he leaves the room. Moments later

I hear him in the living room, talking to Jono, and to his mother, and laughing. And I am stuck in the kitchen, trapped within myself, unable to join them. Always, unable to join them.

That night, I take off my earrings and I put them away in their box. I get into bed, alone. Inside my heart is a vast, hollow space.

Andrew is downstairs, watching something on TV, and I know he will stay there for a while, until I have gone to sleep. Perhaps, if I had behaved differently, we would have had sex tonight. Perhaps those earrings were more than just a present, perhaps they were a bigger gesture, a held-out hand. But I have blown it now. I have slapped that hand away.

And so on we go.

I close my eyes tight and the tears slide into my hair. Is this it? Is this all there is for me? To be useful till I am no longer useful? To be grateful for my small domestic slice and cling to it, no matter what? To hang on and on, till one day I will end up like Andrew's mother or, worse still, like Mrs Reiber, old and alone.

I see my life run away from me. I see it, skittling down the years like leaves in a breeze. How bitter will I be then, when everything is gone and I am stuck here still in this terrible glue?

EIGHT

Janice comes to visit us the weekend after Christmas. She brings books for Jono and champagne for Andrew and me, but she doesn't bring her boyfriend.

After lunch we go for a walk in the park, and she and I walk and talk while Andrew and Jono kick a ball. Janice doesn't have children, and now, of course, she swears she's never wanted them. She observes Jono with a carefully studied disinterest. I ought to find this refreshing, a break from the intensity with which Jono is normally viewed. I ought to find it liberating; it should free me up to be just myself with her. But the fact is that Janice regards all family life with the same indifference, verging almost on disdain. We are part of the domestic otherworld, Andrew, Jono and me, and as far as Janice is concerned, I am cemented squarely in the middle of it.

'How was your Christmas?' I ask.

'Fantastic,' she says decisively. 'No cooking, no relatives – best Christmas ever.'

The feeling that I am a lesser being somehow pervades me, the dull footsteps of predictability creeping over my skin.

'How about yours?' she says now, with forced enthusiasm.

'Oh, fine. You know, the usual,' I say. 'Have you seen the parents?'

'Yes, I went down yesterday. Getting all the family done in one weekend.'

'Oh.' That is what I am then; something to be *done*.

'Paul's still stuck with his in-laws in Bristol,' she adds, by way of explanation.

'You're still seeing him, then?'

'Of course.'

Janice is just over one year older than me. I remember when she used to roam around the house at night-time, dragging her stuffed donkey behind her, terrified of the witches hiding in the dark. Now, she holds her hardness in front of her like a huge, giant bat, with which to smack us all away.

'Did you see him over Christmas?' I ask kindly. She is my sister, after all.

'He came to Devon the day after Boxing Day and stayed over.' She laughs, triumphantly. 'Told his wife he had to go into work.'

She is my sister, but her harshness frightens me. I don't know what to say.

As if she senses my disapproval she says, 'All men have affairs, you know.'

'No, they don't.'

'Well, most do,' she says. 'Ian did.' Ian was her husband. 'And Paul is. I'm doing no worse than was done to me.'

'That's hardly a justification,' I say, and then, because I don't want to argue with her, 'I worry about you, that's all. I don't want you to get hurt.'

She loops her arm through mine suddenly and I am overwhelmed with a thickening sadness.

'You don't know how lucky you are,' she says. She gestures to where Andrew and Jonathan are now wrestling over that ball, the picture of familial bliss. The shriek of Jono's laughter cuts clean through the cold winter's air. 'Andrew is one of the few men I know who wouldn't have an affair.'

I watch him, grappling with his son. And I see his love for Jono, fierce and absolute, stretched wide across his face.

'No,' I say. 'I don't suppose he would.'

'He's a great dad,' Janice says, with detached finality.

'Yes,' I say. 'He is.'

I almost tell Janice about Mrs Reiber. As we walk, I am hunting for the words with which to mention her. Casually, of course; it would have to be casually, as a bit of an aside. *You'll never guess what*, I'd have to start, or perhaps, *A weird thing happened to me the other day.*

But the story gets stuck before I can say it. There are too many connotations, too many layers.

What are you doing snooping around old ladies? she might ask. And, *If she says she's not your friend's mother, then she's not your friend's mother. Why are you so obsessed? Let it go.*

She might well ask these things; after all, I ask them of myself.

She may not even remember Vanessa. In fact she may not have known about her at all. As children, our social lives were entirely separate, as they are now. And I can't bring myself to have to explain. I can't think how I would explain, not just about who Vanessa was, but about how important she is to me – now, as well as back then. I'd have to reveal the feelings that seeing her mother like that has stirred up

in me, about the frightening parallels I see in our lives. I'd
have to talk about the loss of my own baby daughter.

And I can't do that.

When Andrew is back at work and Jono is back at school
and the tree has been taken down, there is just me again,
pacing the house. My thoughts dance in and out of my head
like nimble demons, and I find myself back at that computer,
typing in Simon's name again. And up he comes, just as
before: partner at Sutton and Wright. I click on the link
and there are the details about his office: where it is, the
phone number. Before I even have time to think what I am
doing, I pick up the phone from the table beside me and I
dial that number.

It is answered almost immediately.

'Sutton and Wright Associates,' chirps the female voice on
the line. 'How may I help you?'

My heart starts to thump. 'Can I speak to Simon Reiber,
please?'

'Just putting you through.' The line rings again, six times.
With each vital ring I think to hang up; I think to chicken
out. I ask myself, *What am I doing? What am I going to
say?* Then the phone is picked up again and my heart kicks
into overdrive.

It's another woman. His secretary, I presume. 'Simon
Reiber's office,' she says.

'Oh, hi,' I say, trying to sound like a client or something,
like I do this all the time. 'Can I speak to Simon, please?'

'Who's calling?' she asks and my heart sinks.

'Rachel,' I say. 'Rachel Thompson.' I give her my maiden
name, but Simon won't remember me. I don't actually know
if he ever even knew my surname, and look how many years

have gone by since then anyway. He won't have a clue who I am.

'Just a moment,' she says, and I expect that to be the end of it. I expect her to come back and say he's not available, or would I like to leave a message? And of course I won't leave a message, I'll just hang up and crawl away from all this, as I should have done in the first place.

But then I hear a faint click and a male voice says, 'Simon Reiber speaking.'

I so didn't expect to hear him speak. I so didn't expect to be put through, and now that I have been, I don't know what to say. I hesitate, and in those seconds I sense the fast impatience of a busy man.

'Can I help you?' he asks, and I am thrown just by his voice. It's a confident voice, a professional voice; last time I heard Simon speak he was a boy still, his voice on the cusp, too deep for his body, too deep for his thin, awkward bones, till it lilted on a pitch and caught him out, cranking up on a high note and sending the blood rushing scarlet into his cheeks.

'Hi,' I say. 'I'm sorry to call you like this. I hope you don't mind.' I pause and he waits. My heart is banging against my ribs. I take a deep breath and look out the window, at the cold dank grey of a January day. 'You probably won't remember me. I'm Rachel Thompson. I was a friend of your sister.'

There is a short, awkward silence in which I close my eyes. I think of Mrs Reiber chasing me away, saying, *Go. Just go . . . Just leave me alone.* I think of the suspicion in her cold blue eyes. *What do you want from me?* she asked.

And I said, *I don't want anything.*

I think of Vanessa, dancing, singing, with one arm around

me and the other around Tristram. I think of her body, swaying, bumping up against mine, her body both hard and light, brittle as sticks. I think of her hair tickling my face, her cheek hot against mine. I think of Tristram's arm and mine, linked together around her back, holding her, holding her.

'I do,' Simon says at last. 'I do remember you.'

NINE

It's raining, hard. I come out of Bank station pushing up my umbrella, trying to time its opening with my ascendance into daylight, and failing; rain pummels its way down the back of my collar. By the time I reach the top of the steps my hair is all but soaked, and my shoes too, the suede mopping up the rain like a sponge. I move with the crowd; I have no choice. It's just gone midday, but the Tube was still packed; no one is walking today.

I cross the road and pull into the shelter of a building, and look around, to get my bearings. The rain is hammering down and magnifying the roar of the traffic as it swooshes along the wet road. Just across from the station exit there are roadworks going on, and the splintering crack of a jack-hammer machine-guns through the saturated air. I screw up my eyes, squinting out from my umbrella to read road names, and peer at the map that I printed off Google, soggy now, breaking up in my hand. I see a sign for Lombard Street and head down there, tilting my umbrella against the rain, till I come to the crossroads, and then I wait among the huddle of rain-beaten office workers for the lights to change. Fenchurch Street is straight across.

Simon's office is in a grand, white, stucco-fronted building with columns flanking the entrance, and stands wedged between two much newer buildings, phallic towers of metal and glass, thrusting up at the skyline. 'Sutton and Wright Associates' is etched on a gold plaque to the side of the revolving doors, along with several other company names. In and out of these revolving doors passes a constant stream of people clad in the business colours of black and grey; I am in a different world here, a world so far from my daily round of supermarkets and schools and endless, sundry errands that I had almost forgotten it existed. I feel like an alien. Like a mouse, come up out of the wrong hole. And yet nobody looks at me. Nobody sees me. I could be anyone; I realize this, and it thrills me.

Andrew worked in the City for a while, when we were first together. He worked for an accountancy firm in Cheapside. And when I had my job at the auction house we used to come in together on the Tube; I'd get off at St James's Park and walk, and he'd stay on till Cannon Street. And when we moved out to Surbiton we took the overground in, and went our separate ways at Waterloo. Andrew used to take the Drain and come up at Bank then, just as I did today. I think of him, melding in with the crowd. I think of him and I miss those days; I miss how we were back then. But Andrew hated working in the City; he hated the push of it, the constant, driving shove. It was because of him that we moved out to Surbiton in the first place; it was a halfway point, halfway out. Then he got his job in Guildford, and I kept mine, in Piccadilly. From then on, in the mornings, he went one way and I went the other.

I watch all these people. I watch how they move, fast, clipped, defying the rain. I try to do the same. I march up to those revolving doors, shake down my umbrella, and I am propelled into that building as somebody else comes out. Inside, it is quiet suddenly; plush, like in a luxury hotel. My heels sink into a carpet designed to absorb sound. There are leather sofas scattered about the foyer, and low glass tables, and straight ahead a curved reception desk behind which two girls answer calls in fast, constant rotation. On the desk to one side of them is a tall glass vase filled with lilies; the smell permeates the air like a funeral parlour.

I approach the desk. I wait. My umbrella, folded up and held down beside me, is dripping on the carpet. Eventually one of the girls looks up at me, her eyebrows raised instead of a smile.

'Hi,' I say. 'I'm here to see Simon Reiber, at Sutton and Wright.'

She shoves a registration book at me. 'Sign here, please.' Then she gives me a visitor's badge, which I hold onto, because the shirt I am wearing is silk, and my coat is just too plain thick to stick a pin through.

She keys a number into her control panel. 'Visitor for Simon Reiber,' she says into her mouthpiece, and to me, 'Take a seat. He'll be down in a couple of minutes.'

'Is there a ladies' down here?' I ask, and she points me to the corridor past the lifts. I follow her directions, and once inside I look at myself in the mirror and do my best to repair the damage wreaked by the rain. Other women come and go while I am there, checking their faces before they rush off to lunch, chatting noisily, dashing in, dashing out, slamming the doors behind them.

The rain has made my hair curl up into ringlets, and I do what I can to smooth it out again. When I was a teenager I wore my hair cut short, to just below my chin, and parted on one side. The shorter it is, the curlier it is, and it used to fall sideways across my face in a mass of spirals. I wore a lot of eyeliner back then, too, in a dark plummy colour, which made my eyes look greener, and scarlet lipstick that stood out bold against my pale skin. I stare at my reflection now, and there is a knife of loss digging under my ribs. The make-up that I touch up now is neutral; peachy colours, as advised by the woman in John Lewis. Colours that suit me perhaps, but that certainly don't make me stand out. But why would a woman like me want to stand out? I am what I am: wife, mother, the springboard from which other people leap, the carpet on which they stand. The constant, the unnoticed; the always there.

I think of how different I was when I last saw Simon, and how I will seem to him now. I am forty years old. More than that. I am forty-one.

Back in the foyer I wait for him, my lipstick reapplied, my hair arranged as well as it can be. I sit on one of those sofas, and I try to look at ease. But every time the lifts bleep and the steel doors slide open, my heart lurches. How will I greet him? What will I say? I hardly knew him. He was just a boy; gawky, mixing his records in the half-dark.

When he does approach me, at first I'm not even sure it's him. This man strides towards me, tall and thin still. His hair is not as blonde as it was, and it's cut very short, so that the curl is all but gone. His shoulders are broad inside his suit, which is expensive, as is his blue shirt, and his blue and red tie. At first I look at him absently, but he walks towards me with purpose. And then I know that is him; it is Vanessa's brother.

'Rachel?' he says, and I more or less jump to my feet, and feel the colour flooding into my face. 'It's good to see you.'

His voice is warm. He takes my hand, leans down and kisses me on the cheek.

'Hi,' I say, and my voice is almost a squeak. I am so aware of his height, and of his shoulders in that smart suit, and the general fact that he is a man now. When Vanessa died, I never gave a thought to how Simon must have felt, nor to their mother and father, either. I just thought of myself, and Leanne, and Vanessa's other friends who dropped right out of my life, held there as they had been by such a tenuous thread. I was a teenager, as selfish in my own solitary way as any other. But the people who really loved Vanessa, the people whose lives she filled every day, the people for whom there would now forever be an empty room, a space at the table, a silent, unfillable void – what about them? I am swamped with sorrow suddenly, and with shame for my selfishness. Simon was only fourteen when Vanessa died. What can it be like to grow up with a sister, then have her so cruelly snatched away? I think of Jono. I think of the sister that he would have had, and I try to smile at Simon, but I can't.

'I've booked a table at the Italian up the road,' Simon says, and he does smile, making up for my gaucheness. 'Shame about the weather.'

We don't speak while we walk; we can't. I follow him through the crowds jostling along the pavement, my umbrella slotted under his. And I wonder what I am going to say to him. *Meet me for lunch*, he said on the phone. *How about Tuesday?* He sounded so keen, so pleased to hear from me. I wonder if he ever saw any of the others after Vanessa died; if any of them ever bothered to look out for him, to keep in touch.

The restaurant is busy already; it's a big place with wide glass windows at the front. On the way in he says hi to a couple of people, and I feel them looking at me; I feel them wondering who I am. We stick our umbrellas in the stand by the door and the waiter shows us to a table near the back. I walk carefully, afraid that I'll slip in my wet shoes and make an idiot of myself. There are mirrors running along the side walls and, as we walk, I check my appearance. I wonder what he thought when he saw me. He recognized me; to me, even that is a surprise.

We sit, and I am overwhelmed with the strangeness of this. It is more than twenty-five years since I saw him last, and I have never really spoken to him before. At least, not properly. Not in any real way. Nothing more than the one-liners we all threw his way. *Oh, Simon, put on some decent music, won't you? Oh, Simon, shouldn't you be in bed by now? Or were you hoping to be in bed with me? Come on, Simon, you know you're gorgeous, but aren't you still at junior school?*

'It is so good to see you,' he says again now, and with such warmth and conviction that I am a little unnerved. He's really looking at me, studying me almost; I see his eyes moving across my face, taking in my eyes, my hair, every detail. He'll be thinking how much I've changed, surely; how can he not? And yet he says, 'You look amazing.'

I laugh, somewhat embarrassed. 'I didn't think you'd remember me,' I say.

'Why not?'

'Well, I wasn't there that often – at your house, I mean.' He shrugs, dismissively, and I add, 'Just at those parties. And it was a long time ago.'

I am finding it hard to meet and keep his gaze. He is incredibly good-looking; he has Vanessa's eyes, they are the same shape, the same blue. He has her paleness too, and the same thin nose, though it's more exaggerated on him, more masculine, obviously. What must it be like for him to look in the mirror and see his sister every day, to see her features growing older as he grows older – but as she, of course, never will? Is it a comfort to be reminded, I wonder; does it give a sense of permanence somehow, a sense that even though she has gone, a part of her lives on still, in him, and maybe in his children, too, if he has any? Or is it unbearable, never to be allowed to forget?

'The parties were fun, though,' I say. 'I often think about them, about the things we did. I often think about Vanessa.' I pause, but he says nothing. He's looking at me still, waiting for me to continue. 'Did you keep in touch with any of the others?' I ask. 'Do you know what became of them?'

But instead of answering me he asks me, 'Do you?'

I shouldn't have asked. There was just too much death, too much waste. But he'd know more about them than me, surely? He'd know what happened. 'I heard about Tristram,' I say. 'And Annabel. It was just so sad.'

He smiles a small, one-sided and very wry smile, but his eyes are unreadable.

'I stayed friends with Leanne of course, but . . . I haven't seen her for years.' I realize how bad this sounds. Just saying it makes me *feel* bad. We thought we'd be friends forever, Leanne and I, but look how wrong you can be. 'I often wonder what happened to her,' I say. 'And to the others, too; to Dominic and Fay, especially.'

'I used to go out with Fay,' he says.

'Really?' I look at him, surprised, and he raises an eyebrow.

'Yes, really,' he says. 'For about four years or so. She was my first proper girlfriend. My first true love.' He says this in a voice laden with irony. Such sarcasm is a defence mechanism,

I know, but it makes me uncomfortable. 'But she decided I wasn't the one for her after all. She'll be married to some rich chap now, a few kids, house in the country. Which is pretty much what she'd have got if she'd stayed with me.'

His tone unnerves me. I'm not sure how to respond, but then the waiter comes to take our orders. We haven't even looked at the menus, but Simon orders the veal, medium-rare, as if it's what he always has. 'The fish is good,' he says to me, all warmth again.

'I'll have the fish, then,' I say. 'Thanks.'

'And a bottle of Puligny-Montrachet.' When the waiter has gone away, he says, 'And the last I heard of Dominic he was trying to sell apartments to idiots in Tenerife. But that was a long time ago.'

'It seems we all fell apart after Vanessa died. As a group, I mean. She was like the magnet, holding us together.'

'What happened to you, then?' he says, and there is an edge to his voice. He picks up the restaurant card propped up against the little rose vase on the table and starts turning it in his fingers. He has long fingers, like a musician, and short, bitten nails. I see that he is wearing a thin gold wedding ring.

'Nothing. Nothing exciting anyway.'

'You weren't at the funeral.'

'No.'

'Why not?' he asks, and I sense an anger in him, some-thing deep, simmering below his watchful, guarded surface. 'All her other friends were there.'

Carefully I say, 'I wasn't invited.'

'An oversight, that's all,' he says straight back. 'You should have just come.' He scrunches up that card between his fingers and drops it down. And then he snaps, 'For God's sake, it wasn't a party.'

I feel the colour rising in my face. He is angry with me. He thinks I should have stayed in touch, with him, with the others. He thinks that I just left them; that Vanessa died and I walked away. But I felt my lack of an invite sorely. It was a rejection; a *Keep out, you're not of our world*. That's how I interpreted it. Maybe I should have just turned up anyway. But I wonder, what would have happened to me, if I had stayed in touch? I think of the darkness that seemed to swamp and absorb the others: Tristram, Annabel, Dominic, and Leanne too, to some extent. Maybe I did let them go. Maybe I knew that I had to.

'I'm surprised you even noticed,' I say at last.

'You were one of my sister's friends,' he says. 'Of course I noticed.'

I swallow hard, feeling ridiculously close to tears suddenly. I picture him, the mere boy that he was, looking around at the funeral, seeing who was there, and who wasn't. And I picture myself that day, walking alone in the woods near my college at lunchtime, walking far, far away from everyone else so there would be no one around to hear me cry. And cry I did, in loud, hollow sobs. I remember the sound of it echoing back to me, creepy in the damp autumn air.

'I'm sorry,' I say. 'I assumed the funeral was for family and close friends only. And, as I wasn't invited, I assumed that didn't include me.' And in case I sound petulant I add, 'But you know I liked Vanessa enormously.'

Our wine arrives then, thankfully, followed by our food. It is a struggle to eat anything, but I'm grateful for the wine, though I wouldn't normally be drinking at lunchtime.

'So what made you get in touch now, then?' Simon asks. He isn't eating much, either, but the wine is fast disappearing.

Carefully I say, 'I think I've met your mother. Recently, I mean.'

'Oh?' he says.

I can feel my heart starting to thump. 'That is, I think she's your mother. I'm pretty sure she is. But she insisted that she wasn't.'

He sips his wine and waits for me to continue.

'Or, rather, she insisted that she wasn't Vanessa's mother. And when I asked her about you – when I asked if she had a son called Simon ... well, she got sort of upset. Angry, really. She asked me to leave.' Which is, of course, an understatement. I feel a wave of heat, rising into my face.

'She asked you to leave where?' Simon asks slowly. He is watching me with narrowed eyes.

'Her house,' I say.

'You were in my mother's house?'

'Yes. Well, I was in this woman's house. In Kew.' I pause, but he says nothing, just watches me intently. '*Does* your mother live in Kew now?' I ask.

Simon lifts up his glass and puts it to his mouth. And he carries on looking at me as he drinks. Slowly he lowers his glass again, and he says, 'Yes. She does.' And then, 'But what were you doing at my mother's house?'

And so I tell him – the edited version, of course. That I'd dropped my son at his friend's and then popped into the cafe for a coffee, when in came this woman, who left her credit card. I heard her name, but it wasn't till she left that I made the connection, and I ran after her, and caught her up at her house. I tell him it was then that she invited me in. I don't want him to know that I followed her the way that I did. I don't want him to think that I am a person who creeps about, haunted by her own obsessions.

As he listens he holds onto the stem of his wine glass, which he slowly rolls between his thumb and his forefinger. Again I notice how bitten his nails are, which seems at odds with his tightly held composure. He watches me, his face so guarded.

'I was so sure that she was your mother, Simon, and yet she insisted that she wasn't.' Nervously I drink my wine. I feel that perhaps this is territory I have no right to venture into, almost as though I am prying. But I have to carry on. 'I remember your mother was so glamorous, Simon, so ... *vibrant* ... and yet ...' How can I say it? How can I tell him about the torn stockings and the frayed clothes, and just how shocked I was, to see her like that? 'I told her I was Vanessa's friend. I told her my name, not that I'd expect her to remember me, of course, but ... I just wanted to pass on my ... *love*, that's all, and to tell her how much Vanessa had meant to me.' I swallow. 'But she insisted she'd never had a daughter.'

I cannot think what else to say. The restaurant is noisy. All around us people are talking and laughing; the constant bray of the City lunch. And more deafening still is the endless clatter of cutlery on china, the clink of glasses, and the waiters putting down or piling up plates, and shouting to each other over the din. But all this fades into the background. At our table, suddenly, there is silence.

Simon lets go of his wine glass and taps at the base of it with his finger, agitated, tap-tap-tap. He is frowning, the muscles in his jaw set and tight. I wish that he would speak. My heart is racing away now, from the wine, from nerves.

At last he says, 'My mother has found life very hard.' He speaks slowly, carefully, as if picking his words.

'Yes, I'm sure she has, but to deny she is Vanessa's mother – it's like denying Vanessa ever existed ...'

He turns his head slightly, as if to avoid my words. He sighs, and then he picks up the wine bottle, sees that it is empty and puts it back down in frustration. He looks at me again. 'I know,' he says simply.

'But that's just awful.' The words come out thickly. There is a harshness in my throat, tightening it up.

We sit there, just looking at each other. He smiles at me, but it is a small, sad smile, and the sorrow in his eyes is infinite. Suddenly I have this image of him from years back: he's walking through the corridor to the den in their house in Oakley, carrying a beer and sort of half-dancing. I am on my way out of the den, in search of the loo, and we pass each other. He pulls back to make room for me, but I put my hand on his chest anyway and I pat him, affectionately, like you would a pet. *Oh, Simon*, I say, because that is what we all said; we toyed with him. And he put his hand on my hip, low down, not quite so much the kid that I thought he was. He caught me by surprise. I remember the shock of his fingers through my skirt. He smelled of soap and alcohol and boy.

Now I watch as he dips his head into his hand for a second, then runs his hand back through his hair. I see him thinking what to say. For long seconds he just stares at me. Then, 'When my sister died,' he says at last, 'we went through hell. You cannot imagine.' He says this, but he's wrong; I can imagine. I stare back at him and my eyes are burning, locked onto his. 'My mother ... struggled,' he says. There is a long, loaded pause. 'Now she denies she even had a daughter. It would seem to be the only way that she can cope.'

This isn't anything I hadn't worked out for myself. And yet to hear him say it still causes a horrible needling in the pit of my stomach, and across the front of my shoulders, the re-emergence of dread. I remember walking round and round my house in the days after I'd left my dead baby behind at the maternity hospital; I remember looking out the window at the sunlight, and seeing the postman cycling about on his round. I remember Jono running up and down our living room, dragging his dog-on-wheels behind him, up and down, up and down, and the relentless cheer of *Tots TV*. I remember the normality, the seeming predictability of life still moving along, and then suddenly it would hit me again: the panic, the ice-cold fingers of dread, nailing themselves into my body.

Without thinking, I reach across the table and put my hand on Simon's. 'I'm so sorry,' I say and there are tears stinging the backs of my eyes. He looks startled for a second, as though taken aback by my gesture. And then he looks away and stares down at the table, frowning intently. For a long moment he is completely still, apart from a tiny muscle flickering away faintly at the side of his jaw. I watch as he fights for control, and my chest is tight as a drum. I have to breathe slowly to stop myself from crying.

He turns his hand over now and takes my fingers in his, and he holds them tight. 'Thank you,' he says, but this exchange is more than twenty years too late. Again I imagine him at Vanessa's funeral, helplessly locking every detail of it into his young head, to be replayed over and over, an endless, inescapable nightmare. I imagine him looking into the faces of the people who were there, looking for some sort of recognition – verification almost – of his own pain. And I imagine him noticing who wasn't there; and who, in his eyes, didn't care.

'My mother didn't want to see any of Vanessa's friends,' he says. 'They came to the house. They wanted to talk about Vanessa. They wanted to see my mother, and me.' He looks at me with his eyes so clouded, so blue. 'But she didn't want to see them. She started making excuses, telling them she had to go out, or that she was busy.' There is a darkness back in his voice now, lacing the edge of his words. 'Soon they stopped coming. There was just me and her in the house. It was unbearable.'

'What about your father?' I ask.

'They divorced,' he says dismissively. 'They'd more or less split up anyway. Vanessa's death was the final straw.' Again, that sarcasm. He loosens his grip on my fingers and moves as if to take his hand away, but then doesn't. Instead he starts tapping one fingernail against my knuckle, just as he did with his wine glass, earlier. A nervous gesture; I don't think he knows that he's doing it. 'When I started seeing Fay, my mother was furious. Wouldn't have anything to do with her.'

Now he does let go of my hand and sits back in his chair. He picks up the empty bottle again, puts it back down again and says, 'We need some more wine.' Then, before I can object, he says, 'We can't.' He looks at his watch, runs his hand back through his hair, leaving it standing in ruffles, and sighs. 'I've got a meeting at two-thirty.' He drills his fingers on the table now, thinking what to do, what to say. Then, 'Can I see you again?' he asks. 'I'm sorry. I've got to get back to the office.'

'Yes, of course,' I say quickly, but instantly I'm thinking, *How? How will I see him again?* I know nothing about his current life, and he knows nothing about mine; we haven't touched on any of that.

He beckons the waiter for the bill, and when it comes he signs it impatiently. He glances at his watch again, then leans towards me and says, 'I have a daughter; Charlotte. She is five years old and my mother cannot bear to be in the same room as her. I have two boys too,' he adds quickly, 'but she tolerates them. She won't even look at Charlotte. On Christmas Eve I drove all the way up to Kew to collect her and bring her down to our house in Kingham, and the day after Christmas I drove her back again.' He pauses, and I'm thinking, *Just like Andrew; that's just like Andrew.* I almost say as much. Almost, but I don't. 'She didn't speak to Charlotte once. My little girl – my beautiful, gorgeous little girl – asks me why her grandma doesn't like her, but what can I say to her? How can I answer that?'

My feelings must be clear upon my face because, when I open my mouth to speak, he raises his hand slightly and says, 'No, please don't. This is what we've lived with. This is what we've lived with . . . ever since . . . ' Then, suddenly, 'Look, I have to get back. I'm sorry.' He takes a business card from his wallet, and his pen, and shoves them at me across the table. 'Write your number on here,' he says.

I scribble down my mobile number and he puts the card back in his wallet. 'I'm sorry,' he says again. 'I've got this meeting.'

'That's okay.'

'No, really.'

And I say, 'Really.'

Outside the restaurant we are assaulted by the cold and the rain and the hammering grind of the street. The change in air makes me light-headed; I have drunk too much and eaten too little.

'Which way are you headed?' Simon asks as we shelter by the doorway, putting up our umbrellas, buttoning up our coats.

And because I know that he is anxious to get back now,

and because I don't want the awkwardness of the two of us shuffling along together under our separate umbrellas, I point in the opposite direction to his office and the station. 'That way, I think,' I say vaguely.

He looks as if he's about to question me, but doesn't. Instead he says, 'I'll call you.'

And I say, 'Thank you for lunch. It has been good to see you again.'

He sort of flinches, an impatient gesture. And then he leans towards me suddenly and grips my arm. With his other hand he's holding his umbrella, but at a bad angle; rain is already soaking the right shoulder of his coat. I notice this and I look at it, to break the intensity of his stare. 'You will let me see you again, won't you?' he says. 'You won't just disappear again.'

And, taken aback, I say, 'No. I mean, yes. Of course.'

He lets go of my arm as suddenly as he took hold of it and stands back now. 'Yes,' he repeats, 'Of course. Thank you.' But there is a bleakness in his voice, as if he cannot believe me.

I watch him go. He walks fast, one man under his umbrella, vanishing into a sea of men under their umbrellas. For a long while I stand there, with people shoving past me on the narrow pavement. The rain is metal in my mouth, the cold of it creeping like a ghost into my skin. I wonder if he will call me, and how I will see him again if he does.

But you can't let something like this go. You just can't.

And then I start walking too, back to Bank station. It is too wet to go shopping, too wet to do anything other than go home. And besides, the wine is already making my head ache. I need a drink of water, and I think I'll buy a bottle at

Waterloo, but when I get there the next train to Surbiton is about to leave, so I get straight on it, and of course there's nowhere on the train to buy water. I sit there, looking at the rain lashing the carriage windows, with my mouth drying up and a heavy lethargy creeping into my veins. I want to think, but the rhythm of the train lulls me into leaden doze, and so by the time I get home my head is pounding.

I let myself in to the stillness of my house. In the kitchen I pour myself a glass of water, and then another. The morning's breakfast things are still piled around the sink and the dishwasher is waiting to be emptied, but I cannot face any of it. I have to lie down. And so I go upstairs, where my bed is strewn with various items of clothing from this morning's last-minute panic over what to wear; I push them all to one side and collapse down on top of the duvet.

And that is where I am when Jono gets home. The ringing of the doorbell penetrates my weird, kaleidoscopic dreams and wakes me up. I lie there disoriented for a second, and the bell rings again. Slowly I sit up, then stand, and the blood rises dizzily to my head, starting up the pounding once more. Again the bell rings, and again. I know it's Jono; no one else would be so impatient.

'What took you so long?' he barks at me when I open the door, and flings his bag into the hall, barely missing my legs.

'I was asleep,' I say quietly. 'I have a headache.'

He kicks off his shoes, rips off his jacket and drops them down on the doormat.

'Why didn't you use your key?' I ask.

And he says, 'Couldn't be bothered to get it out,' and pushes past me, to go straight into the living room.

I call him back. 'Jono, don't just leave your things here. Put them away, please.'

He ignores me.

'Jono, come and move your things, please.'

'Why?' he grunts from the living room. I can hear that he's turned on the TV.

'Because they are in the way,' I say patiently. 'People will trip over them.'

'There's no one here,' he snaps.

'I'm here,' I say, but I say it quietly. I say it to the walls, to the air.

He switches channels. I hear the grating whine of an American cartoon.

'Jono,' I say again.

'*What?*'

'Come and move your things, please.'

'I'm watching this.'

'Jono!'

I hear him throw the remote control on the floor, and he swears, just loud enough for me to hear. But he comes back into the hall.

'Thank you,' I say.

He flings his shoes into the cupboard and slings his jacket at a coathanger. It slides straight off, to lie rumpled on the cupboard floor unless I pick it up again in a minute, which we both know that I will. He starts kicking his bag along the hall.

I take a deep breath. I try again.

'How was your day at school?' I ask after his retreating back.

He doesn't answer.

And so this is it; I come crashing back to earth with a heavy thump.

*

I clear up the kitchen and start to prepare supper. I put some washing in the machine. I drink a cup of tea, and then another, followed by a glass of water and an aspirin; all of this within the closed five o'clock world of my kitchen.

I chop an onion and throw it into the pan. I add the garlic, the tomatoes, the meat. I put the water on for spaghetti. And while it all cooks I stare out of the window at the dark. Someone has left the outside light on, and in its foggy glow I can see the constant flicker of rain still falling. If Andrew was here he'd pull the blinds down, but I cannot bear to be so totally closed in. And I like the dark; I like its secrecy. I push open the window, to let a little air in, and I can hear the rain now, the faint, whispering patter. The air smells of river water, and petrol.

And now I think about Simon. I recount the details of the day with slow, precise scrutiny. I stand here, within the solitary island of my domestic life, and I picture his face: his eyes, his nose, his forehead, his chin. I put the pieces of him together in my head and I study them.

He said he lives in Kingham, which is a place I have never heard of, but he said he drove all the way *up* from there to Kew, so it must be in the country somewhere, away from London. Not in Surrey; I'd know it if it was in Surrey. Somewhere further out, then. And he has three children, and a wife. I try to picture him in his life, but I can't. All I see of him is these vague, fleeting images from years ago; Simon at fourteen. I hardly know him. I tell myself this and yet there is a pull, as though on the air around me, fingers dragging at my soul. I hardly know him, and yet . . .

I refocus my eyes; instead of staring out at the dark I stare at the glass of the window now, and at my reflection in it, distorted, unworldly. I see myself as a ghost, captured out of time, just passing through this life. I see myself at sixteen, hungry for life, for newness, believing that the world was out there for me, in all its unknown possibilities.

And here I am now, cooking other people's meals, tending to other people's lives.

I turn away from the window and the kitchen crowds in on me.

'Jono, supper is ready,' I call down the hall.

I can hear the false, chippy laughter of American TV.

'Jono.' My voice is hollow, an echo of itself, a repeat on autodrive. 'Jono.'

'I'll come when this has finished.'

'Come now, please.'

His spaghetti is in a bowl, waiting for him. His fork is there too, and his spoon. And his orange juice, and a small bunch of grapes, the small, sweet, red seedless ones that he likes. All ready for him, all waiting. I wait. And eventually, when it suits him, he comes. My son, the lord of this house. He sits, he eats. I sit opposite him, I watch him eat. I make conversation. I watch gratefully as each strand of spaghetti disappears inside him, and I ask: how was school, tell me about your day, do you have any homework?

And he reacts as though I am interrogating him.

'Why do you want to know?' he complains. 'Stop going on.'

And I say, 'Jono, I'm only asking.'

'Well, don't,' he says. 'You ask me the same things, over and over.'

'Jono, I'm your mother,' I reply. 'I care.'

He frowns at his plate, his cheeks flushed and puffy as a toddler's. I get up and turn to the sink, and start clearing up.

*

I see myself inside a vacuum, sucked in until the sides are all gone. I see my face, pulled long, trapped on the same old words. I cannot move, I cannot breathe. I see myself growing old, putting out plate after plate of food for those who grudgingly come to eat it. I hear myself, pleading for a return. *How are you?* I plead, at the door, on the way out, on the way in. At the bottom of the stairs, the top of the stairs, in the morning, again at night, on the phone. Soon, it will always be by phone. My shrunken face, talking into the nothingness: *How are you?*

And Jono, wherever he is, however far from me, however longed for, never, not even once, asking me the same thing back.

Andrew is going to be late. He phones me to tell me so.

'I've got to get this report out. I don't know what time I'll be home,' he says in a warning tone, the same sort of tone that a plumber or a builder might use to brace you for a ridiculous quote. He uses this tone because he expects me to object. After all, I would have done once upon a time. Only nowadays I realize that I am just as much on my own when Andrew is in the house as when he is not.

'Oh' is all I say.

And then he asks, 'How's Jono? How did he get on at school today?'

'Okay, I presume. He didn't have a lot to say.'

Now it is Andrew's turn to say, 'Oh.' Then there is a pause, during which I can hear him tapping at a keyboard. 'Well,' he goes on, 'I'd better get on, or I'll be here all night.' And then, as if it is an afterthought, he says, 'And how are you?'

And, as usual, I say, 'Fine.'

*

And so there are just Jono and me in the house, but Jono is busy with his homework. I cover Andrew's supper with a bowl and stick it in the fridge, and then I move about the rooms, picking this up, putting that away. I move slowly; my headache is more or less gone now, but the memory of it hangs there like a threat. And then, faintly within the quiet of the house, I hear the muffled ringing of my phone and my heart jumps. I know it's Simon. It could one of any number of people, but I know that it's him. My phone is in my bag still, in the hall. By the time I get to it the ringing has stopped. I dig my phone out and stare at the screen. One missed call, it says, and up flashes the number, a new number. And then the voicemail message pops up. I sit on the bottom of the stairs and my heart is thumping. Jono is just across the hall in the dining room, doing his homework. I press the voicemail answer key and put the phone to my ear.

I hear his voice, familiar now. 'Rachel,' he says, 'hi. It's Simon.' He pauses, as if thinking what to say, then, 'I hope this isn't an inconvenient time. I just wanted to thank you for seeing me today. I'm sorry I had to rush off like that. It was so good talking to you. I'd really like to see you again.' There is another pause, and then, 'I don't want to put pressure on you of course if you'd rather not ... but, well, I do hope you will return my call.'

The self-doubt in his voice pulls at my heart. Again I imagine him at Vanessa's funeral, looking around at all those familiar faces, at all those people who'd piled in and out of his house at the weekends, all of them there except for me. I saw Leanne's invitation to the funeral; she'd put it on her dressing table, up in her room. The very idea of a funeral invitation seemed strange to me. It was a small, square card with coiled silver lettering, much like you'd get for a wedding invitation or a christening. *A celebration of the life of Vanessa Lydia Reiber* it read, or something like that. I suppose Yolande must have gone through Vanessa's address book, though surely some of the others would only have heard the arrangements via word of mouth. Not everyone would have got an invitation. I wouldn't have been the only one who didn't, and yet why did I act as if I was? Why did it feel as if I was? Leanne and I could have gone together, but she never said anything along the lines of *Are you coming?* Just as afterwards, when she talked about it, she never said that I was missed. No, it was very clear to me that I wasn't included. I was an outsider. I knew and adored Vanessa, but I was the audience on the other side of the rope, reaching over. I never had the chance to become more than that.

Maybe I should have just gone to the funeral anyway. I wish I had gone now, but I was too hung up on my sense of rejection. And Simon was right, I did just disappear. I thought it was everyone else, but looking back now, I see that it was me.

I sit there at the bottom of the stairs and am flooded with a wave of regret, not just about the funeral, but over the loss of all those friends: Vanessa, Leanne, Tristram, Annabel . . . And for the loss of myself as I was back then; so free and alive under the light of so much fun. It all came to a stop so suddenly. It came to a stop and what did I do? I went to college, to university, I worked hard, I travelled, I married, I had a son . . . I did a lot. But I don't think I ever really had fun again. Not real, pure fun, like I did back then when I was a teenager, before I became aware of how quickly the good things can be snatched away. I feel as far away from the girl I was then as it is possible to be. I feel the loss, like an imprint inside my bones.

In the dining room Jono slams his books shut and scrapes back his chair. I stand up quickly and, like a guilty child, I hide my phone behind my back. The dining-room door flings open and he almost walks into me. He stops short, as though faced with something unpleasant. I see the shutters come down in his eyes.

But still I force a smile. 'Finished your homework?' I ask in my good-mother voice.

'I'm going on the PlayStation,' he says by way of an answer and manoeuvres around me, to run off upstairs.

'Okay,' I call up after him. 'Not too long now, though; it's getting late.'

Then I walk back to the kitchen, taking my phone with me, and close the door. I sit down at the table and store Simon's number in my phone. And then, before I have time to change my mind, I press the call button. His phone rings for quite a while, for much longer than mine, which switches to voicemail after just seconds, and I sit there with my heart hammering, panicking suddenly. I try to picture him in a home environment, with his wife, with his children. I try, but I can't.

And then he answers. 'Rachel,' he says. 'I was afraid you wouldn't want to speak to me.'

'Of course,' I say. 'I just didn't get to the phone in time.'

'It was good to see you today.'

'It was good to see you too.'

My heart is pounding. I feel like a teenager, stuck suddenly for words.

'I'm sorry I had to rush off,' he says. 'You must think me so rude.'

'Not at all, really.'

'I feel very bad for abandoning you like that.'

'Really, it's okay.'

There is a pause. In it, I notice the silence of the background at his end, and I wonder where he is. Then, 'Are you always this forgiving?' he asks and there is something in his tone, in his choice of words, that disturbs me, but then I remember suddenly that he said the same thing to me once before, or something similar. At one of those parties, at that stage in the night when everyone was drunk and crashing out, he tripped me up. Not deliberately; he was sitting on the floor near the door to the den with his legs stretched out, and as I stepped over him he moved. I tripped, and would have landed on my face, but he sat forward, caught me and steadied me. 'Forgive me,' he said dramatically, his voice thick with beer, and when I laughed he leant back again. 'Of course you will,' he said. 'Rachel is always so nice. Rachel is always so forgiving.'

These memories. These abstract little things, forgotten for so long, spinning back now to life.

'Rachel,' he says now, 'can I see you again? Soon? I've got a case on this week, but Monday maybe, or Tuesday? We could meet after work perhaps; would that be possible?' He talks fast, nervous now. 'I feel so bad that we couldn't talk longer at lunchtime. And . . . I really do want to talk to you, Rachel.'

I sit there at the table in the oppressive silence of my kitchen, and my heart slows to a hard, dangerous thump. 'Tuesday should be okay,' I say.

And he says, as though he really means it, 'Thank you, Rachel. Thank you.'

When we hang up, I go straight upstairs, switch on the computer and look up Kingham. And I see it there, with all its tourist-board photos. *An idyllic village in the heart of Oxfordshire*. There are photos of the pub and the village green, and an abundance of Cotswold-stone houses, complete with rose-filled walled gardens and golden thatched roofs.

This is where Simon lives, with his wife, and his daughter called Charlotte, and his two nameless sons. Which is his house? I feel I am looking at it on the screen, I feel it is one of these buildings. I feel it must be. I stare all the harder. In some pictures there are people, and so I search for him. I find a photo from a couple of years ago of a village fair. He's there, I know he is. I stare and I search. It's a hell of a commute to London. At least an hour and a half to Paddington, and then on from there by Tube. So two hours, I reckon, at least, door to door. And another two hours back home again, to his wife, his daughter and his sons and their rose-covered cottage in their idyllic Cotswold village.

There is even a residents' notice board. I scrutinize the messages. Some dispute over parking around the pub, another over the removal of a bench on the green. There is a fete planned in May, with an invitation for children to come forward for the parade. I see messages posted by Harriet, Louisa, Clare and Jane. Which one of these is his wife? Which one? I look up everything I can about this place, which I had never heard of until now. I look it up on Google maps. I trace the route by road to London, to Kew, to Surbiton.

I stare and I search until my eyes burn. And then the voice of reason snaps into my consciousness: *What am I doing?* I shut down the computer. I turn away from the screen and look at the window, at the black of the night and the rain still beading against the glass. From the spare room I can hear the fuzzy roar and blast of a million aliens exploding at will on the PlayStation, long after he should be in bed. I wonder if Andrew is sitting at his desk still, with his tie loosened and his jacket slung over the back of his chair, frowning over the importance of random, faceless numbers. Or will he be making his way home now, standing on the platform at Guildford station, sheltering from the rain? I picture him, huddled under his umbrella, wrapped up in his silence. And I picture him bringing that silence home.

Inside my heart is a dark and secret place. I close my eyes and imagine myself trapped within a vast cave, and in that cave there is a deep and still lagoon. I pick up a pebble, I throw it, and I watch it disappear. I watch as the black surface of the lagoon ripples open and then closes again. I see myself, standing at the edge, ready to dive.

TEN

On Saturday I take Jono to Oliver's house. He's been invited for a sleepover, and I drop him off there, mid-afternoon. Jono is anxious, I can tell, and it strikes me that there is something wrong about being nervous to see your friends. It's as if he's stressed at having to perform and is worried that he'll get it wrong somehow. He'd never admit anything like this to me, but that is the impression I get, and it seems to me to be very sad. I think back, and wonder: was I ever like that as a child? And the answer is: no, I'm sure I wasn't, not at that age.

Now maybe. But now things are different, every social interaction a weighing-up and a judgement, a laying-out of assets to be displayed. I have a handful of real, close friends who I have known forever, but they live in Yorkshire and Buckinghamshire, and Bath now. I hardly ever see them. We speak on the phone. We meet now and again, and I love them as I have always loved them.

But it is the people you see every day that shape and colour your world.

Jono isn't the only one sleeping over. Oliver has room for Isaac and Luke, too. They are there already; Amy tells us so when she answers the door.

'They're in the games room,' she tells Jono. 'Go on and join them.'

Jono looks at me. It's the same look he gave me on his first day at school.

'I'll see you tomorrow, darling,' I say. 'Have a good time.'

The look in his eyes breaks my heart. I see how much he needs me, and yet how he wishes that he didn't. He tries to appear nonchalant and starts walking down the hall, his body stiff and awkward.

'You're going to be busy then,' I say to Amy, with a big, forced smile. I feel her watching me watching Jono. I feel her making notes.

'Not at all,' she says breezily. 'We've people coming later; friends, with their children. It'll be quite a party, I think. The children will have a ball.'

She smiles her polished, confident smile and I suppress a flicker of irritation that she didn't tell me before that there would be other people here. Isaac and Luke I knew about, because Oliver told Jono, but a houseful? I picture poor Jono, stuck in a house full of strangers. We're not like that, in our family. We're just not like that. We don't surround ourselves with people, we don't just gang up – the more, the merrier. We're quiet people, however much we may all wish that we weren't.

But still.

I take from my bag a piece of paper on which I have already written my mobile number, and hold it out to her. 'Andrew and I are out tonight, but you can call me on my mobile,' I say. 'If there's any problem.'

She slowly unfolds her arms, takes the piece of paper without looking at it and folds her arms again, so that my phone number dangles carelessly from her fingers, soon to be forgotten, soon to be misplaced. Her smile is a little less benign now.

'Why would there be a problem?' she says.

I am loath to leave. Every fibre of my body is screaming to see Jono one more time before I go, to ask if he really wants to stay, to take him home with me if given the chance. But I am fussing. And social mores dictate that I must leave my child in this house full of unknown people, and trust that he will be fine.

I walk away from there, worried that he will be thirsty, hungry, homesick, shy ... I worry as though he were a three-year-old. I worry because it is my duty to worry, my purpose, the very essence of myself. My love and fear for Jono wrap themselves snake-like around my throat and squeeze. It is all I can do just to keep walking. Panic spots an opportunity and sends out its spores, shooting prickles into my hands. What would I do without Jono? What am I without Jono?

And there is the real fear.

I fold my arms across the front of my body and walk. My car is parked just a short way from Amy's house, but I walk slowly, in no hurry to go home. I need some apples, and maybe some bread, things I could buy from the shops near the station. And so I have an errand, something to do. A distraction.

And into my head suddenly comes this bizarre image. Last summer we went on a short holiday to Cornwall. We stayed in Fowey, and while we were there the regatta took place. The village was packed with people night and day and there were all sorts of celebrations going on. Most of the people were from London; they had descended on Fowey in their hordes. And the thing that I noticed most was how they all knew each other, these people. There were literally hundreds of them; boaty types with lean, tanned legs wearing shorts and sailing jackets in blue or red or yellow, and rubber shoes on their feet. I remember how the women called to each other and to their kids, standing tall as they did so, one hand sheltering their mouths, as they bellowed out their instructions in crisp London accents: *Posy, Ned, Hugo, we're off to find some lunch now*. Not at all afraid of their own voices. Not at all afraid of being heard. They acted as though they owned the place. And I remember their children, mucking around on the shingle, dragging boats and dinghies in and out of the water as though they'd done it all their lives, which they no doubt had.

We watched them, Andrew, Jono and I. We watched them from our spot in the shade down at the water's edge, and in the streets, and again in the restaurants. They moved through the village en masse, filling every space with their presence.

'They're just another tribe,' Andrew said. 'You get the skiing tribe, the football tribe, and this is the yachting tribe. Some people just go around in tribes.'

I watched them, repelled and envious in equal measure. We three, we have no tribe. We have nothing to protect us from ourselves.

I buy my apples, my bread and one or two other things. I buy a ridiculously expensive string bag in which to carry them and walk out of the shop, feeling just a little like I've been had.

I think of Jono, and I hope that he is settling in, that he is happy enough, mixing with Amy's tribe.

Sometimes, when I was growing up, there were parties across the road at Leanne's house. Cars would arrive and clog up the street. Music would go on, until the early hours. I'd lie in my little bedroom with the window open, and I'd hear the laughter. The next day Leanne would have purple bruises like thumbprints under her eyes, and she'd feel sick, and shake a little, as though from the cold, never mind that it was hot. It was always hot; they were always summer parties, always spreading out into the long, sultry nights.

And the next day my parents would be tight-lipped and drawn with disapproval. They'd go about their Sunday routine a little slower, a little quieter than usual.

'Would you like a cup of tea, love?' my dad would ask my mum.

And she would sigh and say, 'Yes. Yes, I would, thank you. I'm too tired for anything today.'

'I think we'd better all have an early night, tonight,' my dad would say, pointedly.

Later, they'd be out the front, supposedly watering the plants. I'd see them, with their hosepipe and their watering can, each of them with their eyes fixed across the road.

'Bit quieter tonight,' my dad might say.

And my mum would add, 'I should think so.'

And I believe that they were repelled and envious in equal measure, too.

And now, as I make my way along the road like a tourist with my overpriced goods in my overpriced bag, I realize that is how we live, too. I am the child of my parents, as Jono is cursed to be the child of me, and of Andrew. I think this, and my heart is caught with a sharp and scratching anger. I do not want to live my life in a perpetual audience, forever on the sidelines. I do not want it for me, and I do not want it for my son.

I walk fast, angry now. Angry with myself, with all of us. Suddenly I wish that we could be the ones down on the shingle in Fowey, the ones that the quiet people watch. When I met Andrew I knew that he was kind, honest, decent. I thought that I would be safe with him, but I know now that there is no such thing as safe; there is only fear and denial.

We are in denial.

When our baby girl died, we bundled ourselves up and pulled ourselves together as though we could just carry on like before. After all, there never was a real baby, an *actual* baby that you could see and hold, just a swelling of my belly and an image on a screen. The cot went back in the loft. The buggy went back to John Lewis. We still had Jono. We were just as we were.

Only we weren't.

I reach the junction where the road curls round to Mrs Reiber's house, and I look down there, half-expecting to see her. I stop myself from walking down there, but I think of her, sitting in that gloomy house, with just her own denial for company. And again I feel so angry, so *frustrated*. I think of Simon coming here, to Kew, to visit his mother. I think of him driving around these same streets – walking, probably, along this very same pavement. And I think how dangerously easily life can become stilted and stunted, never moving on, just a series of daily routines running one day into the next. I see the frightening similarities between his mother and myself, and the thought appals me.

Tonight, as we have no Jono, Andrew and I are going out to a restaurant. After all, that is what you do when your child is at a sleepover; you make the most of it. You cannot stay at home; you cannot avoid each other without your child there to hide behind.

So we are going out.

I take my time getting ready. It feels like a big deal, a test almost. In the shower I exfoliate, I condition my hair. I rid my body of excess hair and excess dry skin; I buff and I preen. And then I stand naked in front of my full-length mirror and I look at myself; at the whiteness of my skin with its smattering of freckles, at the roundness of my breasts and my thighs, and at my mother's tummy: soft, pliant, used. I am the giver of life and the taker away.

I do not like to look at myself. I do not like to be naked. My body is no longer a source of pleasure, but an object of functions; I inhabit it, but it is not me. But now I try to look at myself objectively. I turn sideways, I pull in my stomach. I do not have a bad body, but I have a body that has been neglected. I have a body that has not been loved for a very long time. And when I look at my nakedness I am reminded of that.

But tonight I make an effort, to see what happens.

And what happens is that Andrew drives us to the Italian restaurant out past the golf club, and we walk in and are seated at a small table near the back. At the table next to us, on one side, sits a youngish couple, clearly very much in love. All evening I am aware of the way that they keep holding hands across the table and the way that the man strokes his strong, fine fingers across the backs of hers. And he smiles at her, and doesn't take his eyes off her. I notice that she is wearing an engagement ring, but no wedding ring. *Just wait*, I can't help thinking, *just you wait*. She sits on the same side of the table as me, and I have to turn surreptitiously sideways to get a good look at her, and then of course

I wish that I hadn't. She is young, and unselfconsciously beautiful, her dark hair sleek and shiny, her olive skin shown off to perfection by her red strappy top. The tables are close together and she is well within Andrew's vision. He only has to move his eyes a mere flicker to the right and he can look at her properly, and so every time he picks up his glass, or raises his fork, I think that this is what he is doing.

On the other side of us sits another couple, a little older than us this time, and even more jaded. They barely speak to each other, but oh boy, do they drink, bottle after bottle. It strikes me as somewhat unfortunate that we three women should all be seated on the same side of our tables, with our backs to the walls, and thus be presented in a row as the various stages of disillusionment.

The restaurant is popular, and the larger tables in the middle of the room are taken up by people out in groups, couples out with other couples, chatting, laughing, having fun. From my seat I can watch them, and see all that fun they are having. Andrew, as he has his back to the room, can only look at me, or the wall behind me, or that beautiful girl to my left. Or the other woman, to my right, of course. I smile, and do my best to engage him. I feel that we have entered a show, and that now we must play our parts.

We make polite chat. We talk about Jono mostly, of course, and the house, and our plans for the summer. Or, rather, our lack of plans for the summer. We cannot afford much; our money is all being spent on Jono's school. And the truth is I don't much like summer holidays; to me, everything that is wrong with us is magnified when we are away, when we are stuck together for a week, the three of us, dependent and bound. I picture us, trudging around foreign streets in mutual silence, or saying, *Look, Jono, look at the man over there with the bird on his shoulder*; or *Look, Jono, do you see how rickety that building is?* And Jono, sullenly, painfully, snapping back, *Yes, yes, I know, I can see, you don't have to go on.*

Once, when Jono was younger, we went on a package holiday to a hotel with a children's club. It was hell. Not for Jono so much, but for us. We had to deliver him to the club at 9.15 in the morning and we didn't see him again until five. The hours in between were interminable. We pined for him. We counted the seconds. And when we got him back again, we fell upon him with our anxious questions: *Did you have enough to drink, what did you have for lunch, did you put your sun cream on, stay in the shade, wear a hat?* We smothered him with neurotic love, till the joy was squashed right out of him. Poor Jono. He doesn't want to be with us, but we can't bear to be without him.

So when Andrew sits opposite me now, saying, 'We could go to France, maybe, and stay in a caravan on one of those sites with the big swimming pools. I know it's not very exciting, but it wouldn't cost too much if we just had a week, and Jono would like the pools,' I cannot raise much enthusiasm. I cannot think of anything worse than the three of us being holed up together in a caravan, surrounded by other noisier, happier families who are good at that sort of thing, spilling out their fun and their laughter and multiple children, along with their bicycles and their barbecues, and all the other families that they came with or just happen to meet up with while they are there . . . I cannot think of anything that would make me feel more alone. But Andrew is hardly enthusiastic either, really; he makes the suggestions okay, but it's as if he feels that it's what is expected of him. There is a huge shadow of negativity behind his voice. His tone reminds me of those old people you see waiting in pairs at bus stops, when one might comment on the good weather we're having and the other will come back with an *Ah, but we'll pay for it later*. When did Andrew start speaking like that, as if there's a condition and a price to be paid for everything? 'If we booked early we might get a good deal on the Channel tunnel,' he's saying, 'or maybe we could look at the ferries.'

Of course I am supposed to take his idea and run with it. It is my job to add the enthusiasm. *Oh yes, that'll be lovely*, I'm supposed to say, all bright-eyed and eager. *Jono will have a great time. It doesn't have to cost a lot. We can do our own cooking; it'll be fun, it'll be cosy* . . .

And then he'll do that thing of tilting his head to one side and drawing in his breath slightly, as if having second thoughts now. *Oh, I don't know, though*, he'll say in his bus-stop voice, *it would have to be pretty cheap this year*.

I'll look around, I'll say. *I'll look on the Internet, get some brochures* . . . I'll wheedle and persuade. I'll perform as if it was the best idea ever, and then he, Mr Purse-Strings, will concede. And won't he feel like the big man then.

Isn't that the way it goes? Isn't that what's expected in the shunting and shifting that keeps a marriage going? Like we are an old train with rusty wheels in need of constant oiling. If I did perform like that, we would have a good evening. We would have something new to talk about, to share, to get excited over. We would lean closer across the table, my face would become animated and, therefore, attractive. He might even tell me that I look pretty when I smile. If I could bring myself to perform like that, we would have a chance.

But I can't.

I find myself comparing him to Simon. Or, rather, comparing

this situation to my lunch with Simon. I think of Simon's long, slender fingers scrunching up that piece of card, or tapping at his wine glass. And clutching my hand. *It's so good to see you*, he said. And, *You look amazing*.

And here is Andrew, going on about caravans. He eats as he talks. I see the food moving around inside his mouth. I see the dark speckles on his chin and his jaw where he shaved this morning, but could have done with shaving again, tonight. I wish that he would look at me the way Simon looked at me, and I hate him because he doesn't.

'I do not want to stay in a caravan,' I say, and he shuts up now. His face colours a little, and irritation tightens his jaw. 'I mean, why would I want to stay in a caravan? I'd end up cooking, and cleaning, and mopping the floor, just like I do at home. Only in a caravan.'

'I thought it would be fun for Jono,' Andrew says in a hurt voice.

And I say, 'When does Jono ever have fun with us?'

We carry on eating in silence. I become even more aware of the loving couple to the left of me, and the not-so-loving couple to the right. Andrew is driving, so I drink most of the wine, but it doesn't make me feel good; it makes me feel prickly and on edge, and even more on my own.

Eventually Andrew says, 'Well, do you have any better suggestions?'

'We could just not go on holiday,' I say flippantly. 'And spare ourselves the misery.'

'I'm sorry that you feel like that,' Andrew says and his face stills and shuts down. What I want, what I really want, is for him to grab my hand across the table and say, *Come on, we'll have a good time*, or to tell me that he loves me, or even just that we'll be okay. That would do; if he would just tell me that we'll be okay. But he says none of these things, and so I goad him further, I dig myself into a hole.

'I'm sorry too,' I say. 'But it's true. When do we ever have any fun?'

My voice is too loud, and I see him glance to the sides. Shame and loathing twist inside me. I hate myself. He makes me hate myself.

'I'm sorry that you find me so boring,' he says coldly. And then he turns away from me, to signal for the bill. The evening is over, ruined – as ever – by me, and my need for more than this. My need for more than just politeness, and parenthood, and just getting by. I feel my face hot, from the wine, from frustration. We cannot talk. We can never talk. But neither can we even argue.

In the car I say, 'I do not find you boring. But I do want to have some fun. And I do not want it always to be about Jono.'

After a moment he says very quietly, 'You know, you can be incredibly cruel sometimes, Rachel.'

And quick as a flash I say straight back, 'So can you, Andrew, so can you.'

We do not speak again, all the way home. I stare ahead to avoid looking at his stony face, and the tears burn fierce and useless in my eyes.

I lie on our bed, naked apart from my underwear, but it's my best underwear. Black lace, optimistically bought, not so very long ago. In a different frame of mind, I would just put on my nightie and clean my teeth and curl myself into the loneliness of the dark, but tonight I am determined. I am teetering in a dangerous place, and if Andrew had any feeling for me at all he would know it, he would see it, and he would do his damnedest to bring me back. That he might not see it or, even worse, might see it but still not care, is too terrifying for words. So I lie here, and I wait.

He is a long time downstairs. I hear him in the kitchen getting a glass of water. I hear him go into the living room and turn on the TV. My heart bats against my ribs like a trapped bird.

'Are you coming up?' I asked when we got back from the restaurant.

And he said, 'I'll be up in a minute.'

He says I am cruel, but how cruel is he? I lie here with my teeth gritted and my entire being a boiling, hurting mass of rejection. I resist calling to him, though that is what I used to do. I used to go to the top of the stairs and call down, *Andrew, what are you doing? Andrew, will you come up to bed?* Like a nag, or worse still, as if I was begging. Begging, for my husband to come and be my lover, to *love* me.

I will not beg.

Once, I accused him of being gay. Oh yes, he's right, I can be cruel. I lay beside him, desperate to be loved, to be held, to be *wanted*. But all I got was his eternal coldness, the frigid politeness of an indifferent arm around my shoulders. I wriggled against him. I prodded his ribs. He lay on his back – that arm around me as still and unyielding as a dead man's.

I sighed. I wriggled some more. His breathing deepened as he started drifting to sleep, and I dug my finger hard into his side.

'Ow!' he yelped, and turned to me at last. 'What did you do that for?'

I wanted an effect. I wanted to hit home. 'Tell me something,' I said in a voice that scratched out hard and hateful. 'Are you gay?'

He looked at me, his eyes cloudy with tiredness. 'I am not gay,' he said slowly and precisely. And he turned over, and went to sleep.

I wait, and I wait.

I can't stop the tears, creeping into my eyes. They are the mean, redundant tears of a forty-one-year-old woman, messing up my mascara. I reach over the side of the bed and grab my hand-mirror, and a tissue, and then I lie back down again, on my back, and blot at my eyes. I hold the mirror above me and look at my face, and as I look, more tears slide out. How did I come to be like this? I am still young enough, pretty enough; it should not be over for me. I feel that I am being slowly killed; that the price I am paying for this mother-hood and this marriage is the draining away of myself.

And what kind of price is that?

The night sinks on. He will be asleep, in front of the TV. I am too raw to move, too full of fear now. I drag the duvet over my body and close my eyes. It is over. I know it, as I have known it for a long time. It's over, yet what can I do?

What can I ever do, when there is Jono?

I wake with a jolt. My eyes are sticky, glued up with mascara tears. I think that I am still alone, but I stick out a foot and there is Andrew beside me. That he managed to slink in somehow once I'd fallen asleep fills me with a deep, slow rage. It is like having a stranger in my bed. He sleeps beside me, but he is not with me. His very presence simply reinforces my aloneness.

I turn over and prop myself up on my elbow. He is sleeping on his side, curled away from me. I listen to the steady rhythm of his breathing, and I wonder how it is that he can sleep so easily when I am wide awake now. I pull back the duvet and look at him, this man that I have loved, this father of my son. I study him, the planes of his back, the curve of his spine, and my heart is a tight, hard knot. I cannot remember the last time we had sex, but when we did that's all that it was – sex. A pushing and a shoving and a grunting, until it was done. I lay underneath Andrew and I looked at his eyes, and I saw how hard it was for him to hold my gaze, as if he was embarrassed somehow by what he was doing. I saw how he held himself back; his lower half did the work, but his head – it wasn't with me. We didn't connect. It was just an act, like animals might do in the park, a bodily need and therefore slightly shameful, as if it was something that mummies and daddies shouldn't do. As if it was something that people who had given birth to dead babies shouldn't do. I felt as if I was the source of shame. Me. It is my body that produced the dead baby, after all. Why would he want to make love to that?

So I look at him now, and anger and frustration and self-loathing wash through me in waves. I want to touch him. I long to touch him. I move closer, till my face is almost against his back. The tiny hairs on his skin rise as though to a magnet and tickle my nose. His skin is so warm, the scent of it so familiar, and yet so out of bounds. I want to curl into him and press my body against his, but how can I? How can I, when he has rejected me so?

Andrew is up before me. He has things to do: the fence to fix at the end of the garden, and the area behind the shed to clear. Such things will take him a good many weekends. I wake up and I am alone. For a while I lie there and I imagine what it would be like always to wake alone. Would it be so bad? Would it really be any worse than this?

I picture Andrew sneaking quietly out of bed so as not to disturb me, and then doing his best to avoid me by occupying himself outside. Did we row? Is that how he sees it? To my mind, it would be better if we did row, instead of this constant simmering tension.

I get up and put on my bathrobe. I am still wearing last night's underwear, like an unwanted whore. I glance in the mirror and see my messy hair and my streaky, mascara-blackened eyes. What a sight my face must have made upon the pillow. What a sorry, pathetic sight.

I walk down the hall to Jono's room. I push open the door and I can smell my child, both his presence and his absence. His bed is still rumpled from yesterday, his pyjamas flung upon the floor. Even though he is not here, he fills this room. It will always be his room. I cannot imagine ever leaving this house, when Jono has grown up; I cannot imagine there not being this room for him, into which I can go just to be close to him. Suddenly I remember Vanessa's room, with its white furniture and blue walls and the little silver moons dangling from her light shade; I think of her clothes all squashed into her wardrobe and her shoes piled up underneath, their heels sticking out in random spikes, and of all the half-used bottles of lotions and potions on her dressing table, her make-up and her hair brushes, clogged with their catch of hairs. I think of the dirty pair of knickers kicked under her bed one night when we were there – *Oh my God, don't look at those!* – and of her old teddy bears lined up like an audience on the top of her bunk beds, to be sat upon, and squashed or shoved out the way, by us. I think of the old travel sweet-tin that she used as an ashtray, with its little graveyard of lipstick-tipped cigarette butts, pressed down into the ash. And I think of the smell of her room, the smell of her perfume and her clothes, the smell of teenager and stale cigarettes, and just of *her*.

What did her mother do with all that stuff? What would I do, if it was me? I would keep it, all of it, I couldn't bear not to. But how long does it take for a person to fade from a room, till the scent of them is gone, even from their pillow and their clothes? I think of Mrs Reiber making the decision to leave that house in Oakley, and I cannot imagine it. I cannot bear to imagine it.

I pick up Jono's pyjamas and tuck them under his pillow. I straighten his duvet. I walk to the window, collecting up discarded, dirty clothes along the way, and look out. Andrew is out there, down the end of the garden, banging nails into the fence. As I watch he drops his hammer, puts his hands on the backs of his hips and stretches out his back. Then he stands there for a few moments, staring at his work. I wonder what he is thinking. He cannot be thinking about the fence. He picks up the hammer again and whacks it hard against the wood.

'Oh, Andrew.' I whisper his name and my breath clouds the glass. He turns his head for a second as if he can sense me watching him, but then he's back to his task, banging out his anger. What will become of us? What will become of me? The familiar prickles of dread start creeping their way through my body, leaving me open and numb. What will Andrew and I do when Jono has grown up and left us? What will I do with myself then?

I turn away from the window and look around the room at Jono's things, at his bookcase crammed with old *Beano* annuals and sticker books, with picture books from toddlerhood that he still won't part with, and puzzle books that he's been through again and again, in different-coloured pens; the books that he actually reads are piled up beside his bed. I look at all his Lego models in their various states of collapse and at his marble run, bending over and snapped in half like a wrecked fairground ride, the marbles like tiny bodies, fallen out from underneath. There's his old collection of football cards scattered about on the floor beside his drawers; the old lunch box I gave him, in which to keep them, is discarded next to them and now contains a large stone, three Lego wheels and the remains of a dead spider. And everywhere his toys – so many toys – stuffed onto, beneath and beside his shelves. I spy a lone sock dangling out from his Scrabble box and retrieve it. I pick up the worn old bear that my mother gave him when he was two, and prop it up on his pillow.

What will I do when Jono is gone?

I sit on his bed, with my clutch of dirty clothes held tight in my arms.

I should get a job, I know. I should never have quit work in the first place, but what is the point in admitting that now? At the time it seemed the right thing to do. It seemed the *only* thing to do. Jono was all that mattered. He still is. But what will happen to me when he no longer wants me?

Andrew has never said, *Why don't you go back to work?* Even now that money is tight, even last night when I sat there complaining that I didn't want to stay in a caravan, he didn't say, *Well, perhaps if you got a job we could afford something else.* No, he didn't say that, though he must think it at times, surely, as I do. But we made our pact together, we made it in shock and fear, and we stuck to it. We did what we thought was best for Jono – never mind what it meant for ourselves.

Jono, Jono.

I cuddle his clothes to my chest; I feel their worn softness. I press them to my face; I breathe them in.

I could teach. It's the obvious thing; I've got a first degree in French. I could venture out again, into the world, and find something else to fill the void. But that would mean facing up to the fact that my child no longer needs me every minute of every day. It would mean allowing myself to let go, and how can I ever do that?

I picture myself, in business clothes and with a briefcase, opening my front door. And I picture myself, stepping out into blackness. I close my eyes tight, I see myself falling into space, falling and falling, my arms and my legs spinning, Mary Poppins-like, through the air. My chest and my arms ache with my need for Jono, to hold him, to clutch him, to never let him go; but there I am, spinning away into darkness, forever spinning away.

ELEVEN

I tell Andrew I'm going out with my old school friend, Gina. And I say that I had told him ages ago, but that he must have forgotten.

'So you'll have to come home,' I say. 'To look after Jono.'

But I still end up leaving the house before he is home on Tuesday. He rings me to say he won't be home till eight, and my train leaves at seven-forty. So I leave Jono struggling over his maths, with strict instructions not to move till his dad gets in, and my mobile number, Andrew's mobile number and Mrs Jeffries' number next door written down on a piece of paper, in case of an emergency.

'You're sure you'll be okay?' I ask.

And he says, 'God, Mum! What can happen to me in half an hour? Do you think there's going to be an earthquake or a hurricane and the house will fall down? Or do you think a meteorite is going to come crashing from the sky and land right on top of me?'

It's only an eight-minute walk from our house to the station and I half-expect to pass Andrew along the way, in case he did manage to get back a little earlier. I half-want to see him, so that I know Jono won't be on his own for long, and I look out for him among the sea of grey suits disgorging

themselves from the station entrance and out onto the pavement. I look out for him, but I'm ready to duck my head
and dodge back behind the crowd in case I do see him. I
stay on the other side of the road and walk past the station,
and approach it from the far side, just in case. Not that
Andrew would even notice me. He'd be in his own world,
the mechanical world of the march back home. And, anyway,
I am not doing anything wrong. I lied about who I'd be out
with tonight, but that was just to avoid a long explanation.
Had Andrew shown a little more interest in me in the first
place, maybe I wouldn't have had to lie at all.

I phone Jono from the train.

'Yes?' he says when he answers.

'Hi, darling, it's me,' I say.

'What do you want?' he grumbles down the line.

'Just checking you're okay. Are you still doing your homework?'

'No, I'm answering the phone.'

'Dad will be home in a moment,' I say. 'Call me if there's
any problem, or if he's late.'

'*Yes*,' he says and hangs up.

Simon is waiting for me at Waterloo. I see him before he sees
me. I see him standing outside WH Smith under the clock,
scanning the crowds coming from the other direction. He
checks his watch; he shifts his weight from one foot to the
other.

'Tell me where you live,' he said on the phone.

And I said, 'Oh, out in Surbiton.'

'Shall I come to you?' he asked. 'Is there somewhere we
could go for a drink perhaps? I don't want to take up too
much of your time.'

But of course I said, 'No, it's fine,' I said. 'I could meet you at Waterloo.'

But now I know that Waterloo isn't his station. And I also know what a long commute he has to get back home.

'Hi,' I say now, and he turns round to me, startled, relieved.

'Rachel,' he says, 'hi.' He bends and kisses me on the cheek, and he half-holds me as he does so. For long seconds his cheek is against mine, his arm around my shoulders in a gentle embrace. For some reason I feel sudden tears prickling at the backs of my eyes.

'We'll just go to the South Bank,' he says. 'Is that okay?' He walks fast and so I do too; I don't want to slow his pace. I feel a sense of urgency in him, but he doesn't say much as we walk, other than 'How are you?' and 'Thank you for meeting me,' and 'I hope the train didn't take too long.' Small talk, to which I respond in kind.

We stop at a bar by Queen Elizabeth Hall.

'Will this do?' he asks. 'I realize you probably don't have long.'

'This is fine,' I say. 'But you're probably in more of a hurry than I am. You've got to go all the way back to Kingham.'

'Not tonight,' he says. 'That's just at the weekends. I stay in town most of the week.'

I sit at a small table and watch him as he goes to the bar to order our drinks. And I think how naive of me to imagine him slapping back and forth all the way to Kingham twice a day, two hours here and two hours back again. Of course he wouldn't do that every day. I picture myself, sitting at my computer and studying his route, working out how long it would take him, what time he would have to leave each morning, and I wonder why it is that I have to be so obsessive.

'Where do you stay, then, in town?' I ask when he comes back with our wine.

'I've got a flat just along the river,' he says, and I think, *Of course*; someone like Simon would have a flat. People from his sphere so often do; they hole the wife and kids up in some idyllic house in the country, which they themselves will visit at weekends, and keep a flat for themselves in the city. To live like that is just normal for someone from Simon's world. I think of the other boys I knew back then in the Vanessa days; the ones who idled through her house with their cotton shirts and their public-school accents, with their constant supply of dope and their easy expectation of sex. I think of the ones who survived and the ones who didn't, as though their teenage years were a sort of weeding-out process. I try to imagine the men that the survivors will have become now, and into my head pops an image of all those fathers at Jono's Christmas concert, all those alpha-men with their alpha-families living their golden, alpha-lives.

Would I recognize any of those boys if I walked into them now? Would I have recognized Simon? He is from a different world from me; I see it clearly. I see it, and it thrills me, it draws me. It is the same world that Vanessa would move in now too, had she lived. Picture it: the house in the country, the beautiful children, the trips into town. I imagine the clothes she'd wear, the ease with which she'd walk into the kind of shops that I would never dare enter. And the shop assistants wouldn't sneer at her; they'd flock around her, it would make their day just to serve her. The differences between Vanessa and me would be even starker now than they were back then, and, just as I was back then, I would still be looking on: envious, infatuated, enthralled.

And yet here I am now, with Simon, getting glimpses of

that world again. He tells me how Isobel, his wife, wanted space and fresh air in which to bring up the children, and yet ironically their eldest, Theo, will soon go away to school. 'And eventually the others will join him, and there will just be Isobel and her horses at home all week,' he says and I hear the cynicism in his voice, but it is a cultivated, world-weary cynicism at odds with his nervousness. Behind his apparent ease and his smooth manners he is coiled, pent-up. 'What about you?' he asks. 'Tell me about your life.'

But I find that I can't. I don't want to talk about it; my life seems all too mundane. 'I'm married; I have a son, Jono. He'll be thirteen soon.' That's all I can say. Meeting Simon is a step out of my world; the two cannot cross, or meet. And anyway, I'm sure he only asked out of politeness.

But now he says, 'I hope I didn't make things difficult for you, asking you to meet me like this.'

'No, no of course not,' I reply, and to steer us away from Andrew and Jono and all things home, I go on, 'I wanted to see you. I can't stop thinking about what you said, about your mother, about her pretending she never had a daughter. Simon, it's heartbreaking.'

Simon smiles at me, but it's a sad smile of acknowledge-ment. 'It is,' he says, simply. He picks up his wine glass and drinks, and again I notice the bitten skin around his nails, in such contrast to the rest of his appearance, which is so immaculately groomed. When he puts his glass back down he continues, 'I adored my sister.' And, as though even he finds it hard to believe now, 'And so, once, did my mother.' The sarcasm in his voice does nothing to conceal his pain.

'Simon, everyone loved Vanessa,' I say. 'Your mother most of all, surely.'

He stares at me, and the intensity of his eyes is so unnerving, so blue, so like his sister's. He holds his hand out across the table towards me, palm up. Without even thinking, I respond, and place my hand in his. He closes his fingers around mine, warm, strong.

'Thank you,' he says. 'For your incredible understanding.'

Tears prickle the backs of my eyes. For a moment we are silent, but he holds my hand, and he stares at me. And then he says, 'You cannot imagine what it means for me to be here with you. It is such a long time since I have been able to speak to anyone about my sister, and to someone who remembers her, too. I am so glad that you got back in touch.'

I cannot break his gaze, though there is a lump burning in my throat now and my eyes are starting to swim. He squeezes my hand.

'I'm sorry to upset you,' he says. 'Please, forgive me.'

Forgive me.

Again I see him as a boy, drunk and tender, and always there in the background, basking in the light of his sister. She never told him to go away. She never said, *Get lost*, or shut him out. She loved him, as he loved her. A tear spills over and slides down my cheek, followed by another. With my free hand I wipe them away.

Simon leans towards me. 'I'm sorry,' he says again.

I try to smile, but I cannot speak and the tears are coming thick and fast. I sit there, feeling slightly ridiculous, unable to help myself, and *he* was the one who was supposed to be upset.

'Rachel,' he says now. 'Will you come to my flat? It's not far. We could be there in five minutes.'

And so we leave. After all, we cannot stay there, with me crying my eyes out. I think what an embarrassment I am, but he walks with his hand across my back, caring, protective. Such gentleness makes me want to cry all the more, but I try to pull myself together. We walk fast in the cold, clean air, further up the South Bank towards the Tate Modern. It is hard to talk when we are walking; I feel we are suspended somehow, out of all time, out of all grounding.

He says to me, 'Are you okay?' And again, 'I'm sorry.'

And at last I am able to say, 'Simon, *I'm* sorry. Really, I didn't mean to cry all over you.'

His hand stays on my back.

His flat is in a newish block above some shops by the Oxo Tower. We walk into the steel foyer and he presses the button for the lifts. I have the strangest feeling of having slipped outside one life and into another. I am looking down. I am looking down and seeing everything in microscopic detail; I am taking it all in, making notes, colouring it all in, not missing a thing.

We emerge from the lift. The corridor is surprisingly short and contained; just three doors lead from a cream-carpeted, cream-walled hall. He puts a key into one and we enter an open room, half-kitchen, half-living room, divided by a sort of marble breakfast bar, and beyond that, a huge, wall-sized window looking out across the Thames to St Paul's and the City. I think of the view from my kitchen window at 117 London Road, Surbiton. I think of Jono, grumbling over his maths and recoiling from my affection, and of Andrew coming in from work, tired, impassive, remote. I cannot believe that I am here.

I stand there, staring at that incredible landscape, while Simon goes straight to the fridge and takes out a bottle of wine, and then to a cupboard from which he fetches two glasses.

'Rachel,' he says when he hands me a glass, 'the last thing

I want to do is upset you. I really am sorry.' He takes a sip from his glass, then puts it down there on the counter, so that he is standing opposite me empty-handed, vulnerable. 'I couldn't bear it if you went home tonight and I didn't hear from you again.'

I smile at him, but it is a wonky, watery smile. Carefully I put my own glass down next to his. He is looking at me so seriously, so anxiously, and my heart is stretched tight inside my chest. I cannot think what to say, except, 'You're Vanessa's brother. I am hardly going to let you go.' And then my eyes are welling up with tears again, and slowly, very slowly, he reaches out an arm and puts it around my shoulders. A little awkwardly I move closer to him, and he puts his other arm out so that I am held there, within the circle of his embrace. He holds me gently, tentatively, and I hear the restrained sigh of his breathing. At first I am not sure what I ought to do, but gradually I ease towards him; I put my arms around his back and rest my head against his chest. His arms tighten around me. I feel the soft cotton of his shirt against my cheek, and I can smell his aftershave, warm and vaguely familiar, like the scent of expensive leather. His heart is thumping under my ear. I feel him dip his head and kiss my hair, and I close my eyes.

We stand there like that for ages, as if neither of us can bear to move, for fear of breaking the moment. I feel the gentle rise and fall of his chest as he breathes, and the warmth of his mouth, still pressed against my hair. I open my eyes, and my eyelashes catch on his shirt; I close them again. Vaguely, in some distant part of my mind, I am thinking, *What now? What next?* But I cannot answer. I do not dare to answer.

Eventually he says, 'I want to show you something.' And he moves just fractionally, and as he does so I drop my arms and pull away a little, aware suddenly that I had been clinging to him. He loosens his own hold more slowly, leaving his hands on my arms for a moment longer, as if reluctant to let me go. 'Please,' he says then. 'Sit down. Make yourself at home. I won't be a moment.'

The room is open-plan. Apart from the door we came in by, there is only one other door, across the far side of the room. This is where Simon goes now, and for a few minutes I am alone. I wander into the centre of the room, all the while looking out of that window. You could look at that view forever. If you lived here, that's what you would do; you'd spend your whole time looking out. For some reason I think of that claustrophobic and poky room at the back of Mrs Reiber's house; I think of the contrast. And as I sit myself down on one of the two soft leather sofas, I think of myself sitting down on her cracked old sofa, and again I have that feeling that I am little more than an impostor, inching in on their lives.

Just go, Mrs Reiber said. *Who are you?*

I sit on Simon's sofa, and I wait for him to reappear. I am facing the window, and I look at all those lights, hazy against the night sky. Between me and the window is a long, low table, on which are what I take to be work papers, roughly stacked, and the sports section of the weekend paper. I look around now; the wall on which there is neither window nor door is lined with asymmetrical shelves, most of which are piled with ring binders and box files and loose, dog-eared sheets of paper, untidily shoved in. The hi-fi is there too, and a pile of CDs, and there is a glass box-shaped photo holder, one of those ones that holds a picture on each of its sides and you can turn it over and turn it around; the picture facing the front at the moment is of a couple of small children playing outside somewhere: his children, I assume. For some reason I don't want to see these photos, and anyway I don't like those photo frames. They remind me of a toy Jono had when he was small, a sort of Rubik's cube for toddlers with pictures of animals on, and you could twist it and move the picture around. Jono hated it because whenever he put it down, he was putting it down on some animal's face. He couldn't put it down without picking a loser. I wonder whose photo is on the underneath side of Simon's picture box, and if, like Jono, he can't sleep unless he religiously turns it around each day.

This is very much a man's flat. I wonder how long he has lived here, if 'lived' is the word you would use, for a place you stay in half the week. More than half. He must spend most of his life here, but there is nothing like a home about it. I wonder how it feels for him to be here while his wife and children are somewhere else. I wonder if his wife visits when she is in town. I picture her, breezing in, dumping her shopping on the floor and collapsing down onto the very sofa on which I am sitting now. I imagine her, somewhat cold-hearted, somewhat aloof, preferring her horses to her children. *Ghastly view*, she might say, looking out as I am now across the skyscape of concrete and brick and steel, the Thames down below a dirty, inky streak. *How do you stand it up here? Can't wait to get back home. Pull the blinds, won't you, darling? And fix me a drink?*

I have her voice, I have her eyes, I have everything about her inside my head.

The door in the wall opens now and Simon comes back in, carrying something small and protected in his hands, much like you might carry a small animal, a bird maybe, something delicate and precious.

'Sorry to be so long,' he says, and I watch as he walks towards me. I watch the way he walks, the studied ease, the smooth movement of his body inside his well-cut, expensive clothes. I notice the way the hems of his trousers perfectly cover the laces on his hand-made shoes, even as he walks. Yet as he sits down beside me I immediately sense his tension again. 'Look,' he says, and very carefully, apprehensively almost, he opens one hand to reveal what he is holding in the other: a photograph. Three photographs; he gently spreads them, fan-like, to show me there are three, and then closes them back together. He holds them out now, so that I can see that first one.

I move closer, and I say, 'Simon, oh my *God*!'

We sit there, side by side, looking down at that photo, which he grips tight between his fingers and his thumb. My hand is on his arm, also gripping tight.

'Oh my God,' I whisper again.

For there is Vanessa, smiling at us, her hair tied back in a one-sided ponytail, the length of it cascading down over one shoulder. She's wearing a red and white checked shirt and beside her on one side are Tristram, Leanne and Fay. On the other side of her are Annabel and Dominic. They're all there, all squashed together, grinning for the camera. Annabel has two fingers up behind Dominic's head, sticking up like mini rabbit's ears – how dated that gesture seems now – and Leanne's eyes are half-shut. Leanne, who I have not seen for years and years: here she is, wearing her old yellow sweatshirt and that stripy scarf around her neck that I remember so well. They're in the living room in that house in Oakley – I recognize the background. They're all there. They're all there except me.

'It was my birthday,' Simon says. 'I got the camera for a

present.' Slowly, he moves that photo to the back, and shows me the next one. It's much the same, only he's in it this time and Dominic isn't; Dominic must have taken the picture. But there is Simon, squeezed in between Vanessa and Fay, his cheek pressed up against his sister's, the two of them so very, painfully alike. I see him and I remember him instantly, his boyish face, his wavy, soft blond hair. I see them side by side like this, I see the blue of their eyes and how very, very young they are, and my heart twists and buckles into a raw, tight knot.

'And this one,' Simon says, and he turns the photos again. This last one is just of Vanessa and Tristram, and it's the most poignant of them all. They're falling together in a hug, their faces lit with laughter, Vanessa so fair and ethereal, Tristram so much bolder in his features, his hair and his eyes so dark. I want to stare and stare. I cannot stop staring. I never thought I would see Vanessa again, ever, in any shape or form. She lives with the others inside my head, a ghostly dream of a person, but I never thought I would see her again like this, so real.

How can the dead be dead when you see them laughing like this, so human, so alive? I look at this picture and I can smell Vanessa's hair; I can smell her perfume and the pepper-mint of her chewing gum. I hear the breath of her laughter and the plastic chink of her bangles clattering together as she throws her arm around Tristram's shoulder. I hear the brush of their clothes and feel the warmth of their bodies; Vanessa's sharp, china boniness against the gentle, fallible strength of Tristram. I hear Tristram calling out to Simon, 'Go on, boy, let the camera roll.' And Vanessa laughing again, the sound of it deep and easy and free.

I move my hand from Simon's arm to his hand. I clutch

the fingers with which he is holding the photo; I move his hand and the photo closer to my face. I lean down; I look harder, as though I might see more of Vanessa somehow, and of Tristram. As though I might see the pores of their skin and the flecks in their eyes. I stare and I stare.

'Rachel,' Simon says eventually. He is holding the photos with the hand that is nearest to me; he has to turn now in his seat to touch me with his other hand. Gently he brushes the hair back from my face. 'Rachel,' he says again.

I struggle to raise my eyes. Vanessa's face is a magnet, drawing me down. I look at Simon; I look at the paleness of his face and the intense sadness in his eyes, and I look down again at Vanessa, so happy, so without fear.

'How can you bear it?' I say.

'I can't,' he says. 'This is all I have.'

I look at him again. His hand is still on my hair; again he strokes it back from my face, carefully, gently. Absently, he takes a strand and runs it through his fingers. 'I took these photos with my camera. They are mine. I kept them in my bedroom, in a drawer.' His eyes move from mine to that piece of hair that he is twisting now through his fingers. He frowns at what he is doing; he concentrates. I watch his face and I see him swallow, hard. 'I came home from school one day and my mother had got rid of all Vanessa's things.' He pauses and the frown on his face deepens. Again, he swallows.

I dare not speak. I dare not breathe.

Eventually he says, 'I was just a boy. It didn't occur to me that she would do this.' His voice is thin and fragile and so very precisely controlled. 'I thought Vanessa's room would always be there, with all her things, waiting for her to come home.'

'What about your father?' I ask. 'Why didn't he stop her?'

'He didn't live with us any more.'

'Well, what did she do with all her stuff?'

Simon's eyes move from my hair to my face now, and I realize that I must be gawping at him in horror. I blink, and try to soften my stare.

'I do not know,' he says simply. 'I just came home and it had all gone. She wouldn't talk about it. Rachel, I went mad, shouting at her, pleading with her. She would not talk about it. Soon after we moved house.'

'To Kew?'

'No, no. I never lived in Kew. My mother moved to Kew when she married again, though that marriage didn't last, either. No, we lived in Dorking for a while, in a horrible, horrible little house, just the two of us.'

'Oh, Simon.'

'It was a very bad time. Fay was the only thing that helped me through it, but in the end she went, too.' His hand moves from my hair to my face now; very gently, he touches my cheek. 'But I'm sorry,' he says now. 'You don't need to hear all this.'

'Simon, I do.'

'Rachel, you are so kind,' he says. He smiles at me so sadly, and he lowers his hand from my face now, so that he is holding the photos in both hands again, as if he might put them away. 'I wanted you to see these photos,' he says. 'They are all that is left of my sister.'

'But your mother would still have some photos of Vanessa, surely.'

'They're all gone. Everything's gone. She wiped my sister right out of our lives.' He fans the photos apart and snaps them shut, like a hand of cards.

There is something like panic rising up inside my heart. 'But your father, then?' I persist.

'I haven't seen my father for years.'

'But it's just so wrong.' I put my hand on his. I stop him taking those photos away. I look down and there is Vanessa laughing up at me, so beautiful, so real. I want to keep looking at her. I want to look at her forever and ever, and never stop looking at her. I don't want her just to be gone, cast out, as if she never existed. 'I can't stand it,' I say. 'I just can't stand it. Your mother ... she can't do this. She can't just *forget* her ...' I'm breathing so hard I can barely talk now and I have to force the words past the hard lump in my throat. 'Simon, you don't just forget your *child*. You *can't*.'

You can't. No matter how hard you try. No matter how much you pretend that you've forgotten. I close my eyes to stop the tears, but all can see is myself in that delivery room, half-lying, half-sitting on that bed, with my knees bent and that hideous hospital gown pushed up, and the midwife peering down between my open thighs as if delivering dead babies was what she did every day, while the contractions rolled like waves, one on top of another. It felt as if my baby was dragging her nails down my insides, trying to claw herself a grip, clinging, clinging against the tide.

'Not long now,' piped the midwife in her cheery nurse's voice. 'Nearly over.' I wanted to snap my legs shut on her face.

It wasn't nearly over. It would never be over, never.

And then I think of Andrew. I see his face, after they'd wheeled me back down to the ward and drawn the curtains around my bed, as if somehow that would shield me from the fact that the other women in the room still had their babies, their real live babies, still safely inside them. I see his face as he stood there beside the bed, staring at me, useless, the skin on his cheeks pale and drawn and sickly. I see him searching for the words with which to convince me somehow that he had the first idea of what I was going through. I see his mouth moving on a silent wobble, I see the reddening of his eyes.

'Rachel, I have to go now,' he said at last, his voice pleading and weak. 'I have to go and ... and ... I have to get Jono.'

My head is in my hands. My head is bursting with the rage I feel towards Andrew, a rage that buzzes and presses against my skull till I can't think, feel, can't see anything else.

Vaguely I am aware of Simon's arm around my shoulders, holding me, stroking me. 'Rachel?' he is saying. 'Rachel, are you okay?' But I can't answer and I can't open my eyes. My head is a boiling, churning, fizzing mass.

'We won't forget her,' Simon is saying. 'I won't forget her, and you won't forget her.'

These are the very words that Andrew should have said to me, but he didn't, he just didn't.

Simon holds me close and my face is buried in the warmth of his chest. He strokes my back, he strokes my hair. Over and over he whispers, 'You and I, we'll never forget her, Rachel, never.'

I don't know who starts it, but we are kissing, then; small kisses at first, small, searching kisses, on the cheeks, on the mouth. But then the kisses grow deeper and I haven't kissed like that for years. You don't kiss when you've been married too long. The kissing just dries up. Like too many other things, it just stops. The very thought of it becomes almost distasteful, but here I am now, kissing like I'm sixteen again, kissing Simon, kissing him till the pressure in my head starts to melt and run.

For a second he pulls away, just a fraction. I open my eyes and look into his. I see them deep and blue and charged. My heart is a balloon inside my chest, swelling up and up. And then he's kissing me again, with both arms around me now, one hand holding my head and the other on my back. Then he moves that hand on my back, he moves it just slightly so that he's touching my side, and my body jolts like it's been shocked. He moves it again and I'm practically quivering under his fingers. And still he kisses me, gradually pushing me backwards till we're lying down on that sofa and my arms are up around him, pulling him down to me, holding his warm, hard body as tight as I possibly can against mine; and all thoughts of Andrew, all miserable, guilt-ridden, suffocating thoughts of Andrew, are punched right out of my head like a fist through glass.

I think of when we were young, back at those parties. I think of everyone getting off with everyone else. It didn't matter who you were with; you just went with it. You went with the moment, with the pure bliss of the feeling; with the bliss of being young, and so eternally alive. Sometimes I think the girls slept with the boys just because they didn't know what else to do with them; they were like kids in a sweet shop, working their way through the pack. It never got that far for me. I was too uptight, too watchful. But here I am now, just like them at last. Just like one of them.

Simon props himself up on an elbow, and starts yanking off his tie and shrugging off his jacket. Impatiently I wait, I tug at his shirt. He bends and kisses me as he gets first one arm free, then the other, then he pulls away again. He's about to speak. I know what he's going to say, he's going to suggest that we go through to the bedroom, but I can't do that. I won't be able to do that. If I did, I wouldn't be able to do anything when we got there; I'd wake up from this. I'd chicken out. And I don't want to chicken out. I want to just do it – fast, here and now. So I grab at his head: I pull him back down. I manage to kick off my shoes and slide my legs up around his, letting my dress scrunch up around my thighs. He groans into my mouth. He pushes my dress up further. I am shaking, literally shaking now, my teeth chattering against his as he kisses me. I reach between us and start undoing his belt; like a whore I start pushing down his trousers. I cannot think. I will not think.

He twists sideways, stretching a hand down to try and grapple with his shoelaces. 'Shit!' he mutters. 'Sorry.' I let him sit up. And while he's dealing with his shoes, I wriggle out of my tights and pull my dress up off over my head. And before he can really look at me I pull him back down to me again, clutching him to me as he gets rid of the last of our clothes. I arch my body under his, and loop my legs up around his back. And down he comes, thrusting into me. I watch his eyes; I watch how they flicker. I see the moment. I see it, I feel it, and inside my head all else is blown away. There is just this. Me and him. Now.

I used to say, if the opportunity arose, that one man was much like another.

On girls' nights, for instance, after a few drinks, when inevitably the conversation would get around to *what if?*

What if you got the chance?

What if you met someone?

What if you could be sure you'd never be found out?

Or in idle, rambling speculations with a friend, or with

Janice even, I'd say, 'But in the end, when it comes down to it, it's just another man humping on top of you. It would be fine, until you got to that point, but then it would be just the same.'

But it isn't the same.

'He'll end up like your husband, wanting his socks washed and his dinner cooked. And surely one husband is enough in any woman's life.'

But now I know, it really isn't the same.

I lie there, on that sofa, with all of London spread out there below me, and Surbiton seems so very many miles away. I half-cover myself with a cushion, and curl up my legs. I want to believe I am sixteen again, but sadly I am not, however much Simon tells me I am beautiful, however much he kisses me, kisses my tummy, my breasts, my thighs. He tells me I am beautiful, and I feel that I am beautiful, as I have not done so, for a very long time.

He leans up on one elbow, half beside me, half on top of me. He trails his hand over my skin, and kisses me, again and again.

'Rachel,' he says. 'Rachel, Rachel. You were worth the wait.'

And then we talk. We talk as we will go on talking, every time we meet now, at every opportunity. We talk about Vanessa, and the old days; about the things we all did. And about the things that *they* all did, without me; the parties at other people's houses to which I wasn't invited, the trips into town, the gatherings after school. I was on the edge of their group, don't forget, just a hanger-on, a friend by association. But Simon talks as if he *has* forgotten, as if he thinks I was always there, right in the middle of things. *Remember the time we stayed at Annabel's dad's house, and Tristram got completely pissed and fell in the swimming pool unconscious and we had to fish him out?* he says. And, *You know, it was the quiet evenings I liked most, when there were just a few of us, all curled up on the sofa in the den, watching videos.*

And of course I was never there for those things. I listen, and I feel the old envy, creeping in.

But he talks as if I *was* there. And so I feel as if I could have been. I listen to him talking, and I see myself, just slotting in. I see myself laughing at Tristram as he falls back, drunk, into the water. I see myself squeezing in on the sofa between Vanessa and Simon, grabbing a handful of popcorn and saying, *Ssh! I can't hear!*

And I see myself missing the last train back from London after seeing some band in Camden, even though I was jealous as hell at the time that it didn't even occur to Leanne to get me a ticket. But I imagine myself now, lolling on the cold concrete floor at Waterloo station along with the rest of them, waiting for the 5 a.m. milk train back to Oakley, with the sound of whatever music it was that they'd just listened to, still pounding in my ears.

And then I'm back at Simon's house again, after yet another party; I'm with him when he walks into his bedroom and catches Leanne and Tristram going for it in his bed. I'm right there alongside him, slamming a hand up in front of my face in embarrassment. I'm with him; I'm there. I'm laughing.

I'm there too at all those backstage parties that Annabel's dad was always getting them in to, the ones I heard so much about from Leanne; and at the Christmas Eve party that they had in Oakley the year that it snowed really hard, when they all went out onto the green for a massive snowball fight –

there I am, tumbling on the ground, shoving a snowball down Vanessa's neck. And how much better it is to think that I was there with them, rather than stuck at home with my parents, my sister and maybe a grandparent or two, missing out on all the fun. And then we're on the green again, in summer this time; Simon talks and talks, and so clearly that I picture myself with them all, lying back on the grass and doing nothing, just counting the stars in the clear night sky.

I'm there as he talks. I'm there in my head. I'm back in that beautiful world.

TWELVE

The train chugs me back to Surbiton.

I sit there in a carriage half-filled with the tired-faced late-workers, and the after-work drinkers breathing out their sour, petrol breath, and the small groups of tin-eared teenagers chattering over the rattle of their iPods, their voices rising at the end of each sentence so that everything they say is a question, to be answered by another question, and I am hot from running, hot from Simon. I am *wet* from Simon. I sit there, looking like a housewife and feeling like a whore, with the wet of him still taking its time to seep out of me, and soak into my clothes.

There was no time to shower. There was barely time to dress. The trains to Surbiton are frequent, but the last one leaves Waterloo at 11.20 or so, and if I missed that I'd really be in trouble; but Simon and I, we lay there on that sofa and the time just ticked on by, till suddenly I *had* to leave and it was such a rush, then, such a panic. Simon threw on his trousers, his shirt and his shoes, but no underwear and no socks, and dashed downstairs to hail a taxi out in the road behind his block, while I scrambled a little slower to get into my clothes and then followed him. He got into the taxi with me; for some reason I hadn't expected that.

'Waterloo,' he barked at the driver, 'fast.' And he threw himself back against the leather of the seat beside me, flushed, and breathing hard.

'You haven't got a jacket,' I said. 'You'll be cold.' But he just shrugged dismissively, and I thought what a stupid, motherish thing that was to say. And I felt self-conscious suddenly under his gaze, aware that my hair must be a mess and my make-up mostly gone. And I was too tense, too anxious about catching the train, to be able to think of anything to say. What *could* I say? Andrew was creeping into my head now, and Jono, and the enormity of what I had done.

I sat forward in the seat. I watched the street lights, the buildings, the cars race by.

'You'll be okay,' Simon said and I looked at him. 'The train,' he said. 'You'll make it.'

'Oh.'

And then we sat there, staring at each other. He took my hand and he squeezed it, and I still couldn't think what to say.

The taxi leant as it hurled around the bend at the back entrance to the station, flinging me sideways against Simon. For seconds he caught and held me, for sweet, fast seconds, and then the taxi jerked to a stop. Before I could get out my purse, Simon dug some money from his pocket and shoved it at the driver, and then we were out and running across the concourse at Waterloo, slowing only to check for the platform number. I had a minute, less than a minute. Clumsy and awkward and frantic now, I ran on and slammed my way through the barrier.

'Call me,' Simon shouted after me, his voice caught and harsh from running. 'Call me when you're on the train.'

And when I did call him at least five minutes later, after

I'd found a seat and got my breath and tried to calm my pounding heart, he was still there, at Waterloo.

'I'm sorry you had to leave like that,' he said, and I pictured him there without his jacket, without his socks, watching as the train disappeared. 'I'm sorry you had to leave at all.'

Now, I look at my reflection in the black of the window beside me and see myself distorted and wild. I take out my little mirror from my handbag and peer into it. I inspect myself; I see the flushed redness around my mouth, and on my chin and my cheeks. And I see the burn in my eyes. You can *see* what I've been doing. Anyone could see it. *Andrew* will see it. I don't have any make-up with me except for my lipstick, which I take out now and apply, but my lips still appear smudged around the edges, and swollen. And who am I, covering up what I have done with a bit of lipstick, when I have another man's scent – another man's *bodily fluids*, for heaven's sake – still warm upon my skin? From nowhere a shot of hysteria bursts up inside me and breaks out on a cracked laugh, which I try to hold back. The man sitting opposite me glances up at me from his newspaper, and then quickly glances away. And really, there is nothing funny in all this, nothing funny at all. But I feel like I am a player; here are my movements, here are my lines, my cues to speak and respond. Nothing seems real. Not my home and my life within it, or this thing that I have just done.

It's late and dark, and I ought to get a taxi to take me the short distance from the station to my house, but I cannot bear to be hurrying home now. And so I walk, and I walk slowly, conscious of the sound of my shoes on the pavement. Our street is long and straight and we live about halfway down; I find my eyes pinned to the distance, waiting for my house to come into view, and when it does, irritation and dread rise and mingle within me: the lights are on. Andrew is still up.

I put my key in the door and my heart is thumping.

Strangely, the way I feel is the way I imagine I would feel if it was my parents I was coming home to, rather than my husband. I feel like a naughty child or a teenager, about to be found out. And of course I don't want to be found out, but at the same time I also feel slightly defiant. After all, I may have betrayed Andrew, but hasn't he betrayed me too, in shutting me out, in driving me to this?

The house is quiet. For a moment I think that maybe he is in bed and that I might yet avoid him, but as I start to climb the stairs I see that he is in the study; the door is partially open, and there he is hunched over a pile of papers with the computer screen glaring away beside him.

I stop on the stairs.

'Oh,' I say. 'I didn't think you'd still be up.'

He doesn't turn. He shuffles his papers and says, 'There's a discrepancy on the credit-card bill. I can't make it match my accounts.'

And isn't that a disaster for an accountant.

For a few seconds I stay right there, several stairs from the top. I know that he will not look up unless prompted, and that it would be perfectly easy for me now just to go straight into our room, and then quickly into the shower. And yet some demon has me stepping slowly up the last few stairs and loitering at the study door. He sits with his back to me, but I can see part of his face as he moves his head from side to side as he reads through those papers. I see his tiredness; I see his far too familiar frown. And I see how the tension increases in the set of his shoulders as I stand there behind him and watch, and wait.

'It's very late,' I say at last. 'Can't you leave it for now?'

And without looking up he says, 'No. The bill is due tomorrow.'

'Oh.' I stand there a little longer, and I see his shoulders lock a little tighter.

See me, I think. *Smell* me. You must *know*.

Eventually he asks, 'Did you have a good evening?'

And I say, 'Yes. Yes I did. I had a very good evening, thank you.'

And that is all.

Slowly, I get undressed. I feel that I am inside a layer of glass and any sudden movement will break my shelter. I take my time in the shower, carefully washing my sins away. And yet Simon is still on my body. I am changed, moulded to a different shape, stamped by another man's mark.

Andrew will know. How could he not?

I lie in our bed and I can smell the faint scent of Simon's aftershave, still on my hair. If Andrew were to hold me, or to lie close to me, surely he would smell it, too. But it is a long time till Andrew comes to bed, and clearly he has other things on his mind.

He creeps in beside me and I hear him sigh.

I turn my head on the pillow, so that I am facing him. I am wide awake. Too tired, too wired to sleep. Tonight I have crossed the line; I have done what I thought could never be done. I have broken out, however shadily. And now I stare at my husband, and my husband stares at the ceiling.

'Are you okay?' I ask, because one of us must speak.

He doesn't answer straight away. He doesn't look at me. Then, after a while, he says, 'Yes.' Followed by, 'They've charged us the wrong amount on the gas bill. I'll have to phone them up tomorrow.'

I watch as his eyes gently close. I watch as he drifts into sleep. I wonder if it has ever occurred to him that I would, eventually, sleep with someone else. And that he could let it happen, and that he could lie there now, apparently oblivious to the fact that it has, astounds me.

I think of Simon, kissing my mouth, my neck, my chest. I think of his body, so hard and urgent, driving into mine. I think of his hands lacing with mine and of the sound of his voice whispering, *Rachel*, *Rachel*, over and over, as if he would never, ever get enough of my name. And of the intensity of his eyes; of the paleness of his skin and his beautiful face. And I think of my own body, jumping into life. I think of what I have done and I relive it, every moment. And I do not feel guilty. Oh no. I do not feel guilty, I feel justified.

Simon calls me in the morning at a quarter to nine, after Andrew and Jono have gone and I am standing naked in front of the bathroom mirror, contemplating my body, seeing it with new eyes. My mobile rings and I clamour downstairs to answer it, chucking out the contents of my bag with scrabbling fingers; clumsy, giddy as a sixteen-year-old. My heart pounds; my voice comes out breathy, fast.

'Hello.'

And he says, simply, 'Rachel.' And never again will my name be an accusation, an apology, a weary plea of denial. Now, it will always be something else. 'How are you?' he asks, his voice tender, and gentle, and slow. I picture him scrubbed and immaculate in his pristine suit, sitting behind a large oak desk, his office door closed to the world. I am crouched at the bottom of the stairs, still naked, huddled against the wall, lest the postman should come to the front door, and peer through the glass, and see.

'I'm fine,' I say, and I screw up my eyes and flinch at my lack of a better reply. 'How are you?'

He laughs, quickly, softly, then says, 'I was worried about you getting home.'

'It was okay, really.'

'There was no ... problem?'

He means with Andrew. He means with Andrew, who sat at his computer and did his best to avoid noticing me at all. 'No,' I say. 'No problem.' And a spider of hurts creeps its barely-there trace across my heart, strengthening my resolve.

I can hear him breathing and think that probably he can hear me, too; I try to breathe more quietly, and I wish that I could think of something to say; the right thing, the witty, sophisticated thing.

Then he says, 'Can you be free, today, at lunchtime? It's short notice, I know, but I had a meeting that's been cancelled and I – I want to see you again.' He talks quickly, as if there's some thread of doubt in him, as if he fears I might say no.

And just as quickly I say, 'Yes of course. I'd love to.'

I meet him outside the Oxo Tower because I cannot remember exactly where his flat is. I am there just moments before him, and I lean on the railings by the river and watch the view to stop myself from watching, too eagerly, for him. But still some instinct has me turning, just before he approaches. I see him walking towards me, smiling at me, and deep within me rusty, long-forgotten senses curl and flicker into life. I cannot believe I am doing this. I cannot believe I am here. I feel as if I have stepped into somebody else's body, and somebody else's life.

He is carrying a picnic bag from some fancy delicatessen. 'I sent my secretary out,' he says when he reaches me, and kisses me on the cheek. 'I hope you don't mind.'

But we don't eat anyway, at least not until afterwards. We go straight up to his flat and I am wired, every nerve in my body fired up. There is a voice in my head saying, *See it, do it*, and mentally I am recording all this. Recording *everything*; every play of the light, every scent, every sound. His fingers on my skin, the weight of his body, pressing down on mine. I feel his touch like a bruise – so aware am I, after feeling nothing like this for so long. It's like having sex with a stranger, but that's because it *is* sex with a stranger. While one voice in my head is so frantically making notes, there is another voice telling me that I am a fool to trick myself otherwise. But what do I care? What do I care, when it makes me feel like this?

And how easy it is to have an affair.

Suddenly, those days that stretched out so empty before me have a new purpose, and I can be free at the drop of a hat. An hour here, a couple of hours there. I keep my phone right with me always; I jump to its command. Like a Girl Guide, I keep myself prepared. I can get from my house to Simon's flat in just over thirty minutes if I get a fast train, if I time it right.

And with Simon's flat being so close to his office, he can nip back home often; on his way back from court, say, or from meeting clients. He can build in a little extra time. Sometimes he calls me unexpectedly.

'I can escape for half an hour,' he might say. Or 'I can be at my flat at one-thirty. Can you make it?'

And it is worth it, even for half an hour. Even for less.

Oh yes, I take to it like a duck to water. I take to it like it is the answer to all my woes, a plug to fill the void.

And it isn't just the sex. We talk too. *He* talks, constantly, about his sister, about the old days. And that helps to justify it, too. He *needs* to talk. We meet, on stolen lunchtimes and sneaky afternoons, and we lose ourselves in the sort of fast sex that we would have been having back then, though not with each other. And then he talks, about all those people and all those parties from so long ago, and even if I wasn't there I can go along with it, I can picture it. I knew those people. I can pretend. He laces me in, and takes me back to those heady, vibrant days before everything became so serious and precarious and tainted with doubt.

And Andrew simply doesn't notice. He is gone all day; he has no idea where I am or what I do.

I become a little careless. I leave my phone lying around, and on it all my stored messages from Simon, the ones I cannot bear to delete. One day, when Andrew is working at home for some reason, my phone rings when I am in the shower. I'd left it on top of the chest of drawers in the bedroom, and I hear it ring, but in the time it takes me to switch off the shower and grab a towel, Andrew is there before me. I yank open the bathroom door just as he picks the phone up, and the ringing stops.

'Missed call,' he says as I stand rooted to the spot, water running from my hair and my heart pounding. He is looking at the screen. 'S.R.,' he reads. 'Who is S.R.?'

But he doesn't wait for an answer. He doesn't really want to know. He hands me the phone and wanders back out of the room, leaving me dripping shower water all over on the floor and wondering what would have happened if he'd got there just two seconds sooner and answered it. Would he then just have said, 'Some man for you,' and passed me the phone? Would he even have been at all suspicious?

THIRTEEN

'They used to fight sometimes,' Simon tells me in a plaintive voice. 'My mother and Vanessa.'

'Oh, Simon, all mothers and daughters fight.'

It is a Thursday, sometime after two. We are lying on his bed and under my head I can feel the hardness of his chest, the beat of his heart, and the deep vibration of his voice as he talks.

'I know,' he says. 'But sometimes they'd *really* fight. Screaming and shouting and slapping at each other. They'd go wild, both of them. Vanessa especially.'

'You probably remember it worse than it was,' I say because it is hard for me to imagine this version of Vanessa. The Vanessa I knew was so calm, so serene. 'You were very young.'

'I hated it when they fought,' he says. 'I didn't know what to do. My mother threw Vanessa out once. Literally. They were having this horrendous row and my mother grabbed Vanessa by the hair, dragged her down the hall, opened the front door and literally hurled her out. Vanessa skidded straight down the steps and lay there screaming. My God, the noise.' He shudders, and I feel it, under my ear. 'They always made it up afterwards of course, but ... sometimes I wonder if that is why she behaves the way she does. My mother, I mean. I wonder if it's guilt.'

'Oh, surely not, Simon. Surely not.'

But he says, as if he hasn't heard me, 'I wonder if she's just screwed up with guilt.'

'She's screwed up with grief,' I say. 'And *love.*'

He sighs, and I can feel his mood, sliding down. This room doesn't help. It's so claustrophobic. We lie here in the daytime, but it feels more like night. The window in here is small and quite high up, and covered with a grey blind made from a heavy, canvas-like fabric. I have tried to pull that blind up before, but the string that operates it is twisted and too thin for the weight of the material; it cranked its way up awkwardly, and then the view that from the living room is so magnificent seemed all wrong for such a small window: too busy, too crammed. And so mostly the blind stays down, and I tell myself we are cocooned in here, shut away from the rest of the world.

Simon is silent now, lost in his thoughts. Soon he will be going back to work, and I lie there, counting out the seconds, trying to stretch them longer.

I look around the room. I know it well now: the heavy cotton bed linen, which is sometimes burgundy, sometimes silver-grey; the ceiling with its lowered central square around which the downlights are recessed, casting out an angular, muted glow; the walls that are painted the palest, palest grey, in stark contrast to the black slatted doors of the huge built-in wardrobe. A week or so ago I found something belonging to his wife inside that wardrobe: a pale-blue cashmere cardigan, hanging there among all his suits and shirts. I found something of hers in the bathroom, too, in the cupboard under the sink: a small make-up bag containing a travel-sized bottle of cleanser, a pair of tweezers, mascara and a tube of tinted moisturizer. Emergency essentials, and all of them recently used.

I wonder about his wife. I wonder what she is like, that he has never been able to talk to her about Vanessa in this way. Because he hasn't. I just know he hasn't.

Simon sighs again, and stirs, and I am broken away from his embrace. He reaches out an arm to his bedside table and picks up his watch. 'My mother did love Vanessa,' he says. 'And Vanessa loved her. But don't we always hurt the people that we love?'

One day, after we have made love, Simon has to make a work call. He takes the phone into the living room, and closes the door. I hear his voice, business-like and abrupt. While he is gone I look inside his wardrobe again, at that cardigan. I look to see if it has moved; if it has gathered fluff or evidence of more wear, but it hasn't. So I scan the shelves for anything else that is new, or that I may have missed before. There are his socks on one shelf, his pants on another. A couple of jerseys, folded up. Three pairs of shoes on the bottom, below his suits. Everything is so minimal, so neat. At the back of the wardrobe there is a safe the size of a microwave. This, I imagine, is where he keeps all his important things, his passport, his financial stuff, the photos of his sister, though I will never know, of course. I cannot ask. And on the shelf at the top of the wardrobe there is a small suitcase, which I imagine he uses for business trips, and visits to his house in Kingham. There is a leather luggage label attached to the handle, with his name on it, and the address of this flat. I wonder if there is anything inside the case, but I cannot get it down, of course. He would hear me.

But still, look and you will find.

Inside the bathroom cabinet there is now a pot of moisturizer that wasn't there before. I open the lid and discover a long blonde hair wrapped around the rim. And so I know without a doubt that his wife has been here, and been here long enough to need her things. Simon hasn't mentioned this, of course, but why would he? We don't talk about our families. I don't want us to talk about our families. But once I left my scarf here, left it for days, because each time I came here I kept forgetting to take it away with me again. And so there it sat, tidily folded up on his kitchen counter, between his mail and the fruit bowl for the best part of a fortnight. And now I wonder, did he quickly hide it when his wife turned up, and then get it back out again for me? Does she hunt around looking for evidence of me? Does she have her suspicions, or does she not even care?

And those things in the bathroom: did Simon hide them away, thinking I wouldn't find them? Or were they simply put away out of tidiness? The whole flat is tidy – ridiculously so. I suppose he is hardly here. And a woman comes in on Saturdays to clean for him. She changes the bed too, and does his laundry, all of it. She hangs his shirts back up in his wardrobe, all clean, all pressed, all in order. She gets his groceries in, too, and puts them away. She even arranges his fruit in the fruit bowl. I laughed when he told me.

'My God, what is she like?' I asked, picturing some scarily officious housekeeper type.

But of course he said, 'I don't know. I've never met her. I'm not here at weekends.'

I know his full address now, in Kingham. I have it written down on a little slip of paper, in my purse, though with no name attached to it, of course. I copied it down from a letter on the pile on the kitchen counter in his flat one day when he was in the bathroom. There were lots of letters there with his other address on, pieces of correspondence to do with insurance, schools, credit cards, all stacked up, waiting for him to deal with them.

His house doesn't have a number, it has a name. Roseberry House, Mill Lane, Kingham. I picture it, some idyllic golden-stone cottage with roses around the door, children playing in the garden and a couple of horses gambolling out the back. But if it is so idyllic, why would he choose to live here in London instead of there?

I look up Kingham on the Internet again. I scroll through the photos of the church, the village fete, the old, golden-stone houses. I find a little map, hand-drawn and very basic, but there it is: Mill Lane, leading off the road behind the church.

I know his wife's name, and the names of all his children now, though I wish that I didn't. His wife is called Isobel; his children Theo, Alistair and Charlotte. I cannot help but know.

Simon shows me a photo of Charlotte one day. 'Look,' he says, 'look,' practically shoving it under my nose. 'See how she looks like Vanessa. Doesn't she? Doesn't she look like Vanessa?'

And so I have to look. I've seen other photos of her, of course, on that hideous photo cube on the shelf in Simon's living room. Seen photos of all of them, of Charlotte and Theo and Alistair, and Isobel too, with her perfect cheek-bones and perfect, shiny blonde hair; seen photos of them all laughing and horsing around together, having such a jolly, wonderful time. Seen that photo of Simon too, with his arm

around Isobel, smiling at Isobel. I don't want to see any of
these pictures, but see them I do. How can I stop myself?
They are *there*.

And now this photo of Charlotte.

'See how she looks like my sister,' Simon says, but I can
only look for traces of his wife. Oh sure, the hair is long and
fair and wavy, and yes, she is pretty; yes, she is delicate. But
how can I fall upon this picture of another woman's child?

Simon knows nothing about me, about Andrew or Jono. He
knows nothing about my life, these last however many years.
I tell him nothing, and he doesn't ask. I come to him empty,
the canvas onto which he can paint all his pictures of Vanessa.
I lie in his arms and in his bed, and I convince myself I am
some sort of redeeming angel, that I am here to set him free.
I almost believe I have a duty to do this. After all, how could
I possibly walk away?

He talks about his sister. He loops me into that world.
For an hour here, half an hour there, the past twenty-five
years of my life disappear. I step out of my life. I can be
someone else.

And yet the thing that I know – and that I have always
known, right from the very beginning – is that although we
have this momentous thing in common, this love of Vanessa,
this shared romanticized memory that fate has brought us
back together to share … the thing that I know, the thing
that eats away at me, that sits on my shoulder whispering
and whispering its poison into my head, is that it is his
mother with whom I really empathize. His mother, living her
cold and loveless life in that house in Kew. His mother, who
one day fetched a roll of bin bags and threw out every single

thing belonging to or reminiscent of her daughter; every item of clothing left in the airing cupboard, every shoe left down in the hall, every half-used bottle of shampoo in the bathroom, along with the toothbrush, the box of tampons, the cotton wool for cleaning her face. And the school reports and the library card, the passport even; and that favourite mug in the kitchen cupboard, the one with the multicoloured spots like giant Smarties all over it, which sat there on the shelf untouched now, while all the other mugs around it came and went, and came and went. Out it went. Out everything went. The clothes, the old toys, the bedding that still smelled of her. Out. Out. Out.

But it still wasn't enough. Vanessa was still there, haunting the air, haunting their lives. So the house had to go, and the marriage, too. And what must it have been like then for Mrs Reiber still to have Simon to look upon, Simon with his blond wavy hair and his blue eyes, his fine bones and his tall, slim body? What must it have been like to have one child left, so very much like the other, and so be reminded constantly of what was gone, and of what remained?

She is the one that I really feel for: Mrs Reiber, whose only way of coping with the ceaseless roll of day after torturous day is to pretend that she never had a daughter at all. Mrs Reiber, who loved her daughter so much that no comfort will ever be found.

FOURTEEN

In March it is Jono's birthday. This year it falls on a Sunday, which means his party will be the day before. This year I have booked an hour and a half of bowling, followed by a pizza. He has invited eleven boys, those that he is friends with and those that he would like to be friends with. They arrive in ones and twos and threes, dropped off by parents who mostly can't even be bothered to stop and speak to me. Some of the boys barely even speak to Jono; instead they cluster in their little groups, bored, so rude that I want to slap them. All morning Jono has been anxious and agitated, dreading the whole thing. It breaks my heart to see how hard he tries, to see how he swings from frowning bewilderment one minute to desperate, hysterical laughter the next. We are not natural performers in our family. We don't put on a good show.

In the restaurant, Andrew and I sit at a small table away from the boys, from where we can sip our coffee and watch them. We watch how they compete to be the funniest, the smartest, the most important in the group. Food is flicked, drinks squirted through straws. One boy is jeered at for his haircut, another because his phone's out of date. *They're just boys*, Andrew says, but I sit there tense, wishing it was over.

When Jono isn't looking, one of them tips pepper all over his pizza, which of course everyone thinks is a huge joke. Jono doesn't know why they are laughing at first, though he joins in and laughs along with them, making them all laugh even louder. And then he takes a bite.

'Oh, for God's sake!' I snap, seeing Jono's face flush scarlet and his eyes flood with tears as he breaks into a cough, and I start to stand, to go over there, to tell them all to just grow up and behave like humans, not animals, but Andrew sticks out his hand and stops me.

'Don't,' he says, 'you'll embarrass him. You'll make him feel like a baby.'

And then we have to pay for the whole thing. Bowling and dinner for twelve. Andrew sticks it on his credit card, trying not to flinch. Bang goes that week in a caravan that he was so keen on.

Jono is quiet in the car on the way home. I glance in the mirror and see him staring out the window. He looks exhausted.

'You okay, Jono?' I ask.

He grunts a reply.

And Andrew says, 'Did you enjoy yourself then, old boy?'

'Yes,' Jono lies automatically.

'Good,' Andrew says decisively. 'That's all that matters.'

Jono carries on looking out of the window. For the rest of the journey we are all silent.

And then the next day Jono has to perform all over again, for his family this time. My parents arrive in time for lunch, bearing presents and an excess of birthday bonhomie. Andrew's mother is already here and has been since yesterday morning, when Andrew drove all the way to Leicester and back to fetch her. She sits on the sofa from which she has barely moved since she arrived, radiating displeasure.

At least she didn't come to Jono's party, though he was terrified that she would.

'Come along,' Andrew said, doing his best to persuade her, while Jono glared at him, absolutely horrified. 'You'll enjoy it.'

But, 'No, thank you,' she said pointedly. 'I don't want to get in the way.'

We had a row about her, of course. We always do. No, not a row, exactly; a *disagreement*. Andrew doesn't do rows. He wanted her to come for the week.

'It'll be nice for her,' he told me, as I stood in the kitchen last Sunday evening, chopping up beans. 'It'll give her a break.'

'It won't be nice for me,' I said.

'Come on now,' he said, in the kind of tone that you'd use on a truculent child. 'She doesn't see much of Jono.'

And, like a truculent child, I responded, 'What about her precious cat?'

'It'll go into the cattery.'

A whole week with her watching me, judging me, poking around in my business? No way. Absolutely, no way.

I wouldn't be able to see Simon.

I stopped what I was doing and looked at him. And I said, 'I assume you'll be taking the week off work, then?' And I saw it cross his eyes, that hesitation, that doubt. It hadn't even occurred to him that he should do that.

He pushed his hand back through his hair and lowered his eyes. 'Well, I'd *like* to, but I'm really busy at work at the moment. I just don't know if it will be possible ...'

'Well, then.' I picked up my knife and my beans and carried on chopping.

'Rachel,' he said, 'it's not that much to ask, is it? She could come up for Jono's birthday and just stay on for a few days . . .'

It wasn't going to happen. It just wasn't going to happen.

'Andrew,' I said, without looking at him, 'if you want your mother to come and stay, then make it when you can take the time off to entertain her. She is your mother, after all.'

'She doesn't need entertaining,' he said. 'It'll be nice for her just to be here.'

I snorted. I couldn't stop myself.

'For God's sake, Rachel, she's my mother.'

'Yes,' I said, 'but she's not staying all week unless you can get the time off work.'

I could feel him glaring at me. I ignored him, and carried on chop-chop-chopping at those beans.

'I don't understand you,' he said at last. 'What do you have to do all day that means you're too busy to be hospitable to my mother?' He walked out of the room without waiting for a reply.

But no way could I give in, and go a whole week without seeing Simon. And so Lois is here just for the weekend. On Monday Andrew will have to go into work late, after he has taken her back to Leicester.

'She could always go on the train,' I said.

And Andrew said, 'Don't be ridiculous. I'm not sending my mother home by train.'

'That's up to you, then,' I said.

But Andrew, who likes to have the last word, snapped back, 'Well, actually it's not, really, is it?'

I don't know what he told his mother. No doubt they will have discussed me on the long, cosy drive down from Leicester.

And now she sits on my sofa, puffed up with umbrage, while Andrew dances in attendance, doing his best to please her and make up for the failings of his wife. I hate the way he acts so falsely jolly. I hate the way he says, 'Come on, Jono, show Grandma what you got for your birthday,' and, 'Tell Grandma what we did yesterday, Jono; tell her about the bowling,' thus heaping yet more pressure on poor Jono to perform.

I imagine what it must have been like for Andrew as a boy, tiptoeing around his mother, learning to keep his feelings in. When he told her we were getting married, she responded with a drawn-in breath and the advice to *Think carefully*, even though we'd been living together for years. Andrew actually told me this, though I'd really rather he hadn't.

I cannot feel connected to Lois. I do not feel that I am connected to Andrew, even though I am of course; I am bound to him forever, as Jono is bound to us both. We will never be free. I picture the ties that bind Jono and me as being like ribbons; red, silk ribbons they are, in my mind's eye. Sometimes I picture myself cutting those ribbons – snip, snip, snip – and then I see myself, not him, just floating away.

If only it were so easy.

But the ties that bind me to Andrew are of coarser stuff, more tangled, more barbed. He is the father of my son. He knows what I know. Our love for Jono tangles and traps us like wire. We share a child, but we share a dead child, too. That fact is always there between us, unspoken.

I loiter in the doorway of my living room, observing this family gathering; my son, my parents, my husband and his mother. I observe the strangeness of their interaction; the way Lois just sits and stares at Jono because, much as she loves him, she doesn't know how to talk to him. The way that Andrew, hovering anxiously beside her like a go-between or a circus host, can't stop clicking his mental fingers, willing Jono to turn his tricks. My parents, sitting side by side on the edge of the other sofa, making chat – endless cover-the-gaps-up chat – and sipping their tea while it's still too hot, sensitive perhaps of an atmosphere. And Jono, struggling in the middle of this, desperate to escape to his PlayStation.

And I am reminded of when they all came to visit on Jono's third birthday, and the conversation then was all about a new baby sister, and *Won't it be lovely, Jono, to have someone to play with?* I didn't loiter in doorways, then; I sat on the sofa, glad to take the weight off my feet, proud to show off my growing bump, with Andrew perched on the arm beside me, his hand resting on my shoulder.

All of these people in this room – do they ever think about my baby?

After she died, my parents came back to visit. They put on brisk, efficient smiles. My dad built a train track with Jono, and my mum said, 'Do you have any ironing I can do?'

No one talked about what had happened. About what should have been, but now was gone.

We sat in the living room, drinking tea and watching Jono, praising and encouraging him as he pushed around his trains. We got on with things.

And I tried to be grateful for what I had.

For a while we tried to have another baby. For a while, that seemed like the answer, and we went at it hammer and tongs, Andrew and me, not in love, but in desperation. As if we could get another baby in quickly, and then we need not feel the loss so. Much like people do when a pet dog dies: they rush straight out and buy another, and more often than not they get one of the same sort – another Labrador, say, or a collie. And apart from the fact that the new one is a little younger, you really can't tell the difference. Fido, Bonzo, Spot . . . who's to know? It's a dog, that's what matters.

Though in our case, of course, it would be a baby.

And it would save having to explain things to Jono. Oh sure, there'd be a time delay, but Jono was young; he wouldn't understand about that. We could fob him off. *It takes a long, long time for a baby to be made*, we could say. Or, *There was a little delay in getting the right parts, but she's all there now, you'll have your sister soon*. Or, perhaps, *And guess what – it's going to be a little brother instead*.

Rather than what we did end up telling Jono, which was that he was so perfect that we couldn't possibly make another one as good as him.

So we went for it. Andrew filled me up and filled me up, but like a clapped-out old machine, my womb just never kicked back into life.

Soon, sex became something to apologize for. It became something to dread. I saw Andrew's eyes slide away from mine as I lay underneath him. And I felt myself hope and die, and hope and die. Again and again and again.

I thought of going to the doctor, but I couldn't bear it. I couldn't bear the thought of all those medical fingers poking and examining me, of the questions, the tests, only to be told the blindingly obvious: that I'd shot out my last decent egg. That my chances were up – over.

Once, when I lay on my bed sobbing my heart out because I'd got my period yet again and I'd really thought – *really, really* thought – there was a possibility that I wouldn't be getting it that month, Andrew sat down on the bed beside me. I saw the resigned slope of his shoulders, the years fading by in his eyes.

'We've got Jono,' he said. No, he didn't just say it, he *pleaded*. 'Rachel, we've got Jono.'

When I am with Simon I can forget all of this.

When I lie in Simon's arms on the crisply ironed sheets of his bed, or stand wrapped in his bathrobe looking down at London in all its promise and anonymity; when I help myself to a coffee by pouring fresh beans into his expensive steel coffee-machine and taking milk from his immaculate fridge in which his housekeeper has arranged salads, cheese, pâtés and hams in neat, clinical order; or when I stand under his shower and feel the water hit my skin and mix with the scent of his Roget & Gallet soap, a scent that will stay with me all day ... I can forget. I can slip right out of my life.

Sometimes, when we have very little time, he stares at me hungrily, not taking his eyes off mine for a second as he yanks off his tie and kicks off his shoes. We have done it against the kitchen counter with most of our clothes still on, fast and brutal; we have done it on the sofa countless times, with that view a spectacular, cinematic backdrop. We do it when we can. I will go to his flat just for ten minutes with him: a quick, potent fix.

I do not think about Andrew when I am with Simon. Even Jono becomes oddly distant, temporarily stilled within my head. The house, the domestic, the endless silent ache ... all of it just fades away. What we have, Simon and I, is an escape. We are clawing back something lost, reclaiming something precious. We do not talk about our day-to-day, our separate daily lives. We talk about Vanessa, and the old days. And

Simon talks with the same passion and urgency with which he makes love to me. 'You remember her,' he says to me, over and over, touching my face, searching my eyes as if he cannot believe I am really there. 'You knew her too.'

And I can become the girl that Simon remembers – or *thinks* he remembers – from those golden, enchanted days. I can be the girl I always wanted to be.

FIFTEEN

I have something of Vanessa's.

It is an item of clothing; a soft blue cotton jacket, not denim exactly, but that sort of thing. In fact it's more of a shirt than a jacket, but you'd wear it over things. Vanessa wore it over things. The strip of lining down the front behind the buttons, and just inside the cuffs, is pink-and-white-striped velvet. Vanessa wore it with the cuffs turned back, so that you could see that lining. She wore it open, with a little vest top underneath and her jeans. And on her feet her brown suede pixie boots with the tassels at the back, and looped through the waist of her jeans that brown leather belt with the blue mosaic clasp. I loved that belt, even though half the pieces were missing. She'd have her hair tied back, in a long French plait, if there was someone around to do it for her, or that side-of-the-head pony tail, like she has in that photograph with Tristram, the one that Simon showed me. Or else she'd just leave her hair down, and that's how I loved it best, left to ripple and flow around her shoulders in a mass of Pre-Raphaelite waves.

I acquired this jacket from Leanne. Vanessa had left it at Leanne's house one day, and there it stayed, waiting to be collected. It hung from the back of the chair in Leanne's room, along with a varied assortment of other clothes. And I'd see it there, when I came over on a Sunday afternoon and listened to Leanne's tales of the night before. I'd see it there, and sometimes I'd try it on. It didn't look half as good on me as it did on Vanessa, but I loved it anyway. And I remember it *smelled* of her, and it continued to smell of her, for years and years, long after she'd gone.

I asked Leanne if I could borrow it. *Do you think Vanessa would mind*, I asked, *if it's just for a night?*

Oh, sure, Leanne said, barely even listening.

I'll bring it back tomorrow, I said, but I never did.

I only wore it the once, to some party or other at college, and then it hung in my room, not from the back of a chair, but in my wardrobe, hidden. Leanne forgot all about it. As far as I know, Vanessa never knew I had it. Maybe she never even realized she'd mislaid it.

I couldn't wear it again, in case Leanne saw see me in it, and then she would remember and no doubt ask for it back. And so I hid it away, and took it out just to look at it and touch it, and to smell its precious smell. The longer I had it, the more I couldn't bear to part with it again.

And then Vanessa died.

Now, one morning when Andrew is at work and Jono at school, I hunt for this jacket. It was relegated to storage long ago, when I left home. I packed my old books along with various other relics and keepsakes from childhood into two cardboard boxes, which are now in the loft, untouched for all these years. And the loft is not a place I would normally go.

The entrance is via the landing ceiling. We have one of those hook-down ladders, and it takes me an age to work out how to hook it down. Then gingerly I climb up. I've been up the steps before once or twice; I've even gone as far as to stick my head through the hole while Andrew was in the loft, getting down the Christmas decorations. But I've never actually climbed the last bit, right into the roof.

I reach the top of the ladder, put my arms inside the hatch and heave myself up, not thinking about how I will get down again.

There's a mass of stuff up here. This is Andrew territory. I stand on the boards that he's put down across the beams; I see the shelves that he's rigged up for the various things that he deems to be useful. I see things divided into sections, evidence of his constant project-making. Here are the old broken appliances that he thinks to fix one day, though anyone in their right mind would throw them out: the old radio; an old cine-camera that belonged to his dad; our ancient record player for which you can no longer get a needle. And here are the records that can no longer be played on that record player, all stacked up and gathering dust. There's the old TV, and a mini drinks fridge that was won in a raffle and will never be used. There are bags and bags of Jono's old clothes, and his baby toys; I spy his box of Duplo and his pull-along dog. Pushed back under the eaves is Jono's white-painted changing stand, his high chair and baby-bouncer. And the cot. I cannot bring myself to look at the cot.

I focus on the task in hand.

I find my old boxes tucked down behind a crate of Andrew's own college books. His books, I notice, show signs of recent disturbance, whereas the lids on both of my old boxes are covered in dust. I have not touched them since the day we moved into this house, and then merely to move them. I have not looked inside. I am not even 100 per cent sure that the jacket will be there; it is very possible that I didn't pack it up with my stuff after all, but maybe left it at my parents' house. Maybe it has even been thrown away. This last thought twists in me, and fills me with dread. When I moved my things out of my parents' home I didn't want to cling to my past. I'd moved on. Leanne and I had grown apart. I'd been through college and just come back from a year in Paris; I was with Andrew, I had a future to look forward to. I thought about Vanessa still, but as a memory, more distant then than she is to me now, somehow. But in my twenties I was too busy looking forward, whereas now I have become entrenched in looking back.

I reach down to lift the lid off the first box. I am incredibly nervous; afraid that I won't find this jacket, but just as afraid that I will. I don't know how I will feel when I see it again. But this first box is full of old school books and valentine cards and exam certificates, all stuffed in, never to be looked at again. I have no desire to look at them now.

What if the jacket isn't here? What if it did get thrown away? But I pull the lid off the other box and there it is. I find it straight away, wrapped up in a paper bag. And suddenly I remember putting it in that paper bag and tucking it away, as though to rest. The bag is crisp and brittle to the touch now, and I'm afraid that the jacket will be rotten, or full of moths. I lift it out carefully and peel the paper away. And I unfold the jacket. The blue has faded to a dirty white along the creases, and the velvet of the lining is rough now under my fingertips. And it smells musty and stale. I'm *disappointed* by the smell. I feel robbed by it. I thought that if I were to find this jacket I would fall upon it, holding it to my face and breathing in the scent of Vanessa, filling my head with the memory of her. Instead I find myself recoiling slightly. I wish I had left it hidden and untouched, instead of finding it like this. It is a reminder of what is gone, that is all; of what is vanished and turned to dust. I wish I'd let it stay as it was in my memory, the first time I tried it on, so soft, so new, so still of *her*. Now it is the stuff of jumble sales; it is dead man's clothes.

It seems incredible that this jacket, and those three photos that Simon showed me, can really be all that is left of Vanessa. A whole life, reduced to this. Suddenly I think of Mrs Reiber, that day she came into the cafe in Kew; I think of her with her fur coat and her cut-glass accent and her stockings all worn to shreds. She is Vanessa's *mother*. She held her in her arms. How – *how* – can she wipe out her own daughter like that? How can she pretend that she never lived at all?

And yet what *can* you ever do? How *can* you move on?

All of Vanessa's things would be like this jacket now; turning rancid through purposelessness and decay. How unbearable would it have been to see that? To have tried to keep her alive through *things*?

I ought to give the jacket to Simon. I think of him, showing me those photos. *They are all that I have of her*, he said. *They are all that is left*. I know I ought to give it to him, but I don't know that I can.

I sit there on the attic floor and there is a fist in my heart, pressing, pressing hard. I hold that jacket in my hands, fragile and useless as a dead baby. And then, as if it was a dead baby, I put it away again; I wrap it back up in that paper and put it back in that box and I close the lid. I wish I had never got it out.

SIXTEEN

Two weeks after Jono's birthday I meet Janice for lunch in Covent Garden. Naturally, she was too busy to come and see Jono, what with her work and her boyfriend, though she did send him something in the post. Janice hates family gatherings and avoids them at all costs. Being single, and childless – or child-*free*, as she would put it – she can do that. She can make that choice.

And so we arrange to meet on this Saturday, as though by seeing me she is also somehow discharging her duty to Jono, her nephew and, let me add at this point, her godson. To be honest, I wouldn't normally mind this, in fact it's a logic I have happily gone along with for years. *It's a big day for you, too*, she said to me once, *so you and I should go out for lunch*. A present for Jono and lunch with me, and we're all happy, aren't we? Especially as it I means I don't have to put on the stilted, uncomfortable display of happy families that a visit to my house would entail.

But today, taking the train up to Waterloo, I am too aware of the usual purpose of my trips into town these days, and too aware also of the fact that today, being a Saturday, Simon wouldn't even be there. I picture his flat, silent and empty, and then I correct myself and picture that strange unknown woman in there, changing the bed sheets on which we have lain, cleaning the bathroom, replenishing the fridge. It wouldn't be so bad if I had a key, if I could let myself in there, just to be close to him. And I did suggest this. One day, just a week or so ago; it was raining and we'd arranged to meet, but he was late and for twenty minutes or more I was left standing in the foyer like a hooker, waiting, waiting. 'Perhaps if I had a key . . .' I said on the way up in the lift, trying not to sound annoyed.

But he laughed. 'You're sounding like a wife,' he said, and my insides, my heart, my soul, every part of me turned to ice. 'Come on,' he continued, putting his hands on my hips and shoving up my skirt, kissing me, driving me out of the lift and into his flat and his bed, 'you don't need a key.'

And now I sit on the train to Waterloo, and I think of him leaving London last night, rushing back to Kingham, to be with his wife. I picture him waking in bed with her this morning, the country sunlight streaming through the window. I picture a vast table in the kitchen, laden with fresh bread from the Aga, eggs from the hens, and butter and jam; I picture the children rushing in, golden-haired and beautiful, calling, *Daddy! Daddy!* And I mind. Believe me, I mind.

I get off the train and walk towards the river, just as I would if I was going to Simon's flat, but instead of carrying on along the South Bank I take the steps up to Waterloo Bridge and start crossing over. It is a calm, still day and London is bathed in soft, pale-grey light as the weak sunshine reflects off the concrete. It is mild, too, for March, and the tourists and day-trippers are out in their droves. I have always loved this walk across the bridge; the view of the Houses of Parliament to the left and the City to the right, but today in my heart I feel a hollow, dragging ache. If I look to my right

I can see the Oxo Tower, and I find that I can't stop looking. I want to see Simon's flat. I want to know if I *can* see it from here, if I can make it out and identify it. Because if I can, I will have it then, marked forever in my head. Every time I cross this bridge, *every* time, I will see it.

I run over onto the other side, dodging through the traffic. I can't help myself. Like the tourists looking at the view, I am there, one hand shielding my eyes, peering as far as I can.

I can't see it, though, no matter how hard I try. The Oxo Tower stands out as a landmark, but the buildings around it merge into each other, a jigsaw puzzle of grey. It annoys me that I can't see it. I feel as if I am being denied, as if Simon's flat and all the buildings around it are closing together and shutting me out. And so I carry on walking now, though I can't stop myself from turning and turning again, looking back, to see if from a different angle I might get a better view.

By the time I cross the Strand and start walking up Wellington Street I am all out of sorts, angry with myself, angry with Simon. I think of him wandering down the lane into his village with wife, kids and dogs in tow, meandering at leisure, comfortable in his world. I picture them, stamping the mud off their boots at the village pub; I smell the wood-smoke from the chimneys, hear the crackle of wood upon an open fire. I picture this idyllic world that I will never be part of, and I am shot through with a bolt of envy. And I wonder how it is that he can lead such a double life, moving from London to the country and from the country back to London again with such apparent ease, picking up and putting down his family as he goes, and picking up and putting me down, too.

But of course what Simon and I have is not of the real

world. It is a fantasy, born out of loss and longing, a fabricated illusion of a life. I am not real to him. How can I be?

I shove my way through the crowds now and feel as I have always felt: like the outsider, the one on the edge of other people's lives, seeing, stealing what I can. By the time I meet Janice at the cafe on the corner of the Piazza I am sunk in the grip of self-loathing.

She doesn't make it any better.

I am there first, and I get us a table under the awning so that we are half-indoors, half-out, with a view of the crowds gathering around the street performers across the square. I sit there with my drink, watching all this fun and activity while I wait for her, a good fifteen minutes. When she does at last arrive she swoops in, pushing past the other tables, knocking people with her bag.

'Sorry,' she says as she collapses down into the chair opposite me. 'Had to speak to Paul. His bloody wife's giving him hell.'

She does nothing to keep her voice down, and around us people glance over their shoulders, take a good look.

Bitterness, and some dark sense of irony, has me quoting, 'They always go back to their wives in the end, you know.'

'Not always,' she snaps back. 'Ian didn't.'

'No,' I say. 'But if there are children involved.'

'For God's sake, Rachel, children are not the be-all and end-all.'

I am struck by her vehemence and feel a rush of heat to my face. It is not a good start. We look at our menus in silence.

And then, as if it is a natural follow-on, she says, 'How is Jono?'

'Fine,' I say. 'Thank you for his present.'

'I take it he enjoyed his birthday?'

'Yes, thank you.'

Why do I feel so patronized by these questions? So put-in-my-box as the good little wife and mother, as if she knows everything about the world and I know nothing – *nothing* – beyond the limits of my own domestic walls? Her questions are an end to conversation, not a start. They distance me from her. And yet she is my sister. We are both screwing other women's husbands. We have so much more in common than she thinks.

'Do you remember my baby? My other baby?' I do not know where these words come from; they are out of my mouth before I even know I want to say them. And now that they are out, I stare at her, just as shocked as she is.

'Yes, of course I do,' she says.

'Good.' I nod my head. 'Good.' My heart is thumping and I am perilously close to tears.

'Why do you ask?' she says, but then the waitress appears beside us, butting in with her oblivious cheer. 'Salad,' Janice snaps at her.

And I say, 'Same,' and take a deep breath, and try to get a grip.

'Why do you ask?' Janice demands again when the waitress has gone. She is leaning closer to me over the table now and watching me with narrowed eyes. I am reminded of how things were when we were children; of how she'd demand and intimidate me till she got her own way, so that we always had to watch her programmes on TV and play her games, games that she would always win. And of how she'd sneer if she ever caught me crying. This, perhaps, is why I don't tell her things now.

And yet I need to. I need to tell someone.

'It's something we've never talked about, that's all,' I manage to say. To avoid her eyes I look out across the Piazza. Some guy on stilts is balancing a tray of glasses on his head; the crowd whoop and sway as he staggers among them. 'No one ever talks about it. About *her*.'

I can feel her staring at me. 'It was a long time ago, wasn't it, Rachel?' she says at last, though her voice is gentler now, I will give her that. 'Why bring it up now?'

I don't answer. I can't. I watch that clown, weaving around. Suddenly one of the glasses topples and slides off the tray. It smashes on the ground and the crowd jumps back, squealing. The clown loses his balance for a second and another glass falls, and another. The show is in chaos.

The waitress comes back and slaps down our salads.

'Rachel,' Janice says quietly, 'what's this all about?'

I turn and face her. *Nothing*, I could say. *I was just thinking, that's all*. And I could change the subject. We could talk about her work, her boyfriend, the complexities of a hectic, single life. I could ask her about her holiday plans, her progress in painting her flat. And my life could stay where it always stays, skirted over briefly in a series of mundane surface issues, and then we would part, as we always part, done until next time.

Or I could tell her.

Inside my chest I can feel my heartbeat, ticking away like a clock.

'You remember Leanne?' I say tentatively.

'Yes, of course I do,' Janice replies, spearing salad onto her fork. 'You asked me that recently. Why?'

I watch as she shoves lettuce, goat's cheese, olives and tomato into her mouth, getting the eating over with quickly.

My own food sits there untouched. 'Do you remember her friend, Vanessa? Did you ever meet her? Did I ever . . . talk about her?'

Of course she never met Vanessa, and of course I never talked about her. I never talked to her about anything. She quickly shakes her head as she sticks a piece of bread into her mouth, and raises her eyebrows for me to continue.

'Well . . . she was Leanne's friend from school, and I became friends with her, too. She had all these parties . . .' I am stalling. I am having second thoughts.

'And?' Janice prompts in that schoolmistress voice that she used so often when we were little, when I'd have to stand in front of her, stumbling over my excuses for borrowing her pens or her doll, or whatever, without asking. *And?* she'd demand, hands on hips. *And?* till I confessed, and what a mistake that always turned out to be.

I lick my lips, not even sure what I want to say.

'Eat your lunch,' Janice orders, and so I cut up a piece of cheese, stick it in my mouth. She watches while I chew and swallow. It feels like cardboard in my throat. '*And?*' she asks again.

'Well . . . she died,' I say.

And Janice mutters, 'Oh,' and puts down her fork.

'When I was at college,' I add quickly.

'Oh,' she says again. And she watches me, and waits for me to continue.

'And recently I – I got back in touch with her brother.'

'What did you go and do that for?' she asks as if it was the most stupid, ridiculous thing.

And as if it was the most stupid, ridiculous thing, I say, 'I don't know.'

'Did he want to meet you?' she demands.

'Yes,' I say.

And she says, 'Well, don't.' Followed by, 'There's only ever one reason why a man wants to meet a woman.'

'No, there's not!' I am knocked by her cynicism, though, really, I should have expected it. What did I think: that we'd have a sisterly heart-to-heart? That she'd offer me her support and understanding?

'Don't meet him,' she says. I stare at her, wishing I had never started this. She stares back at me and then states disparagingly, 'You already have.'

For a few strained moments neither of us speaks. I prod at my salad with my fork, while Janice sits back in her chair, arms folded, and observes me.

And then she says, 'Are you sleeping with him?'

I don't answer. Suddenly it seems like none of her business. And I think how quickly we fall back into the roles of our childhood.

She leans forward, and says it again, a little louder this time so that if the people at the other tables weren't listening before, they certainly are now. 'I said, *Are you sleeping with him?*'

'*I heard you,*' I hiss. My face is burning. I don't know if I want to slap her or cry. 'You think things are so hunky-dory with Andrew all the time – well, they're not. Believe me, they are not.'

'And you think the answer to that is to sleep with someone else?' Her hand is on the table now and she curls her fingers into a fist and starts rapping a knuckle against her water glass. 'Is he married?'

And I can't stop myself from retorting, 'Is *Paul* married?'

'I cannot believe that you could be so stupid,' she snaps.

'And I cannot believe that you can be such a hypocrite,' I snap right back.

'You have a family,' she says, and, as if it needs spelling out some more, 'you have a child. And a husband who loves you.'

'You see what you want to see,' I say.

'You stop it, Rachel, you stop it right now.'

I glare at her with my eyes burning. I can't believe she is telling me what to do as if I was five years old again.

'You should be ashamed of yourself,' she says.

We part on bad terms.

I push the remains of my salad around my plate in sullen silence while Janice signals to the waitress for the bill. And then we pay and put our purses back in our bags.

'Well then,' Janice says when we are outside the restaurant, ready to go our separate ways. Usually we would wander around the shops together for a while, but not today. Not after that. 'Give my love to Andrew and Jono, won't you?' she says sarcastically.

'I wish I'd never told you,' I say.

'I wish you hadn't, too,' she says. 'Rachel, how can you be so *selfish*? I won't let you do this – you're my sister!'

'And you're my sister. I thought you might understand.' We stand there, glaring at each other. I think of how I've had to listen to her going on about Paul, I think of all the lies she's quite happily had him telling his wife. But it's one rule for Janice and quite another rule for me, obviously.

'Andrew doesn't deserve this, Rachel,' she says.

'So what are you going to do?' I have to ask. 'Are you going to tell him?'

'What are *you* going to do, Rachel?' she asks and, having got in the last word, she turns and walks off into the crowd.

*

If I had a key to Simon's flat I would go there now. I would make myself a coffee and curl up on his sofa and try to find myself some calm, some peace. Just being in his flat would be enough; just having somewhere to go, to be close to him. Somewhere I could think, and try to steady my head.

But I have no key, and nowhere to go except home.

For a while I hang around Covent Garden, looking in one or two shops for the sake of something to do, but I feel all wrong, so out of place among the hordes of animated teenagers and tourists crowding the narrow walkways. The general merriment grates at the blackness of my mood, and so reluctantly I start wandering back to Waterloo.

I can't believe I was so stupid as to try and talk to Janice. She won't tell Andrew. Surely she won't. If she did, she would be the one to hurt him. But nor will she forget, either, or let it go. And what am I supposed to do? Tell Andrew myself, or just stop seeing Simon? Neither is an option. And I'm certainly not just going to go and do whatever Janice tells me. How can she think to preach to me, when what she is doing is no better?

I know an affair can't drift on and on, forever. But nor can a stagnant marriage, either. I feel trapped whichever way I turn. Jono's face rears up inside my head, a reminder of my guilt. How could I ever leave Andrew? And yet I will not stop seeing Simon. I cannot. I think of the emptiness of the days before I met him and I am flooded with panic; I cannot possibly go back to that. And why should I?

I cannot leave Andrew because of Jono, but does that mean I should resign myself to a life without love, without happiness?

But then I think of Simon, down in Kingham with his wife and family. I think of how he easily he shuts down his life here in London every weekend and goes back to them. And he'll have plans with them, of course he will; they're probably talking about them now as they walk across the fields together, or snuggle down back home in front of an open fire. I am not part of his plans. There is no need for me to be. I am here in London; his family is tucked safely away down there.

I walk back across Waterloo Bridge and my eyes are fixed on the Oxo Tower. I need to talk to Simon. I need to talk to him just because I cannot bear the thought of him being so cosied up with his wife when I am here, feeling like this. I have never called him at weekends before, but he's never actually told me not to. And I'm sure he could speak for a short while; I'm sure he could find a way.

I walk faster, and as soon as I am across the bridge I run down the steps to the South Bank, away from the noise of the traffic. My heart is hammering as I ring his number, but he can always pass me off as his secretary or something with a work query, or his housekeeper even. Somewhere there is an irony in that.

The phone rings, but he doesn't answer. Instead of leaving a message I ring again, and again he doesn't answer. So this time I do leave a message. I say, in as neutral a voice as I can manage, 'Hi, this is Rachel here. Could you call me, please? As soon as possible.'

And then I loiter about, hoping that he'll call me straight back. For twenty minutes or so I wander past the booksellers and the skateboarders, phone in hand. It's all I can do to stop myself turning around and walking east along the river, towards his flat, but what is the point in that? What is the point – but nevertheless I do turn anyway, and start walking under the bridge, back up the Thames. And I'm willing him to ring me. I'm wondering if I dare call again if he doesn't. I walk towards his flat, as if I'll find myself some solace just by walking the familiar route. And I'm just outside the Oxo Tower, wondering what to do now, when at last my phone does ring.

But it's Janice.

'Where are you?' she barks, and I wish I'd checked the number before answering.

'Nowhere in particular,' I answer somewhat frostily. 'Why? Where are you?'

'I'm at home,' she says impatiently.

'Would that be alone?'

'Yes,' she snaps. 'That would be alone.' Then, 'Have you thought about what I said?'

I don't answer. I mean, what on earth does she expect me to say? But I do turn around and start walking back to Waterloo.

'I mean it, Rachel. You stop seeing him, do you hear me?'

'I hear you,' I say. 'And perhaps you better stop seeing Paul.'

'For God's sake, Rachel, do you have to be so childish? This isn't about me.'

'But why isn't it about you?' I half-shout into the phone. 'I mean, tell me, what's the difference?'

'There's a huge difference,' she snaps back. '*You've* got a family worth saving.' And she hangs up, leaving me wishing that I had done so first.

I take the train back to Surbiton and walk the ten minutes back to my house with a horrible, sinking feeling dragging at my heart. It is starting to get dark, and the end-of day gloom settles heavily over my shoulders. Simon hasn't called me back. I rang his number twice again from the train, and both times it switched straight to his voicemail. He'd turned off his phone.

The light is on in our living room, and as I walk up the pathway I can see Andrew there on the sofa, slumped down in front of the TV, watching the football. Somehow this makes me even more depressed.

I hate this time of day, always have done.

I open the door and call out, 'Hello', but nobody answers. I take off my boots and hang up my coat, and then I just stand there for a minute, bracing myself. I can hear the faint fire and judder of the PlayStation from upstairs; Jono is up in the spare room. And from the living room comes the quiet, monotonous roar of the football, broken every now and then by Andrew hissing *Yes!* or *Oh, no!* at the TV. And yet here in the hall, the sound that I hear most is the silence. It greets me like a wall.

Again I check my phone. I cannot believe Simon hasn't called me. Was it really too much to ask that he should escape just for a minute or two? It is nearly half-past five and I wonder what he is doing. If they were out for the afternoon, they will be back at home now; there are children to feed. They will be warm and snug in their country home, drinking tea, resting, before doing whatever it is they will be doing tonight.

He could have phoned me.

Maybe he still will, but for me it will be a surreptitious phone call now, if he does; I'll have to lock myself away in the bathroom, I won't be able to *talk*.

I feel myself, fitting in and around things. I feel myself, clutching at air.

Slowly I climb the stairs.

'Hello, Jono,' I say, from the doorway of the spare room. He is gripping the controller of his PlayStation, his eyes transfixed upon the screen. Not for even a second can he look away.

'Hello,' I say again. 'Have you had a nice day?'

He grunts. He says, 'What's for tea?'

And I watch him for a moment; I watch how he frowns, so intent on zap-zap-zapping at whatever monsters there are on that screen. I see the flush on his face, the glare of his eyes. I hate the PlayStation. I didn't want to get it, but he pleaded and pleaded. *I've got nothing else to do*, he cried, *no one to play with*. And so guilt had me giving in; guilt that we'd sent him to a school too far from home for there to be friends nearby. And guilt that he is an only child.

I wonder what it would have been like if I'd had my baby daughter. I wonder what she'd be like now, filling our house and our lives with her girlish laughter and chat. Had she lived, none of us would be so alone.

Downstairs, I force myself to venture into the living room. Andrew is sitting forward in his seat now, glued to the screen. It would seem that the match is reaching its climax. I stand beside the sofa.

'I'm home,' I say, because it appears that he hasn't noticed.

'Have a good day?' Andrew asks, without looking away from the TV.

'Not particularly,' I say, but he doesn't hear. Somebody has just scored a goal. Andrew sits back in his chair, lets out a sigh of disgust. The referee blows his whistle and the commentator starts shouting over the crowd. The game is apparently over.

I stand there a while longer. Eventually Andrew says, 'How's Janice?'

'She's fine.'

'You've been seeing a lot of her lately.' There are people talking on the TV now; men in suits with slicked-back hair and ruddy faces, ex-footballers and the like, ripping apart the game. Andrew watches them. And he listens to them. Or so I think.

'Not really,' I say.

'Well, you seem to be going into London a lot.'

I look at him. Andrew never comments on how I spend my time. 'I don't always see Janice,' I say. 'I have other friends. And sometimes I go shopping.' I hear myself sounding defensive and my heart starts beating a little faster. 'Why?' I can't stop myself from asking. 'Do you mind?'

'No,' he says somewhat wearily, still looking at the screen. 'I don't mind.' And then, more pointedly, 'I didn't mean to pry.'

Finally, at nearly ten o'clock, I get a text message from Simon.

I'll call you on Monday is all that he says.

SEVENTEEN

On Monday, as on every Monday, Andrew gets up as soon as the alarm goes off. He groans and drags himself out of bed. Instantly I am wide awake, though I pretend that I am not. I lie there with my eyes shut, listening to the sound of the shower running, and my entire body is tense with the cold reality of what I am doing.

Andrew comes out of the bathroom and quickly he dresses. And then, as usual, he comes round to my side of the bed, leans over, places one hand on my shoulder and gently shakes me.

'Rachel,' he says. 'Rachel.' And like the thorough, reliable person that he is, he will not go until he knows that I am awake.

I have no choice but to open my eyes. And there he is, my husband, peering down at me.

'Okay, okay,' I say, and I stretch and turn away.

I hear him go down to the kitchen. It is my cue then to go and wake Jono. And so I put on my bathrobe and make my way along the landing. Jono's door is shut, and when I open it his room is dark and silent, and redolent with the scent of boy. He is lying on his side, still in the deepest of sleeps, with his face squashed against the pillow and his mouth slightly open. His forehead is furrowed into an intense, fixed frown. As I watch, I see his eyes flickering slightly beneath their lids as he dreams.

I kneel down beside him and watch him as he sleeps. For these few moments before I must wake him, and before the daily hell of the morning breaks loose and he is ripped away from me, I can look upon him and I can love him, as I have always loved him. I can wallow in that love; I can steal it and feast upon it, before he sees me and pushes me away. These moments are mine. I look at him; I gorge myself. My beautiful, beautiful boy. I would never hurt him, never. I tell myself this, and guilt floods like cold water through my veins. Jono loves his father. He loves us both. When he was younger he used to come into our bed in the mornings; we'd hear the creaking of the door as he pushed it open and the soft pad of his feet upon the floor. Then nothing for a moment as he stood at the end of our bed, wondering if we were awake. And if we were, we'd pretend that we weren't; we'd wait. And then we'd feel the duvet lifting off our feet as he climbed in and snuggled his way up the middle, coming to rest like a tight sausage between the two of us.

We were happy, weren't we, the three of us? We were a family, however small. When Jono stopped coming into us like that, we felt his loss like a void. There was a gap in the bed that it seemed neither of us could cross.

I move closer to him now, and I feel his breath across my face as he exhales. I move a little closer still, and he opens his eyes suddenly and jolts as though shocked. Quickly his eyes come into focus and he pulls away from me.

'What are you doing there?' he demands.

'It's time to get up,' I say.

He sticks out a childish hand to hit me away, and turns over. Slowly I stand up, and I lean over him, and as Andrew did to me, gently shake his shoulder.

'Go away,' he mumbles.

'Come on, Jono, it's time to get up.'

And again he says, 'Go away.'

I time things, so that Andrew is going out of the door just as I come downstairs. The kettle is still warm and I make myself a coffee. And I think of Simon, sitting on the train up from Kingham, on the long, early Monday-morning commute from one life to another. I wonder how they part, he and his wife. By now they will be used to it; she probably doesn't even get up to see him off. Perhaps he even leaves her sleeping in bed with a kiss, as Andrew used to me. Not for a moment do I think that Simon really loves his wife, nor she him. Otherwise how could they live apart as they do? At the very least they must have some arrangement, some blind eye to turn. I cannot be the first woman Simon has taken back to that flat, however much I'd like to think that I am. I try to detach myself, to think myself offhand, relaxed about it all. I remind myself what it was like back in that house in Oakley; how sex was passed around like an affectionate hug. It is only uptights like me who make such a big deal of it.

I try, but the truth is that I am still just as uptight as ever I was.

And now I picture Simon as I have come to know him; I picture him standing in front of that huge window in his flat, coffee cup or wine glass in hand, staring down at the vastness of the city below him. I picture the paleness of his skin with its smattering here and there of fine, blond hair; of the way the sinews in his arms stand out against his thinness.

And of his laugh, which hides such a mass of insecurity, and of the easy, polished way that he talks. I think of these things and I love them because they remind me of another world, another time. But what do I really know of him apart from vague, broken memories? And what does he know of me? What could he ever know? We connect on such a loose, transient fantasy; that is all. But then I think of him hiding away those pictures of his sister, hiding them away from his mother – and from his wife, too, for all that I know. I think of the coldness there must have been in his life since Vanessa died.

And I think of the creeping, elusive coldness in mine.

Surely there is some necessary purpose in this? Call it fate, or whatever you will, but think back – think back to those months after Vanessa died, when I'd take the bus after college to Oakley and walk about the green and stare up at her house, willing, *willing* something to happen, for there to be some sign, some reason for me to have known her and loved her as I did ... Surely, now, surely, this is it?

Trance-like, I set about preparing Jono's breakfast things as I do every morning: his toast, his cereal, his milk. I put it all out on the table, and then I walk back out of the kitchen to call up the stairs, 'Jono! Jono! Are you ready?'

And I wait for him. I hover in the kitchen in my bathrobe and I wait. And while I wait, a question strikes me suddenly, out of the blue: what difference would it make to Jono if I wasn't here, waiting on him like this, day in, day out? And the answer is this: not much, probably. Not to Jono. The difference would all be to me.

'What have you done with my PE shorts?' he demands when at last he stomps his way into the kitchen.

'Jono, I haven't done anything with your PE shorts.'

'Then why aren't they in my bag?'

'Perhaps you didn't put them in your bag,' I say.

'I did,' he wails, and he picks up a piece of toast and throws it down again. 'They were in there yesterday.'

'Perhaps you left them at school,' I suggest.

And he replies, in a voice that tells me how stupid he thinks that I am, 'How can I have left them at school when I didn't even have PE yesterday? *Duh*.' And he takes a gulp of his drink and slams the cup back down, so that milk slops over the side and onto the table.

I feel my heartbeat, picking up its pace.

I glance at the clock.

'Jono, you have less than five minutes before you have to leave. Please eat your breakfast. And if you can't find your shorts, you'll just have to take another pair for today.'

'How can I take another pair? I don't have another pair!'

'A pair of your home shorts,' I say, as steadily as I can.

He stares at me, his face stricken with panic and disbelief. 'I can't do that!' he howls. 'Everyone will laugh at me!'

I watch my son, as he hurries up the road, shoulders bent under the weight of his bag and the heavier weight of his woes. I see him struggle with his sports bag, and my heart aches for him, and for myself. I would go with him to the coach stop and help him with his bags, but of course that would not do. The net with which I would catch him is the net with which I trap us both, after all. And so I just stand there in the doorway, watching until he disappears from view.

And then I go back inside, take my phone from my bag, turn it on and wait.

To make less of a deal of the waiting, to have something to do, I go and have my shower. I time things: ten minutes in the shower; ten minutes to moisturize my face and my body, and to get dressed; ten minutes to dry my hair. Half an hour later I am still waiting. I make another coffee, and some toast, which I am unable to eat. By now, Simon will be in London. He will soon be pulling in to Paddington and crossing down to the Underground. He has had plenty of time to call me.

I walk about the house with my phone in my hand. Every time I pass the mirror in the hall I stop and look at myself and force myself to smile, to try and ease the stress and the tension from my face. And I speak to myself; I say, *Hi, Rachel here*. Or, *Hi, how are you?* I practise. I modulate my voice, lest my true feelings should come ripping through.

I need to be calm, at ease. I need to be *nice*.

He will be at the office now. I will not wait any longer.

I call his mobile. He answers after three rings and says, 'Rachel, *hi*,' as if everything is okay.

'I was waiting for you to call me,' I say as pleasantly as I can.

'I've just got in,' he says, as if that's an excuse. 'Now what can I do for you?'

I picture him, still warm from his wife and the comforts of his effortless weekend life, and jealousy needles its way over my skin.

'I need to see you.'

'Sure,' he says. 'Now let's see . . .' He pauses to check his diary, to find some little space in which to fit me in.

'Today,' I state.

'Is everything all right, Rachel?' he asks at last.

And I say, 'No. I need to see you.'

'I've got a meeting at eleven-thirty, but it should be fairly quick. I can meet you at the flat at one.'

'Thank you,' I say, and when I hang up the phone I look

at myself in the mirror again. My face is taut and drawn, and again I force myself to smile. I wonder how I compare to her, his wife.

First, we have sex. That is, after all, why we are here.

But Simon doesn't have long. He was nearly fifteen minutes late, and he has to be back for another meeting at two. He rolled himself gracefully away from me and went straight into the shower. And now I sit on his bed and watch him as he gets dressed to go back to work.

'Did you have a busy weekend?' I ask, but what I really want to know is why he didn't call me.

'Fairly,' he says. 'Charlotte's got a new pony, and she wanted me to take her out on it. And friends of ours came down on Saturday and stayed over.'

Friends of ours.

Instantly I picture them, these friends who come down from London. I picture them with their loud voices and their kids of the same age; I see them all piling out of the car in their weekend clothes, so *glad* to have escaped out of town. I see how they kick off their shoes and curl up on the sofa; I hear their voices: *My God you're so lucky to have all this. Don't know how I'll bear to go back. If only we weren't so tied to the schools* ... I see them rounding up the kids and the dogs for an amble across the fields after lunch, and what an enviable sight they would make together, these two families. But mostly I see them in the evening, gathered around the table over dinner once the kids are in bed. The candles are lit now; oh yes, there will be candles everywhere, warming the glow on their faces. And how they all talk now, the four of them, their voices growing ever louder on Simon's good red wine; how they talk and how they laugh about the old days: so many old days, so much to share. For they will have known Simon and Isobel forever, these friends who came down for the weekend.

I watch Simon's profile as he stands in front of the mirror to put on his tie. I watch the thinness and the deftness of his fingers as they thread the thin end of the tie through the loop and pull it straight; fingers that have been on me, exploring me. It is a thick, silk tie that matches exactly the line of violet threading down the stripe of his shirt. He'd have bought them together, to match. Probably he didn't even have to go to the shop. Probably they arrived together, this shirt and this tie, in a carefully wrapped package along with several other coordinated shirts and ties, from some shop in Jermyn Street, where he has an account and where some assistant periodically pairs up a selection and sends them off to him. He would have these invisible people doing things for him like that, just as he has his housekeeper emptying his bins and seeing to his laundry; his housekeeper, whom he has never even met.

How remote it all is, his life. How untouchable.

Inside my heart there is a dull, persistent ache.

'Quite a houseful then,' I say, and I hear the sarcasm in my voice even if he doesn't.

But I think that maybe he does hear it, because he doesn't respond. He gives the knot of his tie one last little push, then checks his watch. 'Rachel,' he says. 'I have to get back soon.'

'We don't even have time to talk.' Suddenly my eyes are filling with tears. They come in a rush, spilling over fast, and I gather up a handful of his expensively covered duvet and wipe them away.

Simon sits down on the edge of the bed and looks at me. 'What's wrong?' he asks and he reaches out a hand to find mine, buried in a clutch of his duvet. I am so aware of the neatness of him, the perfection of him, dressed and clean in his suit and his shirt and his tie, and of the rumpled mess of me.

'My sister knows about us,' I say.

His hand, although it stays holding mine, stiffens a little; I feel his fingers straighten against mine.

'Does this matter?' he asks carefully.

'I don't know.' I use my other hand to wipe my face. I am still crying. I feel my cheeks and my eyes puffing up.

Simon looks away from me. He stares down at the duvet, a frown upon his face. Eventually he says, 'I do not want to come between you and your family, Rachel. You know I wouldn't want to do that.'

But I think that what he is really saying is, *And don't you come between mine.*

He looks back at me with gentle, concerned eyes, but his body is tense. He is aware of the watch on his wrist, silently marking time. He is aware of his need for an exit. I feel it in him; that metaphorical glance over the shoulder, the plan to run.

'Of course,' I manage to say, and I try to stop myself crying. I try to regain a little poise.

'Will she tell your husband?' he asks now, getting straight to the point.

'I don't know.' My hand, clutching his, is hot. I feel his fingers try to ease away from my mine, but I do not let them go.

He sighs. 'What do you want to do?' he asks.

'What do you mean, *What do I want to do?*' I wail. 'I don't want to do anything! Why? What do *you* want to do?'

He flinches at the rise in my voice.

'Rachel, don't let's argue,' he says. 'Please. Don't let's spoil things.'

'Don't *spoil* things?'

Again I think of him enjoying his lovely weekend with his lovely wife and his lovely children and his friends down from London ... I think of how he didn't call me, and it wasn't because he was too busy. Of course he wasn't too busy. He *chose* not to call me. I am compartmentalized. We haven't talked about *love*, or any kind of future. All that we have talked about is the past, and the transient, fantasy world that we have created from it.

But what would I do without this escape?

I see him looking at me now with his blue eyes so unreadable, and I am gripped with fear.

'I don't want to upset you,' he says in his beautiful and tender voice. 'I don't want to make things awkward for you ... with your husband.'

'I thought this was what you wanted,' I whisper.

He closes his eyes. 'It is, Rachel,' he says. 'It is.'

He left me in his flat. He didn't want to, I could tell. But he had to get back to work and there was I, still sitting in his bed, still naked.

I watched him, torn between leaving me and not leaving me, but in the end he had no choice.

'I think you can trust me to set the alarm,' I said, but I wondered. Was it that he didn't want to leave me, or that he didn't want to leave me in his flat?

He leant across the bed to kiss me on the cheek. How polite. How very formal.

'I'm sorry I have to go,' he said, as he has said to me many times. 'I'll call you.'

And, too eager, I asked, 'When?'

'Soon,' he said. 'We'll talk more soon.'

And it will hang between us now, this need to talk.

I have never been alone in his flat before. The silence when he is gone is strange and unfamiliar. I have the overwhelming feeling that I don't belong here, but it is a feeling that mixes inside me with longing and envy.

I take a quick shower and dry myself on one of his thick, soft towels. I straighten the bed, and dress. And then I walk about the flat; I look in the cupboards and the drawers. I see his socks, all neatly rolled, his pants laid folded and ironed. I see that blue cardigan still hanging in the wardrobe, and I find an umbrella that I somehow missed before, tucked in at the side of the shelf above the hanging rail, near the back. It's a woman's umbrella, striped purple and black. I check the items in the bathroom cabinet and I scrutinize them for signs of further use, though there are none.

The housekeeper has left Saturday's post on a pile on the kitchen counter, next to the newly stocked fruit bowl. Of course Simon hasn't had a chance to open his mail yet, so I can only read the envelopes and guess at their contents; they appear all to be business letters, officially labelled. And now I trail my eyes along the shelves stacked with legal books and files; I know already there is nothing here of interest to me, but I look again, anyway. And inevitably I pick up that photo cube. I see the laughing faces of his beautiful children; I see the confident, knowing look in the eyes of his wife. I see how strands of her dead-straight hair flutter across her forehead. I see how she smiles at the camera as she hugs her small daughter close to her, cheek to cheek, in a squeeze. *Look at me*, she is saying. *Look at me and see how you will love me.*

I put the photos down and move over to the window. I wish that this view was mine to stare at forever. I wish that I lived here, high above the world. I wish that I could come and go, without complication, without depth. And I wish that it was me in that photo, clutching *my* daughter. *Then see me too*, I might cry. *See me too.*

My sister knows about us, I said, but I didn't need to tell him at all. I told him because I wanted him to care. I wanted him to cling to me and say, *What will we do?* I wanted to chug us forward, into another phase. Stupidly, I was testing.

But there is no other phase. This is it. The world that we have conjured together is thinner than a breeze. So easily it could be gone, and then I will have nothing.

I leave him a note. *It'll be fine*, I say, scrawled on the back of an unopened envelope on top of his pile of mail. *I'm sure my sister won't tell. I'm sorry, I was just upset.*

And I sign my message: *love Rachel.*

EIGHTEEN

The next day, when I have seen Jono off to school, and cleared up the kitchen and put on the dishwasher, and shoved a load into the washing machine, I phone Janice. It is coming up to a quarter to nine and I am still in my bathrobe. She, however, has been at work since eight. Somehow this difference between us makes my lie seem more real; I am the meek one, as always, buckling under.

'You need not worry,' I say stiltedly when she answers her phone. 'I won't be seeing him again.'

I hear her sigh of relief. And then there is a long silence while I imagine she considers the likelihood of my words.

To convince her further I say, 'And it really wasn't anything anyway.'

My heart beats into the silence. I am ready to take back my words, to scream into the phone, *Oh, but it is something. It's everything. And who are you to sit in judgement on me, my dear hypocritical sister?*

And in my head I see her, when I was nine and she was ten; I see her marching home from school three steps ahead of me with her long hair pulled back in a ponytail and flicking horse-like from side to side behind her. I see the upturned tilt of her head, I see the stomp of her feet. And

221

there is me, running along behind her, grizzling, *Please, please don't tell them*, because I had been told off in front of everyone by the headmistress for talking in assembly, and *she* had been there two rows behind me to see it and now *she* was threatening to tell our parents.

Please don't tell, I wailed, and the fear that she would had me grovelling to her for days.

You should be ashamed, she scolded, hands on hips, watching me squirm. *I was ashamed. And they will be ashamed of you, too.*

She who used to steal the pick-and-mix in Woolworths, and get away with it.

I think of this and I am nine years old again, with the old resentment knotting itself up inside me.

At last Janice speaks. 'You don't realize how lucky you are to have Andrew,' she tells me now in her schoolteacher's voice. 'And Jono.'

'Yes,' I say. 'Thank you. Well, goodbye then.'

And I hang up, because I do not need to hear how lucky I am. I have heard it too often and it simply doesn't wash any more. They are words to keep me down, that is all.

Still, she believed me. But then why would she not?

The nail on the little finger of my left hand is chipped and jagged. I pick at it. I pick and I pick until it is split right across, split too low, so that the pink and tender skin below the nailbed is unwillingly exposed. I probe the soreness and it sings as though electric, raw and sensual, disproportionate to the size of the wound. Like gum pain, I cannot leave it alone. I pick, I feel it throb. And I sit there at my kitchen table wrapped in the cloying heaviness of my bathrobe, like just one of so very many housewives, marking down the years.

And I think of Janice, busy with her life, doing whatever

it is that she wants to do, because, after all, she is Janice. Her sense of entitlement marches full steam ahead of her, waving its flag in your face.

I have no such flag. I am a wife, a mother. And that is it: the beginning, the middle, the end.

Late last night Simon sent me a text, saying simply, *Thank you for your message.* That is all. What am I to read into that?

Now, having dealt with Janice, I sit here, still in my bathrobe, toying with the phone in my hand. I watch the minute hand on the clock above the door, as it ticks its way round. The washing machine quietly whines in the corner, and from somewhere, out in the street, I can hear the distant scream of a road drill. But it is my heart that I am aware of, thumping out its fear.

Already I have texted Simon back. I reinforced my message: *I'm sure everything will be fine.*

But how will it be fine?

I saw it in Simon's eyes: the instant pulling-back.

And now I picture him again, fresh from his weekend with his wife, his children, his friends . . . I see them all; I see their clothes and the way that they move, so at ease, so sure of themselves as they tramp across the fields . . . and I see how they laugh together at jokes I will never share, and how they talk, so animatedly; those conversations of which I will never be a part.

I see, and I am so bruised with longing and envy.

The clock clicks to half-past nine.

My grip on Simon is tenuous, but I cannot let it go. Without him what would I do? I see my life stretching ahead of me, vacuous, numb.

I dial his number.

When he answers I say, 'Simon, I'm *so* sorry about yesterday. I think I was having a bit of a bad day.' And I laugh, a quick, throwaway laugh, a roll-your-eyes oh-my-God-what-am-I-*like*? kind of laugh. Like a flash in my head I see Fay, curled up on the sofa in the den at the house in Oakley, her legs, clad in maroon woolly tights, drawn up so that her chin is on her knees. We were teasing her – I forget about what – and she slaps her hands across her face, hiding her eyes. Her thick brown hair falls forward, then she throws back her head, tossing her hair back again, smooth and luscious as chocolate. She takes her hands away from her face and spreads them at the sides of her head like starfish. *Oh my God, what am I like?* she squeals, her eyes sparkling like black jewels. And she laughs, that fast, infectious, runaway laugh.

And here I am in my worn and stained bathrobe, copying her. I think what an actress I am and something splits inside my heart.

'That's okay,' Simon says and I hear the ease slide back into his voice. 'We all have bad days. But your sister—?'

'I've spoken to her,' I say quickly. 'Really, it's fine.' And again I manage that laugh.

'You're sure?' Simon asks, and his voice washes over me, warm, soothing.

And I say, 'I'm sure.'

We arrange to meet the next day. The thought of it gets me through Sainsbury's. It gets me through the washing, the tidying, the cooking. It gets me through the heartache of Jono's bad mood when he comes in from school, and through the hours of waiting for Andrew to get in from work, and then avoiding him when he does.

It gets me through the silence.

We make love on the sofa this time. To be back in his bed, after last time, would be too awkward, too much a reminder of my little scene. Today I am on form. I did my hair, chose my clothes well. And when Simon started to say, 'Are you sure about—?' I kissed him full on the mouth, stemming his words. And we did it fast and hard, blanking out any doubts.

But afterwards, when we are lying there semi-naked, the demons start creeping back in.

'What happened with you and Fay?' I ask.

And he says, 'Why do you ask?'

'I was just thinking about her, that's all.' I keep my voice light and idle.

Simon sighs. 'I was young,' he says. 'Too young. And my mother ... well ... I told you about that.'

'Do you ever keep in touch?'

'No, sadly. We did for a while, but ...' Again he sighs. His arm is around my shoulder; absently he draws his fingers in a circle on my arm. 'She was my last contact with Vanessa.'

I hear the sadness in his voice, and jealousy for Fay snakes through me.

'Until now,' I say pointedly.

He turns his head and kisses me. 'Until now.'

'What about your wife?' I can't stop myself from probing. 'Where did you meet her?'

'Isobel?' he asks in surprise, as if it had slipped right out of his head that he'd even got a wife. 'I've known Isobel for years. I met her through friends.'

Friends.

I lie still, staring out the window, at the clouds trekking fast across the cold March sky. The jealousy slithers, and tightens, and snares.

'Does Isobel know about Vanessa?' *Isobel*. Her name is alien, distasteful in my mouth.

'Of course she does,' he says. 'Why do you ask?'

'Do you talk to her about Vanessa?'

Simon's hand, on my arm, stills. It is a while till he replies, as if he is carefully choosing his words.

'Not really,' he says at last. 'Not any more.'

'But you used to?' I can't stop myself. 'Like you do with me?'

Very slowly, Simon pulls away from me. And now he is looking at me intently, but I cannot look back. I am afraid to see the expression in his eyes. He says, 'Isobel knows about Vanessa, but she didn't *know* her. There is a difference.'

'Does she know about me?'

'*No*.' He pulls right away now. He isn't even touching me. 'Rachel, what is this about?'

But I can't stop. 'What would she do if she did know about me?' I bite into my lip, bite so hard that I taste blood. *Stop it*, I am screaming in my head. *Just stop it!*

Simon sighs. He sits forward now, resting his elbows on his thighs, dipping his head into his hands. 'Do we have to talk about this?' he asks.

And I look at him. I look at the curve of his spine and the width of his shoulder blades, at his skin, so pale, stretched tight across muscle and bone.

'I'm sorry,' I say, and tears spring like needles into my eyes.

He turns his head to look at me again, and this time I hold his gaze. What would I do if I never looked into those

226

eyes again? I look into his eyes and I see my youth; I see myself at sixteen, walking into his house, walking into his world. I see his sister coming towards me, her eyes just like his, that clear, startling blue. *Welcome,* she is saying and for such a short, sweet time I see a life of unimaginable glory; I see the hope, the possibility that it could be mine.

'What do you want, Rachel?' Simon asks quietly.

I try to smile, but my face won't oblige. 'What I want . . . What I want is to stay here forever.' The words come out husky, and I swallow. I correct myself. 'For one night. I want to stay here for one whole night.'

'Well, I'm sure that can be arranged,' Simon says. 'I'm here during the week.'

As if it was that straightforward. As if it should be enough for me that he is here during the week.

NINETEEN

Easter looms ahead now, with Jono off school for three whole weeks, and the thought of the long weekend to get through. Andrew will be at home for four days. We are to do family things: a visit to a museum, a walk in the country. Things that Jono will hate, though we convince ourselves we are doing them for him.

Yet it is not the prospect of my Easter that gets me down, so much as the thought of Simon's. He, of course, will be in Kingham for the long weekend, unwinding in the bosom of his family. There will be Easter-egg hunts, no doubt, and proper country walks. And there will be friends, of course, popping down, staying over; there are bound to be. For four days he will forget about me.

I meet him on the Wednesday before Easter, when Jono is at a friend's for the day, this friend being some boy called Luke whom he's never mentioned before and who lives all the way out in Weybridge. I drive Jono over there; it takes us an hour to get through the traffic and to find the house, which is enormous, and set back on a dark, tree-shrouded road. I recognize Luke's mother from Stephanie Rawlings's class get-together back before Christmas, though she didn't bother to acknowledge me then. Now she greets me with a polite smile, but doesn't ask me in.

'Come back for him at four-thirty,' she instructs me, as though I am a tradesman.

Normally it would irritate me, this dismissal – this welcome for my son, but not for me, into the world beyond her heavy oak front door – but today I do not care. I am in a hurry anyway. I am going straight to Weybridge station to get the train to London; I have the train times, the platform number, all worked out.

At first Simon didn't think he could be free, but I pleaded with him. I said it's so hard in the holidays, with Jono around; I can't just come up at the drop of a hat. And this is the perfect opportunity, we can't let it go. So he had to move meetings, cancel a lunch.

'It was worth it, wasn't it?' I say now as we sit on his sofa eating the sashimi and hand-rolls that we had the sushi restaurant in the basement send up to us. I met him at London Bridge this time and walked with him back to the flat. It is a grey, damp day, but I was early; I had time to kill. And we made love as we always do – love? *is* it love? – and now we sit and we talk as we eat.

'Wasn't it?' I say again. I am asking. I'm not *sure*.

He is distracted. There is something on his mind, I can tell. I wonder if it is because I made him change his plans. I wonder if it is because of me.

'Wasn't what?' he asks absently, biting into a shrimp roll.

'Wasn't it worth cancelling your lunch so that you could see me?' I try to sound coy, as though I am merely teasing.

'Yes,' he says automatically. 'Of course.' But then he is silent again for a while, frowning at the view from the window as he eats.

I pick at a piece of marinated tuna and try to pretend that everything is okay.

After a while he says, 'I'm going to Kew tonight. To see my mother.'

'Oh,' I say, and I wait for him to tell me more.

'I try and see her every couple of weeks or so,' he says, and I wonder why he has never mentioned this before. 'It would be impossible if I was in Kingham all week, but while I'm here . . . Though I don't know if there is very much point.'

'Of course there is a point,' I say.

'She is never particularly pleased to see me.'

He doesn't look at me as he talks. He stares ahead out of that window; the cloud has thickened since this morning and London is weighed down now under a heavy blanket of drizzle. I try not to feel hurt that he hasn't mentioned these visits to his mother before. I try not to take it personally. *Of course* he visits his mother.

'I want to ask her to come for Easter, though I know that she won't,' he says and he kind of laughs then; a quick, humourless sigh of a laugh. 'Isobel doesn't want her to come anyway,' he says, and I am alert to the bitterness in his voice, but who is the bitterness aimed at, his mother or his wife? 'She says why should we bother with her when she's so rude to Charlotte?'

I watch him; I see his face so closed and guarded. He is fiddling with a little stick from the sushi, and it snaps now, between his fingers.

'And I suppose Isobel is right,' he says. Then, after a pause, 'But she is my mother.'

'Of course she is,' I say indignantly. 'And you're all she's got.' I want to be different from Isobel – is that what drives me? Or is it the thought of Yolande Reiber, once so flamboyantly, confidently glamorous, and now so diminished and alone?

'*I'm all she's got*,' Simon parrots back to me, his voice broken and sarcastic, like a boy repeating the punchline of a very bad joke. 'She has three grandchildren, if she'd only care to acknowledge them.'

I hate it when he talks like that. It makes me realize how little I know him. It makes me feel small.

He sighs; he seems to sink into himself. I see our time together fizzling away; I see the threat of the long weekend.

And I say, 'I could come with you, if you like.'

He turns to look at me, and his expression is so incredulous now that I have to backtrack.

'I don't mean to see your *mother*,' I say, although I did mean that, actually. I meant that exactly, but I see from his face how unlikely he thinks such a suggestion to be; how *wrong*. 'I mean I could meet you afterwards, in Kew. We could go for a drink or something. If that would help.' And now I really feel stupid. He is still looking at me as if this is the most ridiculous idea. But then his face clears a little and he shrugs.

'Okay,' he says. 'If you want.' Which hardly amounts to enthusiasm.

I feel like I put him on the spot. I feel as if he couldn't say no, though in his head he is with Isobel; it is her opinion, and her judgement, that matters to him.

I am back for Jono at four-thirty, as instructed. The rush hour is beginning already and he is quiet in the car as we crawl our way through the traffic back to Surbiton.

'Have a good time?' I ask.

He grunts, his standard reply.

I try again. 'Would you like to have Luke back to our house next week?'

'I can't,' Jono mutters, staring out the window. 'He's going to New York. Everyone's going on holiday except me.'

'Not everyone, surely,' I say.

'Yes,' he snaps. 'Everyone.'

I look in the mirror at him and see his face so scrunched up with misery, and this after spending the day with a friend. I wonder what became of the sweet, happy little boy that he used to be, and my heart bleeds and tears. And I question the rightness of sending him to a school where everyone else has so much more than him, but where these people that he refers to as 'everyone' have become the norm. They are his norm, I realize, and we've made it that way. We shoved him among them, and now I can only watch as I see him measuring himself against them, and falling short. I do not know what to say to him. We drive the rest of the slow journey home in silence.

I've planned to meet Simon in the pub by the station at nine-thirty, but I leave home much earlier than that. I phone Andrew at work and tell him I'm going to a last-minute mums' get-together; I want to be gone before he gets in.

'Really?' Andrew says, and immediately I realize how unlikely it is that there would be any kind of class get-together in the school holidays, when he knows as well as I do that most of the others will be going away.

I hesitate for a second. Just a second, but even so I could kick myself. Instead, I pinch my arm, digging my fingers in hard.

'Yes,' I say. 'It's Amy Lewis's idea,' as if that, somehow, is validation.

'Right,' he says. And then there is an awkward pause, in which I pinch my arm a little harder and rack my head for something more convincing to say. Then, 'I'm surprised you're going when you hated it so much last time,' he says.

'I still have to go,' I reply. 'I still have to make the effort.'

I am in Kew soon after half-past eight. Simon, of course, will be coming by train. I wonder if he is here already or if I will see him, walking down the road to his mother's house. I drive around the streets a while, then pull over on the main road just near the station approach, but a little way down past the crossing. There are double yellow lines on the road here and I am not meant to stop; I put my indicator on and keep the engine running and get my phone out, so that I can look as if I have stopped just for a moment to answer a call. Simon doesn't know what car I have, and I am far enough away for him not to see me, I hope; I wouldn't want him to think that I was watching out for him, that I was prying. The drizzle has turned to rain now and my view through the windscreen is obscured. I switch the windscreen wipers up a speed and tilt myself downwards, so that I can scan the people huddled under umbrellas, as intermittently they swarm away from the station approach and spread out to go their separate ways. I cannot see faces, but I would know Simon. I would know him by the way that he moves, and the cut of his clothes.

For twenty minutes or so I loiter like this, with the engine running and the car steaming up, but it seems that I have missed him. He must be at his mother's already. Slowly I drive towards her house. I drive past it, and pull over just a little way down. The lights are on downstairs; there is no way of knowing for sure that Simon is in there, but of course he must be. Perhaps she has cooked him a meal, and now

233

they are eating it. But then I think of her picking out her slices of ham at the deli, with that diamond ring conspicuous, heavy on her finger as she points and chooses. Mrs Reiber wouldn't cook. Her kitchen looked as if it hadn't been used in years. But I picture the two of them inside that house together, struggling to talk. I wonder if they are in the room at the front of the house, sitting on formal chairs, drinking tea from delicate, porcelain cups held on saucers. I try to imagine them there, and to imagine that room, its furniture, its shadows and corners, the way the lighting would yellow their faces. I take my foot off the brake and roll the car forward a little; I can see clearly the drawn curtains of that room, but no particular shadows beyond them, no sign of movement. But perhaps they are at the back of the house, in that small, strange room beyond the kitchen. I picture them cooped up in there, too close, too stifled by the tension of Simon's anger, and his mother's blank denial. I let myself dream and I picture myself in there too, sitting on that cracked leather sofa beside Simon. *Please, Mrs Reiber*, I am saying, *you cannot deny your own daughter. You're hurting yourself. You're hurting your only son.* And meekly she concedes. She softens before our eyes. I picture Simon smiling fondly at me as he squeezes my hand. I picture myself sorting it all out, necessary after all.

I shouldn't have come so early. It's a long time to hide and wait and it's cold in the car. The windows have steamed up again, and I turn the blower on full blast. At ten past nine I move away, and drive closer to the station in search of a parking place. At nine-thirty I walk into the pub and look around, but he isn't there. The place is almost empty. I go back outside and stand under the doorway to shelter from the rain, and wait.

As soon I see him I know it is a mistake. He is clearly tired and probably just wants to go home. I watch him walking towards me and I think what an effort you have to make when you are seeing someone new. He drags a smile onto his face and I fix one onto mine.

'Hello,' he says. 'Sorry if I'm late.' He puts down his umbrella, shakes it and kisses my cheek.

'Do you want to go in here?' I ask doubtfully because it seems all wrong suddenly, after the earlier intimacy of his flat, for us to be meeting here, like strangers, in such an anonymous, public place. I want him to come up with somewhere else. I want him to say, *Look, there's a little place I know nearby, much cosier; we'll go there.*

And then, maybe, the evening would be okay.

But he just says, 'Yes. Sure. Might as well, now we're here' and walks in ahead of me, and up to the bar.

There are just locals inside, just the few determined ones on such a foul night as this. They watch us as we order our drinks, more bored than curious, but suddenly I am self-conscious. We take our drinks and sit at a table as far away from the bar as possible, by an unlit fire. Simon has his brief-case with him; he places that, and his raincoat and his umbrella, next to him on the spare chair.

'Did you come straight from work?' I ask, stating the obvious.

'Yes,' he says. 'Actually it was hard to get away. I didn't get to my mother's until nearly nine. A bit of a short visit.'

I wonder how I could have missed him.

But then he adds, 'There was a huge queue for taxis at Richmond. There always is when it's raining. I should have realized and come on the Tube.'

He must have got to her house just before I did, then. I

wonder how he would have reacted if he'd got out from his taxi and seen me there, parked up outside. Shame at the thought whispers through me, and I pick up my glass, and drink.

And then I say, 'How is your mother?'

'Fine,' he says automatically. Then he shrugs and quantifies, 'As fine as she ever is.'

'Did you talk to her about your plans for Easter?' I cannot keep an edge from creeping into my voice. *I* want to know his plans for Easter. I want to, and yet at the same time I don't. I really don't.

'She won't come and visit us, if that's what you mean. She won't do anything, go anywhere. She just sits in that house, hiding herself away.' He picks up his gin and tonic, pretty much downing it in two gulps. 'Still, I expect we'll have a better time without her.'

We. He says, *We'll have a better time* ... Does he not realize what he is saying? It isn't *we* – it's him and his wife.

'It must be hard for her,' I say.

'She makes it hard. For all of us.'

'Yes, but to be constantly reminded of Vanessa—'

'Look,' Simon says, 'I really don't know if I want to talk about it tonight.'

My insides tighten as though I've been punched.

'I'm sorry,' he says. 'I'm tired.'

And so we try to talk about other things, but there are no other things.

I should never have suggested meeting him. I drive back to Surbiton angry with myself, angry and tearful, sobbing out my frustration in the car with no one to see, no one to hear. I'm losing him. I'm losing him and I can't bear it; I don't know what I'll do, what I'll *be* when this is over.

And it will be over. It never could last.

He'll just get on with his life, but what will I do? How can I go back to before? How can I grow old knowing that that was it for me; my fantasy, my dream of escape, all gone?

When we'd finished our drinks he asked if I wanted another. He asked me politely enough, but it was written all over his face that he hoped I'd say no. And so I did.

And then he had to walk me to my car, before he walked himself back to the Tube.

'I can drop you back at Richmond,' I said. 'Won't that be quicker?'

But he replied, 'I am not very good company tonight. I think I'd better just let you go.'

'When will I see you?' And I could hear it, scratching at the edge of my voice: desperation.

'Soon,' he said – wearily? Gently? I don't know; I could not tell. 'I'm taking a couple of extra days off next week—'

'You didn't tell me!' I flinch when I think how I sounded, barking at him in the street like a harridan.

'I didn't realize I had to,' he replied. But then he must have seen my face, how hard I was trying not to cry, because he said, 'Rachel, it's just a couple of days. I'll be back on Thursday.' And maybe that would have consoled me a bit, but then he went on, 'I just need to be with my family for a while. Can't you understand?'

I stood there beside my car, my throat tight, unable to answer, unable to breathe.

'I'll be back on Thursday,' he said again. He put his hand on my arm. 'Rachel, *please*.'

Please what? Please understand? Please don't make a fuss? Or please just let me go?

'Do you *want* to see me?' I managed to say.

'Yes,' he said. 'I do.' He moved that hand on my arm. He stroked it upwards, towards my shoulder. 'I'm sorry,' he said. 'I'm very tired. And seeing my mother ... seeing my mother upsets me.'

He tilted his umbrella and it knocked against mine, sending the rain spilling off, a sharp downfall between us. It reminded me of the first time I met him at that restaurant in the City. Then he was the one full of doubt, not me.

'I shouldn't have come,' I said. 'All this creeping around ... it isn't enough.'

'Rachel ...' Now he was pleading. 'Don't let's argue.'

'I want to spend a night with you. A whole night.'

'Rachel, you will.'

'When?'

'When I come back,' he said. 'Whenever you want.'

'Next Friday,' I said.

'I go home on Fridays.' *Home*, he said. *I go home.*

'Yes, but you will just have been home, for several days. And it can only be a Friday. It's the only night I can be away, all night. That or a Saturday.'

How tired he looked. How cornered.

'But please,' I said, turning away, and opening the door to my car, 'don't let me force you.'

He grabbed my arm again. 'Don't let's part like this,' he said. 'Next Friday ... next Friday will be fine.'

And I cling to that. I cling to it with open, clumsy hands, grabbing, clutching at air.

I cling to it when Andrew, Jono and I plod our way across the Surrey fields, the three of us in walking stretched out in a line, Andrew at the front, then me, then Jono. Each of us concentrating on the walk, and the effort of keeping ourselves apart. See how we smile for the benefit of passers-by, Andrew and me. See how we smile at all those other families taking in the air and the view; those sprawling, rambling families with their uncles and aunts and cousins and dogs scattering out across the path.

'So how was it this time?' Andrew asked me when I got home the other night, and I was so upset and so distracted that I merely stared at him blankly. 'Your class get-together,' he said with emphasis. 'How was it?'

He knew I'd lied. He knew there was no class get-together. I could see it in his face, and yet I didn't care. Whatever he thought, I just didn't care.

This time of year is always hardest. Easter is a time of fecundity. The sun is out now, there are buds everywhere, blossoming, bursting into life. After our walk we stop for lunch at a village pub complete with pond, a whole variety of ducks and a large white goose. The ducks have chicks, and the goose soon will have; she waddles by the water, her belly weighed low and swollen. It is warm and we sit outside. It seems that everywhere I look there are pregnant women, stripping off the disguise of their winter coats and showing themselves off. Pregnant women with glowing skin and ripe, able bodies, everywhere.

I can't stand it.

Jono wanders over to the pond and starts feeding his chips to the ducks. I watch him and I am choked with tears. How sad he looks throwing chips half-heartedly at the water, such an awkward parody of his younger self. He used to love to feed the ducks. *More bread!* he'd squeal. *More bread!* He'd

chase after them, holding a crust out in his hand, and the
faster they ran, the faster he would too. And Andrew and I,
how we laughed with joy as we watched him. We could never
get enough of watching him; our hearts would burn with love.

'That's our son,' Andrew says.

'What?' I am not sure I heard him right.

'That's our son,' he says again, quietly. 'We made him.
Doesn't that count for something?'

I look at Andrew and he is watching me with dark, unreadable eyes. A sudden flush rushes upwards, into my face.

'Of course it does,' I say quickly, dismissively.

I turn back to Jono now, but Andrew is still watching me.
I can feel his eyes practically boring right into me, and my
heartbeat picks up its pace and starts skipping inside my
chest. There was a time when we could read each other's
minds, finish each other's sentences. I remember this and try
to blank all thoughts from my head.

'Then where do you go when you go away from us?'

I *think* this is what he says. It could have been *Where did
you go on Wednesday?* or *Where did you* really *go on
Wednesday?* I don't know. I cannot be sure, because suddenly
I feel unwell. The flush in my face turns to pins and needles,
creeping its way across my head, and a wave of nausea rises
up inside me. I don't know if I am going to faint or be sick.
I have to rest my head on my hands on the table and keep
swallowing, keep swallowing hard. Through cotton wool I
can hear Andrew saying, 'Rachel? Rachel, are you okay?'

Soon it passes. Soon I can raise my head again, but the
sunlight is too bright, too harsh in my eyes. I feel wiped out,
nauseous still.

Andrew is still looking at me, but with concern now. 'Are
you okay?' he asks again.

'I need to go to the loo,' I say, and carefully, on legs that feel too weak, too feeble for good use, I make my way through the crowded tables dotted about the garden, and into the pub, to find the ladies'. Once there, I lock myself in a cubicle and sit down. My heart is thumping. An impossible, shocking suspicion is beginning to dawn on me. Another wave of nausea washes over me. I cannot, I will not think.

At the sinks I wash my hands and pat cold water onto my neck and my cheeks. I look at myself in the mirror and my eyes stare back at me, wide and startled as a rabbit's. I try to look normal. I try to compose myself, to brace myself to go back outside to Andrew, but I am shaking, light-headed with panic.

I have been gone a long time. Jono and Andrew are waiting to go. Jono is sitting with his back to the table, his body slunk down in the chair and his arms folded across his chest. He scowls when he sees me and says, 'Where've you *been*?'

And Andrew's concern is tempered with irritation now. 'You were gone over ten minutes,' he says as he fiddles with his car keys, clearly itching to go. 'What were you doing in there?' As if he wants details, as if he should even ask.

His irritation sparks mine.

'What do you think I was doing in there?' I snap at him. 'I must have a bug or something.'

The drive home is unbearable. I feel every bump, every curve in the road. Jono is sulking, and between Andrew and I the tension is stifling. No one talks. I close my eyes and shut myself into silence, and the minute we get home I go upstairs to our bathroom and throw up.

I was sick like this with Jono. And with ... *her*.

But I cannot think like this. It isn't possible.

I sit on the edge of the bath, appalled.

How hard we tried, Andrew and I. For months and months and years and years. Screwing each other dry until every ounce of hope, every ounce of love and joy, was gone. I thought my fertile days were over. I pictured my insides withered and useless, like so many rusted old pipes. My periods came, but as irregular and unpredictable as a cruel joke, their purpose merely to taunt me. I have not had one for quite some time.

And now this. It cannot be so. It simply cannot be so.

TWENTY

And yet it would appear that it is so.

At first I try to convince myself that I am merely suffering from a bug, but for much of the time I am okay. Then all of a sudden the sickness will swoop, a fast surge of hormones, stampeding their cling to my womb. My nipples hurt. Far quicker than I could ever plan to – literally, within hours, it seems – I am losing weight.

For the remainder of the Easter weekend I lie in my bed, or move slowly, trance-like around the house. Andrew and Jono think it is a bug. They avoid me, lest they should catch it themselves.

What am I to do?

The full horror doesn't sink in. How can it sink in when I am too numb, too out of it, simply too plain shocked to think?

Andrew goes back to work on Tuesday and there is just Jono and me, filling the hours of our days. Jono needs a haircut, and new shoes; we have the dentist to see. I stretch these trips out, planning one destination for each day, taking us to Thursday.

I am seeing Simon on Friday. The necessity of seeing him

now flashes up, marking the end of the week like a beacon. He cannot back out.

And yet what will I say to him? Should I even say anything at all when this could all be over so soon, no more than a false alarm? I dare not think how he will react. I didn't use contraception because I didn't think I needed to, yet how foolish that sounds now. But look at all those that times I thought that I was pregnant before, with Andrew; all the times that I hoped, and kidded myself, only to be so cruelly disappointed. I didn't think I *could* get pregnant; I thought my body was done, finished.

I send Simon a text, a reminder. *I will see you at seven-thirty, Friday*, I say, and that is all I say. Oddly enough, all other words have left me.

And more oddly still, as though he senses some crisis, he texts me back, simply, *Okay*.

I tell Andrew I am staying at Janice's. This should not seem too odd, as I have done it before, several times. We might go out for dinner, Janice and I; see a film or a play.

And when Andrew starts to question me, to repeat my words back to me as if he hasn't heard me right, *You're going to stay with Janice . . .*, I am so fraught, so tense to the point of wrapped-up, inverted hysteria, that I snap for a second.

'Yes,' I screech at him. 'I have been ill . . . I have been at home all week . . . Is it too much that I have a night off, a night away?'

And he looks at me as he always looks at me when I rail at him so. He looks at me as if he loathes me.

'No,' he says, his voice as dead as fallen wood. And that is all.

*

The irony is that part of me wishes I wasn't staying with Simon for the whole night now. The idea has lost its appeal. It would suit me more, now, simply to curl up under my duvet and bury myself away. I cannot think ahead, but I cannot think what to do right now, either. If I am pregnant – and how I torment myself with the word *if* – the chances are that it will not hold, it will not last. It could all be over at any moment, before anyone need know. Before even I need know, for sure, if I can just keep my head blank. It is but a cluster of cells at this stage, after all. A cluster of cells that my body will, most likely, expel.

And wouldn't that be the best outcome? It is the only viable outcome.

I do not want to, but I cannot stop myself thinking about my baby daughter and picturing her tiny limbs, doll-like, smooth as plastic. I picture her eyelids half-closed over blind eyes, the lashes perfectly formed. I picture her curled up inside me, her thumb in her mouth, so far grown from a mere cluster of cells, so far grown and yet so dead.

I could not bear that to happen again.

I arrive at Simon's with my overnight bag at bang on seven-thirty. I am feeling tired, and queasy, and more than a little anxious. We have not made any plans as such and I don't know what I am expecting, but when he opens the door to me he is still in his work clothes and he is on the phone.

With his free hand he gestures at me to be silent. I stand just inside the door, with my bag at my feet.

'I know,' he says into the phone. 'Yes. I'm on my way there now. I will, yes. I'll call you later. Bye, sweetheart.'

Sweetheart?

He clicks off the phone and sighs. And to me he says,

'That was Isobel. She thinks I'm going to some law function. I told her I'd just come back to get changed. I didn't expect her to call.' And then he adds, 'I hate lying to her.'

What does he expect me to say to this? Does he expect me to sympathize with him? To apologize, even? It is not much of a greeting, and not a good start.

'I don't exactly enjoy lying, either,' I say.

'Of course not,' Simon says quickly. 'I'm sorry. None of this is ideal.' And now he kisses me on the cheek politely, far too politely, and says, 'How are you?'

I do not reply. I walk further into the room, and automatically my eyes are drawn to the window, to the million lights brightening up the darkening city sky. I have not yet decided if I will tell him tonight that I might be pregnant. *Should* I tell him, when I am not even sure myself?

There will be a thousand ponderables, a thousand things to explain. Not least of all, how could I let this happen? And what will I do about it now? A ripple of foreboding works its way down my spine. I think of Jono at home, and of Andrew. I think of my life in a multitude of small, banal and familiar details: the roughness of the carpet under my bare feet in my bedroom, the jagged edge that I have to avoid on the shelf in the airing cupboard where I keep the sheets and towels, the pocket of cold air that collects in the corner of the windowsill in the living room, causing a constant draft. I think of these things and I am swamped with sorrow.

How did I ever think I could possibly belong here, in this transient bubble of a place, so far removed from the reality of my world? I wanted so much to be here. I wanted so much to have this one whole night.

I cross my arms across my chest and try to suppress a shiver.

'You're cold,' Simon says, coming over to me and putting his hands on my hips, a restrained and hesitant embrace. He looks at me closely now, alert to my mood.

'I'm hungry,' I correct him, which is true; I am hungry, with that sudden, light-headed hunger that you only get when you're pregnant. I look at him and our eyes lock and hold.

'We'll eat,' he says. 'We'll go out. I'll be ready in five minutes.' But he keeps his hands on my hips and his eyes on mine. I wonder what he sees, because he is certainly searching for something. I wonder if he is thinking what I am thinking: that we need to have sex first. We need to just do it, however awkward this suddenly feels.

I try to smile, but I am a whisper away from tears.

'Fine,' I say. I half-close my eyes and lean towards him. I put my hands on his chest and he reacts as I want him to; he starts kissing me, touching me, unpeeling my clothes. He pushes me down to the sofa, moving fast; as if, like me, he wants to get it done. My head is swimming with hunger and hormones and a deep, intangible misery. I cling to him, but I cannot get a grip; I cannot feel where I am. I am detached, my arms, my legs, my body as distant as if the cords have been snapped. I so want to lose myself in him. I press my face against his chest, fill my head with the scent of the skin. The tears are brimming in my eyes now, and running sideways into my hair. I feel that I am starting to drown.

When it is over he rests his weight on his elbows and looks down at me. He studies me with his beautiful, opaque eyes and says, 'I am not making you happy.' He states it as a fact, and the acceptance of sadness in his voice brings the tears to my eyes again.

'I am not making you happy,' I reply, but that isn't what I want to say at all. 'I'm sorry,' I say. 'You have made me happy. You've made me so happy. I don't know what I'll do when this is over.'

He looks down at me, and I have no idea what he is thinking. What I want him to say is, *It will never be over*, but he doesn't. He trails the fingers of one hand across my face, wiping away the tears, smoothing back my hair. He looks down at me with such concern.

But he doesn't say it.

And so I tell him, 'I think I'm pregnant.'

I say it for a reaction, and my God, how I wish I could take the words back. In a split second I know I have killed it. His hand stills on my hair. He is naked above me; naked and vulnerable as a boy. His eyes freeze on mine. Those eyes, so blue, so like his sister's . . . How I wanted those eyes to look at me. How I would have done anything to have them looking at me.

Slowly he removes himself.

He rolls onto his back, and we are side by side on the sofa, each of us staring at the night sky.

'Are you sure?' he asks.

And irritation at the question has me saying, 'No, I'm not sure. I said I *think*.'

'But . . . why would you think?'

'Oh, come *on* . . .' I roll over and face him, thus hiding my nakedness.

'I mean . . . *how*?' he says, his voice both thin and sharp with incomprehension. He does not look at me now. He is staring into space, his mouth twisted in shock.

I know exactly what he means, but even so I say, 'How do you think?'

'But I mean . . . My *God* . . .' He flips himself over so that he is facing me. 'Rachel,' he says. 'I've got a *family* . . .'

'So have I,' I say, hot tears burning my eyes again. 'Simon, I didn't do this on my *own*.'

'No,' he says. 'No, I know. But ... I mean, surely you would have said if ... I just assumed you'd taken care of things—'

'Well, you shouldn't just assume,' I snap.

'No,' he says. 'I shouldn't. But surely ...'

'Look,' I say. 'I didn't think I could get pregnant. I lost a baby a few years ago. I thought that was it.' I cannot meet his eyes when I tell him this, though I feel him looking at me in a kind of ... *horror*. Sometimes I had wondered if I would ever tell him about my baby, and if I did, what the circumstances would be. I imagined a deep and intimate closeness, his arms around me, protecting me from pain – *So that is why you were moved so much by my mother*, he would say, understanding at last.

Now, he almost laughs in disbelief. 'You mean you left it to *chance*?'

The outrage in his voice makes me flinch.

'I didn't think I could get pregnant,' I repeat.

'You didn't think ... Oh Jesus.' He sits up, and pushes his hand through his hair. 'Oh Jesus!'

And so we go on. *How? Why?*

On and on.

Eventually, when it is apparent that we will not after all be going out for dinner, I have to say, 'Look, I've got to eat.' And I am feeling so sick, and my blood sugar is so shakily low, that I have to pull on my clothes and go over to his fridge and eat whatever I can find; the needs of my body taking over, proving my point. I stand there, half-dressed, shoving down rye bread and ham, while Simon watches me, quizzing me, looking for holes in my claim, looking for an escape.

'It could be your husband's,' he says.

'It couldn't,' I say.

'But it could be,' he insists, leaving me in no doubt of how easily he has gone from his wife to me and from me back to her, able to switch and change without a thought.

'It is not my husband's,' I say.

He stares at me. 'How – how far gone are you?'

'I don't know. Not long.'

'It could sort itself out then,' he says, and what a fine choice of words that is. 'If it's early days.'

'Yes,' I say stiltedly. 'It could sort itself out.'

He nods decisively, as though evaluating the odds. I see the lawyer in him, weighing things up. 'And have you thought about what you will do if it doesn't?'

How carefully he says these words, and yet I know full well what he would have me do. And, surely, it is the only thing to do. Just whip it out and carry on; each of us going our separate ways, he back to his perfect little arrangement with his family, me back to the emptiness within mine. How I longed for another baby. How I longed and longed, till the life seeped out of my marriage like the air from a balloon. The irony leaves me numb. I am unable to speak.

'Rachel,' Simon pleads gently, desperation lifting the pitch of his voice, 'this could *ruin* me.'

We talk into the night. I regret my decision to stay. My overnight bag sits by the door, intrusive, out of place. But I cannot go home. I am stuck here, trapped within my lie.

Simon works his way though a bottle of wine. I could not drink even if I wanted to; the mere thought of it makes me feel sick. He puts on his bathrobe and calls down for sushi, but now it sits uneaten on the counter on its takeaway tray.

He starts talking about his family. He tells me Alistair was born two months premature; for the first three weeks of his life he was in the neonatal unit at Queen Charlotte's Hospital.

Queen Charlotte's? In Chiswick?

Yes, he says. *We lived in Hammersmith then, before we moved out.*

Before we moved out.

Somehow I never thought of it as a joint decision, that she should be closeted in the country with the children and the horses, while he should stay up here. But he talks about it now and I picture them, making that decision together. I see them, holding hands over a bottle of wine. And what they did, Isobel and Simon, is save themselves from the grief of a marriage slowly dwindling. Who cares what goes on midweek; they have the weekend. They have each other anew. How I envy them their foresight. How I envy them, and how I loathe them now, too.

And he tells me how he worries about Theo, who will be going away to school soon. The school is good for tennis, he says, and Theo is excellent at tennis – well, he would be; these children, these perfect children, they'll be good at every-thing – but is it right to send him away? And do I even care? He tells me all this, walking about the flat with this nervous energy driving him, distracting him; he tells me, as if he actu-ally thinks I might want to hear.

Do I care? Of course I don't care. The more he talks about his family, the more I hate them. And not once does he ask me about mine. About poor Andrew and poor Jono, stuck at home in Surbiton, so badly dealt with by me. I would not talk about them if he did ask. I would not talk about them and I cannot think about them. Instead I sit there on the sofa as he tells me how adorable Charlotte is, with her penchant for riding, and her love of owls.

'You see, I love my family,' he says at last, as if it is necessary to stress this point. 'Please understand, Rachel, please . . . I can't do this.'

And I want to say to him: but what about Vanessa? What about the fact that I knew her and Isobel didn't? What about us, and the history that we have? All those parties and all those laughs when we were kids still . . . what about that?

But I don't say it. I look at him, pacing about the flat, and I know that it isn't the past that really matters to him. It is the now. It is his wife, his children. My little part in all this is not so important after all.

Eventually I can talk and listen no more and I have to go to bed. I pick up my overnight bag and take it to his bedroom, and now it sits on the floor there, beside the bathroom door, still equally out of place. I realize that I do not know on which side of the bed I should sleep, so I assume the left side, nearest to the bathroom. I am so tired now, to my very bones. I go into the bathroom to shower, and when I come out I can hear Simon talking on the phone.

'It was dull as hell,' he is saying, his voice miserable and flat. 'I wish I hadn't gone.'

The bedroom door is ajar. I creep over to it and I can see him, sitting on the arm of the sofa. He is hunched over with his elbows resting on his knees. The hand that isn't holding the phone is rubbing at his head. He looks pale, and forlorn.

'I miss you,' he says. 'I should have just come home instead.' And then, 'I will, yes. I'll get the earlier train. I love you.'

I sit down on the edge of the bed. My heart is thumping

and there is a cold, hard pressure deep inside me. *I love you*, he tells his wife, but he doesn't love her so much that he couldn't screw me. Anger, fast and fleeting, rushes into my head, but very quickly it is followed by fear. This is it. We are over, Simon and me. We are over, and I am pregnant.

I sit there for a long time, and he stays where he is too, long after he has said goodbye to his wife. The flat is silent. The clock up on the chest of drawers flashes past the minutes in neon green: 12.20, 12.21 ... I dare not move. I can barely breathe. The pressure inside me spreads and grows into panic, fierce and raw.

What will I do?

I grip my hands in my lap, digging my nails into my skin, hurting, hating myself.

Eventually I hear him move, and he comes into the bedroom and stands there, just inside the door. His hands are in front of his chest, not folded, but loosely clasped, as if he is about to pray. I stare up at him, though my eyes are burning with hot and useless tears. His own face is anguished. He wants me to speak first, to bail him out and make this easier for him, but how can I? How can I just let him go?

'Rachel,' he says at last and his voice is thin and pleading. 'I'm *sorry* ...'

He opens his hands in a *what-can-I-do?* gesture. I stare at him. I cannot speak.

'Please try and understand,' he pleads, and I do understand. I understand that he does not want another baby. He does not want a broken home. He wants to keep his wife and children in Kingham, and for me now to disappear. It was an affair we had, that's all. A fantasy; nothing more.

Nothing real.

'I should go,' I manage to say at last.

'Rachel, you don't need to go,' he says. 'It's late. You're tired.' He comes closer to me and sits on the bed beside me. He puts his arm around my shoulder and pulls me towards him. I lean against him, wooden, too numb to yield. He sighs into my hair. 'I will support you,' he says, and then quickly, in case I mistook his meaning, he adds, 'while you ... do what you have to do. If the ... problem doesn't go away.'

I close my eyes. I squeeze them tight. Inside my head I see with cinematic clarity every moment that I have spent with Simon, every look, every movement, every word exchanged. Already I am replaying it as I will, no doubt, replay it again and again, for evermore, torturing myself. And then, bizarrely, another image springs up, sudden, grotesque: I see my baby girl, but not as I usually imagine her to be, had she lived, with her brown eyes laughing and her cheeks all pink and fresh and plump. Oh no. I see her as a doll instead; a porcelain doll, brittle-faced and chipped, with empty dark holes where her eyes should have been.

We sleep side by side without touching. I didn't think I would sleep, but exhaustion swoops down like a blanket, blotting me out. I wake up with a jolt in the early morning; for seconds I have forgotten everything, forgotten even where I am.

And then consciousness claws me back.

Simon is already up and dressed, clearly anxious to be gone. His travel bag is open on the bed and into it he is putting a book of some sorts, and a small, square package from Liberty. I watch him for a second before he looks up at me, and sees that I am awake. I sit up, pulling the duvet up over my chest. I am horribly aware of how unattractive I must appear, sleep-blurred and tear-stained, whereas he, of course, is as immaculate as ever.

'I didn't want to wake you,' he says, and I wonder if he was hoping to sneak off and leave me there. But would he want to do that; would he want to leave me in his flat on my own, now that it is over? And we have unfinished business. There is no avoiding that.

'I can make you a coffee,' he says, but he glances at his watch.

'Don't let me keep you.'

He flinches at my tone. 'Rachel, I'm sorry. I didn't want it to be like this.' He looks at me beseechingly, but all he wants is for me to let him go. He zips up his bag, presses closed the lock. 'We'll talk,' he says. 'Next week. Things will be clearer then. This might all . . . go away.'

'And would that make a difference?' I ask bleakly, and I draw my knees up under the duvet and hug them to my chest. I cannot stop my body from trembling.

'Don't let's part on bad terms,' he says, but how does he expect us to part? With a shake of the hands and a pat on the back, and off we both go on our separate merry ways? It's so easy for him.

'What about Vanessa?' I ask; I can't stop myself.

For a moment he looks confused. 'What about her?' he asks, but then surely he sees the horror on my face, because he sits down on the bed for a second and touches my arm. 'Rachel, I am glad you got back in touch,' he says. 'Meeting you again was . . . well, it meant a lot to me. Really, it did. But I have to think of my family.'

My throat is so tight I cannot speak.

He stands up again and looks at his watch, more obviously this time. 'I have to go,' he says. 'But please, take your time. We'll talk soon.' And then he adds, as if he had just remembered, 'Oh, but my housekeeper will be here soon. I think she normally arrives just before nine.'

And that is my cue to be gone, before then.

How strange it is, to be leaving this flat for the last time.

As though I am an automaton, I check the cupboard in the bathroom, his wardrobe, the drawers, the shelves in the living room; I need to be sure that I will remember every detail, every single detail, exactly as it is. I find that he has seven pairs of socks, neatly rolled in his drawer, and another five pairs in his laundry basket, along with an equal number of pants and shirts and various items of gym kit. He has two tickets for a show at the Lyceum in May in the letter rack on the shelf next to his hi-fi in the living room, and a bill for a recent trip to The Ivy. I do not want to find these, but I hunt, and I do. I also find a note from his precious daughter, folded in half and used as a bookmark in an old A–Z, stuck up on the top shelf, wedged in right at the end: *to Daddy*, it says. *I love you lots and lots and lots. From Charlotte.*

It strikes me as strange that he would leave me here alone, for however short a time. He must know I will look. I can only think that he doesn't care.

At half-past eight I am standing in front of that window, wallowing in the view. My heart, now, is a cold, hard place. I am merely observing, recording it all, locking it all in.

I am gone before the housekeeper arrives. Perhaps I even pass her, down on the South Bank. Maybe she is scurrying in as I am scurrying out; maybe I pass her among the early-morning tourists anxious to beat the queues, and the newspaper vendors, and the party-goers – some high still, some just coming down – staggering their way home through the shift workers and the office cleaners and all these other faceless, unknown people, hurrying by.

I walk against the tide, slowly, on legs of clay.

TWENTY-ONE

Jono and Andrew are out when I get home. It is just gone ten; I assume they will have gone swimming, as they often do on a Saturday morning if there are no school sports matches to attend.

I walk into the house, grateful for the silence. The familiar smell of my home hits me. I step over Jono's shoes in the hall and Andrew's briefcase and go straight upstairs, to my bedroom. And there I look in the mirror and see my face, pale and taut and haunted, my hair a wild, slept-on mess. I did not shower again this morning at Simon's. When he had gone I stayed there in his bed, gripping my knees to my chest in a tight, hard ball for ten, maybe fifteen minutes. And then I quickly dressed, and made my last mental inventory of his things.

I collapse down on my bed now and close my eyes, just for a second. My heart is a heavy, leaden weight. I would like to sleep. I would like to sleep and sleep for a very long time and let all of this be gone, but how can I? Andrew will be back soon, with Jono. I need to compose myself. I need to cut out my heart, and carry on.

And so I drag myself together. I quickly shower, and dry my hair, and cover the pallor of my skin with make-up. And then I gather up an armful of washing from the basket and take it down to the kitchen, and stuff it into the machine. Andrew has cleared away the breakfast things, but left a trail of crumbs along the counter and an empty milk bottle, unrinsed, in the sink. The sight of the cream congealed around the rim of the bottle and the milky streaks on the glass makes me retch, but I cannot use the sink without moving the bottle; I turn on the tap, full blast, and water gushes into the bottle and splashes up and out again, spattering the metal of the sink with milky spray. My stomach clenches and heaves and I have to lean on the edge of the sink, gulping in air, waiting for the sickness to pass. And I'm angry then; angry that Andrew could just leave this bottle here for me to deal with. He knows I can't stand milk at the best of times. And why does he half-clear up, but leave me the dirt? There is a splodge of jam on the surface just next to the sink – surely he must have seen it there. How hard is it to wipe the surfaces down, as I do, constantly?

And to me this is synonymous with other things. Andrew tends to his shed and his projects and his jobs that don't need doing, and he neglects the things that matter, the things that really need care, that affect our daily lives. He neglected me, and the things that mattered to me. *That* is why this has happened.

He let it happen.

And how am I to carry on living with someone who simply didn't care enough not to let me go? But what else can I do?

And as for the fact that I might be pregnant – I can't even think about that. I can't think of it as real: it is a cluster of cells at most, a hormonal glitch. Soon it will bleed its sticky way out of me and I will be as empty as before.

*

'How was the film?' Andrew asks, and my head whirrs and clunks, searching for a response. 'The film,' he says again. 'How was it?'

I am crouched down by the washing machine, dragging out its tangled contents and transferring them to the basket. I make much of the task, and so avoid his eye. I cannot, for the life of me, think of a single film that is on at the cinema at the moment.

But Andrew isn't going away.

I pick up the towels and swimming trunks that he so casually dumped down on the floor by the machine when he returned with Jono from their trip to the pool, and shove them into the now-empty drum. I need to stand because I have been crouching for too long, but I know that when I do stand I will be dizzy. Frantically I clutch at the momentary clear space in my head.

'We ended up going to a little cinema in north London,' I say, thinking quickly, thinking very, very quickly. 'Saw some obscure Hungarian film.' *Hungarian?* Do they even make films in Hungary? 'Janice's choice,' I add, as if that should say it all.

I think he'll quiz me. He'll at least ask what it was called, or what it was about, but instead he says, 'Is Janice going to your parents' tomorrow?'

My hand, on the dial of the washing machine, freezes. It's my dad's birthday tomorrow, his seventieth. My mum has arranged a family lunch; even Janice can't wriggle out of that one. I hadn't forgotten, but I hadn't made the connection in my head. Janice yesterday, and Janice tomorrow. How *stupid* of me.

'Of course she is,' I manage to say.

*

I try to ring Janice, but there's no answer at her flat and her mobile goes straight through to voicemail. She's probably with Paul or gone out for the day, but she'd have her mobile on surely? Yet I try her and try her, and each time it's the same. I leave her messages to call me, but she doesn't, and so I keep trying her again, but still she isn't there. Panic swirls around inside me along with irritation, and frustration.

What am I going to say to her anyway?

Listen, Andrew thinks I was with you last night ... Do me a favour, will you, and just say that the film was rubbish.

How can I ask her that?

Look how she reacted when I tried to talk to her about Simon. She'll be furious when she knows that I used her as a decoy. And she thinks that whatever was going on between Simon and me is over.

It *is* over, but how can I tell her that again and have her believe me?

She *has* to believe me. She has to back me up.

Yet she will not even answer the phone, and I cannot help feeling, however irrationally, that she is ignoring me deliberately. I am too muddled and too queasy and too plain miserable to think anything else.

And so we arrive at my parents' house at one o'clock prompt the next day, the three of us, doing our best to behave like the devoted family that everyone supposes us to be. Andrew is good at duty; it requires no passion, no spontaneity, just the functional predictability of carrying out a certain role. He is dutiful in all his roles, be it son, son-in-law, father, husband. Oh yes, he is a dutiful husband. Never let it be said that Andrew isn't *dutiful*.

And here is Jono, the showpiece of the family, psyched up

for another performance. He stares out of the window and frequently sighs in the car on the way there, a faint but audible whisper of a sound floating across the otherwise heavy silence. And when we get out of the car he sighs again, and puts back his shoulders, as though bracing himself.

And then there is me, keeping up the rear. I am feeling sick, and resentful, and prickling up with an almost *dare-you* dread. I look at Andrew as he locks the car and puts his key in the pocket of his jacket, and I hate him. I hate him for his role in this inadequate family that we have created; for the silence in the car, the silence that we inflict upon Jono. I hate him for his emotional deadness; for his inability to see the suffering of his son, and the suffering of his wife.

But here we are the three of us, bound by our charade.

Both my parents are at the door the second we ring the bell. I suspect they were watching out for us and their eagerness needles me with a twinge of guilt. I know how much they love us. Not just me as their daughter – in fact, especially not me in particular – but this family that I have melded myself into and provided them with. First they swoop upon Jono, my mother fairly choking his head off with the fierceness of her embrace, and bombarding him with the promise that he'll sit next to her at lunch so that he can tell her all about school, and my father ruffling his hair till the poor boy is squirming; *No, no*, my dad insists; *he'll sit next to me, and talk to me – after all, it is my day.*

How they do love him, my dear, precious son. I see it, and the guilt inches a little deeper. This should have been enough for me. It should have been, but it wasn't.

It isn't.

And now they move on to Andrew: a pat on the back from my dad, a clasp of the shoulders and a kiss from my mum.

'Good to see you,' my dad says. 'Good to see you.'

'Come on in,' says my mum. 'Let me get you a drink.'

I am last; the mere provider of these other, newer and therefore more appealing members of my small family. My mum pecks me quickly on the cheek and says, by way of greeting, 'I've done Jono some peas, as I know he doesn't like broccoli. And there's some ice cream if he wants it, as well as Dad's cake, for pudding.'

It is always strange, coming back to the family home. Things that I remember as new – the cream-coloured tiles in the kitchen, with the acorn pattern every third one along; the green carpet in the hall, two unfortunate shades darker than the one in the living room; the gas fire with its panelled pine surround – seem so excruciatingly old and out of date now. And so they mark the passage of time; they highlight the ageing of us all: of my parents and, more disturbing still, of me. I want to come back here and find everything unchanged. I want there still to be time.

And how small the house seems to me now, as though it has shrunk over the years. We crowd into the kitchen while my dad pours us drinks and my mother fusses over vege-tables that will have been boiling away for too long already, and over the gravy, which she swooshes around with a wooden spoon in a vast, warped roasting tin balanced precariously on one side of the hob. It is so hot in the kitchen; steam has blotted out the windows and is running down the glass in random tear-like trickles. The heat and the smell of the cooking are oppressive; I cannot breathe without breathing it all in, and we are too close, all of us; in proximity and in need and in history. Far, far too close.

'Happy birthday, Ron,' Andrew says, and he raises his glass.

My mum turns away from the gravy, her thin cheeks scarlet from the heat. She wipes one hand down her apron and the other one back over her hair, smartening herself up, before picking up her glass. 'Yes, happy birthday, Ron,' she says, before downing her wine as if it were water.

The nausea in my stomach grips and pulls.

'Happy birthday, Dad,' I manage to say. 'Where's Janice?'

'Running late,' my mother replies, the flippant phrase at odds with the quick tightening of her lips. 'She called just before you arrived. I think we'll have to start without her.'

So her phone works well enough now, I think. And she'll have picked up my messages, and all my missed calls.

'She'll be here soon,' my dad says, and he beams at each of us in turn. And then he fixes his attention on Jono. 'Now then, young man,' he says. 'How about we go and open my presents?'

While presents are being opened, and food is being dished, I extract myself from the others and walk about the house, taking my handbag with me. It is cooler away from the kitchen, though the smell of boiling vegetables comes with me, clinging to my clothes and my hair. I take myself upstairs, ostensibly to visit the bathroom, but really I am just looking around as I always do, seeing what, if anything, is different.

But I find everything as it always is; a little older, that is all. The real change is all in me.

There is the ceramic oval bearing my name entwined with rosebuds, still nailed to my bedroom door, just as Janice's still hangs on hers. The same floorboards creak underneath my feet. My bed is made up as if ready for me; my old, discarded teddy bears sit propped up against the pillow. And on my chest of drawers my ancient white plastic jewellery box, turned cream now; a small pink vase; and the red and blue glass dish that I bought on holiday in Spain. My mother has kept these things, things that I didn't want any more and left behind me, discarded, when I moved out. She has kept them all, and each week she will polish them and arrange them and be reminded of me. The thought of it fills me with regret.

I never gave a thought to my parents' feelings when I finally left home; I simply packed up my stuff and left. They weren't at home when I came back for the last of my things; and I didn't even leave a note. I was too busy, too preoccupied with my own life, with my future in all its potential glory. I turned my back on all this without a second thought, and yet here is my mother, twenty years later, still plumping up my teddy bears, still hanging on to the rubbish that I left behind.

Loss is loss, in whatever its form.

And what became of that glorious future that I saw for myself? There, too, is loss.

I can hear them downstairs; the comforting ho-ho-ho of my father's laugh; the clatter of pans in the kitchen and my mother calling out, *Won't be long now*; the softer, familiar and yet so alien tones of my husband and my son – these two so connected to me and yet so distant, so *other*.

I move over to the window and look out at the street and my heart is raw. I see myself at five years old, at seven, at twelve . . . running back and forth across the road to Leanne's house; I see the two of us out on our roller skates, clinging to each other, sliding all over; and then with our hula hoops when they were in fashion, belly-dancing them around our

hips, or balancing them, rolling them down the street. I see
Leanne making her weary way home from school in her
ridiculous school uniform – the blazer, the hat, the pleated
skirt right down to her calves, so out of place here in Ashcroft.
I see her bedroom window across the street; I look and I see
the flick of the curtain, the flash of the light – the sign to
tell me that she is home.

Loss is loss.

My mum is calling from down stairs. 'Rachel? Rachel?
You all right up there? Lunch is on the table.' Her voice is
a mixture of concern and irritation; the perennial tone of
motherhood.

'I'm coming,' I call back, as lightly as I can. I look in my
old mirror above my chest of drawers and force a smile onto
my face in preparation. My pale skin is even paler than usual;
the blusher I slapped on my cheeks to give me some colour
stands out clown-like, the shadows under my eyes a stark,
contrasting mauve. I remember when I was pregnant with
Jono: everything about me seemed to bloom. My hair became
thicker, my eyes brighter, my cheeks plumper, and rosier. My
body loved being pregnant, and my spirit too. I was serene;
the very picture of health.

It was the same the second time, too, ironically. I carried
on blossoming even as my baby withered and died.

There is nothing of the bloom about me this time.

Before I go back downstairs I try calling Janice again, but
she doesn't answer. She'll be driving. Janice never answers
her phone when she's driving.

'You're very pale,' my mother says critically, when we are
seated at the table. 'Are you not well?' She is at one end of
the table, and I am to her left; Jono is next to me, and beside

him at the other end is my father. Andrew sits opposite me, and next to him is the empty space for Janice. And so my mother, and Andrew, are perfectly positioned to scrutinize me.

'I'm fine,' I say. 'A little tired, that's all.'

'You're not eating much,' my mother observes.

We are having prawn cocktail, my mother's fail-safe starter. Only instead of the usual seafood dressing she has mixed the prawns with salad cream, and I am finding its sour acidity hard to swallow.

'Just waiting for Janice, that's all,' I say, and as if on cue the doorbell rings.

'Ah, here she is,' my dad says. His face lights up, and I am hit by a flash of annoyance; did he look that pleased to see me? Did he even notice me behind the more appealing presence of my husband, and my son? And what does Janice ever bring with her but her lateness? But this is no time for petty jealousy.

My dad pushes back his chair to get up and answer the door, but quickly I say, 'I'll go,' and beat him to it.

I open the front door to Janice and blurt out, 'I tried to call you.'

It comes out like an accusation, and she steps back on the doorstep, eyebrows raised. 'I've been out all weekend,' she says defensively. 'What's the matter?'

But then my dad is in the hall, with my mum behind him, both of them calling out their hellos, and my chance is gone.

'I need to speak to you,' I say quickly, and Janice gives me a strange look and walks past me.

'Sorry I'm late,' she says to my mum. 'Traffic was hell.' And to my dad, 'Happy birthday.'

And back we all go to the dining room. Janice sits down

and eats her prawn cocktail while we all look at her. I am feeling hot and tense, wondering how long it will be till I can get her alone, and what I will say to her when I do. And I cannot bear the unfairness of it. Janice has been with Paul all weekend; I've no doubt about that. That's why she had no need to check her phone.

My mother starts clearing the dishes and I get up to help. I help her bring through the meat and the vegetables for the main course, too; having arrived late, Janice is let off this task, though I wish she would have the sensitivity to make an excuse to leave the table and find a way of speaking to me. But she doesn't. She just sits there at the table and talks to my dad, and to Andrew.

How long have I got? It feels surreal, farcical almost. I know what is going to happen and I am walking straight into it.

Yet ten minutes, twenty minutes pass and they have talked about Janice's work, my parents' holiday plans, and every little detail of Jono's timetable . . . I am starting to think that maybe my insignificance might be a good thing. Nothing is required of me other than that I should be here, enabling the existence and the presence of Andrew and Jono. Andrew and Jono would not be here, today, if it were not for me, but now that they are here I hardly matter. I am like a chair leg, necessary, but not particularly noticed unless for its absence.

And so my thoughts start to drift.

I think of Simon. I think of his beautiful eyes and his beautiful body, the smell of his skin and the sound of his voice, already so distant. My heart is low in my chest, too hard, too chilled. *We'll talk soon*, he said, but when? He couldn't get away from me quickly enough.

I cut off a piece of beef. I put it in my mouth and I chew.

It takes all my will to swallow it. I can feel my mother's eyes on me, watching.

'Are you sickening for something?' she asks.

'Not at all,' I say and I smile widely. 'This is delicious.'

Andrew is watching me too, now. I cannot read his eyes. I cannot read his expression at all, though once upon a time I'd have known his thoughts before he did. Now he is closed to me – his feelings, if he has any, a mystery. I try to extend my smile to him and it cracks in my face like a grimace.

Very slightly he frowns, and then he looks away.

My father is telling him about the bypass that the council is planning to put around the town. Is it a good thing? Is it not a good thing? What does Andrew think?

I watch Andrew as he considers his reply. He tilts his head a little to one side, he locks his teeth so that his chin is slightly jutting, and he nods faintly, repeatedly, weighing up the odds. But I do not hear what he says to my father. I could not care less if they built one road or ten around Ashcroft, and another fifty right through the middle of it. Andrew shaved this morning as he always does, but he is not as thorough as he used to be and, being as dark-haired as he is, it matters. It shows. There are tiny dark specks appearing on his jaw and, worse still, right up under his nose. The sight of them repulses me. And he is so thin; the hollows of his cheeks becoming more exaggerated as he gets older. Simon is thin, too, but on him the effect is ethereal, somehow, adding to his grace. In Andrew's thinness I see the passing of time; I can imagine how he will look as an old man, and the thought of it fills me with fear.

'So what did you think of the film?' Andrew says and his words slice through my thoughts, clean as a knife. My heart flips in my chest and my ears start to buzz.

He is looking at Janice, and Janice is looking at him. His face is turned away from me, but I have a clear view of Janice; she is frowning at him, confused.

'The film you saw on Friday.' Andrew's face in profile is unblinking, impassive. 'What was it called?'

Janice glances at me, a quizzical sideways flick of the eye. She opens her mouth to speak, and quickly I say, 'I *told* you, it was rubbish. It's not even worth talking about, Andrew.'

My words, in their haste, come out waspish. *I told you* ... like a nag, like a harridan. I flinch at the sound of my own voice, and I am aware that everyone else is flinching too. Andrew is very, very still.

Janice glares at me. She raises her eyebrows and her eyes are as bright and hard as marbles.

Slowly, Andrew turns his face to me. The look in his eyes makes my cheeks burn. 'Then I am so sorry that I even mentioned it,' he says coldly, making an awkward moment even worse.

My mother laughs nervously, a shrill whinny of a sound. 'Any more beef, anyone?' she chirps. 'Andrew, let me get you some more.'

And my dad, following her lead, says, 'Jono, how do you fancy beating me at chess later?'

And Janice still glares at me, and Andrew won't look at me again, for the rest of lunch.

'So what the hell was that all about?'

Janice and I are in the kitchen, clearing up. My mother has just taken a tray of coffee through to the others, in the lounge.

I am rinsing plates, and stacking them in the dishwasher. Janice is standing watching me, her hands on her hips, a tea towel, clutched in one hand, dangling down by her side. 'Well?' she demands.

And what can I say, except the truth, at least in part? I pick up a dish and run it under the tap, hoping that the sound of the water will muffle my voice, should anyone be listening from next door. 'I'm sorry,' I say. It is always best to start with an apology with Janice; I learnt that long ago. 'I told Andrew that I went to see a film with you on Friday.'

'I gathered that,' she says loudly, much too loudly; I turn the tap on harder. 'But would you mind telling me why?'

'Look, I'm *sorry*—' I say again, but she cuts across me.

'It's that man.' She flicks the tea towel in her hand and folds her arms now, across her chest. 'You've been seeing him. You told me it was over.'

'It *is* over. I just – I just had to ... see him about something.'

'You lied to me,' she snaps. 'You're lying to Andrew and you lied to me.'

My hand is on that tap, turning it off, turning it on again. 'I'm sorry,' I say for the third time. 'It isn't that straightforward.'

'Well, it never is, is it? That's the trouble with cheating on your husband.'

'Janice! Please!' I hiss, and I turn the tap on full blast to drown out her voice.

'And I suppose that's what you wanted to talk to me about. You wanted me to cover up for you. How dare you drag me into it?' she carries on. 'How *dare* you use me as an alibi for your sordid little—'

'It wasn't like that!'

'Yes, it was!' she snaps right back. 'It's *always* like that.'

She's right, of course. Cynical, self-righteous, hypocritical

Janice – she's right and she knows it. She glares at me and I glare at her, and I'm searching for something to say, for some justification . . . It's on the tip of my tongue just to *tell* her. Then maybe she'd understand, maybe she could even *help* me. She is my sister, after all.

I think I'm pregnant.

It's there; it's on the tip of my tongue. I'm about to say it. She stares at me as if waiting.

'I—'

But then my mother walks in, pushing the door open noisily and plonking down the tray on the counter. 'Goodness!' she exclaims. 'What are you two arguing about out here? You're making an awful lot of noise!'

Would I have told her?

Here, in my mother's kitchen, with my husband, my parents and my son just the other side of the wall? Would I really have told her? Panic – *horror* – shoots down my arms, sending pins and needles stinging into my fingertips.

What was I *thinking* of?

My mother clatters about with the kettle and the cups, making more coffee for those who want it, and Janice and I stand there and watch her, both of us silenced. I am so weak I can barely hold myself up.

We were making a lot of noise, my mother said, but they didn't hear what we were saying, surely? Please God, surely they didn't hear?

But if they did hear, my mother wouldn't be out here now fussing around us making coffee and saying, 'Come on now. Come and sit down. I'll finish the dishes later.'

Would she?

I cannot believe I so nearly told Janice. I cannot believe this is happening at all.

I sit down on the sofa next to Andrew, who makes room for me, but doesn't acknowledge me. He is watching Jono playing chess with my dad. My dad is sitting in the armchair with the chessboard laid out on the little table in front of him; Jono is kneeling on the floor. I too pretend to watch. I am feeling punched, stunned by my own insanity. I sit with my hands clasped in my lap, wanting to be good, like a child; wanting to be forgiven. There are tears stinging in my eyes; I have to keep blinking them away, hoping nobody will see. Just in case they do, I sit with a taut smile pinned into the cheeks of my face. I must be happy. I must be okay. Desperately I want comfort, but the person I would have comfort me is the person who has driven me away; the person I have wronged. My husband sits beside me, but I am on my own now.

Andrew drives us home from my parents in silence. From the corner of my eye I watch him; I study his face in profile, his focus fixed upon the road. The tension in the car is excruciating; Andrew's silence is so wilful, so accurate in its aim. What does he know and what does he not know? I cannot tell. The book that was once so open to me is now firmly shut, the page lost.

'I'm sorry I snapped at you,' I say when I can stand it no more. 'At lunch.'

Andrew concentrates on the driving, careful, controlled man that he is. Regularly he checks the mirrors. His hands upon the wheel grip loosely, but firmly. I look at those hands; at those long fingers and those broad knuckles, and I think

273

of Simon's hands with the bitten nails; hands as tender as a pianist's.

'The way you spoke to me is the way you always speak to me these days,' Andrew says, at last.

TWENTY-TWO

I need to know for sure. I cannot focus on anything in this excruciating state of limbo.

So on Monday morning when I am in Sainsbury's I buy a pregnancy-test kit, sticking it in the trolley along with the weekly shop. How my heart thumps as I move slowly along the pharmacy isle, searching shelves stacked with deodorants and tampons and vitamin pills. And how my face burns when at last I find what I am looking for, and lift the box down, and drop it nonchalantly into my trolley, where it lies among the usual tins and vegetables and various packets and cartons. I swear that there are a hundred eyes upon me.

And see how it glides along the conveyor belt when I place my items onto it at the checkout to pay. The shop assistant picks it up, scans it and chucks it with a bored, dismissive flick of the wrist onto the heap of stuff piling up on the other side, too fast for me to pack. I feel the woman in the queue behind me watching, as we all watch. She'll see the standard of my shop: where I spend and where I save. She'll see my organic milk and vegetables, and my economy tin foil and pasta. She'll see my pregnancy-test kit.

One of my friends at school was the product of a late

pregnancy. An *accident*, we liked to joke. I went round to her house once and her parents were ancient. She had a sister, fifteen years older, married and with kids of her own. Her father had false teeth.

If I am pregnant there will be a thirteen-year gap between Jono and this baby – this unknown baby – inside of me. He will be eighteen when she is only five. He will be taking off on his life, when she will merely be starting out on hers. He will be fully grown, a young man, off to university, and leaving me, when she is merely starting at school. In the blink of an eye I see her sweet, trusting face, the softness of her skin. I see her hand held out to me. *Mummy*, she says. *Mummy*.

I want to shake myself. I want to slam my head against a wall and blank out my thoughts. Why must I think of this baby as a she? And yet how can I not? I do not think of her as a new person; I think of her as the one that I lost, come back.

I stuff my shopping into bags, clumsy, angry with myself. How can I even think of having this baby if I am pregnant? How could I possibly see it through?

I ask myself this and yet the answer is obvious: *how could I not?*

I have not used a pregnancy test before. With Jono, and the second time, too, there seemed little point. You know when you are pregnant. You don't need to see a little bit of blue on a stick to point out what you already know. But now ... there is the chance that I am wrong. And should I not hope that I am wrong? If I *am* wrong, I can close this episode. Andrew and I will chug along as before. I will live in the coldness. I will accept that this is it, for me, somehow.

Because what can I possibly do otherwise? I *have* to be wrong. It cannot be any other way.

But I'm not wrong.

At nearly a quarter to twelve, after I have unpacked my shopping in the kitchen, emptied the dishwasher, sorted the post and procrastinated until I can procrastinate no longer, I go upstairs to my bathroom with that little box and I do what I have to do.

And half an hour later I am still sitting on the edge of the bath, too numb, too stunned to move.

Outside, I can hear the distant scream of a car alarm, and the doors of a delivery truck, slamming shut. These sounds sear across my consciousness, magnified. I hear the sway of the wind in the trees, the clattering of bottles being put out for the recycling, and the persistent shrill of a telephone ringing in the house next door. Footsteps come running up the street, growing louder as they get nearer, and for some bizarre reason I think they are coming to *my* house; I catch my breath, wait for the creak of the gate, the ring of the doorbell. Irrationally I think, *I am caught*, and my stomach grips and lurches on a sudden rush of panic. But the footsteps just carry on by, pounding out their pace on the concrete, *boom, boom,* till slowly they recede again, and fade, like the echo of my heart.

And still I sit there.

I start to cry; stupidly, uselessly and horribly noisily, in the confines of my small and functional bathroom. Andrew has left his bathrobe pegged on the hook beside the door. It hangs there like a slumped, dark shadow of a man; redundant and abandoned. I cannot bear to look at it. But his things are everywhere: his shaver by the sink, his towel upon the rail. His toothbrush shares the glass with mine; their two bases meet and cross at the bottom of the glass, but then out they stick, their heads far apart, and facing away. I look away from these things and stare at the floor, and I see where the white tiles are marked here and there by the random stray hairs that Andrew has shed from his body; every day I sweep up those hairs, and every day when he showers he sheds some more. There are traces of Andrew everywhere. This is his home. But it doesn't feel like his home to me; it feels like the place that *I* must inhabit and through which he merely comes and goes like a transient judgemental ghost, a cruel shadow of the person that he used to be, the marker by which I measure my own discontent.

What will I do?

The walls of this room squeeze in on me. I can smell the faint dampness from the sink plughole; the combined familiarity of old soap, old toothpaste and the lemon-scented spray that I use to clean. Saliva rises in my mouth and I have to swallow. I force myself to stop crying; I need to get a grip. I need to think.

I could sleep with Andrew and pass the baby off as his.

It's the obvious thing to do. If I am careful, he need never know. And think how happy he would be. After all, isn't this what we both wanted? And wasn't its absence the very cause of the rift between us?

But could I do it? Could I really do that to him?

Could I lie like that, and maintain that lie for all of our lives?

One day I would crack. One day, in a row, or when faced with his insufferable coldness, I would goad him. I would taunt him, and let it out.

But what else can I do? How can I have this child, and yet how can I not? And what likelihood is there of it ever becoming a healthy child anyway? What chance of this cluster of cells inside me taking form and shape, and holding on in there, and growing and thriving, and living long enough ever to open its eyes to the world and breathe? What if it should just die inside me, like last time?

I cannot do it. I cannot go through it all again.

I need to speak to Simon. He cannot just leave me to sort this out. But his mobile's switched off, and when I call his direct line I get the answerphone. *This is the voicemail of Simon Reiber*, I hear him say. *Please leave your name and message and I'll get back to you as soon as possible, or alternatively dial zero to speak to my secretary*. Again and again.

And again and again I leave him a message.

'It's Rachel,' I say. 'I need to talk to you. Please call me.'

And I can't stop the pitch of my desperation creeping into the word *please*.

I pace the house. I wait for him to call me, and he doesn't. That sense of rejection, that stomach-fisting sense of *exclusion* that goes hand in hand with everything I have ever known about the Reibers and all of their kind, locks and pulls inside me.

I call again; I leave another message.

The day slides by; soon Jono will be home. Agitation – *panic* – prickles inside my head. I phone again and this time I speak to his secretary.

'I need to speak to Simon Reiber,' I say, keeping my voice as calm as I possibly can.

'Who's calling please?'

'Rachel. Just tell him it's Rachel, please.'

And she says, 'I'm afraid Mr Reiber's not available at the moment.'

'Is he in his office?' I demand, too harshly, too insistent.

'I'm afraid Mr Reiber's not available at the moment,' she repeats robotically. 'Would you like to leave a message?'

'Yes,' I say. 'Tell him I need to speak to him. It's urgent,' I stress. And, 'Do you know when he will be free?'

'I'm sorry,' she says. 'I am not able to say. I will tell him that you called.'

And then I know: she's vetting his calls. He's not available *to me*. What did he say to her, I wonder? Don't put any calls through from a strange, desperate woman called Rachel?

He cannot *avoid* me.

Suddenly I picture Simon's mother. I see her face as she threw me out of her house; the bright abhorrence in her eyes. It wasn't just that she didn't want to be reminded of Vanessa, but that she didn't want to be reminded by *me*, a stranger. And I think of Simon's reaction that time I suggested that I go with him, to visit his mother. I recall the look on his face now and I want to squirm. And I think how I listened as he talked about the old days with Vanessa and Fay and Dominic and the others . . . and how I lapped it all up; how I couldn't get enough of it – all those stories and memories of the wild, fun times they had without me.

I am nothing to him. I was nothing to any of them.

I have the phone number of his flat. I have never used it because I have always called him on his mobile, but I have it nevertheless. I wrote it down once, when I was there. I found it written on a travel document, left lying on the counter along with the post. I saw it, I remembered it, I wrote it down. I have the phone number of his house in Kingham, too. *That* number is on all his correspondence. Anything sent out by him goes on heavy, letterheaded paper, and there it sits, the family phone number, right after the family address, at the top of each sheet in Times italic, centred, ten-point.

Would I ever call that number? Would I, if I had to?

Later, when Jono has done his homework and eaten his supper and is now ensconced in his room, doing God knows what, and Andrew is slumped in front of the TV watching miserable men moaning on about the miserable news, I go to bed. *I have a headache*, I say, though no one listens. No one takes any notice. I take my phone with me and I curl up with it, under the duvet. I ring Simon's mobile once more, but it is still turned off. Did he think he could deter me so easily? I dial the number of his flat. It rings and rings. I lie in my bed and I listen to it ringing. I picture his flat; that huge open room, the shrill of the phone bleating through the darkness. I picture the stillness; the view from the window, the lights of the city below orange and blurred. And still the phone rings. I lie on my side with my phone snug against the pillow. I have it on redial. It rings and it rings.

I hear Jono going to bed. 'Goodnight,' I call as he walks past my door, but he doesn't reply, and I am too weighed down to go after him. I hear Andrew go out to the kitchen, boil the kettle, make a cup of tea and take it back to the living room. I follow the change in sound and voices as he flicks through the TV channels. And then there is just me again. The phone rings and rings against my ear.

And finally Simon answers.

He knows that it is me, of course. I hear it in his voice: the guardedness, the lie of his careful *Hello*.

'I tried to call you,' I say. 'At work.'

'I'm sorry,' he says. 'I've been busy.'

'And on your mobile. You've had your mobile switched off.'

'I've been in a meeting most of the day.'

'I left a message with your secretary.' I hear myself nagging and I think: *This is how he will remember me.* I close my eyes and the tears slide into my pillow. 'I need to *talk* to you.'

'You can talk to me now,' he says, his voice as smooth and impartial as a stranger's.

'I *can't*,' I wail. 'I can't talk to you now; my *husband* is downstairs. I need to see you.'

'Rachel—'

'For God's sake, Simon, I'm *pregnant*!'

'Are you sure?' he asks, his voice clipped, cutting to the point. 'Are you absolutely certain?'

'*Yes*,' I hiss. 'I did a test.'

'The test might not be reliable.'

'Oh, Simon, come *on*.'

He says nothing. I picture him, standing in his flat, thinking of ways to fob me off.

'I need to see you,' I insist. 'We need to talk about this.'

'Rachel,' he says at last. 'This is not what I wanted.'

'Oh, I know *that*—' I stop. Andrew is coming out of the living room; I hear the flick of the light switch and the closing of the door as he goes into the downstairs loo. 'I want to see you tomorrow,' I whisper.

'Rachel, I'm busy—'

'You can't just abandon me!' I hear the loo flush, one door opening and another close. I hear the echo of my voice, too loud. 'This is your problem, too!'

'Maybe we could meet after work,' Simon says reluctantly. But just so that I should know where I stand he adds, 'I won't have long, though. I'm going to a client dinner at eight.'

*

We arrange to meet at that same bar, by the Festival Hall. I wonder if there is some irony in his choice, or if it really is just convenient. Also, I wonder why it wouldn't have been just as easy for me to go to his flat, but of course, really, I know why.

He is there before me, sitting at a table on which he has placed two small glasses of wine. He rises when he sees me, and he kisses me on the cheek, as if we are friends.

And then we sit, and the first thing he says is, 'Do you know what you are going to do?'

'No.'

He looks at me, as if waiting for me to say more. And when I don't, his expression turns incredulous. 'Rachel, you know what you *have* to do,' he says.

He is wearing a dark-grey suit, with a slightly lighter grey line running through it, at approximately one-inch intervals. His shirt is blue, the same shade as his eyes, but it is cleverly woven so that where the light catches it, it seems darker, almost two-tone. His tie is blue too, with a solid diagonal grey stripe. He certainly knows how to dress.

'Rachel,' he repeats emphatically. 'You do know what you have to do.'

I am strangely detached, from myself, from all of this. I think of Jono; he will have finished his homework by now. He will be ensconced in front of the TV. *Tell your dad I've just popped out*, I said, *if he's home before me.* I was too fraught to think of any proper excuse.

'See your doctor,' Simon tells me now. 'He'll put you in touch with the right person.' And when I do not respond he says, 'For God's sake, Rachel, I cannot do this. I cannot be . . . involved.'

'But you are involved.'

I watch the colour creep into his face. I remember how he used to blush when he was a boy. *Leave my brother alone*, Vanessa would laugh, batting his flirtatious tormentors away. *He's far too young.*

He isn't too young now.

He clears his throat. 'Rachel,' he says tightly, 'I do not *blame* you. But this is not part of my plan.'

He had a plan? I look at him, curious. I thought it was all easy come, easy go. That, I thought, was part of the appeal of the Reibers. I thought it was only uptights like me who needed plans.

More people arrive to join those already at the table beside us; they greet each other in a noisy burst of screeches and laughter and calls for drinks. Simon glances sideways at them, irritated, and then shoots his wrist out of his cuff and checks his watch.

He leans towards me across the table. 'I did not expect this to happen,' he says.

And I say, 'I know, Simon. But it has happened.'

I am not making this easy for him, but why should I? Who, after all, is going to make it easy for me? He is looking agitated now. He studies me with what appears to be annoyance. Certainly it isn't affection. I stare back at him and there are tears prickling at the backs of my eyes.

'What do you want from me, Rachel?' he says, but it isn't a question. He doesn't really want to know what I want from him. Oh no. He doesn't want an answer at all. It's more of a dismissal, a command, a sort of *Stop wanting from me, Rachel.*

So I say nothing and the tears begin their watery descent down my cheeks.

The flush on his face deepens. He's afraid I'm going to

make a scene. Or is he thinking, as I am, of that other occasion when we were here in this bar? Then, when I cried, he took my hand. *Forgive me*, he said so earnestly, so romantically, and took me back to his flat.

He bites his lip. His hand, on the table, twitches nervously. 'You have to get rid of it,' he blurts out in exasperation. 'Of course you do. I cannot be any part of this, if you are stupid enough to choose otherwise.' He stops. He frowns. He shifts in his seat, clearly discomforted by his outburst. 'I'm sorry, Rachel, but that's the way it is.'

I stare at him. A tear has turned the corner of my chin and is trickling down my throat. My nose is running too, but I do not stop it. I cannot move. I cannot speak. Vaguely I am aware that the people at the next table are taking an interest in us now; out of the corner of my eye I see heads turning to get a better look. I do not care, but Simon does. Simon is squirming.

'Rachel, *please*,' he hisses at me. 'Stop crying.'

But I can't stop crying.

Simon glances at his watch again. 'I'm sorry,' he says. 'I have to go.' And then he puts his hand to his inside jacket pocket and takes out his wallet. This he opens, and tucked inside is a cheque, already written. 'Look,' he says, sliding it across the table to me, 'this might help.'

I stare at him, appalled.

'Take it,' he says. 'Please. And ... do what you have to do.'

Whatever I was expecting it wasn't this: a *pay-off*. I feel as cheap and dispensable as a whore. And like a whore, I slowly reach out a hand.

As soon as my finger touches that cheque Simon relaxes. The deal is done.

'Goodbye, Rachel,' he says and stands to leave. 'And – well . . . look after yourself.'

I watch as he weaves his way through the other tables and pushes his way out of the door. He walks fast, gone from me. He doesn't look back.

I sit there a while. Now that there is no one to cry for, I wipe away my tears. I have no tissue and have to make do with my sleeve. I sniff loudly, and a woman on the next table looks around at me, and then looks away.

I know I shouldn't, but I drink my wine down in three swift gulps. I drink Simon's too, as he didn't touch it. The alcohol melts my head and turns my limbs to water. I pick up that cheque and look at it. I think of ripping it up, but who would benefit then? Certainly not my baby, should she ever have the chance to exist. And so I put it in my purse. It will be no great loss to Simon.

Twenty thousand pounds. Not much for a child's life.

TWENTY-THREE

The train back to Surbiton is packed with people still on their way home from work, but I manage to get a seat by the window, squashed in beside a large man reading a paper; his arms, his newspaper, his legs are all in my space. The man opposite me is also too big for these small seats and his knees knock against mine as the train moves. My feet are cramped between his, pigeon-toed. Repeatedly, obliviously, he treads on my shoes. I feel trapped, crushed, invisible.

I look out of the window and watch the grey of the city chug by. I do not know what I am going to do. I am too miserable to think. Simon's cheque sits in my purse, which is inside my handbag, squashed on my lap. Its presence is like a dirty secret, a pointed finger; confirmation of my shame. And yet I hold onto my bag tightly, lest I should lose it.

And then my phone rings, its tinny, irritating tune shrieking into my gloom. The man opposite me tuts; the man beside me shuffles his newspaper in pointed, exaggerated annoyance. I dig into my bag, drag out my phone and see Janice's number flashing up on the screen.

I brace myself and whisper, 'Hello.'

'Where are you?' she demands straight away, and there is

something in her voice that sends a flick of alarm snaking
its way up my spine.

'I'm ... on a train,' I whisper. 'Why?'

'Where are you going?'

'I'm going home,' I say. 'Why? What's the matter?'

For a moment she is silent and that snake of alarm crawls
deeper. And then she says, 'Andrew phoned me.'

My heart flips inside my chest. 'When?'

'About half an hour ago,' she says woodenly.

'What did he want?'

The man sitting next to me shakes his newspaper as if he
was shaking a dog and clears his throat noisily. I shift around
as far as I can, turning my back to him.

'He wanted to know if you were really with me on Friday
night,' Janice says.

'What did you tell him?'

'I told him,' Janice says, her voice rising now in indigna-
tion, 'that he should ask you that.'

My heart, now, is pounding. 'Well, that pretty much
answered him, didn't it?'

'Well, what did you expect me to say?' Janice yells in my
ear, and the man opposite me tuts and huffs and bangs his
knee against mine. 'I'm not going to lie for you, Rachel.'

'No,' I snap back. 'I know you're not.' Then, 'What else
did he say?'

'He asked if I knew what was going on.'

'And what did you say?'

'I told him to ask you,' Janice replies, emphasizing each
word as if I'm an idiot.

'Shit!' I say.

'This is your own fault,' she says, starting up on a lecture now. 'You've brought it on yourself. And you can't expect me to go covering up for you.'

'Where was he?'

'What?'

'Where was he when he phoned?' I ask. 'Was he at home?'

'Well, I assume so. That's why I called you, on your mobile.'

'Shit,' I say again, and the woman sitting next to the man opposite me blurts out, *Oh, for heaven's sake*, as if she's never heard the word 'shit' before. 'Now what am I going to do?'

'That,' Janice says ominously, 'is for you to work out.' And she hangs up on me.

It's just gone nine when I get home. The light is off in the living room, but the hall light is on and the upstairs, too. I push open the front door and Andrew's shoes are on the edge of the mat, lined up side by side; his briefcase just beside them. The house is silent.

All the way back from the station I have been trying to think up lies and excuses, but there are none. The best I could do is bat it back, and blame Janice; say that she's just making trouble. *Of course I was with Janice*, I could say. *She's just being awkward. You know what she's like; any opportunity to stir things.*

But it won't wash, I know it. Andrew is many things, but he isn't a fool.

And anyway, what is the point?

And so I walk into the house with a leaden sense of fatalism. *What will be will be*, I tell myself over and over. *What will be will be.*

He's in the kitchen, sitting at the table, facing the door; I walk into that kitchen as though into a lions' den, but he doesn't acknowledge me. He is sitting with his elbows propped on the table and his chin resting on his hands, simultaneously condemning me, and blocking me out. His eyes are fixed on the table and his mouth is a grim, taut line. I see him like that and I hate him. Who is he to sit in judgement on me, when he hasn't cared one little bit about the hell that has gone on inside my head for the last however many years? Look at him, sitting there like that; isn't it a little late to start acting as though he cared in some way? Am I supposed to be afraid, I wonder? I almost want to laugh, but it's the dangerous, maniacal laugh of hysteria too loose, too close to breaking out.

I go to the sink and pour myself a glass of water, and quickly I drink it down. I place the glass back down on the counter. My hand is shaking. Andrew doesn't move.

'Where's Jono?' I ask, and there is an echo to my voice. *Where's Jono? Where's Jono?* Always, *Where's Jono?*

And what about us? Where are we?

Where is *she*, who was ripped out of my body nearly ten years ago now, and taken away from me, unseen and untouched, and flung into some hospital incinerator to burn and disappear? Where is she, who promised so much to our small, suburban lives, and destroyed, by her absence, even more?

One, two, three, four seconds pass, then Andrew says, 'He's in his room.' His voice is as tight as the expression on his face.

'Right,' I say, and I make to leave the kitchen again, but now he moves. Now he takes his hands away from his face and pushes back his chair, scraping it gratingly against the tiles, and stands up.

And he says, 'Where've you been?'

Where've you been? Where've you been? Like I'm some errant wife of old and he is my keeper? I laugh, I can't stop myself; a short, wild, humourless burst. He stares at me, and in his eyes I see all the bitterness that I feel reflected back at me, black and raw.

'I want to know where you've been,' he says, biting out the words.

But he's never wanted to know before. Before, he's never even cared. And so I say, '*Out*,' and the sarcasm is thick enough in my throat to choke me. 'I've been *out*. Is that okay with you? And now I'm going to say goodnight to my son.'

I turn and start walking out of the kitchen and my legs are like rubber; clumsy, weak.

'Don't you walk away from me!' Andrew barks behind me, and I can feel him glaring at my back. I can literally feel his anger – and poor Andrew, he doesn't *do* anger – but away I walk, and I'm halfway down the hall before he kicks into life and starts following me. He grabs my arm; I try to pull away and he yanks me back.

'Don't walk away from me!' he repeats, and is it fury or desperation that has him digging his fingers into my arm? I turn to face him and his eyes are as hard and dark as stones. Is this the man who blushed and stammered when he asked me to marry him, who'd get so worked up when he made love to me that he'd leave his hand-prints, pink and bruised, upon my skin? Who sat on the bed beside me when we returned from the hospital having left our dead baby behind, and stroked my back, and told me everything would be okay? He lied to me. He *lied*.

His hand is like iron on my arm.

SUZANNE BUGLER

'Let go of me,' I say, and the colour rises in his face. He drops his hand and takes a step back.

'Tell me where you've been,' he says. 'Tell me where you were on Friday.'

'Andrew,' I say and my heart is racing against my ribs, 'you haven't wanted to know where I've been or how I feel, or anything about me, for *years*. Don't tell me that you suddenly care.'

'Of course I care,' he says in a tone that tells me otherwise.

And I say, 'Well, you've got a funny way of showing it.' Then before he can stop me again, I turn and quickly run up the stairs.

'Rachel!' he calls after me. 'Rachel!'

Jono's bedroom door is closed, but I open it, go straight in and close it behind me. My heart is beating so hard it almost hurts. Jono is lying on his bed in his pyjamas, reading a book. He doesn't look up at me, but I see a frown of acknowledgement cross his forehead.

'Hello, Jono,' I say, doing my best to keep my voice light and steady. 'Did you finish your homework okay?'

He grunts in reply.

I walk over to his bed and sit on the edge of it, by his curled-up knees. I touch his shoulder and feel his body stiffen. I lean over and kiss his head, and he shrugs me away.

'I'm reading,' he says, by way of dismissal.

I sit there a moment longer, ignored. The sorrow in my heart swells and burns.

'Well. Goodnight, then,' I say at last. 'Turn your light out at ten.' And I stand up to leave.

He doesn't reply.

*

I close Jono's door behind me quietly. Andrew is still down-stairs, standing where I left him. I do not know what I am going to say to him, or what I am going to do.

I walk along the corridor to our room, and go in and close the door, and moments later Andrew comes up after me. He enters the room and I see the fury in him, suppressed, buttoned down, as it always is. I am standing by the window, as far away as I can be from him; he stands midway across the room before me with his hands hanging down by his sides like a monkey's. His shoulders are tense and hunched up, and he is glaring at me in a pitiful mix of rage and impotence. He huffs and he puffs, unable to get his words out.

Seeing him like that, so blustered up and helpless, makes me cruel, makes me want to hurt him. *This was his fault*, I tell myself; *his fault*. And so I speak first. 'Do you know how lonely I have been? Do you know what it has been like for me, living here with a husband who doesn't talk to me, and a son who doesn't talk to me, either? It's like being trapped in an emotional *graveyard*!' That familiar look crosses his eyes – that *here we go again* look, and I never, ever want to see that look again. There is a lid lifting off inside my head. I am *done* with this. 'I cook for you,' I say and my voice is thick and sore. 'I clean for you. I look after your son. I feel more like your fucking housekeeper than your wife, Andrew. Do you think I could just live like that forever?'

He finds his voice. 'I am well aware that Jono and I are not good enough for you, Rachel,' he says, biting out the words. 'You make that plain every single day.'

'It's nothing to do with Jono.'

'No, it's to do with you. We're a *family*, Rachel. You, me and Jono. But that's never enough for you!'

'We're not a *family*,' I rail at him. 'We're not a family.

How can you call us a family when one quarter of us is dead, and the remaining three are merely forced together in mutual, suffocating misery—?'

He is trembling now; I see how the cotton of his shirt ripples against his skin. 'Will you never let it go?' he pleads. 'Will you spend your whole life hankering after what we lost? Why can't you just appreciate what we *have* got, Rachel? You'll never be happy.'

'You don't try to make me happy!'

His hands are clenching and unclenching by his sides. 'I've tried, Rachel. Believe me, I've tried.'

'How have you tried? You don't talk to me. You don't make love to me.' I see the colour rise in his face. *Good*, I think. *Good*. 'You're so *cold* to me, turning away from me all the time. Living with you is like a punishment!'

'You push me away.' He bites out the words. '*You* are cold. Every day I live with your misery . . . with your resentment. I don't know what you want—'

'I want to be *loved*! I want passion; I want to feel *alive*!'

He flinches. *Good*. And he says, 'Is that what you got then? Wherever it is that you've been – did you get passion, Rachel? Did you get *loved*?'

He is *mocking* me. There is a bad, insidious flame burning up inside me. I blank out of my mind the shameful, sordid image of Simon handing over that cheque, and push into my head instead the thought of his lean, beautiful body and his expensive clothes, and I cling to that memory.

'Yes,' I say to Andrew just to hurt him. 'Yes, I did.' And I watch the sneer slide right off his face. I am horribly light-headed. All shackles are loose now. 'I *did* find love and I *did* find passion.' Again that image of Simon putting his hand to his jacket pocket, taking out his wallet and pulling out that cheque springs into my head, but I bat it away. *Bat* it away. 'Did you think I wouldn't? Did you think I'd just stick here forever, condemned to rot and die with you, when you are the coldest, the most emotionally fucking frigid person I have ever *met*?'

At some point he has moved closer to me, or me to him, close enough for me to hit him. And I do hit him, slapping at his shoulders with my hands, the left and then the right, the left and then the right again, *slap, slap,* as I spit out the words. 'Did you think this was it for me? Did you really think nobody else would want me?' His hands are on my arms now, holding me off, but still I slap at him. His face is rigid with anger. His fingers are digging into my skin; I twist and wriggle in his grip and hit out at him all the harder. 'Well, let me tell you, someone else did want me.' I am crying now, and shouting. If words were rocks, I would be throwing them. I want to break him. I want to hurt him as I am hurting. 'Oh yes, someone else wanted me all right. And guess what? I finally found out what I've been missing all these years!'

And then he cracks. For years I have wanted him to crack. He lets go of me for a second and his body recoils as if his soul's been ripped out, and then he lunges at me, striking my flailing hands out of the way with his fist. Striking *me*, on the side of my face. I feel the heat of his fist burst against my cheek and my head rolls back, but he doesn't even realize he's hit me. He's grabbed me by the shoulders again and he's shaking me now, shouting into my face, 'Is this what you want? Is it? Is this what you've been missing?' He is rattling me like a rag doll. I feel his breath on my face, hot, fast. 'You want me to show you how I feel? You want to know what it's like, knowing how much you resent me, how much you blame me for everything—'

He stops shaking me for a second and holds me there, gripped in his arms. Dizzily I see that he is crying. I have only seen Andrew cry once before; once, when our baby was born dead. I do not want to see him cry now. I cannot see him cry. I shut my eyes and tilt my head away. From somewhere he gets a second wind; he starts shaking me again. Shaking me and shouting, *You want to know how I feel . . . you think I don't care . . .* Shaking me as if he doesn't know how to stop now he's started; back and forth, back and forth. My head is spinning and pounding and there are lights, bursting in my eyes. I'm going to be sick. My stomach is tight, cramping. I'm going to be sick—

'Stop it. Stop it,' I manage to say, and I'm coughing, choking as my stomach heaves. 'Stop it. Please. I'm pregnant.'

Did I say it to stop him shaking me, or did I say it just to hurt him; one last, piercing strike? I do not know, but instantly his hands still.

I hang there, limp in his grip, and I throw up, a viscous, acid spill, straight down my front. For seconds he still holds me. I catch my breath and see the expressions cross his face: the bewilderment, the disbelief, the horror. And then he lets me go and I slump down onto my knees.

'My God,' he says. 'My God!' His hands are on his face, then his head; he's clutching at his hair, pulling at it, trying to rip it from his head. 'My God,' he cries again, 'what have you done to me?'

And then we hear something, a persistent, dull knocking sound. We both hear it; simultaneously we turn around and there is Jono standing in the doorway, banging his head repeatedly, rhythmically against the door, knock, knock, knock. For how long has he been there? What has he seen?

'No,' Andrew says in desperation when he sees him. 'Please, no.'

And I try to pull myself together. 'It's okay, Jono,' I manage to say, but Andrew jolts and starts pacing the room.

'No,' he says. 'No, it isn't okay.' And he staggers over to the doorway, and Jono flinches and ducks out of his way.

Andrew walks straight past him. He doesn't stop. He goes down the stairs and I hear him pick up his keys, and then the front door opens and slams shut again. Moments later I hear him start up the car.

I am still on my knees. Jono is still in the doorway. I look at him and our eyes meet.

'Jono—' I say, but he turns away from me, goes back to his room, and slams the door.

TWENTY-FOUR

He has to come back. He's taken nothing with him except the car. His wallet is next to the toaster in the kitchen, along with his phone; I see them there when I go downstairs to get a glass of water. I see them and I am flooded with a mixture of trepidation and relief; he has to come back.

I want him to be okay.

Somehow, deep down in some locked, suppressed part of me, I wish that *we* could be okay.

I know it is just guilt making me remorseful, making me sorry now that I have done my worst, now that I have taken all the hurt inside me and thrown it at Andrew. But I want him to be sorry, too. I want him to come back.

I shower, but feel unable to go to bed, and so I put on clean clothes, loose clothes that I know I will end up sleeping in. My movements, my thought processes are slow, and fragile. I creep along the corridor to Jono's room. His door is shut and I can hear no sound; I think he must be asleep. Carefully, as quietly as I can, I turn the handle and push open the door. Jono is lying on his side with the duvet pulled up around his ears. I move a little closer and see that his eyes are squeezed shut. I stand there, and watch him, and then he screws up his face and pulls the duvet up higher.

'Go away!' he snaps at me and turns his face into the pillow.

'Jono, I'm sorry—'

'Go away!' he roars again. 'Go away!' And he keeps on yelling it, his voice damp and muffled by the pillow, until I back out again, and close the door.

'Go away,' he yells one more time, and I hear his voice crack and turn to sobs.

I lean my back against his door and listen to him crying. It is the saddest sound in the world.

How did it come to this?

We're a family, Andrew said, but I stopped thinking of us like that a long time ago. Families pull together, but we three, we've just pulled each other apart.

I stand there, listening, till his sobs gradually subside. What have we done to him, our poor boy?

What have *I* done?

There is a full moon tonight and the sky is clear. I turn off my bedroom light, but leave the curtains open; it is not dark. The moon floods the room in a weak parody of daylight. I lie on my bed and stare through the window at the night sky, and see it black filtered through with silver, like the burn of a white fire. The house is horribly quiet. Outside I hear the screaming of a fox; the scratching of a cat at my neighbour's bin. A car goes by and my heart picks up its beat, but the car does not stop, it is not Andrew. I stare at the sky. I stare and I stare as the hours slide by, and into my head creeps a multitude of fears.

I am woken by Jono, slamming his school bag down the stairs with the force of an elephant. Instantly I am alert; I look at my clock and it is a quarter past seven. Andrew didn't come home.

Jono throws his bag down the last steps; it hits the floor with a hard smack and skids across the wood.

'Jono!' I say, coming out of my room and down the stairs behind him. 'Jono, your books – don't throw them like that.'

How mundane, how *trivial* it seems to care about books right now. Jono turns and glares at me, and his face says it all. And I see how tired he is, his eyes puffy from crying. He grabs his blazer off the banister and shoves his arms angrily into the sleeves, wrenching the material across his back. I try not to flinch as I hear the lining rip.

'Jono,' I say gently, 'you don't have to go to school today.'

He glares at me a moment longer, then shoves his feet into his shoes, squashing down the backs, forcing them on without undoing the laces.

'You haven't even had your breakfast,' I plead. 'Jono, you don't have to go in today.'

He picks up his bag. 'It's better than staying here with you,' he mutters, and opens the front door and leaves it open, and stomps his way up the path.

There is a coil of fear knotted and twisted from my stomach to my heart. What if Andrew has done something stupid, what if he has crashed the car? But Andrew is too sensible, too restrained to do anything rash. And bad news travels fast; it would have reached me by now.

More likely he has driven to his mother's for somewhere to stay. And she, of course, will have welcomed him in. I picture him, sitting on her floral pink sofa in that room stinking of cat, while she plies him with weak tea and the stale biscuits left over from Christmas, and tuts and shakes her head in self-righteous, satisfied sympathy. And the thought of it stokes up the remnants of my anger again; the thought of him *telling* her.

But what will he tell her? That I'm pregnant with another man's child? That we fought? Or simply that our marriage is over.

And it is over. How can it be anything else, now?

I look in the mirror and try to see a mark on my face where Andrew hit me; I search for evidence of his wrong-doing, of *his* guilt. I am a little pink maybe, along my cheek-bone. I hope that it will come to a bruise – and then his guilt will lessen my own.

But he'd need to see it, for that. He'd need to be here.

I sit at the kitchen table, and watch the clock. He will not go far without money. I am tense, my senses wrought, stretched out, listening for his car in the street, his key in the door.

Another half-hour, I think; another half-hour and he will come back.

I think about phoning his mother, just to see that he is there. But what if he isn't? What would I say to her then? What would I do?

And what about work? Andrew never misses work. Maybe he's there. Maybe he's sitting at his desk in yesterday's clothes, having already shoved me out of his mind. I could call him. I don't need to speak to him; I could just wait for him to answer, and hang up. But what if he doesn't answer? What if I get his secretary? What would I say to her? *Oh, hello there, Vicky, have you seen my husband?*

The minutes drag by. It is half-past ten now, only half-past ten.

And then the phone rings, jolting my heart on a burst of

panic. I jump up from the table to answer it, and Janice says in my ear, 'Well, you've really excelled yourself this time.'

It takes me a second to comprehend what she is saying. I just didn't expect it to be *her*. 'What do you mean?' I ask and she laughs a nasty, humourless laugh of disbelief.

'Come on, Rachel,' she says. '*Pregnant*? How could you *do* that to Andrew?'

My heartbeat is booming in my ears. 'It wasn't deliberate,' I say, and how feeble that sounds, how childish. 'But how do you know?' I ask. 'Did he phone you? Is he there?'

'I'm at work,' she says coldly. 'I've had about four hours' sleep. Andrew turned up at my flat at about one o'clock last night. *Distraught*. How could you *do* that to him, Rachel?' she repeats, in disgust.

The condemnation in her voice has my hackles rising. 'It isn't all me,' I say.

'I'm sorry, Rachel, but I think it is all you. Andrew has been nothing but loyal to you, and you repay him by sleeping with someone else and getting pregnant.'

Her words strike me like a slap in the face. So certain, so critical is she of my failings. I am so angry I can hardly breathe. 'Do you not think there might be a reason why I slept with someone else?' I manage to say. 'Do you not think Andrew's coldness might have had something to do with it?'

'Rachel,' she says, as if I am stupid, as if I have *no idea*, 'do you realize what you have done to him?'

'What about what he's done to me?' I retort. 'But anyway, it's got nothing to do with you.'

'Oh, but I think it has,' she says straight back. 'When your husband spends the night crying on my sofa, I think it has a lot to do with me.'

Jealousy flashes up inside me. 'I suppose you liked that,' I say spitefully. 'Having my husband on your sofa.'

For a moment she is silent, except for the steady in, out, in, out of her breathing. And then she says, 'You have stooped to some pretty low behaviour lately, Rachel, but this really does cap it all. And now, if you'll excuse me, I have work to do.'

And yet again, Janice gets the last word.

I am so incensed that I don't know what to do with myself. How dare he go running to my sister? I picture him, turning up at her flat, looking for sympathy. And I picture her, wrapped in just her bathrobe, letting him in. How cosy they must have been, slagging me off into the night. And how much sympathy did she give him exactly?

I bet he didn't tell Janice he hit me. Oh no. He wouldn't look so good in her eyes then.

I call her flat, wanting to speak to Andrew, but not knowing what I will say. He doesn't answer anyway. How do I even know if he is still there? But then I think that he must be; he won't have gone to work from there, surely. He won't have gone to work if he has spent the night crying on her sofa, and he has no money with him and no clean clothes. I phone again, but still no answer. I picture him, mooching around her flat feeling sorry for himself, and letting the phone ring and ring, knowing it is me. Because he will know it's me.

My anger gets me through the day. It stops me having to think and face things. But at five o'clock Jono comes home. He puts his key in the lock, opens the door, slings down his bag and stands there in the hall. I see him listening to the silence; I see his shoulders tense and slump.

'Has Dad come home?' he asks and my anger fails, washed away on a wave of guilt.

I make him pasta for his tea, and loiter in the kitchen while he prods miserably at it with his fork. I am reminded of when he was a toddler; he'd have the same expression on his face then, when things went wrong. When he couldn't fit all his toy animals into his barn, for instance, or when he bit into a biscuit and found out the chocolate drops were raisins. His mouth would turn down, just as it does now, and that frown would wrinkle up the softness of his fore-head.

But how easy things were to fix, back then.

'Jono,' I say gently, when I can stand him pushing his pasta around the plate no longer, 'please eat up. Things . . . will be okay.'

'No, they won't be,' he says and pushes his plate away, hard; so hard it skids across the table and nearly falls off the other side. 'You're lying. You always lie.'

Later, Janice calls me again.

'Rachel,' she says in a quiet, icy-polite voice, 'there is some-thing I think you need to know.'

And of course I think she is going to tell me that she is screwing my husband, now that she has got him on her sofa. I especially think it when I hear her take one deep breath and then sigh it out, slowly, over a count of eight seconds. I am braced, waiting to hear it, ready to hate her, ready to hate them both.

But she says, 'When you lost your baby – and refused to talk about it, and refused to even acknowledge that there was a baby – Andrew had to deal with that all on his own. He had to fill in the form for the death certificate. He had to arrange the funeral. And yes, there was a funeral. Andrew wanted to say goodbye to his daughter properly, whereas you didn't want to know. A priest blessed her body in the hospital chapel. You weren't there, Rachel, but I was. I know what that was like for Andrew, whereas you, I assume, only know what it was like for yourself.'

She pauses and I would speak; I would say something, some *Shut up* retort, only I have no words suddenly. I am shaking from head to toe. I cannot feel my feet. I cannot feel my hands. I sit down on the edge of my bed with the phone clamped rigid to my ear.

'Andrew didn't want to upset you, Rachel, any more than you were upset already. But did you ever think how upset he was? Because believe me, Rachel, he *was* upset. But you shut him out. You shut everyone out. Andrew had to deal with the funeral and the grief and everything else – and as far as I can see, he's been dealing with it ever since; but you – we all had to *protect* you.'

Again she pauses, and again I'm silent. And maybe now she feels a sense of betrayal, of regret, or *something*, because she says, in a softer voice than I have ever, ever heard from Janice before, 'I'm sorry, Rachel, but I think you need to know this. Andrew is not cold. He grieved the loss of your baby just as much as you did, and for you to go home and tell him you're pregnant by someone else – just think what that did to him, Rachel. Just think.'

I can't think. I don't want to think. If I think I see the shadow in my head that will always be there; and that shadow is Andrew, holding our baby daughter in his arms as tenderly as if she had lived and breathed. I shut my eyes at the time, and I shut them again now, but still I see it.

He held her; I didn't.

And then I see him properly; I see the anguish pulling at the contours of his face and the bleakness filling up his eyes. I see his pity, and I don't want to see his pity. I don't want to see him tiptoeing around me, being so patient, trying to pretend that everything is okay. And I don't want to see him gradually giving up on me, and retreating into himself. I don't want to see any of it. I don't want to see him.

'I told him he can stay here for a couple of days,' Janice is saying. 'I don't see what else I could do. But please, Rachel, don't insult him or me by suggesting that either of us is enjoying the situation.'

I sit there on my bed long after she hangs up.

Was Andrew just trying to protect me? Did he keep his feelings to himself, for my sake? Is that really what he thought I wanted?

How can you live with someone, and think that you know someone, and then when something bad happens find that you are in different corners of a triangle, far, far apart?

I didn't want Andrew to protect me, but I didn't want to talk to him, either. He wouldn't have got it right, whatever he did. He was the father of my dead baby. How could I ever see beyond that?

TWENTY-FIVE

All evening Janice's words go round and round inside my head. I move about the house, tidying things that don't need tidying. I sweep the floor, from one end of the hall to the other, through the living room, the dining room, the kitchen. I sweep and sweep, but ours is an old wooden floor, badly restored. Weekend after weekend Andrew was on his knees with a useless old sander, scouring away. We still have the cracks. We still have the draught and the dust that comes up through the cracks. I sweep, and it gets me nowhere.

I turn on the TV in the living room and sit on the sofa, and try to watch. But how can I possibly be still? Janice's voice is in my head, tormenting me, making me see images I don't want to see.

My sister and Andrew in the hospital chapel, heads bowed together like Mary and Joseph. My baby daughter, wrapped in a blanket, in a death-shroud, her skin cold and white as porcelain, held in Andrew's arms. And where am I? Where am I?

Did I shut Andrew out, or did he – and everyone else – shut me out? How could my sister be there beside Andrew when I am not? And when I think back to those numb and thumped-out days, all I see is Andrew and Jono, Andrew and

Jono. As if Jono was a shield to hide behind, or some kind of distracting toy to wave in my face. Andrew and Jono – never just Andrew. I never saw just Andrew again.

And those other people who traipsed through my house being useful in the aftermath – my mother, my father, any friends who were brave enough still to come – didn't they too just shove my son at me, as if to say, *Look, look at this boy, look at what you have still got*?

How could I grieve with no space? How could I open my arms to Jono without longing to hold *her*? How could I ever love him without guilt, without fear?

Jono is in his room. He has been there since he left his pasta, uneaten, at the kitchen table. I do not know what to say to him. I do not know what to do.

Often I have fantasized about leaving Andrew, but I always imagined Jono and I sticking together. I imagined a scenario not unlike the times when Andrew is simply out, or away on business, when Jono and I relax, and watch too much TV, and eat careless, lazy food from the freezer at all the wrong times of day. I imagined how much closer we would be, Jono and I, without Andrew there to create the triangle. With Andrew exiled, the pressure would be off, and Jono and I would be free at last to just be.

But if Andrew created the triangle, it was the triangle that held us together.

Jono's door is closed, shutting me out. I stand there on the landing, listening for sounds from within, but hear nothing. I tap on the door, and I wait. I tap again.

'Jono,' I say, my face close to the door so that he will hear me, 'would you like to have a go on the PlayStation before bed?'

He doesn't answer and I creak open the door. He is sitting on his bed, legs crossed, and fiddling with a little torch attached to a metal key ring, flicking it on, flicking it off. He stares down at the torch, his face bloated with misery.

'What are you doing?' I ask, but he doesn't answer. The frown on his face deepens, and he draws his lower lip in, creasing up his chin. I watch him fiddling with that torch, and my heart contracts. I remember when he got it; Andrew brought it back from a trip to Bath last year. I wipe my hands on my thighs and move a little closer. I strive for normality. 'Have you done your homework?'

Flick, goes the torch in his fingers. *Flick, flick, flick*.

'Have you done all your homework?' I ask again.

'Homework, homework, homework,' he mumbles without looking at me. 'All you care about is homework.'

'I thought you might like a go on the PlayStation,' I say, trying to make it sound like a treat, trying to inject a little light into my voice.

'I don't want to go on the PlayStation. I want my *dad*.'

Still he doesn't look at me, and my heart twists some more. Carefully I sit down on the edge of the bed beside him and he turns away from me, his shoulders raised so that he is hunched right over, almost into a ball.

'Jono,' I say, and I am fighting back the tears now. 'Sometimes things ... happen. Between grown-ups. Things you couldn't possibly understand.' I try to touch him, but he flinches, and curls himself up further. My heart is a solid burning mass. 'Whatever happens between me and your dad, we both love you. We'll always love you.'

I don't see it coming. He moves so fast; like an animal, he uncurls from his ball and rises up and hurls that key ring straight at me, at close range. It hits me on the cheekbone, right where Andrew struck me. It hits me so hard that I hear it crack inside my head like a pistol shot. I feel it like a pistol shot, too, and slap my hand across my face, clutching at the pain.

'Well, I don't love you!' Jono screams and he's lashing out at me now, too, arms and legs flailing like a wild thing. He kicks my chest, my legs, my stomach, and I double over, protecting myself, protecting my unborn baby. 'I don't love you! I *hate* you! I hate you!'

I manage to stagger from his room. My face is bleeding; I can feel it sticky under my hand. I can't stand up straight. I can't even see properly. I feel my way along the landing to my room, close the door behind me and collapse down on my bed. Jono is still screaming, *I hate you! I hate you!* and I hear the thud and the crash as more things are thrown. And I hear him crying, too, in between his screams, sobs loaded with hatred and rage.

I curl up on my bed with my eyes closed. My head is throbbing, but my body and my heart are numb. I need to sleep. I need to sleep and sleep and block it all away.

You think you are bound forever. You think you are tied, to this person and to this person. You think that it really matters. You spend your life, clutching at chains, clinging, clinging.

We are undone now.

TWENTY-SIX

I hear Jono get up in the morning and go downstairs, but I cannot bring myself to follow him. I hear him slamming his bag around in the hall. I hear him open the cupboard and rummage for his trainers; it is Friday, indoor PE day. I sit on my bed and I listen to the faint rustlings as he laces his shoes and puts on his blazer; I hear the click of the front door.

And then he is gone.

He did not eat last night and he did not eat this morning. Because I am his mother, I care about this. I care about this more than I care that he threw the torch at me, that he kicked me, that he hates me.

He cannot hate me.

He did not say goodbye to me, nor I to him. This hurts most, like the most brutal severing of the cord.

I would lie on my bed forever. I would sleep again; I would sleep forever. But in my head I picture Jono, plodding up the street to wait for the school bus with his bag on his back, shoulders stooped, face turned to the ground. My little boy, my little boy. And I picture Andrew, his body bent into the confines of Janice's sofa – *if* he has slept on Janice's sofa – in her dark and poky living room in her dark and poky flat.

I picture his unshaven face on her cushions; she has too many cushions. Too many cushions and too many throws, and everywhere too many candles. I can smell those candles; the cloying spinster stink of wax and hippy oils. How I hate those candles. And I can smell Andrew, too; the sleep smell, the man smell, the smell of his socks and his unwashed hair, cocooned, confined, on Janice's sofa.

I think about them talking about me, and there is a hard, tight knot deep inside my heart.

And I think of Simon, crisp and fresh in his expensive clothes, planning his day, planning his weekend, dispensing me from his life as casually as I entered it. I think of the dreams I spun, the stupid, ghost-driven fantasies. Whatever did I hope there could be?

I cannot sleep again. The demons in my head will not still.

How I longed to be free. How I longed to be free, but I am not free; I am merely alone.

My eyes are sticky and tight from crying. My cheek is sticky and tight from the blood that has congealed on my skin. Some of my hairs are caught in that blood; I try to prise them away, but they are trapped, like spider's legs in glue.

I force myself to rise and go into the bathroom. My body is as slow and stiff as an old lady's. I place my hands on the sides of the sink to steady myself, and peer into the mirror. How ghoulish I look, the wound to my face as bright and overdone as a Halloween party-piece, the bruise raised and purple already, the cut juicy and moist and vampire-red, stark against the pallor of my skin. I take a cotton-wool pad from the packet on the windowsill, dampen it under the cold tap and start cleaning off the blood. The cut is deep, and bleeds anew as I dab at it, and threads of cotton wool attach themselves to the goo. So much damage from one small key ring. I should probably get it seen to, but I won't of course.

I am still wearing yesterday's clothes. When I am done cleaning my face, I undress and shower, then dress again. I go through these things methodically; it is the only way. And then I clean my face again, cover the cut with a plaster, and watch as a red stain rises up and blooms through.

I cannot go out.

I cannot leave the house with my face like this and my life like this. If I thought I was a prisoner before, then what am I now? I drift through the day, unable to think ahead or make plans. There is a blank wall inside my head that I cannot see past.

No one calls me. At some point in the afternoon I phone Janice's flat, though I do not know what I want to say. But the phone just rings unanswered. I wonder when Andrew will come back, for his things at least. I move about the house quietly, half-listening for the door. I want to see him and I don't want to see him.

I turn on the computer, to kill time, and I type in *Simon Reiber* and stare at his name. *I did not know him before*, I tell myself. *I did not know him before*. Not really. He was the brother of a friend of a friend, that is all.

That is all.

I type in *abortion*, and up come the adverts, the religious sites, the cold, clinical facts. I see these listed sites and they are all nothing to do with me; I cannot look any closer. I cannot *read* them. So I type in *late motherhood* and up springs a whole load of information about the dangers and the pitfalls, and all the things that could go wrong. But hey, it's a lifestyle choice. It's all about having a career, and being in control.

But what about me? I have no career, and I am not in control.

So I stop even looking. And I go and find my bag, and take Simon's cheque from my purse, and I tuck it away in the bottom of my jewellery box, where it will be safe. And into my head flashes my last image of Simon, walking away from me. I see his face in profile as he heads for the door, the decisive, impatient movement of his body in his perfectly cut clothes. *Do what you have to do*, he said to me, as if getting rid of a baby was no bigger deal than a trip to the bathroom.

What a fool I have been.

The minutes and the hours tick by. I make fishcakes for Jono's tea, peeling, boiling and mashing the potatoes, and flaking in the fish. They sit on a plate now, ready to be cooked, plump and floury and benign. They are a lie, these fishcakes, they are a con. I sit at the table, and I look at them, and my stomach is crawling with guilt and dread. It is almost half-past four. I do not know what I will say to Jono when he gets in. I do not know what I can do, other than make him fishcakes, and wait.

I watch the hands of the clock click by, and by. I listen for Jono's footsteps on the path, his key in the door. Five o'clock comes, and five o'clock goes. I sit at the table, and I wait.

But Jono doesn't come home.

The coach must be stuck in traffic.

I pace about the kitchen watching the hands of the clock

slowly click their way round to half-past five. On a normal day Jono would phone me if he was going to be late, but of course this is not a normal day.

I go to the front of the house and stand in the living room, where I can look out at the street from the window. The coach has been late before, but not this late. What if he didn't catch it? What if he was delayed at school for some reason and the coach set off without him? But that has never happened before. And surely he would have phoned me. He'd have had to.

I call his mobile, but it's switched off. He only ever puts it on when he wants to call me; he never thinks that I might need to speak to him. So many times I have told him to turn his phone on when he comes out of school, so many times.

I phone the school, but of course the office staff will have gone home now. I get the answerphone, with its various options for redirection. I try every option. I call and call again, till eventually the phone clicks and a woman says distractedly, 'Hello.'

'I'm a mother of a boy at the school,' I say, stumbling over the words. 'My son comes home on the coach. Was there any delay, do you know; anything on at school? He hasn't rung me. He hasn't come home.'

My heart is pounding. The phone shakes against my ear.

'What form is he in?'

'8G,' I say. 'It's Jonathan Morgan.'

'Just a minute.' She's gone for ages. I walk from side to side in front of the window, unable to stand still. There must have been a sports practice or a drama practice; something I didn't know about. Something I should have known about, but have forgotten in all the recent chaos. Jono will be waiting for me. He'll be standing at the school gates, waiting for me.

The phone clicks. 'There were no after-school clubs on today for Year Eight,' the woman says.

'But was there anything else? A drama rehearsal or something? Is there anything he might have stayed behind for?' *Please*, I am thinking. *Please tell me there is something.*

'I've just spoken to the bursar,' she says and her voice is patient to the point of irritation, as if every day there are children who do not come home from school. 'There are no children left in school.'

'Well, could there have been a problem with the bus then? Maybe it broke down or something. How can I find out?'

'We use a very reliable coach company,' she says now, as if I have personally insulted her. 'They always let us know if there is a problem.' Then, as if I am completely stupid, 'Have you tried phoning him? He does have a phone?'

'His phone isn't on,' I say and there is a short silence. I can almost see her rolling her eyes.

'Then perhaps you might phone one of his friends, someone from the same bus,' she says, spelling it out as if I am an idiot.

'Yes,' I say. 'Yes, of course,' and hang up.

But Jono has no friends who get the same bus as him. His friends that I know of live in Kew, and West Byfleet. There is nobody who lives near us. Nobody he sees every day, to walk home with, to chat with, to be in and out of each other's houses with. I picture him, trudging up the road to the bus stop every morning with the woes of the day ahead of him, and I want to fold him in my arms, my baby, my poor sweet baby.

It was different at primary school. At primary school we

walked back and forth with all the others, me talking to whichever mums were going our way – and there were many, always there were many – while Jono ran ahead with the other kids; he was one of them, so happy, so at ease. But Andrew and I ripped him away from all that. The other kids went on to the local secondary school, but that wasn't good enough for our Jono. So we stuck him on a coach each day and sent him fifteen miles out into the countryside, to be among strangers, to be alone.

And where is he now?

This is my fault. He can't face me after throwing that torch at me. He will be in Surbiton, wandering around the shops instead of coming home. I rush into the hall, stick my shoes on and grab my keys and practically run down our road. The coach drops off just near the station – but I've no way of knowing if it *did* drop off. Everything is as normal. Everything is busy and slow and choked up as normal; cars crawling round the one-way system and up past the station. I get as far as the High Street, but most of the shops are shut now, and anyway, when did Jono ever hang around shops? I don't know where he could be. There is a play area at the end of Mitcham Lane, not much of a play area – just a couple of old swings and a seesaw – but we used to go there sometimes, when he was little. I double-back on myself, and as I head there I fancy I can see him, forlorn, his chin tucked into his jacket, rocking back and forth, back and forth. But when I get there the place is deserted. I don't know what to do. I spot a woman walking a dog on the far side of the green and run over to her.

'Have you seen a boy?' I ask. 'A schoolboy, thirteen years old. He's got dark brown hair.' But she just shrugs and shuffles away.

Maybe he is home now. Please God, maybe he is home now. So I run back. My hands fumble and drop the key; I pick it up, ram it in the lock and slam open the door. 'Jono!' I yell. 'Jono!'

And when he doesn't answer I search the house: the kitchen, the living room. I run upstairs to his bedroom. Where is he? Where is he? I pick up the book on his bed and put it down again. I pick up his pyjamas and hold them against my face, so soft, so precious, my Jono, my Jono.

Andrew needs to know. Andrew should *be* here. So I go back downstairs and I phone Janice's flat, but no one answers. I phone Janice's mobile, but *she* doesn't answer. I try to get a grip. I try to think what to do. Maybe Jono's gone home with a friend. Maybe one of his friends will know where he is.

So I dig out the class list and phone Oliver's house.

'It's Rachel,' I say as soon as Amy answers. 'Jono's mum.'

'Oh,' she says. 'Hello, Rachel.'

'Jono hasn't come home.' My voice is as clumpy and splintered as old wood. 'I wondered if Oliver knew anything, if he said anything—'

'Doesn't Jonathan go home on the bus?'

'Yes,' I say. 'But he didn't come home. I thought Oliver might know—'

'Well, did you phone the school?'

'Yes, of course I did. Look, please, if you'd just ask him—'

'Really, Rachel, I don't think Oliver is going to know where Jonathan is. Shouldn't Jonathan tell *you* if he is going to be late home?'

She is telling me off. She is criticizing me as a mother. I feel the blood rush into my head, but there is no time to waste.

'We . . . had a row,' I say.

And she says, '*Oh*.' And then, 'Wait just a minute.'

I hear her lay down the phone. She can't want me to hear what she says to Oliver, or she'd have taken the phone with her. I hear her footsteps disappear down the hall, and then someone starts playing the piano, practising their scales. Up and down the keys go, up and down. I follow the notes and I think my head will explode. 'Come on,' I plead into the phone. '*Come on*.'

After an age I hear her heels again, tapping against the tiles.

'I'm sorry, Rachel,' Amy says. 'Oliver hasn't spoken to Jonathan at all today. To be honest,' she adds, tactfully, hurtfully, 'I don't think they are quite as much friends as they used to be. Why don't you try some of his other friends? Perhaps one of them might know something.'

Who are Jono's friends? I stare at the names on the class list and I hardly know any of them. I think of the boys who came bowling for Jono's birthday; were any of them *really* his friends? I think of them putting pepper all over his pizza for a laugh, and how they clubbed together in their little groups. I think of how hard he tried to join in.

What about that boy Luke that I took Jono to see in Weybridge? I run a shaking finger down the list, find his number and key it in. A teenage girl answers the phone.

'Is your mother there?' I ask.

And she says, 'No.'

'Is Luke there?'

'No,' she says again.

'Do you know where they are?'

'Don't know. Someone's house, I think.'

'Well, do you know when they'll be back?'

'No.'

It is nearly seven o'clock. Jono should have been home before five.

I have phoned every number on Jono's class list. Like a robot I have asked, *Does your son know if Jonathan Morgan was doing anything after school today?*

They all said no.

Once, Janice didn't come home from school. She was fourteen and had had a huge fight with my parents, because they wouldn't let her go to the disco at Ashcroft Youth Club because it was on a school night, and older boys went to the youth club. But that was exactly why Janice wanted to go – because of the older boys. So on the Thursday that the disco was on she simply didn't come home from school. I remember kneeling on the chair by the living-room window and anxiously watching out for her. We had shepherd's pie for tea that night, and I remember prodding miserably at the mashed potato, unable to eat with Janice's place at the table so starkly vacant, while my parents sat there po-faced, not even commenting on her absence. They certainly didn't seem worried.

Soon after it got dark Janice came sloping up the front path. She hadn't gone to the disco; she'd been hiding up the end of our road beside someone's garage. I was so relieved to see her that I didn't even mind it when she told me to get lost. My parents didn't bat an eyelid at her return. They acted as if they hadn't even noticed she was gone. She'd missed her tea; that was her punishment.

They knew she hadn't gone far. They knew she'd be home soon enough.

But how had they known?

Panic spreads and chills inside me, iced water seeping through my veins.

I have to call the police, and yet to do so is to acknowledge that Jono might not come walking up the path at any minute; it makes the fear too real. And once I make the decision that I will call the police I know that I should have done it sooner; I should have done it straight away, when he was ten minutes late, not *two hours*. Anything could have happened. Anything. In deadly clarity I see Jono's body being dredged from the river; I see him slumped under a railway bridge with a gash on his head; I see him glancing over his shoulder as he boards a train – gone, *gone*.

The number for the police station is on a Neighbourhood Watch leaflet, stuck in the letter rack in the kitchen. My fingers fumble and shake as I dig it out, scattering business cards and unpaid bills everywhere. It takes me three attempts to key in the number, and then I lean against the table with the phone jammed against my ear and my heart racing.

The phone is picked up straight away; first there's a voice message, then I'm speaking to a person, then I'm put through to another person, all within fast, terrifying seconds. They're taking details: Jono's name, his height; the colour of his hair, his skin and his eyes; the clothes that he's wearing, the way he carries his bag. I describe him and I can see him, so clearly I can see him. I see his head turning away, the misery in his eyes.

'We'll put a call out straight away,' the woman on the phone says. 'A police officer will be with you very soon.'

And because she says this, I convince myself that they will find Jono. A police car will shortly pull up outside, with Jono in the back of it. This is what she means, I tell myself. That

they will find him from my description and he will with me
again soon.

And so I feel a brief, surreal reprieve. A moment of false
calm, like the silence of the birds before a storm, or the
pulling back of a wave. They will find Jono lurking at the
end of the road; they will bring him back. And while I wait
for this to happen I phone Janice's flat again, and I am angry
this time that Andrew doesn't answer, that he has just walked
away from us – from Jono – and is too wrapped up in his
own self-pity to care what might be happening here. It is
with anger, too, that I finally get through to Janice on her
mobile.

'Where've you been?' I demand the moment she answers.
'I've been ringing you for hours.'

'I've been in a meeting,' she says coldly. 'You know, at
work.'

'Where's Andrew?'

And she says, 'How the hell should I know?'

'Because he's *staying with you*.'

'He's staying in my flat,' she says, her voice tight with
hostility. 'That doesn't mean I'm his keeper.'

'I've been phoning your flat,' I say. 'He won't answer.'

'Well, maybe he doesn't want to speak to you. You don't
seem to understand how upset he is.'

I walk to the front of the house on soft, jelly legs and
stand by the window. Any second now the police car will
pull up, with Jono in the back of it. Any second now. 'I need
to speak to him,' I say and my voice cracks. 'Jono hasn't
come home.'

'What do you mean he hasn't come home?'

'*From school*.'

I hear Janice's footsteps echoing on the hard corridor floor as she walks; I hear the heavy sound of her breathing. There is a slamming sound as she pushes open a door and then she is outside; I hear the distant sound of traffic and the crackle of the wind against her phone.

'What time does he normally get home?' she asks at last.

'About five,' I say. I mean, what time does she *think*?

'He's probably gone round a friend's then, hasn't he?'

'*No*,' I say. 'He hasn't.' My teeth are chattering now, like joke teeth, rattling as I talk. 'He was *upset*.'

'Well . . . Do you think you should call the police or something?'

'I have. They're coming round. Janice, I need to speak to Andrew.'

She sighs. 'I was supposed to be going straight out,' she mutters, as if I am just such an inconvenience. 'Okay. I'll go home and tell Andrew to ring you.'

Trance-like, I watch the cars drive past my house; people coming home from work, people going out. I watch as the police car pulls up outside my neighbour's house, then reverses along the kerb. Two people get out; a policeman and a policewoman. But not Jono.

'You haven't found him,' I blurt out as I open the door.

'Mrs Morgan?' the policeman says. 'Can we come in?' And they usher me into my own living room. The woman sits next to me on the sofa, the man opposite, on the chair. They introduce themselves as Tim and Karen, as if there is the need for first name-terms, as if we are to be together, for a long time.

And suddenly it is official.

'All the patrol cars have been radioed,' Karen tells me kindly. 'If he's out there, we'll find him.'

The hairs on my neck shoot out on end. 'What do you mean, if he's out there?'

'Is there anywhere you can think of that he might have gone? Any favourite places, any friends who might know where he is?'

'I've phoned his friends. I've phoned everyone I could think of.'

'Could we have those phone numbers?' she asks, and I have the list right there, on the arm of the sofa, where I left it. 'And we'll need the contact details of his school, any family, grandparents—'

'Are you going to call his grandparents?' I think of my mum and dad; they'll be pottering about after their supper. Clearing away the dishes perhaps, settling down to watch TV. I think of Lois, sitting in her sickly pink living room with nothing but a cat for company, and all of Jono's school photos lined up in their frames above the gas fire.

'Would you prefer to tell them yourself first?' Karen says.

'Yes. No. I don't know.' How can I tell them? *What* can I tell them?

'And what about Jonathan's father?' Karen asks.

'He – I've been trying to ring him. All day. He's at my sister's. We – had a row.'

I see her glance at Tim. And then she stands, and walks over to the fireplace. 'Is this Jonathan?' she asks, picking up the photo of the three of us from the mantelpiece. It's of Jono's first day at Hensham Boys'. There we are, the proud parents, with Jono in between us in his oversized blazer and his shiny new shoes.

'Yes,' I whisper.

'And is this his father?'

'Yes.'

She hands the photo to Tim, who is busily making notes.

'Could we have his mobile number?' she asks.

'Yes – no. I mean yes, but he left his phone here.'

'But you've been trying to ring him all day?'

'Yes, at my sister's.' I feel as if I am saying the same thing over and over, talking through a fog.

'And that's where you think he is,' Karen says. 'Now where does she live?'

I tell her, and Tim scribbles it down. Then he gets up from the chair and, taking that photo with him, he walks out into the hall. I hear him talking into his radio, but he moves too far away. I can hear his voice, but not what he is saying.

'What happened to your face?' Karen asks, and the heat rushes into my cheeks. I'd forgotten about the cut, badly patched up with a bloodstained plaster, looking much like I've been in a fight. Karen smiles at me sympathetically. 'Is there any reason why Jonathan might not want to come home?' she asks.

And our private hell becomes public. It is out of my hands now.

How sordid my tatty little affair sounds. I do not tell them everything; there is no need. They are professionals, they can fill in the gaps themselves.

'We had a row,' I say. 'My husband left. My son was angry; he threw a key ring at my face.'

I see the sympathy on Karen's face alter slightly, by degrees. I see the cynicism, creeping in.

'Was there anyone else involved?' she asks, pointedly.

'Yes,' I say. 'No. I mean there was, but it's over now.'

*

They search the house. They look for Jono in cupboards and under the stairs, as if I wouldn't have noticed him sneaking into the house. As if I wouldn't have known if he was here.

'Did you see him leave this morning?' they ask.

'I heard him go. I heard him picking up his bag and slamming the door.'

'But did you *see* him leave?'

They poke around in the garden, and inside Andrew's shed.

They find Andrew's phone in the kitchen, and his wallet. They find the wardrobe, still full of his clothes.

'There's a car on its way round,' I hear Tim say to Karen, and then he's talking into his radio again, giving details in police-speak, details that have me thinking, *No, no, you can't suspect Andrew.* Andrew wouldn't hurt Jono. Andrew loves Jono. He's his father, for heaven's sake.

But then my phone rings, and it's Janice.

'He isn't here,' she tells me woodenly.

'Well, where is he?'

Tim and Karen are watching, listening. I am powerless and exposed.

'I don't know where he is,' Janice says. 'He doesn't have to leave me a note just because he goes out.' But she's scared; I can hear it in her voice. 'Oh Jesus,' she says, 'there's a police car just pulled up outside.'

They attach some sort of recorder to both my phones, so that they can listen in on my calls, and pick up any other calls trying to get through. And I sit on my sofa with my mobile in one hand and my landline handset in the other, waiting for Jono to ring me. I stare out of the window as I wait. It is properly dark outside now. I cannot bear to think of Jono out there in the dark. He never goes out on his own after dark. Never, not even up the road to post a letter.

Tim is next door in the dining room, working his way through the list of contacts that I gave him, double-checking any that were missed before. Karen moves noiselessly back and forth between the dining room and the living room, where I am sitting, waiting.

Then she comes and sits down beside me on the sofa.

'We've spoken to a boy called Luke Barrington,' she says. 'He said he saw Jonathan getting into a silver car with a dark-haired man after school. He said he thinks it was his father.'

And that's good, isn't it, that he's with his father? Relief washes over me, rendering me light-headed, dizzy.

She puts her hand on my arm. 'We've put a national call out,' she says. 'All ports have been alerted.'

'Well, they can't go very far,' I say, naively. 'Andrew hasn't got his wallet with him.'

I speak to my parents. I know that the police went round there earlier, to talk to them, and to see if Jono was there, which was daft really, because Jono wouldn't have a clue how to get to my parents' house on his own. I think of their shock at a police car pulling up outside their house and I am filled with shame, especially as I was too much of a coward to speak to them myself, first. But now, I think, I have better news.

My dad answers the phone. 'Rachel,' he says anxiously when he hears my voice. 'Have they found him?'

'Well, no, but they think he's with Andrew.'

'Andrew's got him?' My dad is confused. 'Is Andrew bringing him home then?'

My mother, when she comes to the phone, is more astute.

'I knew there was something wrong,' she says, her voice shrill with accusation. 'When you were here at Easter – I knew something was going on.' Her voice rises further. I don't want her advice, but I'm going to get it anyway. 'I don't know what problems there are between you and Andrew, but whatever they are, you should put them to one side and think about your son. You are such a lovely little family, the three of you. Such a lovely little family.'

She starts weeping down the phone. I don't know how much the police told her, but obviously it was enough for her to form an opinion. I hang up the phone, numb. I wanted support, not blame.

I can't bring myself to phone Lois. She too will have had a visit from the police, but in her case the police will still be there, parked up outside probably, just up the road, discreetly out of view. Hers is the obvious place for Andrew and Jono to go. She will have the kettle on for them; she will have a bit of cake, ready on a plate. She will be waiting for them.

Janice phones me.

'Andrew's got him,' I say.

And she says, 'I know.'

'Well, they'll be home soon. Andrew will just have wanted to see him.'

'Rachel—'

'He's his *dad*' – my voice wobbles and breaks on a bubble of hysteria – 'he has a right to see him!'

'Rachel . . .' her voice is plaintive, and strained. 'He took

328

nothing with him. No money or anything. The police have searched my flat. Rachel, I told them how upset he was. I told them the things he said to me, about Jono being all he's got. He said he'd lost one child, he couldn't lose another. Rachel, I'm *worried*.'

I know what she's thinking. She's thinking of desperate fathers who drive their kids into the woods and rig a hosepipe to the exhaust, and gas their kids to death in the car. She's thinking of dads who flip, and hack their kids to death before hanging themselves. She's thinking of men who douse their cars with petrol, and torch themselves and their kids to death.

She's thinking it, and Karen, tiptoeing about my house looking for clues, is thinking it, too.

But I cannot think it. I cannot. Not of Andrew.

TWENTY-SEVEN

The hours creep slowly by.

Tim has long since left, called away on another job. There is just Karen with me now.

'Is there someone I can call for you?' she asked me some time ago. 'Someone you'd like to be here with you? A friend perhaps?'

But who could I ask? Janice must stay in her flat, in case Andrew should turn up there; likewise my parents. My dad did offer to drive up and sit with me when I last phoned, but I told him to stay with my mum, who was wailing in the background, hysterical, no use to anyone on her own.

Who else is there that I could let in on this nightmare?

'You don't have to go, do you?' I asked Karen.

'No.' She smiled thinly. 'I'm on for the night.'

She makes toast and tea in my kitchen. She dozes in my chair, and uses my bathroom. She is all that separates me from total aloneness.

I talk to her.

I jabber away on hyperdrive, telling her one hundred and one things about Jono; about that dog on wheels that he had when he was little, and dragged about with him everywhere;

330

about how he used to play for hours on end in the garden in summer, stark naked, running in and out of the sprinkler, which he'd put on rotate, dodging the spray; about how proud we were when he passed the exam for Hensham Boys'.

About how much I love him.

I tell her about every place we have been, ever, with Jono in his life. I tell her over and over, while she makes notes, while she probes for more.

'Jono loves the zoo,' I say, and I picture him, his solemn face staring at all those creatures in their cages. 'We park by Regent's Park and walk through. We go every summer.'

But Andrew cannot have taken him to the zoo now. It is nearly half-past two in the morning.

I tell her about the baby that Andrew and I lost.

I tell her how the grief ate away at our marriage, driving us apart. That the joy was taken from our lives, and in its place was left isolation, and fear.

'Is it so surprising that I was drawn to someone else?' I cry, sobbing out my guilt while Karen pats my arm and hands me tissues. 'Is it?'

And then I am silent.

We sit opposite each other: me on the sofa, she in the chair.

'All the patrol cars have their description,' she assures me, yet again. 'There are a lot of people looking out for your husband's car.' I stare at her; I hang on her words. 'They'll stop for food eventually. At a motorway stop. We'll pick them up then.'

Outside I hear the rattle and clink of the milk float, trundling its slow way down the road. I hear the birds, starting up their morning call. I stare at Karen, and Karen stares at me.

And I am thinking, *Surely they would have needed food before now.*

The phone rings and I jump, and drop it in my panic to answer. Like a cat, Karen springs to her feet, ready to intervene.

But it's Janice.

'Have you heard anything?' she demands.

And I say, 'No. I would have called you if I had.'

I want her to tell me it will be okay. I want her to say, *Don't worry, they'll be home any minute. Andrew would never harm Jono, never. Andrew would never hurt a fly.*

But she says, 'He was so upset, Rachel. He can't be thinking straight. Surely you have some idea where he might go? They can't just disappear.'

I don't want to hear this. I cannot hear this. I cannot cope with anyone else's fear.

'The police need to find them,' she tells me. 'They need to be out there, looking.'

Her words swim in my head. A rush of nausea tightens my throat. 'Janice,' I manage to say, 'I don't want to block the line.'

Somebody else is trying to get through; the red light on the phone monitor beeps once, twice. I hang up on Janice, and I hear Jono say, 'Mum?'

'Jono!' I stand up, too fast; the blood smashes into my head and recedes again.

The phone is on loudspeaker and Jono's voice, so young, so tender, fills the room. 'Mum, I'm scared,' he says, and my whole body is jelly; boneless, weak.

Karen kicks into action. She's doing something to the recorder; she's on her radio. She gestures me to sit back down. *Keep calm*, she mouths. *Keep calm*.

I swallow hard. 'Jono, where are you?'

'I don't know,' he says, sounding so small, and frightened. Then, 'I'm worried about Dad.'

'Where is Dad?' I ask, keeping my voice as steady as I can.

'He's ... just over there. He won't stop crying.'

'Jono, where are you?'

'I don't know,' Jono says. 'It's dark. I'm cold.'

Panic buzzes in my hands and my head, and I stare at Karen. *Keep him talking*, she whispers. *We're tracking the call.*

'Does Dad know you're phoning me?'

'No. I don't know.'

'Let me speak to him,' I say, but Karen shakes her head. *No*, she mouths, slicing, slicing the air in front of me with her hand. *No*. So quickly I say, 'Jono, wait. Keep talking to me.'

'He won't stop crying,' Jono says, and he starts crying too now, in short, frightened sobs. 'I don't know what to do.'

Karen cuts in. 'Hello, Jono,' she says gently. 'My name's Karen. I'm here with your mum. You're being ever so brave,' she says, 'you're doing ever so well. Now, we just need to work out where you are and we'll have you home in no time.' And she starts to question him softly: are there any buildings nearby, are they near a road, can he hear cars, are there any lights; street lights, lights from buildings? How long have they been where they are? For how long did they drive?

I stand beside her, helpless, powerless, as Jono gives vague, pitiful reply after vague, pitiful reply. 'It's dark,' he says over and over. 'I'm frightened.'

Another police car arrives at the house, and Karen and I move to open the front door together, taking the phone with us. I am clutching Karen's arm; I will not let it go. A policeman walks into my living room, but we take no notice of him. On the phone Jono is saying, 'We drove up a hill. There was a cafe, but it was shut. Dad said we might see badgers.'

Every hair on my body is standing on end, yanked tight and fizzing. My heart is slamming against my ribcage.

'That's Box Hill,' I say.

It all moves so fast.

They won't let me go with them, but I insist; I am screaming, yanking their hands away from my front door.

'*I am not a fucking prisoner!*'

'There's a patrol car already on its way,' Karen says, her hands interlacing with mine, dodging my slaps. 'They'll be with them, any moment.'

'I want to be there,' I say. 'I want to be with my son.'

'Mrs Morgan,' the policeman says, 'please, calm down.'

I stare at him. He is not even thirty. I think of his mother, and how proud she must be. I think of Andrew's mother, with her photos of Jono crowded onto her mantelpiece; every single photo from every single year of Jono's school life, from gap-toothed reception to pensive, woeful Year Eight.

'*He's my fucking son,*' I scream.

The streets are deserted and we drive fast; a journey that on a summer's Sunday afternoon can take almost an hour takes less than twenty minutes. The miles speed by and I sit upright in the back of the police car, tense, leaning forward, watching through the gap between the heads of Karen and this unnamed male. They are in constant radio contact; in code-talk, in crackle and over-and-out.

The roads around Box Hill are dark, not lit at all but for the cat's eyes, winking up from the asphalt. The roads as we turn and climb higher do not even have cat's eyes, and we creep up into a darkness rendered darker by the ghostly tunnel of the car's full beam.

We used to come here, sometimes, but we'd park at the bottom and walk up. We'd come at the end of summer, collecting blackberries, and when we got to the top we'd walk across to the cafe selling ice creams. It was always packed around the cafe, with cyclists and bikers and people out for a walk. And there was a road, leading off the opposite side from us; that was where all these people had come up from. *There's a pub down there*, Andrew said. *I used to come out here sometimes with my mate Roger. On a summer's night you could sit in the garden and watch the badgers coming out of their holes.*

The car follows the road, winding up and up.

And then the lights are cut out, and we barely crawl, barely purr, into the blackness. Up and round and up.

I stare ahead. The last time we climbed up Box Hill Jono skulked behind, dragging his feet. *It's too far*, he complained. *I don't want to go.* We'd just taken him away from his friends in Surbiton and stuck him in Hensham Boys'.

I see the blue light first, flashing in the dark. I see it against the sky whole, long seconds before we are there. I see it like a film set; like some phoney nightmare into which I must run yelling scripted, clichéd banalities. The blue light whirls and flashes, fairground-bright, a hideous spotlight, blinding into my eyes.

'Turn it off,' I yell, dazzled by the brightness. 'Turn off the fucking light!'

And then I see him: Jono. Standing beside a policeman; his face illuminated, white and tear-stained. His arms are hanging by his sides, just dangling there, as if they have no life. My hands fumble with the seatbelt, with the door; before the car has even properly stopped I am tumbling out and scrambling across the uneven ground, tripping, falling over myself.

'Jono!' I shout, and he turns towards me and his face crumples, collapsing in on itself, and then he's in my arms, his body pliant and weak. He bends in my arms; he wilts against me. 'Jono,' I say, kissing his head, over and over; the top of his head, his soft, honey-sweet hair.

'I couldn't leave him,' Jono cries, and his body trembles in my arms like a frightened animal's. 'I couldn't leave my dad.'

He pulls away from me and I turn with him, and I see Andrew, flanked on either side by two policemen, his hands cuffed together in front of him like a convict. He is wearing just a shirt over his trousers and there is a muddy streak all down one side of his body, as if he has been struggling in the dirt. His hair is dishevelled, and his face is twisted in a grotesque mask of horror; as if his skin is made of wax, and someone has put their hand into the wax, and pulled.

'I want to be with my son,' he pleads as they lead him towards the car. His skin is an unearthly blue in the reflection of the light. His eyes are on mine, red-rimmed, naked in their pain. 'I just want to be with my son.'

A policeman puts his hand on Andrew's head and presses him down into the car. Andrew strains against the pressure. He twists around and he stares at me. 'Don't do this to me, Rachel,' he says. 'Please. Don't take Jono away from me.'

TWENTY-EIGHT

Andrew wouldn't hurt Jono. I know this.

But the law assumed that he would, and slapped a prohibiting order on him anyway. It was the law that took Jono away from Andrew, not me. And now he has to earn his rights again as a father, month by month, hour by hour.

For this I am truly sorry.

Andrew stays with my sister a while longer, sleeping on her sofa; my sister who can barely bring herself to speak to me. Then he stays with his mother, and I need not mention the fact that she will definitely never speak to me again. He is given time off work, as long as he needs, to recover. His position is kept open for him. It would seem that his employer values him more than his wife did.

And then he finds a ground-floor flat, with a garden, in a large old house in a quiet street in Guildford. The garden is big enough for Jono to kick a ball in, and although the flat only has one bedroom, Andrew is keeping that bedroom for Jono, for when he is allowed to stay. Already some of Jono's things are there, and new things bought specially: the new bed and wardrobe, the signed poster of Southampton football team, the magnetic dartboard, hanging on the wall.

Andrew sleeps on the sofa bed in the living room. Jono's new room is kept waiting for him, like a shrine.

Our house is put on the market. None of us can live here any more. Our family is sliced apart.

When I am clearing the last of my stuff from the house I come across Vanessa's jacket, tucked away inside that box. I cannot throw it away, nor do I want to keep it. It is not mine; it never was. It lies on a pile of other stuff in the spare room, a reminder of unfinished business.

Carefully, I wrap it up in some new tissue paper, put it in my car and drive to Kew. And as I drive through those streets again my stomach automatically knots itself up with nerves. It is like a reflex reaction. I have to park some distance from Mrs Reiber's house, and so I have quite a walk, and I make the walk longer by taking a detour and following the road around in a loop, so that I approach her house from the other side. And I know, with every step that I take, that I will never, ever come to Kew again. I walk slowly. I look at the houses. With scorn for myself, I think of how I longed to belong in a place like this. I longed to fit in here. I am more the outsider now than I ever was.

And yet.

It is cool for June and I am wearing a cotton trench coat, open, over a long, loose shirt. According to the doctor I have been pregnant for over four months, and now that the sickness has passed I am starting to show. I am swelling in the middle. Like a plant rising up through the ashes, my baby is starting to grow.

Not that Mrs Reiber would notice anyway. She probably will not even remember who I am, but still . . .

My heart beats a little faster as I walk up her path. I am half-expecting her to close the door in my face, but I am ready for that; I have my words prepared. I do not even consider the fact that she may not be in. I hold Vanessa's jacket in my arms like a newborn child, and I wait.

I hear her footsteps the other side of the door; I hear her fiddling with the lock. The door slowly opens, and at first she stares at me blankly, and then recognition, unwelcome, shadows her eyes. Her face puckers in displeasure, but before she can speak or shut the door in my face I say, 'Mrs Reiber, I have something for you.'

'I'm quite sure you have nothing that I want,' she says, dismissing me as if I was nothing but a salesperson, come knocking uninvited.

'Mrs Reiber, I do.'

I hold out my hands. Vanessa's jacket lies draped across them like a sacrifice.

She looks at the jacket and then back at me, confusion, and fear, in her eyes.

'This was Vanessa's,' I say.

And she snaps, 'No!' and tries to close the door. I stick my foot out, quick, to stop her. 'What do you want from me?' she demands.

'I want to give you this.' My heart is thumping, but I hold that jacket steady. 'I borrowed it years ago, when I was sixteen. I never had the chance to give it back.'

In spite of herself she is staring at the jacket, the muscles on her face working frantically, turning her expression from panic to terror to a longing so desperate, so achingly raw. I watch her with tears needling my eyes. Tentatively she reaches out one shaking hand and touches the jacket with such trepidation, as though it might break, or disappear.

I swallow hard. 'Please,' I say. 'It's yours.'

She snaps her hand back. And she looks up at me with such suspicion. 'What do you want?' she asks again, her voice shrill and sore.

'To give you this,' I say. 'That's all. Please.' I proffer that jacket, and again her hand creeps out. And this time she snatches the jacket from my hands and gasps as she clutches it to her chest, as though afraid I might snatch it back again.

'Thank you,' I say and step back from the door, which she then ducks behind and slams shut.

'Who are you?' she calls from the other side.

'No one,' I say back, though whether she hears me or not I do not know. 'I was a friend of a friend, that's all.'

And I walk away from there, and I try to tell myself that I have done at least something right.

I try to contact Simon, but the numbers of his flat, and his mobile, are no longer in use. I call his office, and his secretary tells me he has gone on a secondment, but she will not tell me where. So I write him a letter, and I post it to his house in Kingham. And in that letter I tell him that I will be keeping his baby.

He has a right to know. He has a need to know, surely.

I do not get a reply.

I write to him again with my new address, when Jono and I move into our new little house in Guildford, less than two miles from Andrew's flat, and one mile from Jono's new school.

And I write to him in November, when our baby daughter is born healthy and beautiful in the maternity ward at Guildford hospital, with no one but me, and the midwife, to see her into the world. I tell him that I have named her Freya.

He doesn't reply.

How strangely the world turns.

On a Sunday in December I pull up in my car outside Andrew's flat to collect Jono, with Freya asleep in her car seat beside me. Andrew and Jono are in the garden; I see them straight away. Andrew's flat is in a large Victorian house, with a garden that runs all the way around it, and a low fence, barely a yard high. They are racing up and down the side of the house, playing with the dog from the flat next door. Jono is shrieking and laughing; I can hear him even before I open the car door. I see a stick fly in the air. I see a small whirl of grey as the dog jumps up to catch it.

I get out of the car and I stand there and watch them, my son and the father of my son. And my heart aches as it will always ache. For a long time they do not know that I am there and carry on playing with this dog, free for a while, unburdened. Then Jono spots me, and Andrew looks up, too. I see disappointment and resignation cloud Jono's face; the *oh no* look of a boy who knows it is time to go. And in Andrew I see the shutters come down, rendering him closed, and wary.

I'm sorry, I'm so sorry, I whisper, under my breath.

Jono turns away from me and picks up that stick again, and throws it for the dog, making the most of his last few minutes. And Andrew starts walking towards me.

'How are you?' he asks guardedly.

And automatically I say, 'I'm fine, thanks. How are you?' He smiles a thin smile, but doesn't answer. 'Really,' I go on, 'how are you?'

I really want to know. I want him to know that I care.

He looks away, back to Jono. 'Jono seems happy with his school,' he says.

'Yes,' I say quickly. 'He's really settled in. He's doing really well. And he's got friends who live just near us.' I am talking too fast, talking too much now. I clasp my cold hands together and stick my nails into my palm.

Jono is getting that dog to do tricks. He knows we are watching. He is putting on a show. Jono loves us; he shows it every day in his kindness to his sister, and his father. *We're still your family*, I tell him. *We still love you.* I tell him this over and over: *We will always love you.*

Is it enough? Can it ever be enough?

He left his old school without a second thought and I saw the clouds lift out of his eyes. We live close enough for him to see his father every day, and if he doesn't see him, Jono speaks to him. Perhaps we all make more effort now.

'He says you're doing some teaching,' Andrew says.

'Oh, just a bit. Just private, you know, while Freya's still so young.' *Freya*. I have never said her name to him before. I watch his closed face and grip my hands a little tighter.

'Can I see her?' Andrew says, and my heart jolts.

But then Jono comes bounding up with that dog yapping at his heels. 'Can we get a dog? Can we, Mum?' he asks, and I laugh and try to catch him in a hug.

'We don't need a dog, we've got a baby,' I remind him and he goes straight to the car, opens the passenger door, bends down and drops a kiss on his sister's cheek.

'She's asleep,' he says, and he starts tickling her chin with his grubby fingers, till she screws up her little face and fleetingly opens her baby-dark eyes. And then he is gone again, back down that garden, the dog following behind.

'Babies are not quite as much fun as dogs,' I mutter, just for something to say.

Because Andrew is standing by the open car door, looking down at Freya with a look on his face that will haunt me forever. How could I ever think that my husband had no feelings? How could I think that he didn't care? Regret clogs my heart like a rock.

'She's beautiful,' he says, and his voice is thick, barely more than a whisper.

I look at him, looking down at my baby, and my eyes are burning with tears. 'I'm sorry, Andrew,' I say. 'I'm so sorry.'

I reach my hand out, to touch his. I feel his skin, soft, dry, so instantly familiar. Tentatively, my fingers creep around his.

He says, 'I wish that she was mine.'

My fingers move against his, are caught and held. He rubs his thumb against mine; he clutches my hand tight, like he will never let it go, squeezing it, squeezing it.

And I say, 'I wish that she was yours too.'

extracts reading groups
competitions books new
discounts extracts
extracts
competitions
reading groups
discounts
books
new
events
reading groups
events
books
new books
extracts
extracts
new titles reading groups
interviews
new
events extracts
extracts
books
discounts
new books events
events
interviews new books extracts
events new
reading groups
discounts extracts discounts
books
www.panmacmillan.com
extracts events reading groups
competitions books extracts new